STARFLIGHT

STARFLIGHT

MELISSA LANDERS

HYPERION

LOS ANGELES   NEW YORK

Copyright © 2016 by Melissa Landers

All rights reserved. Published by Hyperion, an imprint of Disney Book Group. No
part of this book may be reproduced or transmitted in any form or by any means,
electronic or mechanical, including photocopying, recording, or by any information
storage and retrieval system, without written permission from the publisher. For
information address Hyperion, 125 West End Avenue, New York, New York 10023.

First Hardcover Edition, February 2016
First Paperback Edition, January 2017

3 5 7 9 10 8 6 4 2
FAC-025438-18158
Printed in the United States of America

This book is set in Bembo MT Pro
Designed by Maria Elias

Library of Congress Cataloging-in-Publication Control
Number for Hardcover Edition: 2015004693

ISBN 978-1-4847-4786-5

Visit www.hyperionteens.com

*For Carey Corp, a brilliant brainstorming
partner and an even better friend.*

CHAPTER ONE

What if nobody picks me? Nothing can be worse than that.

Solara's pulse quickened, and her palms turned cold. She hadn't considered the possibility that no one would want her, but now, as she scanned the servants area, she noticed only two indenture candidates standing with her behind the gate—an elderly man with more hair in his ears than on his head and a teenage boy who couldn't stop scratching himself. Of the fifty standby travelers who'd arrived that morning, the three of them were the leftovers. The last boarding call would sound in a few minutes, and if she couldn't entice a passenger to hire her in exchange for a ticket to the outer realm, she'd have to wait sixty days for the next spaceliner.

That wasn't an option.

Brightening her smile, she stood up straighter and tried to catch the eye of a woman with her shirttail untucked and a chunk of dried food in her hair. "Pardon, ma'am," Solara called.

"Are you traveling with young children? I can help. All I require is passage to the last stop."

The woman paused midstride, then tipped her head in contemplation. She chanced a step toward the servants gate. "Do you have experience?"

"Yes, ma'am! I practically raised the little ones in my group home."

"Group home?" The woman pruned her mouth and regarded Solara with new eyes, taking in the grease stains on her state-issued coveralls and the holes in the toes of her scuffed brown boots. "Show me your hands."

Solara feigned ignorance as her stomach dropped. "What?"

"Your hands," the woman repeated. "I want to see them."

With a sigh, Solara removed her fingerless gloves and allowed the passenger to read the tattoos permanently inked across her knuckles. She didn't bother trying to explain. It never made a difference anyway.

"That's what I thought." The woman shook her head in disdain exactly like one of the nuns at the home. Then she stalked away without another word.

The old man standing beside Solara invaded her personal space and delivered a light elbow nudge. He leaned in and whispered, "I know someone who can clear your record. He's the best forger in Houston—even the new laserproof ink is no match for him."

Solara rolled her eyes. She knew a dozen flesh forgers. Finding an expert wasn't the problem. "If I had that kind of money, I wouldn't be standing here, would I?"

He flashed both palms and backed away.

Soon a group of businessmen approached the gate in search of stewards for the five-month voyage. Solara hid both hands behind her back and offered her widest grin, but it wasn't enough. They indentured the old man and the itchy teenager instead.

Panic crept over her as she scanned the vacant station and the thick metal doors leading to the boarding platform. There were no passengers left. At any moment, the shuttle would transport thousands of vacationers to the moon's space station, where they'd board the SS *Zenith* and set off for exotic destinations.

Why hadn't anyone chosen her?

She wouldn't describe herself as pretty, or charming, or even entertaining, but the calluses on her palms proved she was a hard worker. She practically slept with a ratchet in one hand and a wrench in the other. Every time the diocese shuttle sputtered and coughed, it was Solara the nuns called on to fix it, even if it meant freeing her an hour early from chapel detention, where she usually knelt in penance for peeking at her data tablet during morning prayers. And when the engine purred once again, Sister Agnes would rub her arthritic fingers and remark that she'd never trained a better mechanic.

Didn't that count more than a criminal record?

Apparently not.

The click of high heels turned Solara's attention to the lobby, where a stunning girl of about eighteen sashayed toward the gate, wheeling a tote behind her. An animal yipped from inside the bag, a lapdog from the sound of it.

The young woman brushed a bit of lint from the lapel of her designer dress, then tossed a curtain of glossy pink hair over one shoulder and called to someone out of sight. "Hurry. If we miss the shuttle, your father will make us wait an hour before sending another one, just to prove a point."

Sensing her last chance of escape, Solara rose onto her toes to wave at the girl. "Miss! Over here!" She achieved eye contact and smiled. "I'm an excellent maid. All I require is . . ."

But it was no use. The girl scowled and turned away.

A deep male voice sounded from the entrance, "I wouldn't mind missing it. I can't breathe in those tight spaces," and a tall boy strode into view.

He'd slung a tuxedo jacket over one shoulder and loosened the first few buttons of his collar. Practically oozing indifference, he moved at a leisurely pace as if the *Zenith* would wait an eternity for him.

Because it would.

Solara had never seen him out of academy uniform, but the boy was easy to recognize. He was Doran Spaulding: heir to the galaxy's largest fuel corporation, first-string varsity football star, and a complete pain in her ass. Freshman year, she'd won a day scholarship to the mechanical engineering program at his private academy—classes only, no room or board—and he'd done his best to punish her for it ever since. Especially after she'd beaten him for the Richard Spaulding Alumni Award. There'd been other tiffs, too, like the time she broke Doran's quarterback arm during a bad landing in pilot's ed class. But that had been an accident, and he'd only had to sit out for half the season. She knew the real reason for his anger had always been the humiliation of losing his father's award to a penniless girl with no family of her own. As if she'd tarnished his precious name by association.

It was clear he recognized her, too, because the instant their eyes met, he stopped and laughed. "Rattail," he called. "Fancy meeting you here."

Reflexively, Solara fingered the squiggly birthmark at the base of her throat, the one Doran had once said reminded him of a rodent's tail. That'd been four years ago, and she still hadn't managed to shake the nickname.

"You missed graduation," he said, though she didn't know why he cared. "I guess all that free education didn't mean much if you couldn't be bothered to take your diploma."

Solara indulged in a small grin, relieved that he hadn't heard the news. The real reason she'd missed graduation was because the academy had dropped her like a flaming brick the instant they learned about her felony conviction. "I tested out early," she said, which technically wasn't a lie. "With a near-perfect score."

He didn't seem to like that. Jutting his chin at the indenture band around her wrist, he asked, "Selling yourself for a glimpse of the Obsidian Beaches? Can't say I blame you. It's the only way you'll ever see them."

She opened her mouth to fire a witty comeback, but nothing came. Her best lines always arrived an hour too late. "Not that it's any of your business, but I'm headed to the end of the line."

"The outer realm?" Doran drew back. "Why would you want to go *there*?"

"For a job," she told him. "The offer came last week."

In the lawless outer realm, mechanics like Solara were hard to come by. No one would care about the tattoos across her knuckles or the grease beneath her fingernails. She'd be revered as a goddess because settlers on the fringe planets appreciated skill over beauty. That was where she belonged, far from Houston's overcrowded high-rise slums and the sweatshops that paid a few measly credits to those with the connections to get inside. She was going west, all the way to the edge of the charted territories, to a new terraform called Vega. Her benefits package included a whole acre of land, all to herself. She couldn't wait to work that soil between her fingers and know that she owned it. Freedom, wealth, and security were right there, waiting for her.

All she needed was a ticket.

"But you can't afford the fare," Doran said, mostly talking to himself. "And the next trip to the outer realm isn't for a year."

"Two months," she corrected.

"No, a year." He smoothed a perfectly manicured hand over his dark hair, then took the opportunity to study his reflection in the nearby ticketing screen. "They're scaling back because there's no demand to visit the fringe planets. Only criminals end up there." Raking his gaze over her, he added, "And vagrants."

All the blood drained from Solara's head.

A year?

Where would she live? How would she support herself? The nuns had practically danced a jig when she'd left because it freed up a bed for one of the teens sleeping on the cafeteria floor. Each day more abandoned kids appeared at the front gate, their parents having fled the scene in the world's saddest game of hide-and-seek. The group home couldn't afford to keep anyone past graduation. No exceptions. Even Sister Agnes, who'd been like a mother to Solara, had pressed a handheld stunner into her palm and shoved her out the gate. *The fringe is a dangerous place,*

Agnes had said. *Keep this in your pocket.* Then she'd told Solara to go in peace and serve the Lord.

It was clear she wasn't meant to return.

Doran brought her back to present company by tapping his chin and peering at her with new interest. "My usual valet is too sick to travel," he said. "I can see that all the proper servants are taken, but you might do." His upper lip curled in a way that made Solara want to hide her face. "I'd have to let you in my suite, but I guess I can live with that."

Before Solara could respond, Doran's girlfriend made a noise of disgust and whined, "Come on, Dory. Not that one. She's so . . . dirty."

Solara's cheeks blazed. She'd taken great care to scrub her face at the public bathhouse that morning, even paying extra to have her hair washed and plaited in the latest style. "*She* is standing right here. And I'm not dirty."

Doran snapped his gaze to hers, his black brows forming a slash above blue eyes cold enough to frost the fiery moons of Volcanus. "Let's get something straight, Rattail. If I agree to finance your passage, the only words that will leave your mouth for the next five months are *Yes, Mr. Spaulding.* If you disappoint me in any way—if my every wish is not brought to fruition—I'll drop your carcass at the first outpost. Do you understand?"

Solara held her breath while a furious pulse pounded in her ears. Five months as Doran's slave or a year on the streets. Unpleasant as it was, the decision made itself.

"Yes," she said.

"Excuse me?"

"Yes, *Mr. Spaulding.*"

"That's better. See?" he said to his girlfriend. "She can be trained." He pointed at Solara's wrist. "Where's the matching band?"

"You buy it from the machine," Solara told him, nodding at the kiosk beside her.

Once Doran transferred the credits to pay her fare, the gate opened with a beep and an *M*-emblazoned bracelet dropped into the collection tray. He slapped the band around his wrist, linking them as master and servant.

"Quit standing there," he said. "You can start by taking Miss DePaul's bag."

But the girl—Miss DePaul, presumably—gripped the handle of her pet carrier with ten red-tipped fingers. "I don't want her touching my things," she declared, and clicked toward the boarding platform.

Doran shrugged and handed Solara his tuxedo jacket. When they reached the boarding entry, he shouted, "The door, Rattail. Open the door!" She scrambled ahead of him and heaved aside the metal barrier. As Doran preceded her through the gateway, he murmured, "Well, you're off to a poor start."

Solara clutched his jacket and resisted the urge to choke him with it. Maybe there *was* something worse than not being picked.

CHAPTER TWO

*T*he beeping awoke her from a dead sleep, but in her foggy
state, Solara couldn't tell where it was coming from. She
scanned the darkness for the source of the awful sound until
a pillow arched up from the bottom bunk and smacked her in
the face.

"Turn off your band!" hissed one of her roommates.

Understanding dawned, and Solara tapped the Accept button
on her bracelet. By now, she should be used to Doran's constant
requests. The sadistic jerk hadn't allowed her a full night's rest
since they'd boarded the *Zenith* a month ago, so he wasn't likely
to start now.

"He's ruining my sleep," another roommate whispered.
"Why does he keep torturing you?"

That was a good question.

Solara pulled on a pair of pants and thought about it. The
obvious answer was his white-knuckled hold on a grudge from

freshman year, the urge to put her back in "her place" after she'd won his father's award. But aside from that, sometimes she wondered if Doran craved attention. He reminded her of a boy in the group home who used to pull her hair. When she'd complained to the nuns, they had brushed off her concerns, claiming that the boy liked her. But she didn't enjoy having her hair pulled, so she'd put a stop to it by sinking her fist into the boy's stomach.

Maybe that was what Doran needed.

After wrapping a blanket around her shoulders, she slipped quietly into the hallway and waited for the motion-sensor nightlights to activate. Soon a thin strip glowed in the middle of the floor. She knew from experience it would take 872 steps to reach Doran's first-class suite from her position in the steerage class level, so she didn't waste another moment getting there. The last time she'd waited too long to respond, he'd fallen asleep, only to summon her an hour later to pull a clean shirt from his walk-in closet. He hadn't been kidding when he'd said he hated small spaces. It made her want to lock him inside a luggage trunk.

She knocked softly on his door. Most valets had key fob access programmed into their indenture bands, but of course Doran didn't trust her enough for that.

Once the door slid into the wall, she stepped inside his suite and immediately stopped short to survey the damage. He'd hosted another party. The empty bottles littering the carpet made that clear. Someone had overturned the sofa and rearranged the furniture in what appeared to be a tic-tac-toe grid, and naturally she would have to clean it up. But that couldn't be why he'd called her in the middle of the night.

Or could it?

She slid a glare toward his bedroom but refused to go in there. If the lingering scent of Miss DePaul's perfume was any indication, he wasn't alone.

"Did you need something?" Solara shouted.

Doran's voice was sleep-roughened when he demanded, "Excuse me?"

She closed her eyes and drew a slow breath. "How may I assist you, Mr. Spaulding?"

"I've got insomnia," he said. "So I might as well make use of it and get some work done for my internship. Come in here and take notes for me."

Solara didn't move.

It was one thing to fetch a T-shirt from his closet, but spending time with Doran inside his bedroom—in the middle of the night? Not for all the fuel in all the ore refineries in all four quadrants of the galaxy.

A rustling of blankets sounded from the other room, followed by a heavy sigh. "Stay there," he grumbled. "I'll get dressed and come to you. But for future reference, anyone who stinks like a toolshed is safe from my advances."

Frowning, Solara lifted a lock of hair to her nose. She'd spent an hour touring the auxiliary engine room yesterday, but she didn't smell like grease. At least, she didn't think so.

He padded into the living room wearing a dark bathrobe that concealed everything but his bare feet. "Feel safer now?"

She answered, "Yes, Mr. Spaulding," and meant it for once.

Doran turned an armchair upright and plopped into it, not bothering to create a seat for her. He flicked a wrist toward the opposite wall. "You'll find a tablet on the desk. I assume you know how to transcribe, considering all the years the head-master let you spend at my school."

Jaw clenched, she nodded.

"I'll dictate from my . . ." He trailed off as a trio of lines wrinkled his forehead. "Damn it. Where's my data file?" With-out giving her a chance to guess, he made a shooing motion with one hand. "I'll have to find it. Wait in the hall. I don't want you to see where I keep my valuables."

Solara suppressed an eye roll. The only thing she wanted to do with his data file was soak it in hot sauce and shove it up his nose, but she obediently waited outside until he reopened the door. Then she powered on the tablet and opened a new document.

"I'm ready," she said.

But Doran had fallen silent. She glanced down and caught him staring at the felony tattoos on her knuckles, his face leak-ing color by the second. The whites of his eyes kept growing until he looked like he'd seen a demon, and Solara half expected him to retreat to his bedroom and pull the covers over his head. She cursed herself for leaving her room with naked hands. She should have remembered to put on her gloves.

"You didn't have those when you were at my academy," he said, tugging absently at his earlobe. "I would have noticed."

"No." Her first instinct was to look at her knuckles, but she fought it. She didn't want to see them. "They're fresh. Only a few months old."

Doran swallowed hard, his gaze never leaving her hands. She found it odd that he hadn't laughed at her yet, not that she was complaining. "That's why you didn't graduate. You were expelled."

"I still graduated," she said. "Just not from the academy."

"What did you do?"

The question made her shoulders go tense. It always did. She knew she could give him the easy answer—she'd been caught stealing. But that wasn't the half of it. As the nuns always said, the devil was in the details. It was the details that shamed her beyond any punishment a judge could hand down. The details hurt like a slash to the heart, and she would die a thousand deaths before sharing them with Doran.

"I don't remember," she told him.

"You're a liar."

"Yes, Mr. Spaulding."

"You have to tell me," he insisted. "It's my right as your employer."

No, it wasn't. She knew the law. "I made a mistake and I learned from it. I didn't hurt anyone. That's what matters."

"How do I know you're telling the truth?" he asked, and swallowed hard enough to shift his Adam's apple. He almost seemed afraid of her, which couldn't be right. Nothing scared the Great Doran Spaulding, except closets and possibly the absence of mirrors. "We've already established that you're a liar."

Solara didn't want to play this game anymore. She would clean Doran's suite and fetch his slippers, but she wouldn't give him a piece of her soul. "If you trust me enough to let me in here, you must know I'm not a threat to you."

"You're not going to tell me?"

"I don't like talking about it."

"Fine, then." He thrust a finger toward the door and ordered, "Get out."

She drew her eyebrows together. Was he serious or just jerking her around? Sometimes it was hard to tell. "But what about the—"

"I don't want your help," he said. "Be at Miss DePaul's suite before breakfast to tend to that thing she calls a dog. Aside from that, I don't care what you do."

Then he stood from his chair and turned off the light in a clear dismissal.

Solara blinked a few times before setting down the tablet and backing out of the room. She returned to her bunk expecting another summons, but she slept undisturbed until the morning alarm rang.

*   *   *

The next day, she couldn't shake the feeling that something was wrong, a sort of prickly sensation in her stomach that lingered throughout her morning routine. There was no logical reason for it. The ship traveled smooth and steady, only two hours from the next refueling post. Her roommates smiled and gossiped about their onboard crushes while braiding one another's hair. Nothing seemed out of the ordinary.

It wasn't until she reached Miss DePaul's suite that Solara realized the cause for her unease. Her wristband had remained silent for too long. Doran hadn't demanded predawn breakfast in bed. He hadn't ordered her to warm his bath towels or set the telescreen to his favorite news program. He hadn't even asked her to pull an outfit from his closet.

That definitely wasn't normal.

She knocked on Miss DePaul's door and tried to ignore the worries nibbling at the edge of her mind. The girl answered wearing nothing but Doran's T-shirt—Solara had laundered it enough times to know. After tucking a gleaming pink lock behind one ear, Miss DePaul hitched a thumb over her shoulder.

"Baby had an accident on the carpet last night. Take care of it before you walk her." She sniffed a laugh and added, "You can't miss it. Look for a reeking pile the exact shade of your hair. I'll be in the shower, so lock the door when you leave."

In that moment, Solara decided to "forget" locking, or even closing, the door. She cleaned up after the dog, then tucked it gently beneath one arm and carried it to the mezzanine, where passengers brought their animals to exercise. By the time she finished six laps around the artificial park and returned the dog to Miss DePaul, the *Zenith* had stopped to refuel and Doran finally sent instructions to meet him outside the auxiliary engine room.

An odd request, but Solara knew better than to question it.

When she slid open the door to the utility hallway, a chill of foreboding prickled her skin into goose bumps. The passage was empty and cool, illuminated by flickering overhead lights that cast menacing shadows on the floor. All engines had shut down, and without the rhythmic hum, an eerie silence hung in the air. She heard only the creak of her new boots as she strode toward the stairwell to Doran's meeting place. She saw him in the distance, but he kept his back to her while she climbed the steely stairs. Even when she joined him on the upper platform, he didn't turn to face her.

Instinct told her to retreat—something wasn't right—but she crossed both arms over her chest and asked in her sweetest voice, "How can I assist you, Mr. Spaulding?"

He turned and favored her with a glance as cold and empty as their surroundings. Wordlessly, he swept a hand toward the service door at the hull of the ship.

At first Solara didn't understand. She gazed through the porthole at the outpost station to watch attendants pump fuel into the ship's massive holding tanks. But then her gaze drifted downward, and she spotted her trunk on the floor. There was no mistaking the government-standard stenciling on the lid: BROOKS, SOLARA. CHARITABLE INSTITUTE #22573.

She was still staring at her luggage when she asked, "What's this?"

"This," he told her, "is where you get off."

She whipped her gaze to his. "You can't be serious."

"Have you ever known me to enjoy a joke?"

"But this is an outpost. There's nothing here. That's why everyone's staying on board."

His casual shrug said that wasn't his problem. "There are other ships. If you're lucky, maybe someone less discriminating than me will hire you."

Solara's mouth went dry. Would he really leave her stranded at an outpost without a single credit to her name? Surely he knew what awaited her out there. She had never traveled beyond Earth before, but she'd heard stories of what girls like her had to do in these situations. She would be at the mercy of every lonely ship hand and oily smuggler who passed through this hub.

Maybe Doran was only trying to scare her.

"This isn't funny," she said in a small voice.

"Who's laughing?" he asked. "By the way, you can keep the boots and clothes I bought for you. They're of no use to me."

She searched his face for a glimpse of kindness, the barest spark of compassion, finding none. As awful as Doran's constant insults were, she'd never believed him capable of this kind of cruelty. She still didn't want to believe it. "You're really going to do this?" she asked. "Leave me here with nowhere to go?"

By way of answer, he brushed past her toward the stairs.

"Damn it, Doran!" she yelled, enjoying a morsel of satisfaction when the echo made him flinch. "We have a contract!"

He spun on her from his place at the top step. "And I warned you what would happen if you disappointed me."

Disappointed him?

The accusation was so ridiculous that it stole Solara's voice. She'd done everything he had asked of her, completed each demeaning task without once complaining. How dare he accuse her of failing to honor her side of the bargain?

Her vision tunneled, and she thrust a finger at him. "I came to your suite in the middle of the night to bring you a glass of water when you were too lazy to walk to the bathroom. I cleaned your girlfriend's vomit off the sofa cushions." Solara's voice raised a pitch. "For God's sake, I even fetched her panties when you two left them in the elevator! I wanted to amputate my own hand after that!"

Doran's cheeks flushed bright pink, but he kept his tone cool. "I don't tolerate liars."

"Liars," she repeated, finally understanding the real issue. She'd refused to share the details of her conviction with him. Well, that wasn't going to change. She ripped off one glove and held her knuckles in his face. "So this is what it's about? You want to know what I did to earn my ink?"

His blue eyes narrowed. "I can't promise I'll reconsider my decision."

"That's okay. I want you to know." She gripped the stair rails and leaned down until she was close enough to smell his musky cologne. "I killed my last boss—buried a wrench in his brain when he tried to fire me."

Doran took one step backward down the stairs, then another.

"But the judge had mercy," she said, holding his gaze as she followed him down the steps. "Because my boss was just like you . . . a total waste of flesh."

"I don't believe you." But Doran's trembling voice contradicted his words.

"That I killed someone?" she asked. "Or that you're a waste of flesh? Because one of those statements is true."

He glared at her. "While you're hustling a ride to the outer realm, I'll be sipping champagne in bed with my girlfriend. Who's the real failure here?"

"You are," Solara said. "No doubt about it." An odd sense of calm settled over her, steadying her pulse and slowing her breath. It felt good to speak her mind, even if each word was a nail in her coffin. "I might have dirt under my fingernails and tattoos across my knuckles," she told him, "but I can fix that with a hot bath and a visit to the flesh forger. You're dirty in a place that can't be washed. You'll never change, and you'll never make a difference. When you die, no one will miss you, because your life won't matter." She followed him down the stairs until they stood nose-to-nose at the base. *"You don't matter."*

If she didn't know better, she'd think her words had stung him. "Don't pretend you're better than me," he whispered. "By the time you afford your first bolt bucket, I'll control all the fuel in the galaxy. The Solar League would collapse without Spaulding, and they know it. If you hadn't been expelled, you would've seen the League president at graduation—to congratulate me."

She shook her head. "You still don't get it."

"You're the one who's deluded."

"You know what? I'm glad you dropped me here." She jabbed a finger toward his forehead to punctuate her final words. "You're not worth my time."

Lurching back to avoid her touch, Doran pointed at the top of the stairs. "Don't let me stop you. Your passage here is unpaid. I'd hate to see you arrested as a stowaway."

But despite her bold words, Solara didn't budge.

Couldn't budge.

Beads of sweat formed along her upper lip, because once she left the safety of this transport, there was no turning back. She would never survive out there. And if she stayed on board the *Zenith* and the crew caught her, they would show no leniency. Not with her conviction so fresh. They'd send her to one of the prison colonies, where she would spend the rest of her life mining the fuel ore that made Doran so rich.

No.

She couldn't lose her freedom over him. There had to be another way.

"Better hurry," he said with a smug smile. "I've traveled on plenty of vessels like this, and they don't take all day to refuel."

While he gloated, Solara scanned the engine room for anything she could smuggle out and barter for passage on another ship. She spotted an upgraded gravity drive, but without the tools to remove it, the device was useless to her.

Think harder, she told herself. *There's always unexpected currency to find.*

Then her gaze landed on Doran's indenture band, the one that joined them as master and servant, and the solution hit like a lightning bolt to the head. That bracelet was the most valuable hunk of metal on board, because he'd linked it to his credit account. And Doran's credit was limitless. Just last week, he'd gambled away a lifetime's fortune in the casino as if it were spare tokens he'd found in a jar. If she overpowered him and took his bracelet, she could use his money to hire a private ship.

Solara chewed the inside of her cheek and sized him up—six feet, two inches of lean, sculpted muscle. His bulk came from a gym, not a work site, but that wouldn't make him any less strong. Overpowering him was out of the question.

"What's the matter?" he taunted, leaning against the stair rail with one booted foot crossed over the other. "Afraid you'll miss me?"

She sneered at him. "The only thing I'll miss is the chance to flush you out the waste port."

He laughed. "You're not very nice for a girl raised by nuns."

Solara was about to retort, *Maybe they weren't nice nuns,* when she remembered Sister Agnes's parting gift—the tiny weapon tucked inside her pocket.

She drew a hopeful breath.

The stunner dispensed a fast-absorbing liquid drug with enough neuro-inhibitors to drop a mule. One touch to Doran's skin and he'd be out cold in seconds. Better yet, when he came to, he'd have a nasty hangover and wouldn't remember his own name. That meant he couldn't tell anyone she'd stolen his band, at least not for a day or two, which was more than enough time to put a few solar systems between them.

Solara reached into her pocket and closed her fingers around the stunner while trying to ignore the sudden guilt tugging at her stomach. This didn't make her a bad person. Doran had left her with no other options—it was life or death. Besides, the toxins wouldn't hurt him.

At least not permanently.

She reminded herself of that as she positioned the button inside her palm and flicked the tiny activation switch. "I'd better go," she said.

Doran nodded. "And soon."

"Thank you for taking me this far. And for the new clothes."

"Don't forget the boots."

"And the boots," she agreed while extending her hand to him. "No hard feelings?"

The peace offering must have surprised him, because his eyebrows twitched. But even after he recovered, he made no move to touch her. He only stood there and tugged at his ear-lobe while refusing to look her in the eyes. It seemed the Great Doran Spaulding was too good to shake hands with her.

Solara solved that problem by grabbing his wrist.

There was just enough time for confusion to register on his face before his body collapsed to the floor, landing with a clang. Solara dropped to her knees and immediately started working the bracelet over his hand. As soon as she slipped it free, she shoved the band around her wrist and made for the stairs. She was halfway to the exit before she realized a snag in her plan.

The bracelet couldn't be used without identity verification, which meant she would need his handprint for the scanners at the retail center.

"Oh no," she whispered, and whirled around to face his sprawling body. If she wanted Doran's credits, she would have to take him with her into the outpost.

Just how was she supposed to do that?

CHAPTER THREE

He awoke to searing pain.

His body throbbed in places he hadn't known existed. Even his teeth had a vicious heartbeat. But it was his skull that screamed the loudest. It felt like someone had peeled back his scalp and coated his brain with molten ore.

What the hell had he done to himself?

He opened his eyes a crack and immediately wished he hadn't. The light was too bright, burning a path to the center of his aching head. Moaning, he clutched his temples while rolling onto his side. A sudden image flashed in his mind of being trapped inside a closet, but when he felt the surface beneath him, it was hard and frigid—metal, not carpet. A quick peek confirmed it. He exhaled in relief. He must've passed out and hit his head. That would explain the unholy pulsing between his ears.

"Hey," whispered someone close behind him. "Are you all right?"

Was he all right? What kind of asinine question was that?

"Fan-damned-tastic," he barked, wincing at his own shouts. He lowered his voice to a whisper. "What happened to me?"

Instead of receiving an answer, he felt delicate fingers probe his scalp. "It's a good thing your head's so hard," the person said, and he realized for the first time that the speaker was a young woman. "Can you sit up?"

"I don't know."

"Let's try," she said. "I'll give you a push."

She cupped his shoulders and guided him into a sitting position, then helped him lean back against what felt like a metal rail. His head pounded at the change in altitude, but the rest of him didn't object.

"Better?" she asked.

"Not really. I feel like my brain's about to explode."

"It's no wonder," she chided as if he'd done something wrong. "After all the Crystalline you drank last night, your liver's probably begging for mercy, too."

"Crystalline?" Was he drunk? He didn't think so, but the waves of nausea roiling inside his stomach forced him to reconsider. "What are you talking about? What happened?"

She didn't say anything for the longest time. When she finally answered, it was with a question of her own. "What's the last thing you remember?"

The odd response made him wonder who he was talking to.

He squinted open his eyes to look at the woman, surprised to discover she was a girl about his age. She had a heart-shaped face with full lips pulled into a frown, and a nose that turned up slightly at the tip. He couldn't tell whether her eyes were green or brown, but they were fringed with dark lashes that matched the color of the intricate braids encircling her head. She wore black pants and a fitted gray top, simple clothes but of seemingly high quality, and peeking out from above her shirt collar was a tiny pink birthmark in the shape of an S.

He knew that birthmark.

"Did you hear me?" she asked. "What do you remember?"

He tried thinking back but couldn't focus over the pain. "I don't know."

"Let's start with something easy," she said. "How many fingers am I holding up?"

"One."

"What's two plus two?"

He shot her a glare. "I'm injured, not deficient."

"Who's president of the Solar League?"

"Haruto Takahashi. These are ridiculous questions."

"What's your name?"

He opened his mouth to respond, but nothing came out.

The answer was on the tip of his tongue, suspended barely beyond his reach. It was like trying to place an old friend he hadn't seen in a while. The realization was there, but it hadn't fully connected. It was probably one of those situations where the answer would come to him as soon as he quit trying to force it.

"I know my name," he insisted. "I just can't think of it right now."

She wrinkled her forehead and studied him. "What's *my* name?"

This time he didn't have the foggiest idea. His instincts told him they knew each other, but not very well. Otherwise her name would be on the tip of his tongue, too.

"Remind me," he said. "How do we know each other?"

Of course she didn't answer him. He was beginning to think she was doing that on purpose. While she crouched there in silence, he scanned her for clues.

She wore a fingerless glove on one hand and cradled the other against her chest. Something about her glove plucked at his senses, a warning of sorts, but the memory wouldn't come. A simple bracelet encircled her wrist, thin and metallic with an M-shaped barcode etched onto the surface. He recognized it at once. The *M* stood for "master." That meant she had an indentured servant. But people only wore those bands while traveling. He glanced around the room, taking in metal walls and a staircase leading to a small platform and an exterior door.

"Are we on a ship?" he asked.

The girl laughed at him. "You drank more than I thought."

"It was your bracelet that clued me in."

She nodded at his hand. "You have the other one."

When he glanced down and noticed the matching *S* band, all the pieces clicked into place. "Do I work for you?" he asked, but the words felt wrong when he spoke them aloud. "No, that can't be right."

"Yes, it can," she said. "And I have the contract to prove it." She gave a scolding shake of her head. "You really *do* need to lay off the bottle before you kill your last few remaining brain cells."

He scowled at her. "Why would I indenture myself to you?"

"For a free vacation," she said with a shrug. "My father doesn't like me traveling alone, so he hired you to take me to the Obsidian Beaches. You said you've always wanted to go but couldn't afford the fare. It was a perfect match." She pointed at the platform above them. "In fact, we were on our way to catch our connecting ship when you got dizzy and fell down the stairs."

The Obsidian Beaches.

He hated to admit it, but her story sounded familiar. He recalled feeling excited to visit the beaches. Everything else was a blur, but at least his memory had begun to return. Just as he'd predicted, full realization would come as soon as he quit trying to force it. However, this didn't mean he was anyone's servant. He couldn't picture himself hauling this girl's baggage or braiding her hair. Assuming he knew how to braid hair.

"I want to see the contract," he told her.

"You can't," she said. "It's with my luggage on the next ship. Like *we* should be."

"But why did you hire me to travel with you? Why not take your friends?"

"My father thinks they're a bad influence," she whispered behind her hand. "He was afraid I'd have too much fun and come home with no tan lines." She laughed without humor. "So he chose you to keep me on the straight and narrow. You're doing an interesting job so far."

He studied the girl and tried to pinpoint the reason for his hesitation. Everything she said made sense, and yet . . .

"Listen," she told him. "I know you're hungover, but we're going to miss our connecting ship if we don't hurry. This outpost is kind of scary." She shrugged. "For you, anyway. With a pretty face like yours, the ship hands won't look twice in my direction."

That made him chuckle, but not for long. The added movement hurt too much.

"So are you coming?" she asked. "If not, I hope you have enough credits to cover your fare, because I only paid your way to this stop."

Did he have enough credits to buy a ticket? He had no idea.

"They arrest stowaways," she added with a raised brow. "Just so you know."

He glanced at his indenture band and wondered if he was being paranoid. All the evidence confirmed what the girl had told him, and he really did want to visit the Obsidian Beaches. Looking at the girl, he figured she didn't weigh more than a sack of potatoes. Even if she was lying, how much harm could she possibly do?

"All right," he decided. "But I still want to see the contract."

"You will, once we're settled in. Can you walk?"

He moved his legs in a brief inventory. They were wobbly but usable. "I might need some help."

She slung his arm around her neck, and together, they hauled him upright. His brain spun a rotation inside his skull. "Steady, there," she said while leading him toward the stairs. "If you throw up on me, I'm adding another week to your service."

"That's a joke, right?"

"Let's not find out."

Once they'd made their way up the stairs, she stopped to retrieve a glove, then kicked aside a discarded luggage trunk and keyed open the exterior door. A burst of canned oxygen washed over him, followed by piercing, artificial light. Right before they stepped out of the ship, he stopped her.

"Wait," he said. "Remind me what my name is."

"It's Doran," she told him. "Doran Zenith."

"Doran," he repeated. Yes, that felt right. "And who are you?"

She looked up at him with a smile so wide it drew out a dimple in her left cheek. Despite the drumming in his head, he couldn't help smiling in return. The girl wasn't beautiful, but she had an honest face, and he finally understood why he must've indentured himself to her.

"I'm Lara," she said. "But you can call me Miss Brooks."

CHAPTER FOUR

As Solara guided her new servant across the outpost floor, she couldn't decide if she was a genius or a fool. Taking Doran's money was a no-brainer. Once she'd hired a ship and reached the outer realm, the Enforcers couldn't touch her. Their jurisdiction didn't extend to the fringe settlements, and as a matter of policy, the settlers didn't extradite.

Everyone knew that.

Taking Doran along for the ride, however, wasn't one of her better ideas. At some point, his memory would return, and she couldn't keep stunning him forever. Her device had only one use left, two at most. Maybe she should ditch him here after she withdrew his credits. That was the smart thing to do.

"I was thinking," she said. "Let's see if we can get you wait-listed for a ship back to Earth. You shouldn't continue on like this."

"What?" His eyes went round. "No!"

"I'll pay for your ticket."

"You can't leave me here!"

"Oh, come on. It's not *that* dangerous."

He cast her a skeptical glance. "What about my 'pretty face' drawing in all the ship hands?"

"Just strike up a conversation with them," she said. "You're a lot less attractive once you open your mouth."

"Very funny." His muscles tensed as a hulking man with a long, jagged scar where his left eye belonged passed by. "I need to get to the Obsidian Beaches," Doran said. "There's something important I have to do there."

"Like what?"

"I don't know," he admitted. "But I remembered it's the whole reason I came on this trip. Whatever it is, it's urgent. You have to take me with you."

She stalled and tried to think of an excuse to send him home.

"Let me rephrase," he added, sharper than barbed steel. "I'm coming with you."

"Excuse me?" Solara came to a sudden stop, forcing him to do the same. "You'll go wherever I send you."

"I'm not—"

"Don't interrupt."

He sealed his lips shut.

"Our relationship is simple," she told him. "I say 'Jump,' and you say 'Through which window, Miss Brooks?' You don't make demands of me. Are we clear?"

Instead of answering, he cringed and used his free hand to grip his temples. Solara decided not to press the issue, because it wasn't any fun taking Doran down a peg when he was in so much pain. But that didn't mean she would let him order her around. She was the master now . . . for as long as this farce lasted.

Once the tightness faded from Doran's mouth, he gave a slow nod.

Solara was about to tell him not to let it happen again when he loosened his grip around her shoulder and whispered, "Please." He swallowed hard and begged with those big blue eyes. "Please don't leave me here."

All the air trickled out of her lungs.

"Take me to the beaches," he said, blinking down at her. "I won't cause any trouble."

How did he do that?

A minute ago she wanted to break his jaw, and now she had to fight the urge to pat him on the head and give him a cookie. That had to be some kind of superpower. She finally understood how he got everything he wanted in life.

Maybe it wasn't such a bad idea to bring him along. The outpost wasn't the safest place to strand someone with neuro-poisoning, and if she sent him back to the *Zenith*, the crew would find out what she'd done. Plus, traveling with Doran would allow her more access to his credit in case of an emergency. As an added bonus, she'd get to make him polish her boots and wash her socks—maybe wake him up in the middle of the night to fetch her a glass of water, too.

She smiled just thinking about it.

"All right," she said, figuring she'd already dug herself a deep enough hole, so she might as well keep on digging. What was one more felony? Doran's memory wouldn't return for at least another day. She could always ditch him then, or stun him again. "We'll go together."

"Thanks."

"Don't mention it. I'm sure you'll make it up to me." She hid a grin and paused to take in her surroundings.

Thanks to movie nights at the group home, she knew that each space station was modeled the same. Along the perimeter, narrow corridors led to the ships docked outside. If the doorway glowed green, it meant a vessel was available for hire. A glance around the hub showed only three green doors, fewer than she had hoped but better than none. The center of the outpost was a wide floor dotted with freestanding vendor booths, an open setup that made it easier for security to keep watch from their platform overhead. Only two structures in the outpost offered the conceal-ment of four walls and a roof: the automated mall, where valuable commodities were kept, and the bordello, where she probably would've ended up if Doran had succeeded in abandoning her.

Solara slid a glare at him.

Suddenly she didn't feel so guilty about spending his money. But first she had to gain entry to the automated mall. No one was allowed inside until proving they had credits to use, which she could only do by scanning Doran's bracelet along with his handprint. After that, she'd be free to buy whatever she needed without scanning him again.

"I want you to come with me to the auto mall," she told him. "There's probably a med-pod in there. We'll buy something to settle your stomach before we board the ship."

He answered with a nod, and she tightened her hold around his waist while they crossed the floor. To avoid drawing attention, she kept her stride casual and leaned into Doran's body as if she couldn't get enough of him. She hoped they looked like a couple, as much as that made her want to retch.

When they reached the auto mall, she placed his palm on the security pad and scanned her bracelet, thankful he was too woozy to notice. Then the doors parted, and she led the way into the market of her dreams.

She'd never seen the inside of an auto mall—or any mall for that matter—but she imagined this was what heaven looked like. Rows of luxuries spread out before her: delicate candies, silken robes, insulated spacesuits, medicines, tools, and even Spaulding fuel chips. She'd hoped to find the chips here, because those slow-burning ore coins were the most useful currency in the galaxy. She was going to buy as many as she could carry.

After she peeled Doran off her.

She helped him to the medical pod in the far corner, a computerized chair behind a thin metal screen that offered patients the illusion of privacy. He lowered to the seat, and she strapped a belt around his chest and lap, making sure to position the buckles behind the seat, where he couldn't reach them. If his memory returned, at least he'd be trapped here for a while. Attached to the chair was a small screen that read, TOUCH HERE TO BEGIN TREATMENT.

"Let's see," she said, scrolling through the medicinal offerings. "Custom-made tonics." She tapped the corresponding button and asked Doran to describe his symptoms. As he spoke, she clicked HEADACHE, NAUSEA, and DIZZINESS.

A computerized voice droned, "Please provide one hundred credits."

Doran looked at his wristband. "Do I have that much?"

"Probably not." Solara lightly patted his cheek while scanning her bracelet. "But lucky for you, I take care of my employees." When the pod dispensed a cup of clear, fizzy liquid, she chirped, "Bottoms up."

She stepped out from behind the screen and headed straight for the fuel chips. It wouldn't take long for Doran to finish his seltzer, and then they needed to go. Each second they spent here was a risk.

She bought the sturdiest shoulder bag she could find and told the computer to fill it with chips. As she watched the tiny coins drop into the sack, an idea came to mind. She fed the machine a leather cord and instructed it to punch a hole in a set of chips to string a necklace for her to wear. She'd seen traders do the same—it kept their currency close.

While her fuel order was being filled, she wandered the aisles and purchased a practical wardrobe and enough boots to last five years. She guessed Doran's size and ordered a set of generic coveralls for him, the kind she'd worn at the group home. It put a bounce in her step to imagine how he'd look as a ward of the diocese.

Next she loaded up on standard medications like pain relievers and antibiotics. She'd heard those were hard to find in the outer realm. After buying a precision tool kit and a set of toiletries, she was ready to have her order boxed. But then a twinkle of light caught her eye, and she saw something that sucked the air from her chest.

It was a dress. No, not a dress—a gown fit for an empress.

Made from the most opulent fabric she'd ever seen, it hugged the mannequin's curves to the waist and flared out to the floor, shimmering like a million dying stars. The effect was mesmerizing. She couldn't identify the dress's color. It was simply made of brilliance.

Solara knew she'd never wear anything so lavish. A gown like that was for people with more money than IQ points. But that didn't stop her from drifting forward and allowing the computer to take her measurements. A moment later, the screen showed her size in stock and offered the dress for five thousand credits.

She gulped and scanned her bracelet.

TRANSACTION APPROVED.

"Thanks, Doran," she whispered. "You shouldn't have."

A shaky laugh escaped her lips. She'd better wrap it up before she completely lost her mind. She returned to the med pod, where Doran pounded a fist against his chest and released a belch.

"Better?" she asked him.

When he glanced over his shoulder, she noticed a difference in him right away. His brow was smooth and his eyes were clear of pain. "Much."

"Good, because you have a lot of packages to haul."

Annoyance flashed behind his eyes, but he clenched his jaw and mumbled, "Yes, Miss Brooks."

It was music to her ears.

Ten minutes later, he wore a set of delightfully dull coveralls and pushed a handcart piled high with her treasures. She led the way, glancing around the outpost at the green doorways to weigh her options, until a voice came over the central intercom and interrupted her thoughts.

"Passenger Spaulding," came the announcement. "Please report to your ship."

Solara's heart dropped into her pants. How had the *Zenith* discovered Doran's absence so quickly? Jerking her gaze to the nearest green doorway, she told him, "That one!" She jogged ahead of him to the corridor and punched the contact button while scanning the temporary sign affixed to the wall.

SS *BANSHEE.* CAPTAIN PHINEAS ROSSI,
SOLE PROPRIETOR.
RING BELL FOR INQUIRIES.
NO SOLICITING—UNLESS YOU'RE
SELLING SUGAR GLIDERS.

There was no information on the ship's make or model, and Solara had never heard of a sugar glider. But beggars couldn't be choosy. She pushed the button a few more times and peered across the expansive hub at the *Zenith*'s boarding doorway, where two stewards argued with each other. Probably debating how much longer to wait before dispatching a search team. Solara's pulse skipped, and she pushed the button again.

Footsteps clamored from inside the boarding corridor, and a boy's furious voice echoed, "Enough! I cranking heard you the first time!" He appeared wearing a scowl that instantly softened when he noticed her. With wheat-brown eyes the exact shade of his skin, he moved his gaze over her from head to toe while a lopsided grin curved his lips. Then he dipped his blond head, sending dreadlocks spilling over both shoulders. "Pardon my language," he said. "I didn't realize I was in the presence of a beautiful lady."

No one had ever called Solara beautiful before, nor a lady, but the compliment didn't touch her. She had known others like him—gorgeous and cunning boys with the same impish twinkle in their eyes. They understood how to twist a girl's heart using nothing but words.

But not *her* heart.

"Passage for two to the outer realm," she said coolly.

At the same time, Doran and the boy repeated, "The outer realm?"

"I thought we were going to the Obsidian Beaches," Doran said.

"That's right," she corrected. "The Obsidian Beaches, *then* the outer realm." She remembered the lie she'd told about her overprotective father. "I only contracted you as far as the beaches. Once we're there, I'll find another indenture to take me the rest of the way."

The blond boy stared at her as if she'd grown a third eye. "That won't be cheap."

"I can pay you in credits," she said. "Or fuel chips."

"We prefer chips."

"How much?"

"At least two thousand per person, probably more."

"I'll give you twice that if we can leave now."

Fair brows shot up his forehead. He raised an index finger.

"Wait here. The captain has to approve all passengers." Before she could ask him to make an exception, he turned and ran down the boarding corridor.

Five minutes passed. Then ten.

The intercom blared, "Passenger Spaulding, report to your ship."

Solara's palms began to sweat. She wiped them on her pants while peering down the dark hallway that led to the *Banshee*. What was taking the captain so long?

Seconds later, she found out.

It had taken him so long because he was older than home-made sin—and twice as terrifying. Like a craggy character ripped from the pages of an ancient seafarer novel, the captain limped onto the hub, every other step a metallic clink that suggested one of his legs was a titanium prosthetic. His eyes looked artificial, too, unnaturally black and scrutinizing her while he stroked a thick white beard. The skin on his face reminded her of a dried apple, withered and caving in on itself, and although his shoulders filled out the broad seams of his jacket, he stooped over and moved with the aid of a crutch.

Solara didn't know what kind of captain she'd expected, but he wasn't it.

"Captain Rossi?" she asked, resisting the urge to look away. His gaze burned as real as any med-ray until she could swear he saw inside her. Maybe he did. "I'm Lara, and this is my servant, Doran. We require passage to—"

"The fringe," he interrupted with a smile that didn't reach beyond his lips. "*And* the Obsidian Beaches, of course. We mustn't forget that."

Solara swallowed a lump of fear. He knew. Somehow he knew she was lying. Her only hope was that he cared more about money than truth. "Yes, and as I told your ship hand, I'll pay twice the fare if we can be off."

He watched her for a few silent moments, continuing to stroke his beard. "In a hurry, are you?"

"Who wouldn't be?" She tried to laugh, but it came out all wrong. Like a twittering bird that had flown into a window. "I've heard the Obsidian sands are so fine it's like walking on water."

The intercom repeated, "Passenger Spaulding, report to your ship," and Solara snuck a glance toward the opposite side of the outpost. What she saw made her insides turn cold. A dozen Enforcers in red uniforms and helmets pointed to the auto mall.

She snapped her head around and faced the captain. "Do we have a deal or not?"

His onyx gaze missed nothing. He looked at the Enforcers and then down at Solara's gloved hands. Her chest rose and fell in gasps; her thighs tensed to run. If he said no, she would bolt to the nearest ship and take her chances. When the wait had become unbearable, he said, "Ten thousand chips."

Relief flooded over her, so strongly that she would've kissed him if there were time. "Agreed."

The captain gestured to someone behind him in the corridor, and the boy with the blond dreadlocks approached. "Help Lara's manservant with the luggage," the captain said. "Be quick about it. We ship out in five minutes."

* * *

Solara learned that the blond boy's name was Kane, and he seemed to love nothing more than the sound of his own voice.

"This is the galley," he said, leading the way inside a small kitchen with an adjacent dining area. A rectangular table was bolted to the floor, and seating consisted of long benches positioned on either side. They were bolted down, too. Everything was—chairs, tool chests, even waste receptacles. On the *Zenith*, furniture could be moved, but that ship was larger than most high-rise hotels. The *Banshee* offered only four levels, and the combined engine room and cargo hold occupied one of them.

"You can have breakfast and lunch whenever you want," he went on. "But everyone eats dinner together in the galley. Captain's orders." Kane rested a hand on her shoulder, leaning in as if they were old friends. "He's a few centuries behind the times."

Solara glared at his hand, and he withdrew it.

"I'm the cook," he said. "So don't expect high cuisine."

She sniffed the air and picked up the acrid scents of dried onion and cumin. The crew probably ate a lot of chili. "That's all right," she told him. "I'm not picky."

"I knew I liked you for a reason." He winked, then flashed a toothy grin that slowly faded when she didn't reciprocate. Clearing his throat, he turned to continue the tour. Only then did Solara set a smile free. It had to be killing him that she didn't respond to his charms.

"That's the crew's storage hold," he said, pointing to a metal door on the right. "And the washroom's up there at the base of the stairs. Water's in short supply, so you're allowed one shower a week. In between, stick to sponge baths."

She nodded. It'd been the same at the group home.

They climbed the stairs to the residential level, where Doran sat on the lounge floor, counting out ten thousand fuel chips. The room was so unusual that it stopped Solara short at the threshold.

"Wow," she breathed, unable to hide her amazement.

Instead of flaking gray walls, the space was surrounded by murals depicting an alpine landscape of dark evergreens. In keeping with the forest theme, a cluster of chairs encircled a holographic fire pit, and on the opposite wall she noticed a shelf of books—real books, the kind nobody printed anymore. On the other end of the room stood a multipurpose gaming table much like the ones in the group home, though this set probably wasn't missing half of its billiard balls. Beside it, she spotted a small cage with a dormant hamster wheel and bedding made from old rags. But whatever creature had lived there was gone. She recalled the sugar glider mentioned on the sign and figured the ship mascot had died.

Kane pointed at the murals. "It's the Black Forest," he said. "Or at least how the captain remembered it from when he was a boy. He says it's mostly gone now." Kane shrugged. "I didn't grow up on Earth, so I wouldn't know. Anyway, this is where we spend most of our time."

"I can see why. It's an amazing room."

Doran shushed them from his spot on the floor. "Three thousand, two hundred and fifty-seven," he said, and pushed another coin into the massive pile he'd built. He glanced up and greeted Solara with narrowed eyes. "I unpacked your things, but I still haven't found our contract."

"It'll turn up," she promised. "How's your head?"

He didn't seem to appreciate the change in topic but grumbled, "Fine. The tonic is still working."

"You shouldn't sleep in long stretches tonight, just in case you have a concussion."

At the warning, he rubbed a nervous hand over his scalp.

"I'll wake you," she said. "Every hour, on the hour."

"Are you sure?"

"Believe me, it's the least I can do."

When she left to resume the tour, she heard a coin scrape across the metal floor, followed by Doran's count of "Three thousand, two hundred and . . . and . . ."

"Fifty-eight," Kane supplied. "But why aren't you—"

"No," Solara interrupted before he could suggest that Doran use the currency scale. "I thought it was twenty-eight," she lied. "Make sure you get it right. The captain won't appreciate us shorting him."

"Well, I'm sure as hell not starting over," Doran snapped.

"Excuse me?" she said. "I don't think I heard you right."

Doran mumbled a word that would make an escort blush, followed by "One"—scrape—"two"—scrape—"three . . ."

This trip was going to be fun.

"The ship's quarters are down here," Kane said. "We all double up, even the captain and the first mate." He made an apologetic face and opened the last door in the hallway. "This is the only room we have left."

At first, Solara didn't see the problem. The space was clean and bright with stark-white walls and a double bed situated in the corner—lavish when compared to her narrow cot at the group home.

Kane scratched the back of his neck and took a sudden interest in his shoes. "I don't know what kind of relationship you have with your servant. . . ."

"Oh." Now she understood. "Not the kind you're thinking of." She'd rather sleep with the crusty old captain than share a bed with Doran. "It's not a problem. He can take the floor."

Satisfied, Kane turned back down the hallway and climbed the steps to the bridge at the top level. This area was narrower than down below, its ceiling tapered to a point so the only place she could stand without hunching over was in the middle of the room. To the left, a tall brown-haired man with glasses teetering on the tip of his nose was bent over a metal table that had been fused to the wall. About thirty years old, he appeared to be studying solar charts.

He met her gaze and grinned—a real smile that reflected in his eyes. It'd been so long since Solara had seen a gleam of genuine kindness that her heart melted, and she liked him at once.

"This is Lawrence," Kane said, lifting a hand toward the man. "Our first mate."

"Call me Renny," the man told her. He pointed at his charts. "I was just plotting a course to the Obsidian Beaches. The captain said your final destination is the fringe, but he didn't specify where."

"Vega," she said, and leaned in to look at his charts. She recognized the Solar Territories from interstellar geography class. The Milky Way was divided like a dartboard into four sectors with Earth as the bull's-eye and five rings moving out from it. The tourist rings were the closest, then came the colony planets, ore mines, and prison settlements, in that order. The Solar

League headquarters were on Earth, along with most of the galaxy's industry and wealth, so the farther away you traveled, the more rustic the surroundings. The fifth ring was the fringe, or the outer realm, which the government hadn't annexed yet. She tapped a spot on the chart and told him, "Vega's in the same sector as Obsidian, but a few rungs out."

"Good. That shouldn't be too—"

"Kane!" interrupted a shrill feminine voice that carried up the stairs so loudly it rattled a loose bolt in the floor. "You scum-eating son of a crotch smuggler!" Footsteps clattered up the metal planks, but Kane didn't seem concerned. He crossed one foot over the other and studied his fingernails. "I'll have your guts for bootlaces!"

"Go ahead!" he shouted. "But you'll have to reach up my ass to get them!"

Solara retreated a pace until her back met the wall. She braced herself, waiting for the owner of that enormous voice to appear, but a tiny young woman stepped onto the bridge, wearing a bathrobe that dragged on the ground. No taller than Kane's shoulder, the girl craned her neck to glower at him. Her tawny complexion and long blond dreadlocks were nearly identical to his, but dripping water onto the floor. Solara wondered if the two were siblings.

"You took my laser blade again," the girl shouted. "My only day for a shower, and now I can't shave!"

"I didn't touch your blade."

"Really?" The girl stood on tiptoe and scrutinized his jaw. "Then where's the dandelion fuzz that usually grows on your chin?"

Kane sighed. "Fine. I used it yesterday."

"I knew it!"

"But I put it back in your shower caddy." Kane gripped his hips. "I didn't bother asking, because I knew you'd never let me have it."

The girl curled one hand into a fist and shook it menacingly. "I'll *let you have it*."

"Check your caddy, you lunatic!"

"I told you, it's not there! The only other person—"

Suddenly the argument came to a halt and all eyes shifted to Lawrence, who blushed and dropped his gaze to the floor.

"Renny," the girl said. "Turn out your pockets."

The first mate dug into his pockets and emptied two handfuls of odds and ends onto the table—casino chips, a wristwatch, mismatched earrings, key fobs, dice, folded pieces of paper, and a pink laser blade.

He offered a sheepish grin. "Sorry. You know I can't help it."

The girl stomped forward and snatched her blade off the table. Then she flung her wet dreadlocks behind her and set off down the stairs.

"Hey," Kane called after her. "You owe me an apology!" When she didn't respond, he jutted his chin at the pile of knick-knacks on the table. "Is that my watch?"

"I don't know." Renny handed it over. "Probably."

Kane raised the item for show and told Solara, "There's a lockbox in your quarters. I suggest you use it, because Renny's got sticky fingers." He pointed down the stairs. "And that delightful girl is Cassia, the other ship hand."

"Is she your sister?" Solara asked.

He barked a laugh. "God, no. I'd hang myself."

Renny lifted an object from the table and inspected it beneath the light. Inky black and flawlessly round, it might resemble a marble to someone who hadn't trained for several years as a mechanic. But Solara knew what it was.

"Is that the *Banshee*'s tracker?" she asked. "Removed from its port?"

Renny and Kane shared a knowing look before the first mate tucked the item back inside his pocket. "Yes," he said. "It's broken."

Solara didn't believe him. Trackers withstood even the worst collisions, and it was illegal to remove one from its designated port. The only reason to do that was if someone didn't want to be found. Not that she was complaining. She didn't want to be found, either. But regardless, she resolved to bolt her bedroom door that night.

Clearly she wasn't the only one with secrets.

CHAPTER FIVE

Dinner consisted of dried beans stewed in rehydrated tomatoes. Solara could tell the food was reconstituted because of the rare times when farmers had donated fresh, albeit half-rotted, produce to the diocese. Even bruised and overripe, tomatoes in their natural state were bursting with a sweetness and tang that the dehydrating process couldn't capture. Still, she ate her supper without complaining. It was better than soy-meal, a cheap oat hybrid that tasted like dishwater.

The captain frowned at the untouched bowl of beans next to hers. "Where's your indenture? Everyone eats—"

"Together," she finished, avoiding his black gaze. She'd discerned that his eyes were real, but looking into them still made her uneasy. "I told him."

Doran joined them soon afterward, announcing his presence by dropping a sack of fuel chips on the floor. "It's all there," he said, and blew out a breath. "Ten thousand. I counted them myself."

"Counted them?" the captain asked. "Why didn't you use the machine?"

Doran froze. "What machine?"

"The trading scale," Kane supplied from the far end of the bench. "We'd never get anything done if we hand-counted chips. I told Lara about it."

While Doran glared at her, Solara explained, "But they're not always calibrated just right. I wanted to make sure the captain has his due."

With a disbelieving grunt, Doran took his seat. He glanced at his beans and then peered around the table as if looking for something. "Where's the main course?"

"This is it," she said.

"But there's no meat."

Solara turned to face him, stunned by the sense of entitlement that transcended his memory loss. It must be nice to afford so much animal protein that he expected to have it served at every supper. "If it's not to your liking," she told him, "the rest of us can divide your share."

Clearly he was hungry, because he curled a protective arm around his bowl.

"Now that we're all here, we can get started," the captain said. "Whose turn is it?"

"For what?" Doran asked.

"To ask 'would you rather,'" Cassia said, blotting her lips with a cloth napkin. "We play every night." She dismissed him with a flick of her wrist and turned to Kane. "Would you rather know the date of your death or the cause of it?"

"Can I change the circumstances of my death?" Kane asked.

49

"Of course not."

"Then the date," Kane quickly decided. "What's the point of knowing the cause if I can't change anything? That's a weak question."

Solara agreed with him, but she wasn't about to say so and risk Cassia's wrath. When it came to venom, the scorpions in Texas had nothing on this girl.

"Some people might want to know," Cassia argued. "So they're not always worrying about it."

"Who wastes their time worrying about how they're going to croak?" Kane shoveled a heaping spoonful of beans into his mouth and spoke with one cheek full. "Weak."

Cassia landed an elbow in his side. "Let's hear you do better."

"Fine," he told her, but Renny cut him off with a lifted hand.

"It's my turn," Renny said. "And I've got a good one." After a dramatic pause, he smiled at everyone and asked, "Would you rather find the love of your life, or ten million credits?"

At once, everyone echoed, "Credits," not needing time to think about it.

Renny's shoulders slumped. "Really?"

"Really," Doran said. "Credits are actually useful."

Renny looked at Solara with soft eyes, as if he considered her an ally and she'd disappointed him by not feeling the same way—strange because he didn't really know her. "Even you?" he asked.

She was about to tell him *Especially me* when she noticed movement from inside the captain's left breast pocket. She didn't expect to see a tiny brown head poke out and blink at her with bulging black eyes.

Solara extended an index finger. "Is that a chipmunk . . . in your pocket?" It sounded like the opening line to a bad joke.

"This is Acorn," Renny said, using a fingertip to stroke the animal's fur. At the contact, the creature ducked its head. "She mostly sticks with the captain."

"That's because he's her mommy," Kane said with a chuckle, then shut down his laughter when the captain glowered at him.

"Acorn's a sugar glider," the captain said. "Renny pinched her from a trader when she was a baby, then slipped her in my pocket without telling me. She's a marsupial, so . . ."

"She thought your pocket was her mama's pouch?" Solara pressed a hand over her heart. The poor little thing was motherless, just like her. "That's so sad."

Captain Rossi nodded, not looking pleased. "She bonded to me before I even knew she was in there. Made a mess of my coat."

"She makes a mess of everything," Cassia muttered under her breath.

"That's what the cage is for," Solara said. "The one in the lounge."

"Not that she uses it," added Cassia. "And guess who gets to clean up all her little surprises."

The captain cut a sideways glance at Cassia and reached a thumb inside his pocket to soothe his pet, as if the words had hurt her feelings. "You know she can't be caged in there all alone. Acorn's a colony animal."

"Very social," Renny added with a nod. "We looked it up. She can actually die if she doesn't get enough affection."

"So until we find her a friend or two," the captain said, "she has free run of the ship." He lowered his voice to a rumble and asked, "Anyone have a problem with that?"

Both ship hands faced their bowls and filled their mouths with food. Everyone ate in silence for a while, until Acorn peeked her furry head out again and Renny handed her a bean. She took it between her paws and sniffed it with a tiny pink nose, then began nibbling while making a contented chirping noise.

The captain's mouth turned down. "I wish you'd stop giving her junk food."

"It's not junk," Renny said in a tone that implied they'd had this argument before. "Beans are healthy."

"Not as healthy as insects and—"

An alarm interrupted them, and the captain cocked his head toward the sound in perfect synch with the marsupial in his pocket. "Vessel approaching," he muttered while reaching for his crutch. He pushed to standing with a groan and limped toward the stairs leading to the pilothouse.

"It's probably nothing," Renny told them.

But not a minute later, the captain's voice crackled over the intercom with a single command. "Strap in."

As the crew scattered, Doran jerked his gaze around the galley. "Strap into what?"

"Follow me," Solara said while swinging both legs over the bench.

She ran back to their room and pointed at the front wall, where two harnesses were bolted on either side of the door. Kane had shown her what to do in case of turbulence. They were supposed to sit on the floor and strap their backs to the wall.

A sudden force of inertia tossed them both to the floor. Their bodies collided, but Solara barely felt a thing. She rolled off Doran and crawled to the nearest harness. He did the same, and they buckled in.

Solara tightened her straps and drew both knees to her chest.

"I can't die yet," Doran whispered. "I barely remember living."

"Don't talk like that. It's probably just a debris field."

But then a force of energy passed through her—a vibration, like she'd pressed her whole body to the shell of an engine. The fierce, rattling hum settled in her joints. Her teeth clattered together, making her lips go numb. The discomfort stopped as abruptly as it had begun, but it left a lingering impact because she recognized the sensation. She'd felt it before, several months ago, when she'd tried to run from the Enforcers. It was a cautionary blast, a threat before they fired real ammunition. And if memory served, the *Banshee* would only get one more warning. Her heart pounded and jumped into her throat.

They'd found her.

"Did you feel that?" Doran asked, gawking at his hands. "It was like a million bees crawling over my skin."

The sickening buzz passed through her again. Solara opened her mouth to cry out, but she didn't get a chance. The ship turned sharply and rolled to the left until she was hanging upside down by her harness straps. A discarded cup clattered against the ceiling, making her grateful the furniture was bolted down. The floor trembled with something new, and then a horrible screech rent the air as the ship rocketed forward with enough force to glue her limbs to the wall.

Now she understood why the ship was called *Banshee*.

The room lurched and spun for what felt like an hour before it came to a sudden halt.

Solara shook her head to clear it. Had they landed?

All motion seemed to have stopped, but dizzy as she was, she couldn't be sure. The captain's voice blared through the intercom, and the urgency in his tone sent a pang of fear through her. If a man like Rossi was anxious, it must be bad.

"We made an unplanned stop," he barked. "All hands report to the bridge."

Solara's left arm was pinned awkwardly beneath the harness strap, so she brought her free hand to the buckle and fumbled with the release button. She had to find a place to hide from the Enforcers. Kidnapping was a capital offense, and Doran hadn't been lying when he'd said his family had connections in the Solar League.

Cold sweat slicked her hand, causing her grasp to slip from the fastener until she whimpered and tugged at the strap. She turned to Doran and said, "Help me out of these buckles."

But instead of making himself useful, he sat there with a palm clapped over his mouth, swallowing in noisy gulps like he might lose his supper.

As Solara wiped the sweat from her hand, panic morphed into anger. She should've known better than to rely on Doran Spaulding in a crisis. "Never mind," she shouted. "I'll figure it out myself, since you're totally helpless."

Doran wrenched his head around and fired an all-too-familiar glare at her. "I'm not helpless, and I *do* matter!" He flinched as if he'd startled himself with his own words, and Solara did the same—because he'd just responded to something she'd said on board the *Zenith*.

"What?" She pretended not to understand him while praying it was nothing more than a fluke. If his memory had returned, there was no point in running. He would lead the Enforcers right to her. "Where did that come from?"

Twin lines appeared between his brows. "I don't know. It just slipped out." His tone sharpened when he added, "But don't say that to me. I'm not helpless."

"All right." She released a breath and sat back, pointing at her straps. "Show me."

With surprisingly deft fingers, he unfastened his harness before scooting over to start on hers. But as soon as he reached out, he paused with his fingertips suspended an inch from the buckles. A bloom of color fanned out across his cheeks, and he nervously licked his lips.

Solara glanced down and saw the problem. There was no way to free her from the tight straps without touching her breasts. She rolled her eyes. He was awfully prudish for someone who'd left his girlfriend's thong in the elevator.

"This isn't the time for modesty," she told him. "Just do it."

He got to work, and within seconds, she shrugged out of the harness and stood up. The floor seemed to tilt beneath her, and she gripped the wall for support. It took a few moments for the dizzy spell to pass, but then she regained her focus and opened the bedroom door.

Doran peeked over her shoulder into the dim hallway. "What now?"

That was the million-credit question. Solara didn't know where the ship had landed or what she would find beyond the doorway, but anything was better than cowering in her room. Steeling herself, she led the way into the hall.

"Now we move."

CHAPTER SIX

*N*o free vacation was worth this.

Doran's stomach heaved and his mouth flooded with saliva, but he gulped hard, willing himself not to vomit as he followed Lara through their rusted tin can of a ship. He hated small spaces like this. The metal walls seemed to shrink, contracting around his rib cage until he had to close his eyes to draw a lungful of air. He knew the sensation wasn't real, but that didn't make it any less painful.

For the life of him, he couldn't understand why she'd booked passage on the *Banshee* instead of a luxury liner. This ship was a dump. He shouldn't have to share a room with anyone—or sleep on the damned floor. Hell, his second apartment was larger than this piece of dung.

Wait. Second apartment?

He froze in place as images flashed before him of a bright living room furnished with plush leather sofas and tables made of etched glass. Sunlight peeked between the narrow slats of UV-resistant window blinds, which he instinctively knew concealed a stunning panorama of the city skyline. He'd finessed many a date out of her skirt with that view. He recalled that down the hall and past the guest room was his master suite, with a king-sized bed facing the theater wall, so he could fall asleep watching movies. But that wasn't the best part. He'd had the adjoining room customized to store his clothes—that way he would never have to walk inside another closet.

The luxurious penthouse was his second home, where he'd stayed on weekends or when his boarding academy was between sessions.

Doran smiled. He had more money than God.

So what the blazes was he doing here?

He jogged to catch up with Lara, who crouched at the end of the hallway and peered around the corner like a mouse looking for a place to hide.

Not a mouse, he thought. *A rat.*

Doran didn't know where that'd come from, but something about this girl was off level. She still hadn't produced a contract—possibly because there wasn't one—and twice at supper, he'd caught her glaring at him like she wanted to drive a fork through his head. And why did she want to visit the outer realm? Only two kinds of people ended up there: settlers who couldn't afford to live on Earth and the scum who preyed on them.

Which was Lara?

"Hey," he whispered, making her jump. "I want answers."

She whirled on him and slapped a palm over her heart, then whisper-yelled, "Don't creep up on me like that!"

Even in the faint glow of the emergency lighting, he saw her birthmark thumping wildly at the base of her throat and her gloved hands trembling. It reminded him of the way she'd whimpered and clawed at her harness a few minutes ago. Despite her dodgy behavior, a thread of compassion tugged at Doran's heart. He'd felt a similar panic in the outpost, where she could have left him but chose not to.

"Fine. We'll talk later," he said. "What are we doing?"

She thumbed toward the stairs leading to the bridge. "Listening to hear what's going on."

"Why?" he asked. "Just go talk to the captain. I'd say ten thousand fuel chips entitles you to a status update."

"Not yet," she said. "Not until I know it's—"

A clattering of boots interrupted her, at least two pairs heading quickly down the stairs in their direction. Doran stepped into the main corridor to intercept the crew. Lara grabbed at his sleeve, but he shook her off. If she wanted answers, they wouldn't find them by lurking in the shadows.

"Hello?" he called.

The footsteps halted for a moment, and then the two young ship hands stepped into view. Doran couldn't remember their names, but the girl yelled like it was her job, and the boy had an oily smile that he used on everyone except the girl. The pair seemed to enjoy spitting curses at each other, and yet they stood so closely in the passageway that their shoulders touched.

Doran couldn't quite figure them out.

They blinked at him as if they'd forgotten there were passengers on board. Then the boy flashed that annoying sideways grin and said, "Sorry for the bumpy ride. Everything's fine now." His stomach rumbled, and he pressed a hand over it while making an apologetic face. "The galley's a mess. I'm afraid we'll all have to hold out till breakfast. We're docked here until morning, so you should go ahead and turn in."

"Where's *here?*" Lara asked from her hiding spot around the corner.

The blond girl must've smelled Lara's fear because she retracted her fangs. "An old lunar colony," she said sweetly. "It's abandoned. We come here sometimes when we need a quiet place to . . . uh . . ."

"Sleep," finished the boy. "Captain's worn out, and the autopilot's on the blink."

Lara glanced up and down the hall. "Did anyone follow us?"

Blond dreadlocks bounced as the pair shook their heads, and based on the question, Doran wondered if Lara was worried about privateers. He couldn't really blame her. Organized crime flourished in space, where Enforcers were spread too thin to prevent it. But most convicts were motivated by profit, and like all businessmen, they ran a cost-benefit analysis before attacking a vessel.

"A ship this small won't catch a pirate's eye," Doran told her. "Not enough cargo in the hold. The ship-jackers won't want it, either. Flying this heap to the nearest salvager would cost more in fuel than it's worth." He threw a glance at the ship hands. "No offense."

The girl shrugged. "He's right. We're safe here. So try to get some rest."

Lara agreed, but as soon as they returned to their room, she pointed at the door and told Doran, "Bolt that. I don't know why the captain docked here, but there's nothing wrong with the autopilot."

"How do you know?"

"I just know," she told him. "Trust me."

Trust her? That was almost funny—*almost*. He slid the bolt into place, then leaned back against the door and folded both arms across his chest. "Speaking of blind faith, where's our contract?"

"Around here somewhere," she said, unfastening her braids. "I'll look tomorrow."

"I don't think you'll find it." He studied her reaction by the dim glow of the exit light mounted above the door. Her face betrayed nothing, but she couldn't hide the sudden stillness in her chest. "Because there's no contract, is there?"

"I wish there wasn't. More than you know."

"I remembered something earlier," he said, tapping an index finger against his head. "I have money. Tons of it."

"Congratulations." She rolled her eyes. "I'm sure you'll be very happy together."

"So why would I indenture myself to you, or anyone else?"

With her back turned, she loosened each plait until her hair hung in waves that curled around her waist. Then she spun to face him and puffed a sigh. "Fine. You caught me. I guess there's no use pretending anymore."

Doran settled in and waited for the punch line.

"I lured you onto this ship," she said, "because I couldn't get enough of your scintillating personality."

There it was.

"Kiss me, Doran," she cried, flopping onto the mattress with one arm slung over her eyes and the other clutched to her breast. "I burn for you, hotter than a thousand hells."

He cocked his head to the side. "I think there's an ointment for that."

"Desire like this can't be tamed by medicine."

"I'm glad you think this is funny."

"Listen," she said, and pushed onto one elbow. "We're not friends. You don't confide in me. So I don't know why you came on this trip, or what your motives were. Maybe it had something to do with that job on Obsidian. Maybe not. But in case you've forgotten, I tried to send you back to Earth."

"I haven't forgotten." It was the one hole in his theory that he didn't work for her. "But something doesn't feel right."

"Nobody held a gun to your head and made you board this ship." She pulled a blanket over her legs and used its concealment to remove her pants, then tossed them onto the floor along with an extra pillow. "So let's drop it and get some sleep."

He didn't want to let it go, but what could he say? Lara had a point. She hadn't forced him to tag along. He'd come willingly, and the more he thought about it, the more he believed the Obsidian job was the reason.

A memory teased at him, the barest recollection of a man's voice urging Doran to visit the beaches and pretend he was on vacation. The job was a secret, and the sudden heaviness in his stomach made him believe it might not be entirely legal. That would explain his odd travel arrangements.

He gathered his blankets and made a pallet on the steely

floor. But it wasn't the cold metal that kept him tossing and turning for an hour. He didn't want to believe he would do anything criminal. He wasn't like that, was he?

Doran didn't know, and that scared him a little.

* * *

The next morning he awoke to a sensation of floating, his limbs weightless and free from the hard press of the floor. Yawning, he blinked against the starlight streaming through the porthole, then gasped when he spotted the floor several feet beneath him. He flailed in panic, heart pounding while his muscles tensed to brace for the fall.

But the fall never came.

Soon realization set in, and Doran exhaled in relief. The artificial gravity drive must've died during the night. On a clunker like the *Banshee,* it probably happened all the time. This ship was a death trap. Even something as simple as a gravity drive could be dangerous if it reengaged too suddenly. Anyone who'd drifted above a hard surface might snap his spine when gravity took hold again.

He should wake Lara.

He pushed aside a curtain of floating blankets and saw her suspended above the bed, fast asleep with her lips slightly parted and a fringe of dark lashes resting against her cheeks. The tension that usually hardened her eyes and tightened her mouth was gone, leaving behind nothing but peace. He tipped his head and studied her, struck by how different she looked—almost angelic as a gentle beam of light illuminated her flowing waves of hair.

She glowed. It was sort of mesmerizing.

Because he was only human, he couldn't help noticing that her covers had drifted away, leaving her exposed in nothing but a fitted T-shirt and cotton briefs that rode low on her hips. Her legs were fair and smooth, with gentle curves that tapered to a delicate set of ankles and tiny pink toes. She wore no holographic nail polish to trap his gaze, and yet he couldn't look away. It must've been a long time since he'd seen a girl's naked toes, because he'd nearly forgotten what they looked like.

Doran swallowed hard.

He shouldn't be watching her like this. She was his employer, not some escort on display in the front window of a flesh house. But despite that, it took another minute for him to reach out and tap her on the shoulder.

She came to the same way he had, arms flapping and legs kicking, before she realized there was no force pulling her toward the ground. Then she uttered a curse and said, "Gravity drive."

He snagged her pants and handed them over. "I was about to wake the crew."

"No, let them sleep." She wrestled with the garment, struggling to shove both legs inside without the leverage of her weight. Soon she was floating upside down. "I'll fix it."

He did a double take. "You'll what?"

"Fix it," she told him while zipping up. "And you'll help me."

"Sure," he droned. "I always assist in major ship repairs before breakfast."

Just add this to the day's list of surprises. Who was this girl?

It occurred to him that he didn't know anything about her, like where she'd gone to school or what program she'd studied. Not even her age.

"Are you an engineering student?" he asked.

"Something like that." She pointed to a crate strapped to the floor, supplies she'd bought at the outpost. "Reach in there and grab my tool kit. Then follow me down to the engine level."

They swam like drunken fish through the hallways, propelling themselves with barefoot kicks against the wall. Doran engaged her in small talk and learned that she was eighteen, like him. She'd recently graduated and was on her way to the outer realm for training, though she wouldn't specify what kind.

She was lying, of course.

No eighteen-year-old traveled to the fringe unaccompanied, not for training. But he didn't bother pressing for the truth. If she wanted to risk her neck in the middle of no-man's-land, that was her business.

They reached the ship's bottom level and turned on the lights, which didn't do much to orient him. Half the room was a cargo hold with massive crates bolted to the floor, and three sliding metal doors compartmentalized the other half.

"If this is the engine room," he asked, "where's the engine?"

"There's more than one," Lara told him. "They're kept quarantined, so if a fire breaks out, it won't fry the whole system." She pointed to the first metal door. "Hear that whirring sound?"

He nodded.

"That's the emergency engine. It powers oxygen and heat: things we can't do without. There's usually a backup generator, too. If we run out of fuel, we can hand-crank enough air to keep us breathing until someone responds to the distress call."

Doran didn't say so, but only idiots responded to distress calls. That was a good way to get yourself robbed, sold, or killed. Maybe all of the above. He'd heard about pirates sending distress beacons and then sitting back while the victims came right to them. Smart travelers kept their heads down and minded their own business.

"That's the main engine," Lara said, pointing at the middle door. "It's powered down, otherwise we'd need earplugs." Then she indicated the final door. "There's the room we want—secondary systems, navigation, electrical. All the ship's bells and whistles."

"Bells and whistles?" he asked. "More like rubber bands and Popsicle sticks."

Lara frowned at a flake of rust floating past her nose. "Well. In hindsight, maybe I should've picked a different ship."

She pushed off the steps, sailing across the room, and Doran followed. It took some maneuvering, but they eventually made it to the last door and slid it into the wall.

A warm gust of static blew over them, smelling of oil and dust. It tickled a sneeze from his nose and sent him backward an inch. When he caught hold of the doorframe, he let his gaze wander over the variety of machines mounted to the walls. They varied in size and shape, but each was dulled by layers of old grease, their tubes opaque and gummy with age.

The ship's innards matched its hull—ridden hard and put away wet.

"At least no moths fluttered out," Lara said. She gripped her way around the room until she settled in front of a boxy device that resembled a climate console.

The tiny space made Doran's airway squeeze, so he stayed put. "I'll wait here until you need me."

Nodding, she snapped the grav drive casing from the wall, then began prodding at its wires. It didn't take long for her to find the problem. "The couplers need replacing."

"Easy fix?"

"Five minutes, tops," she said. "But I'll keep it powered off until the crew's awake. I don't want bodies crashing to the floor. That's no way to say good morning."

Doran laughed. The sensation felt foreign, and he wondered how long it'd been since something had struck him as funny.

"Hand me the smallest wrench," she said. After he delivered the tool, she held it between her teeth and delved inside the grav drive. But loose strands of hair kept drifting into her face, tangling among the wires. She growled and mumbled around the wrench, "Help me out, will you?"

Doran didn't want to go in there, but he stuffed down his fear and moved behind Lara to gather her wayward locks. He smoothed the hair back from her head and twisted it into a ponytail, then rubbed the ends between his thumb and index finger. Her hair was freakishly soft, like liquid velvet. Lara shivered when his thumb accidentally brushed her skin, and he noticed chill bumps break out along the back of her neck.

She spat out her wrench. "That tickles."

"Sorry."

He tried coiling the twist into a knot, but the strands were too satiny to hold. Faintly, he recalled that he'd done this before—run his hands through a girl's hair—and liked it. But he'd never felt anything as silky as this. Probably because his girlfriend had damaged her hair by dying it so many glaring shades of pink.

He blinked and saw the girl's face, so stunningly gorgeous that she barely passed for a mortal. A sheet of sleek bubble-gum tresses fell just above the swell of her flawless breasts, and the rest of her was pretty impressive, too. He recalled that she'd even made elevator rides enjoyable, no easy task for a claustrophobic like himself.

"I think I have a girlfriend," he said, grinning. "She has pink hair."

Lara snorted a laugh. "Yeah, I met her. Pink hair and a black soul. You really know how to pick 'em."

"Oh, that's rich," he told her, "coming from a felon."

As soon as the words left his mouth, several things happened at once.

Lara whipped around to face him, jerking her hair from his grasp.

Their eyes widened and locked.

And Doran remembered everything.

It was like he'd yanked a veil from his face, and now free, he saw his past with perfect clarity. He was Doran Michael Spaulding, from Houston, Texas—the original Texas, not the terraformed knockoff in Sector Two. He'd had a brother once, a twin who shared his face. But that boy had died in a ball of flames, and Doran still had nightmares about it. His parents were Richard Spaulding and Elizabeth Kress-Spaulding, record holders for the world's most bitter divorce. His dad owned Spaulding

Fuel, and his mom had moved off world when she'd decided that her second-favorite child wasn't worth raising. Doran still hated her for that, but not half as much as he missed her. He recalled that chocolate made him break out in hives, and his favorite food was fried green beans.

Most important, he was *not* anyone's servant.

He grabbed the wall and used it to propel himself backward, away from Solara—her real name—until he was outside the tiny compartment. The distance was more for her protection than his. Rage boiled his blood, and there wasn't a word vile enough to describe what he wanted to do to her.

"Doran," she whispered. "Hear me out."

"Don't tell me what to do." Before she could advance on him, he slammed the door shut and trapped her inside. "Ever again."

She slapped her palms on the door, piercing his ears with the clank of metal. "I had no choice," she shouted, loud enough for him to hear on the other side. "You were going to leave me stranded in the middle of nowhere!"

"What did you do to me?" he demanded. "Hit me on the head? Drug my food?"

She waited a few beats before admitting, "It was a handheld stunner."

Neuro-inhibitors. That explained a lot.

He shook his head in disgust, recalling the way she'd offered her hand to him after their argument on the *Zenith*. He'd actually felt too guilty to accept it, and now look. She'd trussed him up in workmen's coveralls and plundered his credit account. His first instincts had been right. Once a felon, always a felon.

"Kidnapping is low," he yelled. "Even for you."

Her fists pounded twice against the door. "I didn't have a choice."

"Save your breath." He glanced around the room for a way to wedge the door shut. "I know who I am, and soon the captain will, too."

"Wait, no!"

If he could just find a crowbar to shove through the door handle . . .

"Doran, listen to me," she shouted. "You don't want to tell the crew who you are."

He grabbed a floating bungee cord and used it to tether the door handle to a nearby hook in the wall. The tension wasn't as strong as he'd like, but it should hold long enough for him to alert the captain.

"Remember the buzzing last night?" she went on. "That wasn't the engine. It was a warning blast from the Enforcers. This crew is running from the law." When he turned and prepared to launch himself toward the stairs, she added, "These are the kind of people who might ransom you."

Her warning stopped him cold in his tracks.

He reached out a hand to steady himself against the door, and then he wasn't in the ship's engine room anymore. For a sliver of a second, he was locked inside a dark closet. The air smelled musty and metallic, like mold and blood, and there wasn't enough of it in the tiny space. He panted for oxygen and choked on acrid smoke while the echo of his brother's screams filled his head.

Doran gritted his teeth and told himself it wasn't real.

That closet doesn't exist anymore. It burned to the ground.

He opened his eyes and cemented himself in reality. He was safe.

"You're just saying that to save yourself," he yelled. He couldn't stop his voice from cracking.

"I can prove it." She must've pressed her lips to the door because she sounded close enough to stun him again. "They pulled the ship's tracker. If you don't believe me, go to the bridge and check. The port will be empty."

Doran rubbed his forehead and considered his options. He knew that criminals disabled their trackers, but that didn't mean Solara was telling the truth. He needed to check—alone. He set off through the hallways and stairwells, flinching every time his weightless body thumped against the wall. Waking the crew was a bad idea, at least until he knew he could trust them. When he reached the top level, he gingerly slid aside the pilothouse door and shielded his face from the starlight streaming through the front window.

Once his eyes adjusted to the brightness, he scanned the control panel until he found a red bull's-eye with the acronym SLATS stenciled above it—Solar League Auto Tracking System. He pulled his way closer and dipped his finger into the circular depression where the tracker belonged. The port was empty, just as Solara had said.

"Damn it," he whispered.

Leave it to her to book them on a ship full of fugitives.

As much as he hated it, she was right. Revealing his identity to this crew was as smart as sticking his arm in an ore grinder. Just like the others, they'd hear the name *Spaulding* and see easy credits. His dad loved him enough to pay the ransom, but Doran wouldn't put either of them through that hell again.

Never again.

Somehow he would have to let his father know he was safe, then lie low until the next outpost. His dad would send a private shuttle, maybe even pilot it himself to make sure everything was all right. That was what he'd done last year—walked right out of a shareholders meeting to fetch Doran from spring break during a mutated flu pandemic. Any other man would have sent an assistant. Not Richard Spaulding. He might be ruthless when it came to business, never hesitating to slash thousands of jobs to raise profits, but he believed in putting his son first. And unlike most men of his stature, he backed it up with action.

In a sudden flood of relief, Doran remembered it was his father who'd sent him to Obsidian, for a job that was classified, not illegal. His vacation with Ava had been a ruse to throw off the competition. Once they arrived at the beach, he was supposed to send her home and retrieve a private ship, then continue to a set of coordinates and await further instructions. Now that the original plan had changed, maybe he and his father could travel there together.

Doran blew out a breath. Everything would be all right.

In the meantime, he'd have to play the part of Solara's manservant. The idea made his jaw clench. What were the odds of them sharing a bedroom for the next few days without killing each other?

About as likely as him admiring her toes ever again.

After closing the pilothouse door, he followed the sounds of fists against steel to the impromptu holding cell he'd created on the bottom floor. He released his prisoner with a warning: "Try anything and I'll shove you in the garbage chute, where you belong."

The little rat drifted into the open, shooting daggers with her eyes while her hair snaked out in all directions. Her nostrils flared as she heaved a furious breath. Now that she'd dropped the whole innocent act, she reminded him of Medusa. Which fit her true nature a whole lot better. "Well?" she forced through her teeth. "Believe me now?"

He refused to acknowledge the question, instead turning and launching himself toward the stairs. "I'd estimate we're at least two days from the nearest outpost. If we're going to coexist until then, we need to establish some ground rules."

She smirked and followed. "I'll take that as a *yes*."

"Rule number one, I'll keep the stunner," he said, holding out his palm. The weapon might come in handy if the crew discovered his identity.

"No way." She pressed a protective hand to her side pocket. "How do I know you won't use it on me?"

"Because unlike you, I'm not a lowlife convict." When she hesitated, he told her, "This is nonnegotiable."

"Fine. It only has one use left anyway." She tossed the button-like device into the air between them. "Rule number two," Solara said. "We're not sleeping together."

A snort of derision tore from his throat. "As if I'd share a bed with you."

"Then enjoy the floor."

"Why shouldn't *you* take the floor?"

She flashed a dimple at him. "Because I'm not the one at risk for ransom."

Anger flushed his skin. He couldn't believe he'd ever thought she had an honest face. "You're a real masterpiece, aren't you? How many of my credits did you steal at that outpost?"

"Hey, at least I didn't leave you stranded there—like you tried to do to me."

"Clearly you would've been fine."

"If that's what you think, then clearly you're a pampered horse's ass!"

"You don't know anyth—"

A distant throat clearing interrupted their argument, and Doran turned to find Captain Rossi making his way toward them in the spry movements of a man accustomed to zero gravity, twice as quick in the air than on his feet. Doran studied the captain for any sign that he'd overheard something incriminating, but the only emotion etched on his wrinkled face was annoyance.

Solara waved. "We were just coming to wake you. I fixed your gravity drive."

Rossi's furry gray brows jumped.

"I'll bet you didn't know," Doran said to dispel suspicion, "that our Miss Brooks is a budding engineer."

The captain turned his dark eyes on her, but he didn't say a word. He simply stared until the silence grew awkward, then drew a sudden breath and said, "There's not much I *do* know about our Miss Brooks. I think it's time to remedy that."

Solara paled a few shades and nodded. Judging by the twitch

of her feet, she looked ready to pitch herself out the air-lock—a decision Doran fully endorsed.

"Let's talk over breakfast," she squeaked. It was satisfying to watch her squirm, until she added, "My servant will cook for us."

Doran shot her a warning glare. He didn't cook for anyone. Not even himself.

"He'll clean the galley, too," she said, clapping him on the shoulder. "Our Doran's no engineer, but he sure is a hard worker. I can't wait to show you what he's made of."

CHAPTER SEVEN

"Might as well take off the gloves." Using his crutch for support, Captain Rossi lowered onto the pilot's seat. Its metal springs groaned beneath his weight, and he mimicked the sound while rubbing one knee. "You're not fooling anyone."

He stowed his crutch on the floor between their chairs, leaning close enough for Solara to hear the tinny click of his artificial heart—a Beatmaster 3000, from the sound of it. The hollow tap was a dead giveaway. Lab-grown donor organs had replaced that technology decades ago, meaning the captain had to be at least a hundred years old. He seemed to have a lot of mechanical enhancements. Solara wondered how long a man could keep replacing his broken parts with machines before he lost what made him a person.

She pointed at his knee, which could use an upgrade, too.

"I'll bet you felt better when the grav drive was broken. Less stress on your joints."

"Don't change the subject," he said, powering on the main engine. The ship came to life in a gentle hum that drowned out the sound of his Beatmaster. "I know you're marked. What'd you do?"

Solara dropped her gaze into her lap and used a thumb to stroke the buttery leather of her glove. Did the whole crew know? Had they talked about her, worried she might attack them in their sleep? If so, they'd probably bolted their doors last night, too.

"I didn't hurt anyone," she said.

"I know that." His tone sounded clipped, as if she'd offended him. "The *Banshee* isn't much to look at, but she's where I lay my head at night. If I thought you were a threat, I wouldn't have let you on board."

"Thank you. She's a fine ship."

The captain wheezed a laugh. His chest shook, causing Acorn to flick her long, fluffy tail out of his pocket. "Now I know you're a liar *and* a con." He motioned to her with one hand. "Let me see."

His smile gave Solara the courage to peel off her gloves. She extended both arms while Rossi squinted at the block letters etched onto her skin. He arched an appreciative brow and let out a whistle.

"Grand theft," he said. "And conspiracy. Didn't see that coming."

"It sounds worse than it really is."

"Mmm-hmm. I've heard that before."

"I'm not a thief."

She shoved her hands back inside their casings, but that didn't stop Doran's voice from echoing inside her head. *You're a real masterpiece, aren't you? How many of my credits did you steal at that outpost?*

Just because Doran had money to burn didn't mean she had any right to take it. Her face grew warm when she pictured the crates of supplies downstairs in her quarters. There was nothing wrong with using his money to buy passage—he had promised her that in their contract—but she'd gone overboard with the clothes and tools . . . and the ball gown.

She *was* a thief.

"I didn't say you were," the captain told her. "Inked knuckles don't mean much." He disengaged the *Banshee* from its docking station, and with a slight lurch, they left the moon colony behind. Slanting her a glance, he said, "You met Renny. He'll steal the gun right off an Enforcer's hip, but he'll never wear a thief's mark. He's too good to get caught."

"That's different," she said. "Renny has a sweet spirit. He doesn't want to steal."

The captain lifted a shoulder. "Doesn't stop my pills from going missing."

"What I did was on purpose." She knitted her fingers together. "Kind of."

"Let me guess: the devil made you do it," he said, beard twitching as he grinned.

The devil. What a fitting description for Jace. The nuns had always preached that Satan was a seducer, that he dealt in clever half-truths and betrayed anyone foolish enough to allow him into her heart.

"Yes," she said. "You nailed it."

"Your father?"

"No. I don't remember my father." Like most kids at the group home, she'd been accepted into the custody of the church because her parents couldn't afford to keep her, and neither could the state. The abandonment stung, but at least her mom and dad hadn't thrown her to the wolves the way Jace had done. "He was a friend," she said as a blush crept into her cheeks. "Or at least it started that way."

The captain grunted in understanding. "Ah, yes. Love—the great equalizer. It makes all of us stupid."

A familiar ache opened up behind Solara's breast, but she forced it down. She hated that Jace still had the power to hurt her from halfway across the galaxy. She hated even more that she'd given him that power—dropped her heart right into his waiting hands in exchange for a few sweaty fumblings and some pretty words.

"It'll never happen again," she insisted. "I'm smarter now." She didn't know who she was trying harder to convince, herself or the captain, so she asked, "Can we talk about something else?"

"One more question, and then we don't have to talk at all."

"Fair enough."

He brought the ship around and hit the accelerator, and the *Banshee* shrieked, hurtling them away from the nearest sun and into the black. Light faded and within moments they were surrounded by a veil of darkness. The view sent a shiver down her spine. If anything could make her feel even more insignificant, it was the open void of space.

After programming a navigational course, the captain released the controls and sat back to face her. "What are you really after," he asked, "in the fringe?"

Solara drew a breath and prepared to give him the easy answer: *a job*. But something in his expression caught her off guard. A hint of tenderness shone in the depths of his ebony eyes, like he actually cared. She didn't know if that was the case, but she found herself willing to share the truth with him. And the truth was bigger than simply needing a job.

She was tired of being charity's slave.

When farms donated soy-meal to the group home, that was what she ate. If she outgrew her boots, she made do until someone discarded a larger pair. When her data tablet broke, she shared with another orphan. Nothing belonged to her, not a single sock. Even her underclothes had been handed down.

She wanted to own something, all to herself.

More than that, she craved a purpose—to matter and feel needed. In the outer realm, settlers didn't care about supple skin or glossy pink hair. Practical skills were the real beauty in those colonies, and for once, she would be stunning.

Finally she told the captain, "A new life. That's what I'm after."

He made a noncommittal noise, and she couldn't help noticing that the smile had left his face. "And you think you'll find it there?"

"Yes. Why wouldn't I?"

"Ever been to a fringe planet?"

"No, but I've heard the stories."

"It's a dirty, hard existence," he warned.

"I know that. And I want it."

He tipped his head in a *suit yourself* gesture. "All right, then. I guess we'd best see to our breakfast." Turning to his navigational screen, he added, "I just need to engage the autopilot."

She leaned in to peer over his shoulder. "It's not broken, then?"

"What's not broken?"

"The autopilot," she said, testing him. "Isn't that why we docked last night?"

He shifted a terse glance in her direction, a look that told her not to play games. "You know it's not."

"Yes," she admitted. "I felt the blast." She chewed the inside of her cheek and tried to think of a way to probe for more information without revealing that she was a kidnapper *and* a thief. "Who were they after?"

Gaze softening again, he patted her knee. "Not you."

Solara blew out a breath. That was all she needed to know.

They stood and slid aside the pilothouse door, then instantly recoiled at the stench that slammed into them from the other side.

"Saints on a cracker," she hissed, waving a hand to dispel the fumes. "Only one thing stinks like that."

"Burnt porridge," the captain muttered. "We'll never get the smell out."

He was right. Burnt gruel had magical properties, clinging to walls and surfaces like a hundred-year curse until the reek grew so familiar that you stopped noticing it. In hindsight, maybe she shouldn't have volunteered Doran for breakfast duty.

By the time Solara and the captain arrived in the galley, the whole crew had gathered at the table, Cassia and Kane on one side, Doran and Renny on the other. Each head was bent over a bowl of flawlessly prepared hot cereal, creamy and dusted with a sprinkling of cinnamon. That didn't explain the foul smell . . . until she glanced at her spot at the table and the bowl of soup waiting there. It seemed Doran had managed to simultaneously burn and drown her porridge.

And judging by the smug look on his face, he'd done it on purpose.

"Kane helped with breakfast," Doran told her. "But I insisted on making yours all by myself. I hope you love it."

She faked a smile and settled on the bench beside him. If he thought he'd won this round, he was wrong. She had eaten far worse than this. "I'm sure I will," she said, even as the putrid scent burned her nostrils. Peering down, she used her spoon to jab a lump floating in the gruel. Was that charred grain or a dead bug?

"Go ahead," Doran challenged. "Don't be shy. There's plenty more."

She glanced up and noticed the whole crew watching her with mingled amusement and disbelief. Even Acorn, who was perched on the captain's shoulder, nibbling a chunk of dried fruit, had trained her glassy black eyes on the bowl. Before Solara lost her nerve, she scooped up a spoonful of porridge and shoved it in her mouth.

Sweet mother of God. It tasted like death.

When her eyes and mouth watered in protest, she reminded herself that she couldn't let Doran win. She had to eat it. She tried to swallow three times, but her gag reflex kicked in and forced her to spit the mouthful into her bowl. The bite landed with a plop that splashed her cheeks.

The table erupted in laughter, and Kane walked to the stove to fill a new bowl for her. "I made extra, just in case," he said. He handed the porridge to Doran, who set it in front of her with a grin that made her want to slap him so hard his grandkids would feel it.

"Sorry it wasn't to your liking," Doran told her.

"That's all right," Solara said coolly while wiping her mouth. "I didn't hire you for your cooking skills. I'll find other ways to make you useful."

Cassia snorted from across the table and gave a knowing wink. "I'll bet you will."

Solara's face blazed. She couldn't shake her head fast enough. "No, that's not what I meant."

"Yeah," Doran echoed while pointing back and forth between him and Solara. "There's nothing—"

"Zero judgment." Cassia flashed a palm. "Hookups are the best way to fight transport madness. If you don't rev up those endorphins, the lack of sunlight will scramble your brain."

With a sardonic twist of his lips, Kane leaned an elbow on the table. "So *that's* why you keep a meathead at each port. I thought you just had bad taste."

Cassia swiveled around so quickly she smacked herself in the eye with her own dreadlocks. "Don't talk to me about taste, you wharf-licker!" she yelled. "Your last girlfriend couldn't walk and chew gum at the same time."

"Well, your last boyfriend had a nose like a weasel."

"Maybe it wasn't his nose that made him special."

Kane made a face. "Thanks for the visual. Excuse me while I vomit to death."

"Enough!" barked the captain, and Acorn dived headfirst into his pocket. "If you two can't behave, I'll send Renny to make the Pesirus delivery."

Cassia gasped and sat bolt upright. "Pesirus? That's today?"

The captain pointed his spoon at her. "Only for good little ship hands."

Cassia and Kane turned to each other with manic smiles, argument forgotten, as they bounced in their seats and squealed like children. They drew a joint breath and yelled, "Hellberries!"

Solara shared a questioning look with Doran.

"Those two are weird," he whispered behind his hand.

She nodded. For once, they agreed on something.

Cassia linked her arm through Kane's as if she hadn't just screamed in his face and called him a wharf-licker. "You should come with us," she said to Solara. "Your servant, too. It'll be fun."

The confusion must have shown on Solara's face because Renny explained, "Pesirus hosts a hellberry festival each spring. We have a contract to deliver cane syrup from Orion."

"They add syrup to the wine," Kane added. "To take the edge off. You can drink it straight, but it's a donkey kick to the mouth."

"Hellberry wine," Cassia said, going dreamy. "It's spicy and sweet and makes you warm all over. There's nothing like it."

The captain warned, "Your delivery comes first, then payment, then fun. And take it easy on the drink, you two. We don't want a repeat of last year."

His warning made Solara wonder what had happened last year. When she asked them, Renny and the captain grinned but said nothing while Cassia and Kane blushed ten shades of crimson. They avoided each other's eyes and then suddenly "remembered" they had chores to do. Within seconds, they were gone.

"Must've been good," Solara mused as she watched them retreat. She knew the dash-of-shame when she saw it. "Or hilariously bad."

Renny laughed. "I didn't get a ringside seat—"

"Neither did I," the captain interrupted. "Thank the maker."

"—but I imagine it was both."

Solara found herself wearing a smile. There was a real festival nearby, with food and drinks and games. She weighed the risk of appearing in public against the rewards of sunshine and spiced berries. In the end, sunshine won the battle. "Sounds fun. I'll come along."

Doran nudged her with his elbow.

"Doran, too," she added. As much as she dreaded spending the day with him, it wasn't smart to leave him alone. He might find a way to use the ship's com system to alert the Enforcers. "He's no engineer and his cooking may kill us, but even *he* can haul a few crates of syrup."

* * *

Four hours and two solar systems later, they stood in the bottom-level cargo hold and craned their necks to stare at a mountain of storage containers marked PESIRUS FEST.

"A *few* crates?" Doran remarked. "How much wine can one colony drink?"

Solara had to agree. Judging by the amount of syrup to deliver, the festival must've been more popular than she'd expected. In that case, maybe leaving the ship wasn't a wise move. She bit her lip, peering out the open door of the cargo hold to the rolling landscape beyond.

The view was nearly too gorgeous to believe.

Pure yellow sunlight gleamed above a field of shorn blue-green grass dotted with lavender wildflowers. The terraformed colors weren't quite right, as if someone had overbrightened the saturation on a telescreen. But after a month of space travel, her body craved fresh breezes and warm sunrays more than her next breath. She caught herself leaning toward the exit ramp.

She was *so* going.

"The job's easy," Kane said, thumbing toward a wheeled pallet parked outside. "We just stack everything on there, then strap it down and use the auxiliary shuttle to haul it to the fairgrounds."

"Easy," Doran repeated with a scowl. But he didn't spend another second complaining. He grabbed the first crate and walked outside, then double-timed it back for another.

Apparently he was anxious for fresh air, too.

Kane pulled off his shirt and tossed it over a nearby railing just as his fellow ship hand joined them. Cassia caught her lower lip between her teeth and stared at the dusting of blond hair across his chest before catching herself. Then with an eye roll, she snapped, "Quit showing off for the guests and put on your clothes."

"What?" Kane asked, splaying both hands. "Laundry day's not till tomorrow, and this is my last good shirt." He shot her a teasing grin and flexed his pecs back and forth in a twitchy little dance. "You think I've got something to show off?"

Groaning, Cassia spun around and picked up a box of syrup. Solara moved in to help, but Cassia shook her head. "The captain will flay me alive if I let you do my work," she said. "Why don't you wait outside? It's nicer out there than in here."

Solara didn't need further convincing.

She jogged down the exit ramp until her boots met grass. Once there, she couldn't stop herself from jumping in place to feel the dull thud of soil beneath her feet. She never thought she'd miss something as simple as standing on the ground, but there was no replacing it. Not even the *Zenith*'s manufactured lawn had come close.

Giddy, she raised her face to the sun and pulled in a breath of air. The breeze smelled sweet compared with the stench of burnt porridge, but the effect wore off the longer she stood outside. Then she began to detect other scents—sharp and acrid, like cleaning products—and her smile faded.

She studied the turquoise grass between her boots. She'd never visited a colonized planet before, but some people claimed the terraforming chemicals caused cancer. Others said that if a planet's ecosystem wasn't completely destroyed before terraformation, its elements could mingle with the earth's to create new toxins. She didn't know if any of that was true, but she decided to remain standing instead of taking a seat on the ground.

"Not much to look at," Doran called to her while stacking another box. He flicked a glance at the landscape before marching back up the ramp. "They didn't even spend enough to bring birds here."

Gazing skyward, Solara realized he was right.

Since alien life hadn't been discovered yet, all animals were imported from Earth. And here, not a single creature took to the clouds or perched on tree branches, not even insects. There were no chirps or musical warbles to fill her ears. The quiet was unsettling, and she wondered if her new home on the fringe had imported birds to populate their world. If not, maybe she'd take up a collection to buy doves. And squirrels. Butterflies, too.

She was still making a mental list of her favorite animals when the group finished stocking the supply trailer. They descended the ramp dressed for the festival, Doran in a clean pair of coveralls, and the two ship hands in their usual canvas pants and tops. Kane explained that the auxiliary shuttle only seated two people, so she and Doran would ride on the trailer.

Once they were under way, sitting side by side with their legs dangling over the edge, Doran extended a hand, palm up. "I need some fuel chips."

Solara eyed him skeptically. "For what?"

"Why does it matter?" he snapped. "They're *my* chips."

"Not while they're strung around *my* neck," she reminded him. For a moment he stared at the necklace as if tempted to rip it free, and she covered it with one hand while delivering a warning glare. "I don't need a stunner to break your nose."

"Fine," he huffed. "There's a com-booth at the festival. I want to contact my father."

That's exactly what she was afraid of.

"No," she said. "You can call him from the next outpost."

"But that's days away!"

"So?"

"So by then he'll probably think I'm dead. In case you've forgotten, I disappeared from my ship without a trace."

"I'm sure he can go a few days without hearing from you."

Doran looked at her like she'd sprouted horns. "You don't know much about my family, do you?"

She mirrored his expression. "I must've missed that lesson in school."

"My dad is all I have," Doran muttered, and faced away. "We're close. Close enough that I know he's going crazy wondering if I'm okay."

Solara fingered her necklace and stared at the grass as it moved beneath her dangling feet. She felt a sympathetic tug for Doran, along with a heaping side of envy. Aside from Sister Agnes, no one on Earth would care if she ever returned, not even her parents. Especially not her parents. She remembered telling Doran that no one would miss him because his life didn't matter. But he did matter, at least to his dad.

"All right," she decided. "But I'm coming with you. Not a word about me or what happened on the *Zenith*."

He huffed a dry laugh. "You mean how I tried to help you, and then you stabbed me in the back? Don't worry. My lips are sealed."

"*Help me?*" she repeated, rounding on him as all her sympathy turned to dust. "The way I remember it, you almost helped me into a life of whoring."

"Don't be dramatic," he said. "If it weren't for me, you'd still be on Earth, begging for passage."

She blinked at him in shock. Did he really see it that way?

"You showed more compassion to your girlfriend's dog than to me," she said. "Maybe I made some bad choices since then, but what I did was nothing compared to the way you crushed me under your boot for a month. People don't treat each other like that."

His gaze mocked her. "You're naive. People do far worse."

"Maybe. But I trusted you."

That seemed to get through to him. He took an interest in the ground, hiding behind the dark locks of hair that had fallen across his face. "Let's focus on making it to the next outpost," he said, and tugged at an earlobe. "Then we never have to see each other again."

"Fine by me."

They didn't exchange another word until the cart stopped outside the fairgrounds.

The auxiliary shuttle landed beside them, and Kane disconnected the towline while Cassia skipped—actually skipped—away to collect payment. Their smiles helped lighten Solara's mood. She reminded herself of why she was here: spiced berries and sunshine.

Not even Doran could ruin that.

Hopping down from the cart, she turned to survey the fairgrounds.

The familiar setup of white tents and wooden booths brought a grin to her lips, reminding her of a hundred fish fries and carnivals where she'd sold tickets to raise money for the group home. At this early hour, the festivities hadn't begun, but the mouthwatering smell of fried dough began to sweeten the air. The scent reminded her of Sister Agnes's funnel cakes, fried golden-brown with extra powdered sugar. Wards of the diocese weren't allowed many treats, but that was one of them, and Solara looked forward to it all year.

A sudden prickling of heat stung her eyes. She never thought she'd miss the nuns, but it hurt to know she would never see them again. They had cared about her, in their own way. And in all fairness, she hadn't always made it easy on them.

"Are you crying?"

Doran's voice jerked her back to the present.

"No," Solara said, dabbing at her eyes. She led the way into the maze of tents and called over her shoulder, "Let's get this over with before the fair starts. Then you're on your own."

It didn't take long to find the com-booth. She removed a fuel chip from her necklace and asked the attendant to exchange it for one minute of transmission—more than enough time for Doran to tell his father that he was safe. The attendant gave her change in local currency and unlocked the booth's fiberglass door.

Doran peered inside the closet-sized enclosure and frowned. "It's tight in there."

"You should've thought of that before I paid," she said, and stepped inside.

The compartment resembled an old-time photo booth, with an adjustable seat facing a small screen. Doran sat down while Solara stood with her back pressed to the opposite wall, out of the camera's view. The screen powered up, and Doran entered his father's contact number.

But nothing happened.

"'Transmission failed,'" he read aloud. "'Number not in service.'" He entered the data two more times with the same results. "That's weird. I'll have to try Ava instead."

"Who?" Solara asked, but then the answer came. "Oh. Pink hair, black soul."

Doran glared at her and tapped the new contact information. The second transmission connected almost instantly, followed by a breathy "Hello?" Solara craned her neck to glimpse the screen just in time to see Miss DePaul's eyes fly wide.

"Dory!" the girl cried, then lowered her voice to a hiss. "What are you doing? Are you crazy?"

That wasn't the reaction Solara had expected, and judging by Doran's parted lips, he hadn't seen it coming, either. His girlfriend didn't seem worried about his disappearance, or particularly happy to hear from him.

"I, uh," he stammered. "I need you to send a message to my father."

"Where are you?" she asked, instead of *Are you okay?*

"On Pesirus, but I'm going to Obsidian." He leaned forward and stressed, "I'll be at the next outpost in three days. Tell my father to have a ship waiting so I can do my job. He'll know what that means."

Miss DePaul acted like she hadn't heard a word he'd said. "What happened to the girl you hired?" she asked. "The homely little indenture with the dirty clothes. You didn't"—she gulped—"kill her, did you?"

"What?" Doran jerked back. "Of course not!"

Solara clamped her lips together, trying not to laugh at the idea of Doran using his perfectly manicured hands to kill her. He'd never do it. He might break a nail.

Miss DePaul didn't look convinced. "Then where is she?"

"Right here with me, very much alive."

"She came with you? Of her own free will?"

Doran cast a cutting glance at Solara, and she brought a finger to her lips as a reminder to keep their arrangement a secret. "I didn't kidnap her," he muttered darkly, "if that's what you're asking."

"Then she's more stupid than I thought," Miss DePaul said. "To aid a fugitive when she's already got a record."

Solara's eyebrows jumped in perfect synch with Doran's.

"To aid a what?" he asked.

"Dory, you know I love you, but I can't get involved." His girlfriend twisted a pink lock around her finger. "You understand, right?"

Doran nodded absently while his cheeks turned waxy. Solara waved to get his attention and mouthed *Fugitive?* at him, but he stared right through her.

"Is this a secure line?" he asked.

"Totally," Miss DePaul promised. "And I won't tell anyone you called."

"Yes, please don't. What happened after I left?"

"They're still trying to extradite you for all those indictments on Earth," Ava whispered. "When you took off, they started tracking all the ships that—"

The transmission ended with their prepaid minute.

While Doran groaned and cradled his head between both

hands, Solara processed what her ears were trying to tell her . . . which she still couldn't believe. Doran was a fugitive from justice? Doran Spaulding—Mister *unlike you, I'm not a lowly convict*—had broken the law?

"What did you do?" she asked him.

"Nothing," he whispered. "I swear."

"Sure. That's what they all say."

She remembered how the outpost intercom had repeated, *Passenger Spaulding, return to your ship.* The Enforcers weren't worried about the heir to the Spaulding throne. They were trying to extradite him. And she'd helped him escape.

"The ship that chased us last night," Solara realized, her stomach sinking, "they were after *you*, not me." Which didn't really matter. Because if the law caught up with them, everyone on board the *Banshee* would rot in a lifer colony. "And you just told your girlfriend where we are."

The booth seemed to shrink around her, and for once she understood how Doran felt about closets. She jerked open the door and stumbled outside, blinking against the sunshine while she turned in a clumsy circle. "We have to go," she said. She didn't know where the nearest Enforcer patrol was stationed, or how long it would take it to reach Pesirus, but the clock was already ticking. "What do we tell the crew?"

"Nothing," Doran replied from behind. He stepped out of the booth, looking calmer than any fugitive had a right to be. "They can't find out who I am."

"We're supposed to spend the whole day here," she reminded him. "How do we convince them to leave?"

"Easy. I'll lie." He nodded at the booth. "I just got word that my grandmother's dying, and I have to rush to the nearest outpost for an Earthbound ship. We're paid passengers. You heard the captain; business comes first."

"But you can't go to that outpost anymore," she said. "Your girlfriend knows—"

"Yes, I can." Doran brushed past her and strode back the way they'd come. "Because she won't tell."

"Oh, please." Solara chased after him and tugged his sleeve. "That airhead's already folding like a deck of cards. I'd put money on . . ." She trailed off when a streak of movement in the background flashed between two vendor tents. When she peered between the next gap, she noticed a set of familiar dreadlocks flapping in the breeze behind their owners, who were sprinting toward the *Banshee*'s shuttle like the devil was on their heels.

"Cassia and Kane," Solara said, pointing. "Something's wrong."

She and Doran jogged in that direction, then increased their speed to a full-on bolt when they saw the shuttle doors open and Kane hurtle himself into the pilot's seat. At once, the engines hummed, sending a blast of warm air over them.

"Wait!" Solara screamed while waving one arm.

Cassia made eye contact just before leaping into the passenger's seat. After darting a glance in the opposite direction, she made a *hurry up* motion and pointed at the rear hatch, which had begun a slow rise. Solara pumped her legs harder and faster while fear chilled her skin.

What were they running from?

The hatch was fully raised when she reached it, exposing a narrow cargo area behind the two front seats. Without slowing, she launched her body onto the floor and braced for Doran's impact. He landed half on top of her, knocking the wind from her lungs, and then the shuttle rose sharply while the rear hatch was still open.

"Grab on to something," Kane shouted as he veered the craft hard to the left.

Solara gripped the back of the passenger's seat with one hand and hooked the other around Doran's waist. He wrapped a leg around both of hers, and together they held on for dear life while the hatch gradually closed.

"Attention, Captain," Cassia called through the com-link. "We're coming in hot. The Daeva are here. I spotted them on foot, but their ship is probably nearby." Her voice cracked, and she repeated, "The Daeva are here. Do you copy?"

She pronounced it *day-vuh*, a word Solara had never heard before.

The captain responded with a curse, and the noise of the ship's engines roared to life in the background. "Don't bother landing," he ordered. "I'll meet you halfway. Use the tow cables to dock. With any luck, we'll be long gone before they're airborne."

"Copy that," Cassia said.

"Do you have your pills?" the captain asked, his voice dark as the grave.

"No." Cassia sounded strangled when she answered. "It's been so long since the last time that I hoped—"

He swore again and cut off the link.

Solara tried to swallow, but her throat was too dry. She felt Doran's heart thumping against her shoulder and whispered, "What's a Daeva?"

"I don't know." He was still panting from their mad dash across the fairgrounds. "And I don't want to find out."

That was twice they'd agreed on something.

Soon the floor rumbled and the *Banshee* appeared in front of them. Two metallic cables snaked out from the shuttle, latching onto the main ship with a loud click that shook the hull. A sudden dropping sensation, followed by the *Banshee*'s signature screech, told Solara the ship had accelerated into the atmosphere without bothering to dock the shuttle. There was only one reason for a captain to abuse his equipment like that, and the answer made her shudder.

Once the tow cables had reeled them in, they all clambered out of the craft and through the docking door leading to the ship's cargo hold, then jogged up the stairs to the galley.

Renny was waiting there for them. Sweat shimmered along his brow and upper lip, and his hand trembled as he held out four necklaces made of fibrous cords, each bearing a black pendant no larger than a thumbnail. Cassia and Kane took one and worked the cords over their dreadlocks. Solara noted that Renny already wore his, but he'd tucked the pendant beneath his shirt.

"What's this?" she asked him.

He moved closer and showed her that the pendant was a locket of sorts. He opened it, and inside rested a pea-size capsule.

"Good old-fashioned cyanide," he said. When her eyes widened, he opened his jacket to reveal a pulse pistol tucked beneath his waistband. "We won't go down without a fight. It's just a precaution. If they take you, all you have to do is bite down on this, and it'll be over in minutes."

"A suicide pill?" She stared at the tiny sphere, so innocuous it could pass for a breath mint. Was he actually suggesting she take her own life instead of surrendering to capture? He couldn't be serious. But as much as she wanted to believe this was an elaborate prank, the absence of color in Renny's face wouldn't allow it.

Doran must have felt the same way, because his lips barely moved when he asked, "Who's after us? And what'll they do if they catch up?"

Before Renny had a chance to answer, the ship lost speed, and inertia flung them to the galley floor. Solara cracked her elbow on the way down, sending a jolt of white-hot pain along her nerve endings. She cried out and pressed a hand over the joint while peering around the room for smoke or flickering lights—any indication that they'd been hit. All she detected was a hint of static in the air, but she didn't know if that was a good sign or not.

The captain's voice crackled over the intercom. "I pushed the accelerator too hard and something blew," he said. "Lara, give me a status report from the engine room."

She scrambled to her knees and told Doran to meet her there with her tool kit. But before she made it out of the galley, Renny stopped her and slipped a cord over her head.

"Just in case," he said.

If I can't fix the accelerator, she thought, *we'll all die.*

Her heart pounded and her palms turned to ice. She removed the necklace and gave it back to him, then turned and darted down the stairs when he tried to object.

Now failure wasn't an option.

CHAPTER EIGHT

*D*oran stumbled twice while dashing to the engine room, but the tool kit was wedged under his arm as snugly as any football he'd carried into the end zone. If there was a way to get this clunker of a ship moving again, he'd bust ass to make it happen. He had no intention of eating cyanide today.

He skidded to a halt outside the open doorway and locked eyes with Solara. The damage had to be bad, because she stood there motionless, clutching a hunk of metal at the end of one limp arm while her gaze shone with tears. The whir of moving parts in the adjoining room drowned out the sound of her breathing, but her chest rose and fell fast enough that Doran could tell she would faint if she didn't snap out of it.

"What's the problem?" he asked as gently as he could. He wanted to scream at her—to tell her to quit standing the hell around and do something, but she was obviously under enough pressure. If he pushed her any harder, she might shut down completely.

She didn't move, just dropped her gaze to the engine part in her hand. "One of the rods snapped off."

"Can you fix it?"

"Yeah." She nodded and a tear spilled free. "If I had six hours."

"Jury-rig it," he said. "The repair doesn't have to last forever, just long enough to get us out of here."

She held up the greasy part for show. "Without that rod, there's nothing keeping the accelerator attached to the engine. I can't fix that with duct tape."

"Can you hold it in place?"

"Not once the engine starts turning. Right now it's powered down."

The captain's voice called over the speaker. "Any progress?"

"We're working on it," Doran told him, exactly as Solara said, "No."

"No pressure," Rossi told them. "But we're about to have some very unpleasant company."

"Give us a minute," Doran shouted, and then took hold of Solara's upper arms. She was undeniably smart and resourceful. All she needed right now was more confidence. For the briefest of moments, it occurred to him that this might not be an issue if he hadn't spent so many years tearing her down, but he shoved that thought aside and gave Solara a fortifying shake. "Listen to me," he said. "I watched you work on the grav drive. You're a natural. You'll figure this out, too."

"That was different. It wasn't broken."

"The only difference this time is the stress. If you weren't so panicked, you'd have it figured out already. I want you to take a breath, hold it, and count to ten, and then you're going to try again." He tightened his grip. "Okay?"

Nodding, she puffed out her cheeks and held her breath while he counted down from ten to one. He knew the Daeva were closing in on them, but he forced away his fear and focused on their only chance of survival: getting Solara back in the game.

"Ready?" he asked when he got to one.

She released a lungful of air. "I think so."

"You can do this," he reminded her. "What are the challenges?"

After a moment of consideration, she retrieved a pair of pliers from her tool kit and pointed them at the engine. "First I have to remove the rod that broke off inside the accelerator cradle."

That sounded easy. "I'll do that. You tackle the next obstacle."

He took the pliers and knelt on the floor to retrieve the broken rod. Removing it was much like pulling out a splinter—a very greasy, slippery splinter the size of his thumb. By the time he slipped the rod free, Solara had puzzled out a makeshift replacement.

"It's not quite wide enough," she said while hammering a wrench handle through the broken end of the accelerator. "But it might hold for a few hours."

The intercom blared, "Status report!"

"Almost done," Solara shouted. "One more minute . . ."

"We don't have that long," the captain yelled, and a sickening sound like a foghorn penetrated the ship. "They're trying to board. It's now or never."

Solara scrambled to the engine and placed the accelerator in its cradle, then snapped both fasteners over the extension rods. "If they're close enough to dock," she hollered to the captain, "then they can eat our thrusters. Fire it up!"

The engine began to spin in a noisy rotation, turning faster by the second until its parts formed a gray blur and filled the tiny partition with blistering heat. Doran jogged into the cargo area, and when Solara followed, he shut the engine room door behind them.

"Cover your ears," she shouted over the din.

He had just enough time to comply before an unholy shriek rang out, and the floor vanished from beneath his feet. He skidded on his backside until he hit the wall, then remained plastered there by the sheer force of speed, tangled up with Solara as the ship rocketed into space like a bullet from a gun.

Doran closed his eyes and savored the crush.

Acceleration had never felt so good.

*   *   *

That night, after the captain had docked the ship inside another dismal hidey-hole, Doran and the crew gathered in the lounge to wash down the day's horror with a round of hot buttered Crystalline. But despite cushioned seating and the facade of a crackling fireplace, the mood was anything but cozy.

"They've been quiet for months," the captain said from his chair while petting that ridiculous thing he called a sugar glider. Acorn sat in his palm and curled a long tail around his thumb, oblivious to how close she'd come to nibbling a poisonous treat today. "What were they doing on Pesirus?"

"Waiting for us, maybe," Renny answered. "It's no secret we make the syrup delivery each year."

Doran was tired of tiptoeing around for answers. If Solara wouldn't ask, he would. He leaned forward in his seat and looked the captain right in the eyes. "What are the Daeva, and why are they after you?"

At the question, Captain Rossi tucked his "baby" inside his coat pocket as if to protect her. "When you want someone dead," he said quietly, "you hire a hit man. When you want someone to scream until his vocal cords rupture, you hire the Daeva."

Solara glanced up from the floor, where she sat hunched over the ship's accelerator with a soldering gun in one hand and the broken rod in the other. "So they're snuffers?"

"I guess you could call them that," the captain said. "Since they do kill folks."

"Eventually," Renny added.

"Which one of you are they after?" Doran asked, glancing around the room. He noticed that Cassia and Kane hadn't said much. They sat at the gaming table, each studying a handful of cards, but had yet to make a single play. Kane's eyes seemed especially shifty, never settling on his opponent's face longer than a second. Doran's money was on that one. Maybe he'd seduced the wrong man's wife with that greasy smile of his.

"We don't know," the captain said. "And it doesn't matter."

"Why not?"

"Because we just roasted their hull and sent them spinning." The captain smiled at Solara. "Thanks to you."

"I can't take all the credit," she said. "If Doran hadn't kept a cool head—"

"So you're telling me," Doran interrupted, "that the whole ship is marked?"

Captain Rossi nodded. "For death."

"Worse than that," Cassia muttered behind her cards. "If the Daeva catch you, death will sound like a trip to the candy store."

"What did they look like?" Solara asked, peering at the ship hands. "I never saw who we were running from."

Neither had Doran, so he listened for the answer.

Kane spoke up for the first time, though his gaze never left his cards. "You can spot them by the metal studs on their temples." He tapped a finger against the side of his head. "Prefrontal cortex blockers. Subdues the part of the brain that controls guilt and empathy."

Solara's mouth dropped open. "That's . . ."

"Disturbing," Doran finished.

"And how they do their job so well," Kane said.

That clinched it. Doran was getting off this heap as soon as possible. "How much longer are we stuck here?" he asked Solara.

She powered off the soldering gun and inspected the rod she'd just reattached. "Until morning. I want to reinforce the other side, too."

"How far is the nearest outpost?" he asked the captain.

"From here," Rossi said, "a couple of days."

"Good. The sooner the better."

Solara stood from the floor and motioned for him to do the same. "Excuse us," she said to the others. "Doran and I have to discuss some contract details, since we're parting ways before Obsidian."

He had no idea what she meant by that, but because he didn't want to spend the evening in the company of death-marked fugitives, he gladly followed her back to their room. The door had barely shut when she lit into him.

"This is a bad idea," she whisper-yelled. "We should be heading in the opposite direction, away from where your evil girlfriend thinks we're going."

Doran rolled his eyes. "She's not evil. It was a secure line, and I trust her."

"Well, I don't," Solara said. "And it's not just your neck on the line. As your pink-haired princess pointed out, I have a record. Do you know what'll happen if I get caught?"

"Yes, you'll go to a prison colony. Which, if I'm not mistaken, is preferable to death by torture."

"Not by much."

"You don't know Ava. She won't tell."

Solara shook her head. "You really are an infant, aren't you?"

His anger flared, sending a billow of heat to his face. "We're not changing course, so shut up about it."

To reinforce the message, he turned his back on her and rummaged through her crates of supplies—which technically belonged to him—looking for objects of value. The Enforcers had probably frozen his assets and blocked his father from sending help, so he'd have to find more creative ways of reaching Obsidian.

"Stay out of my things," she ordered. "I'll give you some money."

He would've laughed if his lungs weren't hanging limp inside his chest. A false indictment and the threat of imminent death tended to have that effect. "How generous of you," he said as a glimmer of fabric caught his eye. He smoothed his knuckles over the satiny folds. Whatever it was, it looked expensive. "Is that a ball gown?"

"Not important." She grabbed the crate's lid and slammed it down, barely missing his fingertips in the process. "You need to get your head in the game. A pocketful of fuel chips won't take you far. And then what? Not even *you* can get by on your looks. Not out here."

Her words stirred the anxiety that had already bubbled inside his stomach, but he faked a lazy shrug. "If my father doesn't meet me at the outpost, I'll just go to Obsidian. I have a private ship hidden there. That was the plan to begin with. I was supposed to find it and then travel to a set of coordinates my father gave me."

What he didn't tell her was that the coordinates were in the outer realm. He'd already shared too much, and he didn't want her asking for a ride. The idea of having Solara as his permanent shipmate made his eye twitch.

"Transportation is the least of your problems," she told

him. "If the Solar League wants you extradited, there's probably a reward for turning you in. Have you considered that?"

No, he hadn't. And now his heart was trying to beat its way out of his body.

"Come on, Doran. Use that cool head of yours."

"What do you suggest," he snapped, "since you've got all the answers?"

She took a seat on the edge of the bed and said, "Stay here."

"With you?"

"On the *Banshee*," she clarified, as if there were a difference. "Your passage is already paid. And the crew has no love for Enforcers."

"The same crew who you said would ransom me? The ones marked by a group of sadistic terrorists? That's where you want me to put my faith?"

"Better the devil you know . . ."

"I'll take my chances alone," he decided. If nothing else, at least he would shake those Daeva.

Solara made a face that said, *It's your funeral*, then lay back with both hands folded behind her head. "So what did you do?" she asked. "And don't give me that crank about being innocent, because I don't buy it."

Doran pointed at her gloved knuckles. "What did *you* do?"

As usual, that question put her on edge. "None of your business."

"In that case," he said with a sardonic grin, "I'm innocent."

She blew out a frustrated breath and flopped onto her side, facing the wall.

Even though she didn't believe him, Doran had told the truth. He'd always kept his nose clean for the benefit of the Spaulding shareholders. He couldn't count the number of invitations he'd turned down for wild weekends with his friends at the red-light cities, where a few hundred credits would buy enough debauchery to last a lifetime. And that wasn't even illegal. Plus he'd graduated with honors from the most prestigious academy in Texas—all while balancing varsity football and an internship at his father's company.

The indictment had to be a mistake.

"Why Obsidian?" Solara asked. "That's not where fugitives go to lie low."

Again, he had to admit she was right. The Obsidian Beaches drew more tourists than Planet Disney. But that was where his father had planted the ship, and unless Doran managed to reach him and make other arrangements, it would have to work. "I don't know all the details, but this job is top priority. My father said he didn't trust anyone else to handle it."

Solara rolled over to face him. "That sounds cryptic."

"Not really," he said. "Part of my internship was to visit new planets and bring back ore samples for research. The company kept those missions quiet to discourage competition."

"But the timing is suspicious, don't you think? How do you know this secret job isn't related to your indictment?"

"Because my father wouldn't do that to me," he told her. "Plus there's no reason to do anything shady when we already control the League's fuel supply."

"Successful people can be greedy. They always want more."

The hypocrisy of that statement shocked a chuckle out of

him. "You're wearing a necklace literally made from my stolen money, and you're lecturing me about greed?"

She sat up so fast he thought she might charge him. He flinched back, but she stayed in bed and brought both hands behind her neck to untie the leather cord.

"Here," she said, thrusting the necklace at him. "It's all yours."

He took the fuel chips before she changed her mind. "This doesn't make us even," he said while stuffing them in his pocket.

"Oh, we'll never be even." Her eyes glinted with something wicked. "But that won't stop me from trying." Lounging back against her pillow, she ordered, "Bring me a cup of tea."

"Excuse me?"

"Tea," she repeated. "Now."

"Get your own damned tea."

"Doran," she warned, "on a regular day, I want to push you in front of a bullet tram. But today I was robbed of spiced berries and then handed a suicide pill. So don't test me."

Clenching his jaw, he told her, "Fine. You want tea? I'll make it extra special for you."

He stormed to the galley and rummaged in the cabinets until he found a tea bag. He'd never brewed tea before, but he understood the basic concept: fill a cup with hot water and dunk the bag in it a few times. He returned to their room ten minutes later, tin mug in hand.

"Drink it," he said, then leaned down and added, "I dare you."

The tea wasn't contaminated, but she didn't need to know that.

She handed back the mug while her face turned red with rage. If steam had poured from her ears, it wouldn't have surprised him. "I can't wait until you're gone," she ground out.

"Well, then," Doran said. "We *do* have something in common."

CHAPTER NINE

*D*oran spent the next couple of days avoiding everything on two legs, which wasn't easy when his least favorite pair was regularly stretched out on the bed above him.

Right now Solara was sleeping facedown with her limbs sprawled across the mattress and one bare foot hanging off the edge. She mumbled something in her sleep and punched through the blanket, then drifted off again with her fist dangling above Doran's head.

As if a double bed weren't enough, she had to invade his floor space, too?

He frowned at her gloves, wondering if she ever took the blasted things off. Knowing her, she probably wore them in the shower. Whatever she'd done must've been heinous if she refused to let anyone see her conviction codes. And if that was the case, he'd made the right call by terminating their contract.

He wished he'd caught a better look at her tattoos on the *Zenith* because the curiosity was killing him.

After today, it won't matter, he reminded himself. *I'll never see her again.*

Good riddance.

He ignored the sudden heaviness in his stomach and cleared his pallet from the floor. With any luck, he'd sleep on a real bed tonight—in a room all to himself. Maybe with an adjoining bathroom and unlimited shower privileges. Funny how, a week ago, he never would've considered bathing a luxury. Now he'd trade all the champagne in the quadrant for one long, steamy shower.

Settling for another sponge bath, he made his way to the washroom. When he returned to his chamber, Solara was sitting up in bed, rubbing the sleep from her eyes.

She greeted him with a gravelly "Mornin'," then must have remembered they weren't on speaking terms because she immediately scowled. But with a pillow crease embedded in her cheek and a halo of loose hair sticking out from her braids, the effect was more cute than menacing.

"This is the last time we'll ever wake up together," he said. "You should be happy."

Stretching both arms above her head, she told him, "I'm smiling on the inside."

He found a knapsack and filled it with a handful of toiletries and two changes of coveralls. Since all his luggage was still on the *Zenith*, there was nothing else to pack. "Talk about traveling light," he muttered while tossing his bag in the corner.

Solara picked at a loose thread on her glove. "You can still change your mind."

"I know," he said. But if he wanted to keep his heartbeat steady, he couldn't start second-guessing himself. "My mind's made up."

"Good luck, then." She kept her face turned down as she spoke. "I know we're not friends or anything, but I hope it turns out okay for you."

Doran watched her for a moment. It couldn't have been easy for her to say that, and despite everything she'd done, he felt a stirring of respect for her. "Same to you," he said, and meant it.

They spent the next few minutes avoiding each other's eyes until the captain's voice came over the intercom. "Passengers, report to the bridge."

Doran glanced up. "Guess he means us."

"Hand me my pants?"

He tossed them onto the bed and waited outside until she'd dressed. Then they strode quietly through the ship to the bridge, where the whole crew was waiting for them.

Right away, the silence sent up a red flag.

Cassia and Kane sat with their backs to the pilothouse door, each studying the bolts in the wall. The first mate had taken a seat on the edge of his navigation table, polishing his glasses over and over while the captain stood nearby, leaning on his crutch. No one was smiling—not even Renny.

"What happened?" Doran asked.

The captain gave a terse nod. "There's no easy way to say this, so I won't blow sunshine up your trousers. You've been made."

"Made?" Doran asked. "Into what?"

Solara moved close beside him and stood on tiptoe to whisper, "It means your cover's blown."

Pulse hitching, he glanced around the room and checked for weapons or rope—signs that they meant to hold him hostage. When he saw nothing to that effect, he released a quiet breath. "So you know who I am?"

"We've always known," Renny said. "Since the first night, when the Enforcers hailed us. They were looking for a missing *Zenith* passenger called Doran Spaulding. It wasn't hard to put two and two together."

Doran cocked his head in disbelief. "Why didn't you say anything?"

"None of our business," the captain replied. "But that's not why I called you here." He pulled a data tablet from inside his jacket and handed it over. "This just broadcasted on the emergency frequency. When I said you've been made, I meant on a galactic level."

Doran took the tablet while Solara leaned in to read over his shoulder. It was an all points bulletin with his name and senior picture at the top, the cheesy one of him leaning against a tree with a football tucked under his arm. Beneath his smiling face were the instructions ARREST ON SIGHT.

He read the charges—conspiracy to defraud the government, theft, industrial espionage, obstruction of justice, resisting arrest—but they made no sense.

"I didn't do any of this," he said.

The captain told him, "Keep reading."

When Doran continued to the bottom of the page, the real

blow came, a bullet to the heart that knocked him back until he actually swayed on his feet.

AN ANONYMOUS CITIZEN REPORTED SPAULDING'S LAST KNOWN WHEREABOUTS AS PESIRUS. HIS DESTINATION IS OBSIDIAN, BY WAY OF OUTPOST #8774.

"I changed course," the captain said. "Just in time."

All Doran could do was nod and try to breathe. Ava had betrayed him. She'd said that she loved him, and then she'd told the Enforcers everything. Maybe he'd never intended to move in with her, but he had trusted her. Shared his bed with her. Told her secrets he'd never revealed to his friends, like how he still talked to his mother's picture at night when he couldn't sleep. A lump rose in his throat, but no matter how hard he swallowed, he couldn't push it down.

He couldn't believe she'd actually turned him in.

"There'll be too much heat around Obsidian," the captain went on. "So we'll steer clear and head straight into the fringe."

Pressure built behind Doran's eyes, but he bit the inside of his cheek to ward off tears. He wouldn't lose it. Not in front of the crew.

Solara's hand appeared on his forearm. Her fingers bit into his flesh, the steady grip keeping him upright. She told the captain, "Let's not make any decisions yet."

"The choice is already made," the captain said. "When it affects my ship, you don't get a say."

Doran's ears pounded, forcing the argument to his periphery. He mumbled a hasty promise to compensate the crew for all the trouble he'd caused and then stumbled down the stairs on weak knees. He didn't remember the trip back to his room, but the next thing he knew, he was sitting on the bed, staring at the wall.

What was he going to do next?

He had no way to reach his father. He might be able to send a message to his friends, but if Ava had sold him out, it stood to reason they would do the same. He didn't know where to go, and every minute he spent on the run would make him look more guilty. Maybe he should turn himself in and trust the Spaulding attorneys to untangle this mess.

Too bad he was fresh out of trust.

A quick knock sounded at the door, and Solara stepped inside. She didn't say anything, but he had a pretty good idea what was on her mind.

"You were right," he told her. "Go ahead and say it."

"I'm not here to gloat."

"Yes, you are." He would gloat if their roles were reversed. "Just leave me alone."

"I want to show you something first."

Doran was about to snap at her, but she stunned him into silence by peeling off her gloves and tucking them in her back pocket. Then she displayed her tattoos and gave him an eyeful. It would've shocked him less if she'd stripped nude.

She sat beside him on the bed and held a hand between them. From left to right in bold black ink, the markings read SLPC 33.87, SLPC 43.14.

"It's Solar League Penal Code," she explained. "The first number is for grand theft, and the second is for conspiracy.

What that basically means is that I stole something worth a lot of money and tried to convince other people to help me." She glanced at him. "But only the first part is true."

He waited for her to go on.

"I never told anyone what really happened," she said. "Not even the Enforcers who arrested me. But I'll tell you if you still want to know."

Once Doran managed to close his mouth, he nodded.

"It started with a boy," she said while staring across the room. "He was an orphan like me, but nineteen and emancipated, with a job and an apartment that he shared with a few other guys. He wasn't gorgeous or anything, but he paid attention to me. He always smiled when I walked by." Going quiet for a moment, she picked at a cuticle. "No one ever looked at me the way he did. Like every other girl in town was ordinary and I was on fire."

"Was he your boyfriend?" Doran asked.

She nodded. "He was my first boyfriend. My first love. My first kiss. And my first"—her cheeks flooded with color—"well, *everything*."

"Everything," he echoed in understanding. That was a lot of *firsts* for one boy to take from a girl. Doran could sense where this story was headed.

"Once he had me hooked," she said, "he told me about a group of revolutionaries called the Patron Brotherhood. They were going to change the world—feed the hungry, help the poor, make it so everyone could afford to live on Earth. But to do that, they needed money."

"Of course they did," Doran said. He'd heard of this scam. "What did he ask you to steal?"

"The coolant coils and buffering plates from city trams," she told him. "Worth a fortune on the black market. And there were a bunch of us in on it. We'd steal the parts, and then he would fence them and send the money to the Brotherhood."

"Which didn't exist."

"And I had no idea," she said. "When the Enforcers busted us, I stayed true to the cause. I told them nothing—didn't say a word to defend myself. Not even when they offered me a plea deal."

Doran was willing to bet her boyfriend hadn't extended the same courtesy.

"And the whole time," she went on, "he was pinning the operation on me." She shook her head and scoffed. "In exchange for full immunity."

"And because you refused to talk . . ."

"I took the blame by default." She retrieved her gloves and pulled them on one slow finger at a time, as if telling the story had drained her. "The only reason I'm not in a penal colony is because the judge didn't believe I was the ringleader." She grinned. "I guess criminal masterminds don't sob during their trials the way I did."

"What happened to the boyfriend?" Doran asked.

Solara shrugged and traced a leather seam with her fingertip. "Nothing. I imagine he's still running around out there, looking for new hearts to steal."

Doran didn't like hearing that.

"He told me I was special," she said quietly. "And that was all it took to unravel my integrity. So you can probably understand why I don't like talking about it. Or looking at my hands."

Doran nodded. All that made sense. What he didn't understand was why she'd shared her story with him. "Why did you tell me? We're not even friends."

"Because we're members of a secret club now," she told him. "Both of us were used up and betrayed and thrown away by the people we loved."

"I never loved Ava."

"But still," Solara said.

"But still," he agreed. "I'm sorry that happened to you."

"It didn't happen to me. I made it happen."

Doran glanced at her hands, now concealed beneath black leather. He wanted to confess the real reason he had panicked when he'd first seen her tattoos, but he couldn't get the words past the knot in his chest. So instead, he said, "I guess we're stuck with each other."

She gave him a sad smile, and he realized for the first time that her eyes were hazel, not simply brown or green. A starburst of warm amber surrounded her pupils, giving way to olive-hued irises that were rimmed in glowing emerald. The effect was striking. Odd that he'd never noticed before.

Looking into those smiling eyes, he felt a little less alone.

"Guess so," she said. "Too bad you make lousy tea."

CHAPTER TEN

*I*n the weeks that followed, Solara settled into an unspoken cease-fire with Doran, neither hostile nor friendly. They hadn't shared any more secrets since the day she showed him her tattoos, but he'd stopped calling her a felon. And while she still coerced him into galley cleanup and cargo loading, it was only in the interest of improving their standing with the crew, not out of spite.

Well, okay. Maybe a *teensy* bit out of spite.

She couldn't deny the tingle of satisfaction that came from watching Doran get his hands dirty. With each new chore, his fingernails lost a little more of their sheen. A few blisters on his palms had hardened into calluses, and in her opinion, that was far more attractive on a guy than baby-soft skin.

So really, she was doing him a favor.

"You missed a spot," she told him, pointing at a patch of mildew encircling the bathroom drain. The ship's recycled air was so dry that only the hardiest molds took root, making them nearly indestructible. "That's going to take some serious elbow grease."

Doran took a break from his work to sit back against the wall. He dragged an arm across his sweaty forehead and locked those indigo eyes on her, the heat of physical labor glowing brightly behind his gaze. He released a tired chuckle that lifted one corner of his lips, and for a split second, a tiny pair of angel wings fluttered behind Solara's navel.

She rubbed a hand over her stomach to erase the sensation. She was probably just excited about shower day. Nothing more than that.

"Feel free to show me how it's done," he told her.

"Nice try." She slung her towel over the nearest stall and hooked her caddy of toiletries to the showerhead. "I spent all day turning the engine inside out to find the reason for that screeching sound." With no luck. "This shower has my name on it."

"We paid ten thousand fuel chips for this trip," he said, tossing aside his scrub brush. "And by *we*, I really mean *I*."

"So?"

"So are you sure all this extra work is making a difference?"

"Of course," Solara told him while pulling a hairpin free. "It's endearing us to the crew."

"Doesn't look that way to me," he said. "The captain's getting free labor, and he still won't take me to Obsidian."

She pointed her hairpin at him. "Not with that attitude, he won't."

"*Psh*," Doran scoffed. "I doubt a few smiles will change anything." In demonstration, he flashed his teeth and used both hands to frame a grin. "Not even on this pretty face."

Solara laughed with her whole belly. Lame as it was, that might've been the first joke she'd ever heard Doran tell. "Patience, my attractive friend. I'll get you to Obsidian."

Still smiling, he arched a brow. "I thought we weren't friends."

"We're not."

"Then what are we?"

"You want a label?"

"Yeah," he said. "I think I do."

She thought about it while combing out her hair. They'd attended the same academy, but the word *classmates* implied a certain level of camaraderie that didn't apply to the boy who'd once uploaded a picture of her stained coveralls to his SnapIt account to prove she'd worn the same pair twice in a row. Last month she had considered Doran an enemy, but that didn't apply, either. They were in uncharted territory now, feeling their way one day at a time.

"Cohorts," she finally decided. "That's how the Enforcers would classify us."

He wrinkled his nose. "Cohorts. That sounds sketchy."

"If the shoe fits . . ."

"Or the gloves, as it were," he said, nodding at her hands. "I was right. You do shower with them on."

That wasn't true and he knew it, so she didn't bother with a reply.

"You should stop wearing them. Nobody here cares about your markings. By hiding them, you're giving the ink too much power."

"Oh, so you're a therapist now?" she asked.

"It's just common sense." Abruptly, his lips pulled into a frown, and he stared at his own knuckles in silence. A shadow passed over his face, making Solara wonder what he was thinking. "Believe me," he muttered. "If I can stand to look at your ink, then so can you."

If he could *stand* to look at her?

Her shoulders rounded as she shrank into herself, stung more than she wanted to admit by the careless words. "It's like English is your second language," she said. "And your native tongue is Jackass."

His head snapped up. "What?"

She fisted her gloved hands until the leather creaked, but it didn't stop the ache growing inside her chest. She shouldn't have shared her story with him. It hadn't changed anything. All she'd done was give him the power to hurt her. "Should I be flattered that the Great Doran Spaulding can bring himself to look upon my tattoos?"

"I didn't mean it like that."

"Just get out," she said, jabbing a finger at the door. "You're not going to ruin my shower the way you ruin everything else."

He shook his head in contempt and pushed to standing. As he passed by, he mumbled, "I don't know why I bother trying."

"The feeling's mutual," she said. "I'm downgrading you from cohort to accessory."

"You can kiss my accessory."

"In your dreams!"

The washroom door slammed shut, but the argument wasn't over. At least not in Solara's head. She cursed Doran while yanking off her shirt and throwing it against the wall. Then she did the same with her clothes and boots until she stood naked in nothing but her fingerless gloves. She studied the worn leather and chewed her bottom lip before tearing the casings off and tossing them onto the pile. As much as she wanted to banish his voice, she couldn't help wondering if he was right.

Had she given the ink too much power?

Standing beneath a steaming spray of water, she used one hand to wet her hair while holding up the other for inspection. Soon the heat reddened her skin and reminded her of sentencing day, when the Enforcers had marked her. The law entitled her to topical painkiller, but that hadn't stopped her knuckles from swelling too large to fit inside her gloves. She'd returned to the group home with no way to hide her shame. The other orphans had known better than to ask questions, but they'd whispered when her back was turned. Even worse was knowing how deeply she'd disappointed Sister Agnes, who'd blamed herself for teaching Solara mechanics in the first place. She would never forget the humiliation of wearing her mistakes on both hands like a flashing beacon for the whole world to see.

As punishments went, this one was effective—with plenty of power all its own.

"Screw you, Doran," she muttered under her breath. As usual, he didn't know his ass from his elbow.

She squeezed a dollop of shampoo into her palm, but before she had a chance to put it in her hair, her body lurched forward and she hit the stall face-first. A jolt of pain exploded behind her right cheekbone, replaced by the sharp ache of her backside suddenly meeting the floor. The violence was over as quickly as it had begun, and in the span of two heartbeats, she was sitting on the wet tile, panting in shock.

A metallic taste crossed her lips, and she dabbed her cheek to find it bleeding. She crawled back to the shower and turned off the water, then grabbed her towel. By the time she wrapped it snugly around her dripping body, her brain had recovered enough to process what'd happened. Because there was no noise of impact, the inertia that had catapulted her into the wall must've been caused by a figurative slamming of the brakes. Which could only mean one thing.

The accelerator had come loose again.

She tugged on her clothes while muttering every curse in her vocabulary. When she reached the engine room, her right eye was swollen shut. The good news was that it only took one eye to diagnose the problem. The bad news was she couldn't do a thing to fix it.

"The accelerator's fine," she called toward the noise of approaching footsteps. "But your propellant cell sprang a leak. You need a new one."

Renny appeared beside her, leaning in to look at the lime-green ooze fizzing and bubbling on the engine room floor. The substance's bark was louder than its bite. Once exposed to oxygen, propellant lost its combustive properties—a safety feature to keep the ship from exploding. Each sizzling pop faded softer than the last, and within seconds, it was nothing more than a placid puddle of goo.

"Can we scoop it up and put it back inside?" Renny asked.

Solara shook her head. "It doesn't work that way."

"Where are we going to get a new—" He cut off, eyes flying wide as he glimpsed her face, and shouted, "Oh my god!"

She gently probed her swollen cheek. "That bad, huh?"

Renny reached out to touch her but quickly drew back his hand. "You might need a stitch or two. I'll get Cassia to bring the med bag."

Before he had a chance to page her, Cassia descended the stairs with a limping Kane on her heels. Doran followed behind, navigating the steps blindly while holding a gel pack low on his forehead. The instant he met Solara's eyes, he did a double take and flinched upright.

"What happened to you?" he asked, both brows disappearing beneath his hair.

Solara wished she had a mirror handy because she must have looked spectacular. "I had a close encounter with the shower stall. It's not that bad."

"You sure about that?" Kane asked with a wince.

"Here," Doran said, holding the gel pack toward her. "You need this more than I do." When she refused to take it—because she didn't want anything from him except an apology—he crept closer in the tentative steps of a man approaching a wounded animal. "Really," he said. "Before your face falls off."

She tried smacking away his hand, but it did no good. Doran persisted until she let him rest the pack lightly against her cheekbone. The cool contact brought an instant flood of relief she hadn't known she'd needed. It felt so good she nearly forgot why she was angry with him. But not quite.

"Thanks," she said, reluctantly moving her hand over his. "I've got it."

"The captain wants a status report," Cassia said.

Renny blew out a long breath. "We need a new propellant cell."

"Or . . . ?" the girl prompted.

"Or we're stuck at snail speed," Solara said. "Your two-man shuttle could outrun the *Banshee* right now."

Cassia turned to Renny. "How close are we to a supplier?"

"At this speed?" he said. "Two months out."

Everyone in the group exchanged nervous glances, and Solara imagined they were all thinking the same thing. The *Banshee* was a transport ship, not a military vessel. With no cannons or propellant, they were easy prey for every band of roaming marauders and shipjackers in the quadrant. Or worse. The Daeva might stumble across them.

Solara shivered just thinking about it.

Kane broke the silence with the low voice someone might use to tell a ghost story. "We could go to Demarkus."

Renny chuckled without humor. "Are you volunteering for the job?"

When nobody responded, Solara asked, "Where's Demarkus?"

"Not *where*," Renny said. *"Who."*

"He's a pirate," Kane explained. "Runs the black market in this quadrant. But he won't do business with just anyone. All pirates belong to an alliance called the Brethren of Outcasts." He tapped a spot on his wrist. "They wear a brand to mark themselves because pirate law favors their own kind."

"And if you're outside that circle," Cassia said, "Demarkus is more likely to rob you blind than trade with you. The captain has enough street cred to barter with him, but they had a falling-

out last year."

"Cap'n shot him," Kane supplied with a grin. "Two slugs, right in the chest. Demarkus didn't even drop his pistol. Did skew his aim, though."

"That's how the captain lost his leg," Cassia added.

Renny pinched the bridge of his nose and peered at the puddle of propellant like he could reanimate it if he stared hard enough. "Demarkus knows our faces," he said. "He'd probably sell us into slavery—if we're lucky."

Doran sniffed a dry laugh and glanced at Solara. "Except Solara. Not even this guy would mess with someone who looks as scary as she does right now."

There was a collective intake of breath from the crew, and then all eyes locked on her tattoos. "You know," Kane said with a cautious expression, "that's not a bad idea."

"No, I was kidding." Doran shook his head. "It's a terrible—"

"Wait," Cassia interrupted. She cocked her head, study-ing Solara with narrowed eyes until her lips curled in a smile. "A sweet, young felon. Cute but combative." She nodded. "Oh yeah. Demarkus would love her to pieces."

"That's what I'm afraid of," Renny said. "We can't ask her to get involved. We'll find another way."

"And what other way is that?" Cassia demanded. "There's no salvage yard out here, and we can't exactly put out a distress call."

No one argued, because she was right.

Solara didn't relish the idea of bartering with a bulletproof pirate lord, but like it or not, she would do whatever it took to get the replacement part.

The crew, however, didn't need to know that.

"Let's make a deal," Solara said. "I'll be your go-between with the pirates if you'll take me and Doran to the Obsidian Beaches." Doran made a choking noise, but she silenced him with a glare. "And then to the fringe. Just like we originally agreed."

Twin lines formed between Renny's bespectacled eyes as he stared at his shoes, clearly tempted by the offer and hating himself for it. "I'll have to ask the captain."

She shrugged. "Go ahead. But I won't take anything less."

Not surprisingly, the captain agreed.

An hour later, Solara stood wincing in front of the washroom mirror while Cassia plaited her hair into a facial death grip. The braid's tightness pulled at the corners of her blackened eyes, resulting in an angry expression that said, *Speak at your own risk.* A steady rotation of gel packs had lessened the swelling above her cheekbone, but she still looked as if she'd gone ten rounds with a grizzly bear.

It was a good start.

Solara stepped back and studied her reflection. A black holster hung low on her hips, complete with two pulse pistols she had no clue how to use. The outside of her thigh showcased a sheathed blade. Its curved edge screamed menace, but she'd probably sever her own artery trying to draw it.

"Smoke and mirrors," she said, both palms beginning to sweat.

"You'll be fine." Cassia patted her on the back. "Just don't smile—at all. And say as little as possible. Whatever price they quote for the cell, offer sixty percent of that. Any more and they'll think you're a pushover. Any less would be an insult."

"Sixty percent," Solara repeated while nervous butterflies tickled her belly. She'd never been good at crunching numbers in her head, especially not fractions. And what about pirate law? Until now, she hadn't known pirates had any laws. What if she broke their rules?

"Hey, slow breaths," Cassia said.

Solara hadn't realized she was gasping. "Right. Sorry."

"If you faint among pirates, don't bother waking up."

Oh god. That was not helpful.

The washroom door swung open, and all thoughts of pirates vanished. A tall boy walked inside, dressed in black clothes at least two sizes too tight. His cherry-red hair stood in haphazard spikes, and his eyes were heavily lined in kohl. If a rock star had an affair with a circus clown, this guy would be the result. It took a few moments to recognize him as Doran.

Before a question left her lips, he announced, "I'm your pilot."

"You?" she choked out. "No way. You'll get us killed."

"They won't kill me," Doran insisted. "I'm worth too much."

"But I'm not."

"I'll stay in the shuttle. If the plan works, they'll never see me."

"And if the plan goes south?"

He gripped both hips. "Look, we both know you can't fly a shuttle."

"I can fly," she argued. It was the landing part she hadn't mastered.

"Like the time you broke my arm in pilot's ed class?"

She answered with a glare.

"That's what I thought," he said. "Now, quit arguing and let's go."

He stalked out of the washroom, leaving her with a lump of fear in her throat.

"You'll be fine," Cassia repeated. But this time she didn't make eye contact.

CHAPTER ELEVEN

Solara learned it was disturbingly easy to summon a pirate. After she and Doran put an hour's distance between themselves and the *Banshee*, they cut the thrusters and transmitted the shuttle coordinates to an encrypted radio frequency, along with her name and a request for a propellant cell. According to the captain's instructions, the pirates would come to her. Now all she had to do was survive the wait without crawling out of her skin.

"Are you sure you used the right signal?" she asked, leaning over Doran's arm to check the shuttle dashboard. The piercing scent of hair dye watered her eyes and forced her back into her own space. "They should've been here by now."

"They're thieves, not doctors," Doran said. "They'll come when they feel like it."

She wiped both palms on her pants. "Like you're an expert."

Instead of taking the argument bait, Doran turned to face

her. His expression showed no panic, which was beyond unfair. "Calm down. It's going to be okay."

"I know that."

"Then why are your hands shaking?"

She glanced down and saw that he was right.

"Take a sip of this." He reached inside his jacket and handed over a flask. "The captain said it'd bring you down a notch."

Solara tipped back the flask for a quick pull and forced down a mouthful of liquid flame, nearly retching at the taste. She coughed and pounded her chest. "Thanks," she wheezed. "If anyone corners me, I'll breathe on them."

"Feel better?"

"If by *better* you mean pukey, then yes."

He expelled a heavy sigh and reached for her wrist. "Here, give me your hand."

"What for?" she asked, eyeing him warily.

"So I can help you relax. If you try to negotiate with these people while your hands are shaking, we're screwed."

"Help me how?"

"Just give it here," he snapped. "Why is everything a battle with you?"

She grunted and held her free hand in his direction, making sure to display an extra special finger for his benefit. She didn't know what she expected to come next, but it wasn't the gentle touch of Doran's thumbs massaging her palm. Caught off guard, she flinched upright.

Doran didn't seem to notice. He watched her hand while rubbing it in alternating circles, soothing muscles that had grown stiff from clenching her fists for too long. "My mother used to do this when I was little," he said. "It always calmed me down after a bad dream."

Solara didn't know what to say. Doran was holding her hand. In what alternate dimension was that valid? Crazier still, she didn't hate the sensation. It felt rather delicious, actually. Her whole body responded to the warm contact, coaxing her to relax until she nearly dropped the flask.

"Sometimes I lied about having nightmares just so she'd do this," he continued. "I think she caught on because that's when she stopped."

"Are you two close?" Solara asked. "Like with your dad?"

His thumbs paused for a moment. "No."

"Because she quit giving hand massages?"

"Because she took off. About eight years ago, after the divorce."

"Oh." Solara's cheeks heated. Her comment about the massages was a joke, and now she wished she could take it back. "Took off, as in permanently?"

He nodded.

"Why? Where'd she go?"

"I'm not sure," he said. "But I think my parents hate each other too much to share the same planet. They used to work together—that's how they met. She was the scientist who invented Spaulding Fuel chips. It was a huge moneymaker, but after the split, they couldn't stand to look at each other, and my dad ousted her from the company. Then there was the whole thing with . . ." He trailed off. "Well, I guess she couldn't handle the reminders, so she left."

"Do you ever hear from her?"

"Sometimes." Doran moved his thumbs to the inside of her wrist, delicately stroking between the tiny bones there. His voice turned soft in a way that plucked at her heart. "On birthdays and holidays. But there's not much to talk about anymore."

"I'm sorry," Solara told him, and meant it. She knew how it felt to be abandoned. But unlike her mother, Doran's mom had no excuse for leaving—she had the resources to be a parent, just not the desire. Solara could only imagine how much that hurt. She looked at him with new eyes, and something warm stirred behind her ribs. "I guess we're members of two secret clubs now. My mom left me when I was little, too. And my dad."

Doran stopped massaging her hand and pointed at the flask. When she passed it over, he took a long pull, then winced and coughed. "We need to join better clubs."

"Agreed," she said. "Chess, maybe."

He swore quietly to himself and took another swig of Crystalline. Then his voice went hollow while his eyes fixed on a point in the distance. "Don't freak out or anything, but they're here."

She snapped her gaze in the direction of his, and all the air leaked slowly out of her lungs. Approaching them was the ugliest tank of a ship she'd ever seen, like evil in motion. At least the length of a football field and twice as wide, it probably housed the population of a small town, maybe a hangar of shuttles as well. The battered metal patchwork covering the ship's hull was proof of combat, and the pulse cannons mounted all around the exterior promised they could dish it out as well as take it.

She'd expected a shuttle to meet her, not the whole operation. She wasn't ready for this.

A computerized voice crackled over the intercom. "Set your controls to neutral and prepare to come aboard." Doran did as commanded, and their shuttle jerked forward into the ship's tow beam. Slowly, they closed the distance until a massive rear hatch opened—a dragon's maw sucking them into the belly of the beast.

A tiny squeak escaped Solara's lips.

Doran took her hand and squeezed it hard. "Look at me." When she didn't listen, he physically turned her face. "Before we land, I need to know why you're doing this. We're not friends. We're not even cohorts. So why are you helping me?"

Even facing him, she could see the hangar in her periphery, a dim, cavernous space filled with mismatched shuttlecraft. Her heart hammered. There was no turning back now. "You know why," she told him. "If we can't find a propellant cell, we're as good as dead."

"But you leveraged it in my favor."

"So what?"

"There has to be a reason."

She shook her head at his low opinion of her, though after what she'd just learned about him, it wasn't surprising. If he couldn't trust his own mother, why would he trust a felon? "That's where you're wrong," Solara told him. "Most people don't need a reason to be decent. I'm one of those people. You could be, too, if you made an effort."

That seemed to get through to him.

He released her face as the next command sounded from the intercom. "Passenger Lara. Leave all weapons inside your craft and exit with your hands visible. Any aggression will be met with lethal force."

With trembling fingers she tossed her pistols and knife to the floor, then took a moment to draw a deep breath as the shuttle floated inside the massive metal holding chamber and touched down. A grinding noise signaled the hatch closing, followed by the whir of heated oxygen filling the hangar. When it was safe to exit, a buzzer sounded.

"Thirty minutes," Doran said, unlocking the shuttle door. "And then I'm coming after you."

Solara didn't trust herself to speak, so she nodded and climbed down to the steely floor. She made her way to the front of the enclosure, where two armed men stood guard at the metal door leading to the air-lock. From where she stood, they didn't look like pirates, just ordinary men from the streets. Except better fed.

One of the guards, a bald man with a second pair of eyes tattooed on his scalp, pointed at a circle painted on the floor and told her, "Stand there."

She did as instructed, and an overhead beam scanned her for weapons. Once cleared, she folded both arms, making sure her conviction codes were visible. It worked. She saw the respect in the nearly imperceptible nods of the guards' heads. For once, her ink was actually useful.

"Propellant cell, right?" the first man asked.

Solara nodded.

"Fifty thousand fuel chips."

She pretended to consider his offer while mentally calculating sixty percent. Half of fifty was twenty-five, and ten percent of fifty was five. So thirty? To be safe, she guessed high. "Thirty-five."

"Done," he said. "You can pay inside, second room on the right. I'll deliver the part to your pilot." With the press of a button, he opened the door to the air-lock chamber, a small holding cell that regulated pressurization. But when he tried opening the next door, the one leading into the ship, it wouldn't budge. "Damn thing's stuck again," he muttered.

"It's probably your hatch sensor," Solara guessed. She pointed through the window to the control room, where another guard was frowning at the equipment panel. "Ask your friend if the hangar lights are blinking."

The bald man cast her a skeptical glance, but he did as she asked. A moment later, he touched his earpiece and nodded. "He says it's all lit up."

"Then your sensor needs cleaning," she told him. "It's an easy fix."

The man scoffed at her, nodding across the hangar at the enormous hatch while thumbing behind him. "What does the hatch sensor have to do with this air-lock?"

"It's a safety feature. Think about it. What would happen if both of these doors"—she pointed in front of and behind them—"were open at the same time as the hangar?"

The corners of his mouth turned down. "We'd all get sucked into space."

"Blown into space," she corrected. "So the ship won't let you open the interior door unless it thinks the hangar is sealed." Leaving the air-lock chamber, she began walking toward the hatch and motioned for him to follow. "And if your sensor is dirty . . ."

"Then it sends the wrong message?" the guard said.

"Exactly." When she reached the glassy sensor at the other end of the hangar, she found it covered in a greasy layer of filth. She used her tunic hem to wipe the bulb clean and stood back to show the guard.

"That's it?" he asked.

"Well, let's see if it worked."

They returned to the air-lock, and the interior door slid aside without a problem.

"See? An easy fix," Solara said, beaming a little.

Instead of thanking her for the repair, the bald man peered at her as if she were a puzzle he couldn't solve. Then he held up an index finger and turned his back to make a quiet call. When he faced her again, he announced, "Demarkus invites you to join his table."

Solara's prideful grin faltered. She wanted nothing to do with Demarkus. Besides, nobody had told her about pirate dinner protocol. She might use the wrong fork and start a war. "Thanks for the offer," she said. "But I . . . uh . . . have a long trip back, and my captain needs this part."

Right away she knew she'd put her foot in her mouth.

"Our chief," the bald man repeated as if talking to a five-year-old, "invites you to his table, an honor extended to few outside the brotherhood." He didn't say anything more, but his tone made it clear that this wasn't really a choice.

"Of course," Solara said, tapping her right ear. "Forgive me. I lost part of my hearing in a cage fight last year. I would love to dine with your chief."

The guard ushered her inside with instructions to follow the passageway to the great hall at the center of the ship. She knew she was nearly there when the scents of rust and metal gave way to roasted meat and baking bread. Her stomach gurgled loud enough to be heard over the growing roar of voices, and she mashed a silencing hand over it. She couldn't afford to show weakness here, not even hunger. But as it turned out, her appetite shriveled like a winter leaf once she reached the main hall.

The belly of the ship was madness.

Dozens of long tables dominated the space, their benches filled to the brim with bawdy crewmen. Their laughter, thick with drink, competed with shouts coming from a raised stage in the center of the room where a bare-knuckle fistfight was under way. One boxer strayed too close to the ring's invisible ropes, and a jolt of electricity boomeranged him into his opponent's waiting fist. The fighter's head snapped back, and he collapsed to the tune of mingled cheers and groans. In the crowd, money exchanged hands and the victors rushed to the bordello booth to spend their spoils.

This was what she'd expected from pirates.

Another armed guard, this time a muscled woman with daggers tattooed across her collarbones, approached and asked, "Lara?"

Solara raised her chin. "Yes."

"This way," the woman said while turning into the crowd.

Doing her best to slow her breathing like Doran had taught her, Solara focused on the back of the woman's head while following through the room and up the stairs to the stage. A private table stood opposite the boxing ring, and four men dined there, tearing hunks of meat from long rib bones. Solara identified their leader at once.

It was easy.

Authority draped over him as clearly as the bloodred sash on his tunic. His companions showed deference in the lowering of their heads, which wasn't hard to do when he dwarfed everyone in the room. Demarkus was a mountain of a man, resting his ham-sized fists on the table as he scanned the crowd. There was a certain shrewdness in his gaze, one that warned he had brains as well as brawn. His face, framed by long, flowing locks of chestnut hair, had probably been handsome once. But now scars and lumps marred his skin, sun-leathered and stretched tight over his bones in a way that made it impossible to guess his age. His dark eyes landed on Solara and widened a fraction before sparking bright with interest.

"Lara," he called while standing from his seat. He made a cutting hand gesture, and all the men at the table left without a word. Then he used that same hand to indicate the spot beside him and unleashed an unexpectedly charming smile.

Solara knew better than to underestimate him. She kept her lips in a flat line when she sat down. "Thank you," she said. "I'm honored to share your table."

"The honor is mine." He lowered to his seat while studying her conviction codes. Much like his guards, he lifted an appreciative brow. "Grand theft and conspiracy, at such a young age?"

Tearing off a chunk of bread, she told him, "I take what I want."

"Don't we all?"

"Fair enough," she said. "I forgot my surroundings."

He delivered a long, silent look. "What did you steal?"

"Bullet tram parts," she told him, seeing no reason to hide the truth. "To sell on the underground market."

"You have mechanical training, then?"

She nodded. "It's what I do."

"A useful skill," he mused. "I heard that you fixed the airlock door. We've been wrestling with it for weeks."

"It was nothing."

"And clearly you're a fighter, too." Using an index finger, he traced the outline of her cheekbone. "Who provoked you, little bird?"

She pulled away and met his eyes. "The last man who touched my face without permission."

Demarkus laughed in a rolling chortle that might have warmed her heart if he hadn't trapped her on a ship full of convicts. "I like your fire," he said. "There's no reason to fear unwanted attention from me. There are plenty of women on board who *do* give me their permission." He speared a hunk of meat with his knife and lifted it for show. "You should know that I take care of my own. Plenty of food, a fair share of the spoils, a private bunk. If you swear fealty to me, you could lead your own team in five years' time."

"I'm not looking to join a crew," she told him.

"What if I sweeten the deal?"

"It wouldn't make a difference."

"A signing bonus?"

She shook her head.

"But I need a mechanic," he said. "Is there nothing I can say to convince you?"

"Your offer is flattering, but I'm happy where I am."

"A pity." He took a bite and muttered, "The loss is mine."

They ate in silence for a while, until two young men approached the table and asked Demarkus to settle a property dispute. The pair testified that their dead roommate had promised both of them his laser pistol, but he'd left no written will. They each laid a coin on the table and asked their chief to declare a challenge, whatever that meant.

Demarkus leaned close to murmur in Solara's ear. "What do you think, little bird? If you were chief, how would you decide?"

She made a show of studying the men, trying not to let Demarkus see how his nearness made her shoulders clench. "I would take the pistol for my armory," she said. "Or sell it and use the money to benefit my whole crew."

He chided her in a teasing *tsk, tsk*. "Spoken like a Solar League politician. I thought you'd have more imagination than that."

"How will you decide?" she asked.

"Our law is clear in this case. They'll compete for the pistol in a battle of my choosing." Addressing the men, Demarkus announced, "Long staffs in the antigravity room. Last one conscious wins."

The men bowed and each laid another coin on the table, then backed away.

Demarkus asked her, "You don't know much about pirate law, do you?"

"Nothing at all," she admitted.

"It favors the power of individuals over the group. So the

fittest rise to the top, and the weakest die out. That's how we differ from the Solar League. We maintain order, but not at the expense of our strength. When my chief grew weak, I challenged him for control. Now he works in the galley, and I rule the Brethren in this quadrant."

"Only this quadrant?" she asked. "What about the others?"

"Each has its own chief, and we stay within our territory. It keeps things civil."

"Civil," she repeated. "Sounds kind of boring for pirates."

"Perhaps, but at least our justice makes sense. Can you say the same for the Solar League?" He dragged a finger across her tattooed knuckles. "Among us, your markings are a badge of honor because they prove you're not afraid to follow your own rules. You would do well here, earn riches most men will never lay eyes on."

Not wanting to encourage him, she stayed silent.

Demarkus reached behind his neck and unclasped a gold choker that his tunic had concealed. He laid the necklace on the table so she could inspect its craftsmanship, hammered flat and polished to a high shine. She'd never seen real gold before, at least not this close-up, and her fingertip itched to touch it.

"Go ahead," he said. "It won't bite."

She noticed a script of Latin engraved in the metal. "What does that say?"

"It's one of our oldest tenets."

Of course it was. For criminals, they sure had a lot of laws.

"Try it on," he said with an encouraging nod.

"No, that's all right." She couldn't pinpoint the reason, but something about this felt wrong. "I meant it when I said I'm not looking to join—"

"A bargain, then," he interrupted. "If you put on that necklace and give me the pleasure of seeing you in it, I won't ask you to take it off."

She cast a sideways glance at him. "It'd be mine to keep?"

"For life."

Part of her bristled at the offer, but a much larger part was already calculating how many years of rations it would buy. She brushed a thumb over the warm gold, more enticed than she wanted to admit. This necklace could be her ticket to a comfortable new life.

"All right," she decided, and lifted the gold to her throat.

As soon as she fastened the clasp, a grin broke out on Demarkus's face, so full of cunning that the hairs on her forearm stood on end. It was then that she noticed a second, identical choker around his neck.

"You wear it well, little bird," he said, lips stretched wide over his teeth. "Welcome to the family."

CHAPTER TWELVE

Twenty-nine minutes and thirty-seven seconds.

She should be here by now.

Doran stretched his spine and peered across the hangar for Solara, but the only sign of life was the pirate who'd delivered the propellant cell twenty minutes ago. The guy was bald and had a second pair of eyes tattooed on his dome, and at the moment, he was leaning against a metal door, sucking on a synthetic cigar. His biceps were bigger than his head.

Doran shifted in his seat. Maybe he should wait five more minutes.

But then he remembered the feel of Solara's trembling hand, and he knew he'd already waited for her too long. If she was brave enough to barter with pirates, the least he could do was check on her. A few deep breaths later, he exited the shuttle and approached the guard, who he'd secretly nicknamed Four-Eyes.

"No refunds," Four-Eyes said, the cigar bouncing between his lips.

Doran tucked both hands in his pockets and faked a yawn. "I'm here for Lara. She wandered off half an hour ago."

The man shook his head. "She's dining with the chief. You'll have to—"

A riotous cheer from inside the ship interrupted him, so loud that the metal floor hummed beneath their boots. Four-Eyes touched an earpiece to communicate with someone out of sight, and then his mouth curved into a smile so wide he nearly dropped his cigar.

"Well, I'll be a piss swiller," the man said to himself. "The chief took a bride!"

"Just now?" Doran asked. He didn't give a damn about the chief's love life, but he sensed an opportunity to get inside the ship. "Then let's go toast the poor bastard!" Behind his hand, he added, "There's not enough ore on Mars to put a ring on *my* finger."

"You and me both, my friend."

Apparently, confirmed bachelorhood was all it took to unite them as brothers. Four-Eyes slung his weapon over his back and opened the sliding metal door. Then he hooked an arm around Doran's neck and led him to the source of the festivities, a great room at the heart of the ship. The sight of a thousand bodies stopped Doran short.

He nudged his new friend and shouted, "Where's your chief?"

Four-Eyes pointed above a sea of heads to a stage at the center of the room, where Solara stood beside a hulking Goliath twice her height. Doran had to do a double take. He'd never seen a human being so large, not even last summer during Super Bowl Camp. It was no wonder the pirates had made Demarkus their chief; he could crush a man with a pinch of his fingers. Solara looked like a child beside him, hugging herself tightly with both arms, her blackened eyes round and unblinking.

But the two of them stood alone onstage. Where was the bride?

Mugs of ale started circulating, handed down the tables until Four-Eyes snagged one for himself and handed another to Doran. After they each took a gulp, Four-Eyes lifted his mug toward the stage. "A bit young and slight, that one. Not his usual type." He cupped a hand in front of his chest as if balancing a cantaloupe. "He tends to favor bigger ladies, if you know what I mean."

Doran inhaled his ale, then coughed so hard he almost expelled both lungs. He wrenched his gaze to the stage and paid attention this time, noticing the way Demarkus showcased Solara like a prize he'd won at the fair. She fingered a golden necklace at her throat, which certainly wasn't there half an hour ago. But nothing in her watery eyes led him to believe she'd chosen this union willingly.

"That's my crewmate," Doran shouted.

Four-Eyes laughed. "Not anymore."

"But I know her," he said. "She would never consent to this."

The din of the crowd had died down enough for a few men to overhear. One of them cocked a warning brow and said, "The girl wears his token. She put it on of her own free will, in front of witnesses."

"A token?" Doran asked. "That's what passes for a wedding with you people? She probably didn't understand what she was doing."

The man shrugged. "Ignorance of our law is no defense. They're wed."

"Okay, so they're wed," Doran said. "How do we undo it?"

His question drew the interest of another nearby group, who silenced their conversation to listen in. Four-Eyes studied Doran's face warily before telling him, "There's only one way to break a marriage bond."

"How?" Doran demanded.

"One of us can challenge him for the bride." Four-Eyes glanced at his comrades and let out a barking chortle. "But who's fool enough to do that?"

While the men joined him in laughter, Doran peered across the crowd at Solara, who seemed to have shrunk an inch. Her skin was the color of almond milk, pale white against purple bruises. Soon her eyes met his and widened with the unmistakable relief of a lost soul who'd found her only friend in the world. She lifted her head in an obvious show of strength, but her gaze shimmered. And then her proud chin began to wobble.

Something behind Doran's breastbone cracked in half.

He lost control of his vocal cords and heard himself say, "I'll do it."

For the span of two heartbeats, there was silence all around.

He repeated, louder, "I challenge him."

The pirates must have craved a night's entertainment more than a life of marital bliss for their chief because cheers erupted from nearby, along with shouts of, "A challenge! A challenge for the bride!"

Four-Eyes clapped Doran on the back hard enough to send him stumbling forward a step. "You've got titanium twins between your legs, my friend. What's your name?"

Doran had rehearsed this answer in the shuttle, but it took a few tries to untie his tongue. "Daro," he said. "Daro the Red."

Four-Eyes lifted Doran's hand in the air and hollered at the stage, "Daro the Red issues a formal challenge of combat for the girl!"

"Wait. Combat?" All the blood left Doran's face. He'd assumed the challenge would involve athletics—target shooting, or a race, perhaps. He'd never engaged in combat before, unless varsity football counted. "Can't we do something else?"

But it was too late. Four-Eyes began pulling him through the crowd. Rough palms slapped his shoulders as he passed, while unseen men shouted, "Good on ya, boy!" and "Die well, you crazy bastard!"

Doran's legs went numb somewhere along the way, and he felt like a wooden marionette by the time he climbed the stairs to the platform. His feet seemed to know what awaited him there, because they kept sticking to the planks, forcing him into a jerky dance across the stage until he stopped in front of a pair of boots large enough to house an elephant.

When Doran craned his neck up—and then up some more—to look Demarkus in the eyes, he was grateful he'd used the bathroom recently. Because a few of his internal parts simply let go, surrendering before the fight had even begun.

After Demarkus finished sizing him up, which didn't take long, he beamed as if Doran had given him the best wedding present ever. "So this is my challenger?" he asked with a grin.

"Daro the Red, Chief," said Four-Eyes. The man still had an arm wrapped around Doran's shoulders. "The girl's pilot."

"And her lover," Demarkus added.

"No." The clarity of Doran's voice surprised even himself. He glanced at Solara and said, "Her friend." It felt strange calling himself that, but if combat with a seven-foot-tall pirate chief didn't upgrade them to friends, nothing would.

Demarkus scratched his chin. "How old are you, boy?"

"Old enough. Eighteen."

The pirate brought both hands together and studied Doran like a proud parent. "I command a thousand men. Seasoned fighters with three times your grit. And do you know how long it's been since someone challenged me?"

Doran shook his head.

"Five years."

That's because your men are smart, Doran thought.

"You've got more guts than sense," Demarkus said. "I respect that. Traditionally, the challenged party chooses the weapons, but I defer that decision to you."

Doran turned to Four-Eyes for a translation.

"He's giving you the advantage," Four-Eyes whispered. "What's your weapon of choice? Pistols? Staffs? Clubs?" When that didn't yield a response, he added, "Long blades? Spears? Pulse rifles?"

"None of that," Doran whispered back.

"Good man." Four-Eyes gave a respectful nod. "Bare fists,

it is!" he announced to the crowd below, eliciting a chorus of cheers.

Demarkus rested one meaty palm on Doran's shoulder, then gave it an encouraging shake that rattled his teeth. "Excellent choice. That's how a real man fights." He lowered his head and murmured, "I like your spirit, boy. I'm going to try not to kill you."

If that was supposed to make Doran feel better, it didn't work.

Demarkus strode off toward the boxing ring, leaving Doran to face Solara. She rushed forward and grabbed him by the upper arms. Her fingernails bit through his shirt, but the contact barely registered. Soon he would know *real* pain.

"Are you insane?" she screeched. "He'll kill you!"

The wires in Doran's brain must've crossed because that made him laugh. "Not on purpose."

"Call it off. I'll get out of here some other way."

Doran sobered up then, focusing on her eyes—not the bruises staining her skin, but the rings of color where her honey-eyed irises morphed into green. "If you manage to escape," he said, "and that's a big *if*, it won't be tonight—your wedding night. Do you think marriage is a joke to this guy? He's going to . . . you know . . ." Doran's gaze faltered for a moment. "Expect *things* from you."

Solara's eyes flashed. "I can defend my own virtue, thank you very much. Anyway, it's not like that. He wants me in the engine room, not his bed. He only married me so I'd have to stay."

"That's not much better," Doran said. "Look around. Do you feel safe?"

"I'll figure out a—"

"Damn it, Solara. If I don't do this, you could be stuck here forever. Is that what you want?"

"No."

"Then let me fight him." He shook her off before she had a chance to fuss at him again. "I know I've got no shot against this guy. But I can't just walk out of here and leave you." A bead of sweat trickled down his temple, and he scrubbed it away with his shirtsleeve. "You're the one who said I could be decent if I wanted to, so quit trying to talk me out of it. I'm about to piss myself as it is, and you're not helping."

Solara chewed on her bottom lip. Just when it seemed she was about to argue, she told him, "Men his size are slow. Guard your face and stay light on your feet. Hit the soft parts—belly, kidneys, throat—not the face, or you'll break your knuckles. You won't knock him out, but maybe you can wear him down and trip him. Then kick him in the head before he gets up. Don't be afraid to fight dirty."

Doran nodded, taking it all in. With that strategy, winning the fight almost sounded possible. Or at least that's what he told himself when he turned and joined Demarkus inside the ring.

As soon as he crossed the threshold, a buzz of electricity sounded behind him—invisible ropes to lock him in. While Demarkus secured his long hair in a ponytail, Four-Eyes stood outside the ring and hollered to the crowd, "Witnesses, give heed!" The room quieted, and he went on. "This is a formal challenge of bare-fisted combat brought by Daro the Red against Demarkus Hahn for dissolution of marriage. There are no moves barred, and the last man standing wins." He addressed his chief and bowed.

Demarkus flexed his long fingers and bent his head to the side, cracking his neck. He rolled both shoulders and nodded as if to signal his readiness. Doran figured he should probably loosen up, too, but it was all he could do to keep his wobbling knees locked. The smile had left his opponent's face, and now Demarkus approached in sure steps, his fists raised and ready to strike.

Doran shifted his weight to the balls of his feet in an attempt to dodge the first blow, but a flash of skin blurred in front of him and connected with his left eye. Like whiplash, his head jerked back, sending him flailing for balance. The pain came next, a dull throb around his eye socket that he barely had time to register before another jab sent him tumbling to the floor. He landed hard on his ass, a jolt ricocheting up his tailbone.

The crowd roared with laughter.

What the hell was that? He thought big men were supposed to be slow.

"Get up," Demarkus snapped. His brow was stern, his tone scolding. "They're mocking you. Get on your feet!"

Doran pushed onto all fours and stood up, which lasted for half a second. One right hook to the jaw and he was back on the planks with spots dancing in his vision. This time Demarkus didn't bother telling him to stand up. He reached down and lifted Doran by the shirt until the soles of his boots met the floor.

With his mouth pressed to Doran's ear, the pirate whispered,

"C'mon, boy. I can't keep going easy on you, or I'll lose the respect of my men."

This was taking it easy on him?

"Fight back," Demarkus said. "You should be hitting me right now."

Curling his hand into a fist, Doran grunted and delivered an uppercut to the belly. His knuckles met the tension of flexed abdominal muscles, and Demarkus pulled back and gave him a disappointed look that said, *Is that all you've got?*

"Where's your fire?" the man asked, shaking Doran's shirt. Then his gaze focused on something in the background, and a calculating smile curved his lips. "I can see Lara. She looks worried for you."

A spark of anger ignited in Doran's belly. He pushed against the pirate's chest.

"She's a talented girl," Demarkus said. "A rare find in these parts. I hope you won't miss her too badly, because she's going to love it here. Soon she'll forget you ever existed."

Without thinking, Doran head-butted Demarkus in the mouth, then shoved him backward and punched him directly above the groin. Rage took control, humming all over his skin and making him numb. He hit the man again and again, anywhere he could reach, until one giant fist to the chest knocked Doran down. Only then did he notice the blood trickling over Demarkus's chin.

He'd done it. Doran had drawn first blood.

Demarkus smiled as if he'd gotten exactly what he wanted, and then the fight was on—in earnest. Doran scrambled up from the floor and charged the giant, landing a shoulder in his midsection. Demarkus brought down a hammer of a fist onto Doran's back, flattening him with ease. As soon as his belly met the floor, Doran rolled aside and avoided a kick to the gut. But he wasn't quick enough to dodge the next punch, a thunder jab to his good eye.

After that, Doran spent the match ducking and running with minimal success. He peered at his aggressor through the cracks of his swollen eyelids and the stinging sweat that blurred his vision. He couldn't see his periphery, and Demarkus must've known it because three left hooks came in a row. Doran pushed onto his feet only to tense for the next hit—to the mouth, the nose, the stomach. No part of him was safe. At one point, Doran took a blow to the head so hard he saw the future.

And he wasn't in it.

He began to realize this strategy wouldn't work. He couldn't match his opponent in strength or speed, so attempting to wear him down and trip him was a waste of time. To win the fight, he'd have to find Demarkus's greatest weakness and exploit it. Doran knew the man was arrogant, but how could he use that to his advantage?

To buy himself a few seconds to think, he executed some basic football drills, faking left and darting right while he decided what to do next. He kept hearing Solara's advice inside his head. *Don't be afraid to fight dirty.* His instincts told him that was the key, but how?

Another punch clipped Doran's jaw with enough force to send him back to the planks, where he bounced twice and landed faceup. The adrenaline began to wear off, allowing a torrent of pain to swallow him whole. His face throbbed like an overinflated balloon. Hot blood flowed over his mouth, and when he darted a tongue over his lips, it slid between a cleft of missing flesh. A selfish part of him wished he could pass out so his suffering would end.

Then an idea came to mind.

He *could* pass out, or at least make it look that way.

With an extra-loud groan, he rolled onto all fours and swayed back and forth, even gagging for effect. He stood from the hard planks and immediately let himself tilt to the side until he stumbled back to the floor. Then after one more feeble attempt to rise, he went limp as a noodle and gave up the fight. Almost at once, he heard Demarkus's throaty chortle, followed by the crowd's roar of applause for the victor, their chief.

While the hall erupted in celebration, Doran kept both eyes closed and waited for the planks to stir beneath him. When he felt the thump of footsteps, he snuck a peek at Demarkus's boots and noticed they faced the opposite direction.

Now was the time to come alive.

He belly-crawled a few inches toward Demarkus, who was too busy pumping his arms in the air to notice anything else. Doran glanced up at the juncture of his opponent's widespread legs, pleased to find that Demarkus had left his weakest spot unprotected.

Arrogance, Doran thought, grinning.

He pushed himself onto one elbow while tensing his opposite fist. A few of the men watching from outside the ring had begun to catch on. They pointed wild fingers at him and shouted at their chief in warning. Doran knew he couldn't wait another second. Drawing on all his strength, he thrust his arm straight up and punched his enemy in a vulnerable place that made all men weaklings. His knuckles connected with a satisfying pop, and at once, Demarkus bent at the waist as if an invisible hand had chopped him in half. In slow motion, his massive frame tipped over and landed on the electric ropes. There was a long crackle of energy, followed by the stench of burnt hair, and Demarkus went rigid as he fought to untangle himself. The pain had clearly made him clumsy because it took three tries before he managed to stagger free.

Doran jumped to his feet and quickly pushed Demarkus back onto the ropes. When the man eventually rebounded, Doran was there to deliver another shove—and then another. Each time, the voltage seemed to drain Demarkus a little more, until his head lolled from side to side and his body began to sway. Then, clenching one fist, Doran wound up and punched Demarkus hard enough to send him to the floor with a loud clatter that shook the planks.

The crowd fell silent, and the electric ropes shorted out.

Keeping a wary distance, Doran crept near enough to study his opponent's face—lids shut, lips parted by slow, deep breaths. He didn't know if Demarkus was playing dead or truly out cold, so he stripped off his belt and used it to secure the man's wrists behind his back. Only then did he rise and face the crowd, lifting an arm to declare himself the last man standing.

Nobody cheered.

A thousand pirates blinked at him, then turned to peer at one another in confusion. Hands settled briefly on pistols before drifting up to scratch their owners' heads. The reaction told Doran that they didn't know what to do. Should they honor the victory of an outsider, a boy who'd won by trickery, or avenge their leader?

Solara must've noticed their indecision, too, because she snatched a pulse pistol from the nearest hip and started waving it around. "Stand down," she shouted at the crowd. "According to your rules, no moves were barred. My pilot won his challenge. You're bound by Brethren law to let us go." She tossed her gold necklace onto Demarkus's body, then pointed the gun at Four-Eyes. "You. Drop your weapon and come here."

The guard obeyed.

She pressed the muzzle to his back and ordered, "Tell your crew to make a hole. You're going to lead us to the hangar, and if anyone moves on me or my pilot, I'll ventilate your chest."

Four-Eyes seemed to hesitate, but then he raised both hands and begrudgingly told everyone to clear the way. Like molasses on a pancake, the spectators drifted toward the edges of the great hall and opened a path to the exit, never taking their eyes off Solara. She gave the guard a nudge and followed as he began a cautious stride through the room. Doran fell into place behind her. His eyes had swollen nearly shut, making it impossible to watch the crowd, so he fixed his gaze on Four-Eyes and let Solara scan the others.

Doran's heart thumped while they crossed the floor. Every sound made him flinch, each cough triggering his anticipation of an attack. The journey to the corridor seemed to last a thousand years, and when they crossed the threshold into the hallway, he released a long breath.

"Shut those doors," Solara told him. "And bolt them if you can."

He did as she asked. There was no bolt, so he removed his jacket and tied the sleeves in a sloppy knot around the door handles. It wouldn't hold the crew if they decided to follow, but it might slow them down a bit.

They jogged to the hangar, where Solara ordered the guard to remain inside the control room and open the hatch after they'd boarded their shuttle. She pointed to a box mounted on the hangar ceiling and warned, "If anything goes wrong, I'll start taking shots at your air pump. Are we clear?"

Four-Eyes set his jaw and nodded.

"And since we obeyed your laws, there's no reason to follow."

"No one will come after you," the guard said, then glared at her and clarified, "Today."

That was good enough for Doran. He ran to the shuttle and climbed through the passenger door. "You'll have to fly," he told Solara. He could barely see well enough to fasten his safety harness. "Try not to break my other arm."

She took the pilot's seat and flipped on the ignition. "I told you. I can fly just fine."

"*And* land?"

"Shh," she dismissed him while lifting off. "One crisis at a time."

CHAPTER THIRTEEN

Solara held her breath as she eased the shuttle toward the *Banshee*'s docking station. She cast a longing glance at the switch to dispatch the magnetic tow cables, wishing she could use them to pull her into position. But Doran had insisted that she land on her own. *You'll do fine,* he'd said. *If you can hold a room full of pirates at gunpoint, then you can land a two-person craft.*

She gripped the wheel and asked, "How's this?"

Doran peered out the side window. "Good. Now tap your starboard thruster to bring us around a bit."

She did as he'd suggested. The shuttle rotated into perfect alignment and drifted near the ship. A few slow seconds later, the shuttle nested into place with a slight jolt that shook Solara and Doran in their seats. An automatic smile formed on Solara's lips. She'd performed her first landing without breaking any bones.

"I did it!"

"Told you," Doran gloated while unbuckling his harness. He opened the side hatch and pointed at the propellant cell. "Let's celebrate inside. I'd like to put a few solar systems behind us before morning."

"Good plan," she agreed. They'd kicked a hornet's nest tonight, and the Brethren didn't strike her as the forgiving sort. Still, her chin lifted as she followed Doran inside the ship. She felt more like an action hero than a mechanic. She wished Sister Agnes could see her now.

The bounce in Doran's step told her he was riding the same high, but she had no idea exactly *how* high until he spun around and scooped her into a hug that lifted both her boots off the floor. She stiffened while his laughter rang in her ears, a sound of pure exhilaration she'd never heard from him before, not even during football season at the academy. His reaction forced a giggle out of her, and she told herself the tingly sensation unfurling inside her belly was nothing more than adrenaline.

"We were amazing back there," he said, and set her down. He kept both hands on her hips and pulled back to look at her through one swollen eye. "Can you believe it?"

At the sight of him in the overhead lighting, her smile died and her tingles morphed into sympathy pains. The darkness inside the shuttle had concealed the extent of his injuries, but now she could see that his eyes were nothing more than slits, and the bottom half of his face was covered in a macabre beard of dried blood. She could only imagine how badly he would hurt once the rush wore off.

Guilt swam over her. This was her fault.

"Do I look that bad?" he asked.

She winced as a cut reopened in his lower lip, but then she reminded herself that Doran's happiness was the only silver lining in this cloud. He'd done something remarkable tonight, shown more bravery than she'd ever thought possible, and she refused to rob him of that. "I hate to break it to you," she said. "But you're not the prettiest girl in the room anymore."

He chuckled. "Give me time."

"Go ahead and laugh." She studied the crooked angle of his nose, which was undoubtedly broken. "Because you're going to feel this in the morning."

"Hell, I feel it now," he said, bringing a hand to his ribs. "But who cares? I actually knocked him out. First person to challenge Demarkus in five years, and I won."

Her heart twisted at the memory of Doran lying on the floor, blood pouring from his mouth while she watched helplessly from outside the ring. She hadn't known it was a trick. She'd thought he was dead, and fear had gutted her like a fish. The flashback made her vision go blurry, so she dropped her gaze to his boots. Even those were smeared with red. "Sorry for doubting you."

"Well, don't sound so excited," he muttered. "All I did was bring down a giant with my bare hands."

"A giant who could have killed you." She glanced up to find him frowning at her. "All because I put on that stupid necklace."

"You didn't know any better."

"No, but I should have. Nothing comes for free in life—not food or land or clothes, and especially not gold. Deep down I knew it was too good to be true, but I took the necklace anyway. And you paid for my mistake, Doran. You could have died."

He didn't answer at first. He waited until she met his gaze, then flashed a grin that softened the edges of her guilt. "I'm fine, really. This is surface damage. My devilish good looks aren't lost forever."

"Demarkus hurt you."

"Yeah, but I gave it back," Doran said. "If it makes you feel any better, he's probably still looking for his left nut."

Solara couldn't help laughing. "That does make me feel better."

"Me too."

"Listen," she said. "I'm sorry."

Now it was his turn to avoid her eyes. He fell silent for a while, fidgeting with his jacket's zipper pull until he quietly cleared his throat. "I'm pretty sure I've got more to apologize for than you do. When I tried leaving you alone at that outpost, I had no idea what it's really like out here. I hate to think . . ." He trailed off, peeking down at her. "But maybe we can call it even and start over?"

She nodded. "I'd like that."

"Good. Then it's settled."

"And thanks," she told him. "I owe my freedom to you. You don't know me very well, but nothing means more to me than that."

"Anytime." His gaze moved over her face in a way that made her blush. "That's what friends are for, right?"

Their eyes held for a beat of silence, and the mood shifted.

Solara could swear she felt something electric pass between them. One of his hands still rested on her hip, and she became hyper-aware of its weight and its warmth. But then he seemed to take note of their closeness and stepped back. The moment ended so quickly that she wondered if she'd imagined the whole thing. She couldn't decide whether to feel disappointed or relieved.

"Sorry," he said. "I probably stink like a corpse."

She cradled the propellant cell to her chest and inched toward the engine room. "I hadn't noticed. The only thing I smell anymore is burnt porridge."

"You're never letting that go, are you?"

"Of course not," she told him while striding away. "It's my duty to give you hell. *That's* what friends are for."

*　*　*

Two hours later, when the *Banshee* was sailing smoothly once again, Solara followed the sounds of laughter to the lounge, where a party seemed to be under way. She walked inside and found the crew sitting around the holographic fireplace, leaning toward Doran to hang on his every word. He reclined in his chair, head tipped back with a gel mask covering his face, not that it stopped him from spinning a lively tale.

"And then," Doran said, practically choking on a chuckle, "he told me, *I like your spirit, boy. I'm going to try not to kill you.*"

The captain slapped his knee and heaved a mighty guffaw that shook his chest. In response, Acorn climbed out of his pocket and scampered to his knee, then spread her furry arms and glided to the floor. "I bet he's eating those words right now."

"With a steaming side of crow," Renny added, removing his glasses to wipe a tear from his eye. "I wish I could've been there."

"Me too," the captain said. "I'd give my fake leg to see the look on his face when you punched him in the short and curlies."

"Who wouldn't?" Cassia asked with a grin that transformed her face from fierce to beautiful. She should smile more often. "We'd make a mint if we got our hands on the video feed." She elbowed Kane, who sat beside her, but he wasn't laughing.

Unlike the others, he glared at Doran with an intensity that prickled Solara's nerves. She had no idea what his problem was, but she didn't like it.

"How's our hero?" Solara asked while watching Kane. Their eyes met, and he must've sensed her apprehension because he looked away and offered Acorn a chunk of dried fruit.

"I'm fannntastic," Doran called from beneath his mask, and thrust both thumbs in the air. He sounded drunk, or at least buzzed. "How's our divorcée?"

"Still single, thanks for asking." She admired his relaxed posture. "But I wouldn't mind sharing a sip of whatever you've had."

Cassia stood from her chair to check on Doran. "I gave him some painkillers before I set his nose. He's still a little loopy." She lifted his gel mask to reveal a nose splint, and right away Solara noticed the swelling had subsided.

"Wow," she said. "Nice job. He looks almost human."

"I can't take all the credit." Cassia pointed at a jar on the floor that seemed to be filled with squirming black slugs. "That's the magic of camelback leeches. They drain twice the fluid in half the time."

Solara wrinkled her nose. "Whatever works, I guess. I didn't know those existed."

"I knew the woman who bred the first pair," Cassia said. "She was one of my teachers, and she passed along a few of her healing tricks."

"Lucky for us." Solara's cheeks warmed with fresh guilt when she noticed a pile of bloody rags on the floor. "We really put your skills to the test tonight."

"Hey, listen," Cassia said, and pointed the gel mask at her. "Don't beat yourself up over what happened with Demarkus. You're not the first person to fall for that trick, and you won't be the last. I should've warned you about pirate gifts. They always come with strings attached."

Don't beat yourself up. How fitting.

Solara changed the subject by asking Doran, "Can you stay on your feet?"

"I think so. Why?"

"It's my shower day," she said. "I never had a chance to finish, so my turn's still open. Why don't you take it? You can wash that dye out of your—"

Before she was done, he jumped up and scrambled out of the room, calling over his shoulder, "No take-backs!"

The crew laughed at his retreating form . . . everyone except Kane.

As soon as Doran's footsteps faded into silence, Kane delivered a harsh look to the rest of the crew and hissed, "You know what's going to happen now, right?"

"Yeah," the captain said. "Demarkus will sound like a lady when he talks."

Renny snickered. "Oh, to be a fly on the wall."

"This isn't funny," Kane snapped. "The Brethren will come after Doran, which means they'll come after the *Banshee*."

"Why do you care?" Solara asked him. "You've already got the Daeva on your trail. Compared to them, the pirates are puppy dogs."

"I care plenty," he said, flicking a glance at Cassia. "The Daeva make up one squad, and we can avoid them if we lie low. But the Brethren are everywhere. All it takes is one person to report Doran's location, and we're screwed." Kane turned to the captain and urged, "We have to drop him."

"*What?* No!" Solara said.

"Whoa, there." Captain Rossi flashed his palm. "We're not dumping anyone."

"Every minute he spends on this ship is a liability," Kane argued. "Demarkus will find him. You know it. And I don't have to tell you what he'll do—"

"Hey!" Solara shouted. "You weren't this worried about Demarkus when you served me up on a silver platter to save your ass." She jabbed a warning finger at him. "We had a deal. I installed that propellant cell, and I can rip it out just as easily."

"Everyone, calm down," the captain barked, causing Acorn to scamper behind the nearest gaming table leg. "Nobody's dumping our passengers. And nobody"—his eyes flashed at Solara—"is sabotaging my ship. Are we clear?"

She nodded, but Kane didn't seem ready to give up the fight. He drew a furious breath while a muscle ticked visibly in his jaw. Gone was the seductive gaze and the slippery smile she'd come to expect from him. This boy looked capable of murder.

Without another word, he stood from his chair and stalked to his quarters. The clatter of an object hitting the wall soon followed.

Cassia tugged on a dreadlock and stared after him. "Sorry," she said, as if part of her job involved policing his behavior. "I don't know what got into him."

Neither did Solara. And that was a problem.

*   *   *

She was still puzzling over Kane's outburst when she closed her bedroom door and bolted it for the night. No matter how many times she replayed their conversation, she couldn't make sense of it. Maybe he and Doran had argued. That wasn't a stretch. Doran could teach a class on the Art of Alienation. Or maybe Kane was just a jerk. Either way, Doran deserved to know what'd happened.

Folding both arms, she leaned against the wall and watched him toss and turn on his pallet of blankets, moaning nonsense in his sleep. She decided to tell him in the morning, after the pain medicine had worn off. Right now she would only wake him for one reason.

"Doran," she whispered, gently shaking his elbow.

He stirred with a groan and pulled the covers over his head.

"Get up." After throwing the blanket aside, she tried to lift his shoulders, but it was like moving a boulder. "Come on. I'm taking the floor tonight."

"Hmm?"

"You can have the bed."

One puffy eye opened. "Don't tease me."

"It's all yours. You've earned it."

That was all it took to lure him off the floor. In his woozy state, he needed some help scaling the mattress, but luckily the climb wasn't too high. She swung his legs into place and tucked him in while he nestled into her pillow and made happy noises.

"Better?" Instinctively, she reached out to smooth his hair and caught herself just in time.

He hummed in response, already half-asleep, then mumbled, "There's room for you."

She glanced at the empty spot next to him, and a familiar tickle reappeared behind her belly button. He was right. They could share the bed. But that seemed like a dangerous idea—not because anything might happen between them, but because Doran needed space to heal. What if she rolled over and accidentally elbowed him in the face? She might rebreak his nose, or open one of his cuts.

No, she would take the floor. It was safer down there. For Doran.

CHAPTER FOURTEEN

The next morning Solara yawned and stretched, massaging the knots in her shoulders and feeling a twinge of remorse for all the weeks she'd made Doran take the floor when there was plenty of room on the mattress. She glanced over to see if he was awake, and he blinked at her with sleepy eyes.

"Sucks down there, doesn't it?" he asked.

She ignored his question and looked more closely at him because something didn't seem quite right. His facial swelling had decreased, revealing high cheekbones and allowing his eyes to open all the way. But despite that, his skin was pale and a sheen of sweat glistened on his forehead.

"No offense," she said, "but you don't look so hot."

"None taken." He rolled onto his side with an agonized groan. "You were right when you said I'd feel it in the morning."

"Where does it hurt?"

"Where *doesn't* it hurt?" he quipped, and glanced at the door. "Do you think Cassia has any more of those magic pills?"

"I'll ask her." Solara squinted at the dried cracks in his lower lip, threatening to split open again. "But first you need another coat of oil."

Doran reached for the salve with one trembling hand, but he only managed to knock it to the floor. Since he was too weak, she picked up the jar and applied a thick layer for him. His dehydrated flesh drank the oil in seconds, forcing her to repeat the process and ignore how the slide of her finger across his mouth made her insides dance.

"All better," she said, and before she realized what she was doing, she licked her thumb to erase a smudge of dried blood from his forehead. She didn't know what had possessed her to clean his face with her spit. "I'll go find your pills."

She was halfway to the door when Doran cleared his throat and said, "Pants."

"What?"

"You're not wearing any."

"Oh, good catch." She grabbed her pants from the floor and pulled them on, more surprised by her lack of embarrassment than the fact that she'd flashed Doran her underwear. Funny how comfortable she'd grown in his company. When had that happened?

She padded on socked feet into the galley, where she found Cassia and Renny sitting alone, whispering over their coffee mugs, each unaware of Acorn creeping silently along the wall behind them. The furry sugar glider spread her wings and glided onto Cassia's head, sinking tiny claws into the blond dread-locks. Cassia let out a scream and splashed coffee into her lap while Renny tried not to laugh. He gently untangled Acorn's claws and handed her a raisin before sending her off in the other direction.

Cassia stewed, glaring after the animal. "I hate that little—"

"Doran's awake," Solara interrupted. "He needs more pain meds. You might want to give him an antibiotic for infection, too. He looks feverish."

That distracted Cassia from her rage. Her mouth pulled into a frown as she stood from the table. "I already gave him one."

"An antibiotic?"

Cassia nodded. "Because of all the open wounds."

She and Renny followed Solara to the bedroom. As soon as Cassia took a seat on the edge of Doran's bed, she placed a hand on his forehead. "No fever. If anything, you feel cold."

Doran responded with a shiver and gathered the blanket around his neck.

"Any dizziness?" Cassia asked.

"A little," he said. "But I thought it was from the pills."

"Those left your system hours ago."

"Then give me some more. I'm dying here."

Cassia didn't seem to like hearing that. She flicked a glance at Renny, then refocused on her patient. "Where's the worst of the pain?" she asked. "In your nose?"

"Unh-uh." Doran curled into the fetal position and shiv-ered again. "My belly and my sides. It feels like I did a thousand crunches in my sleep."

"Did Demarkus hit you there?"

Solara knew the answer to that. "Yes. And he didn't hold back."

"Lie flat and pull down the covers," Cassia said. "I want to have a look under your shirt."

"*Yeah*, you do," Doran teased.

That elicited a smile from Cassia. "It's my lucky day."

"Get on with it," Solara said, her face suddenly hot. "This isn't the time for jokes."

"Yes, ma'am," grumbled Doran, rolling onto his back.

As soon as he lifted his shirt, Cassia gasped, but clearly not out of appreciation for his sculpted torso. Her smile fell and she breathed, "Oh my god."

Solara moved closer to see what was wrong. She glimpsed exposed flesh, but Doran's nakedness barely registered. She went blind to everything except the sick patchwork of bruises that bled across his body until she couldn't tell where one ended and the next began. It looked like someone had injected wine beneath his skin.

Her stomach tightened. "What does this mean?"

"Internal bleeding," Cassia said. "That's why he's dizzy. He's lost too much blood."

Doran tugged down his shirt. "Stop talking about me like I'm not here. How are we going to fix it?"

Instead of answering, Cassia locked eyes with Renny.

"You *can* fix it," Doran pressed, volleying a gaze between the two. "Right?"

"We only have a few basics in the med kit," Cassia told him. "Painkillers and antibiotics for common wounds. Not the kind of drug that heals internal damage."

"But there's a drug like that?" Solara asked.

"Tissue-Bond," Renny said. "It's expensive."

"Then we'll buy some."

"It's not that simple."

"Money makes everything simple," Solara snapped. "I've got tons of fuel chips. I'll buy it on the black market."

Cassia nervously twirled a lock of blond hair at the base of her head, too short to fit into her dreads. She glanced at the first mate and said, "You should tell him. If it were me, I'd want to know."

"That sounds ominous," Solara said. "It's Demarkus, isn't it? He runs the black market, and now he won't sell to us."

Renny blew out a long breath and dug inside his trouser pockets to study the odds and ends he'd collected there—a broken necklace, a few liquid-filled capsules, and the small jar of medicated oil she'd just used on Doran's lips. She held out a hand toward Renny, and he finally spoke as he returned the jar. "He put a price on Doran's head. Alive, preferably. But that's not a requirement."

Doran pushed to his elbows. "How much?"

"Twice what the Solar League is offering."

"Wonderful," Solara muttered. Once Kane found out, he'd probably stage a mutiny. *Or cash in on the reward.* She hated herself for thinking it, but after his tantrum last night, she didn't know what he was capable of.

Ever the optimist, Renny pointed out, "It's not personal. Two of Demarkus's men have challenged him since the fight. I think he's worried he'll never have a moment's peace until he kills you."

"Well, that's a relief," Doran said. "I was afraid he didn't love me anymore."

"Can we be serious for a minute?" Solara asked. She yanked the blanket over Doran's body and softly karate-chopped it into place. "None of this is funny. Your whereabouts are a golden ticket right now. If I try to buy your medicine from a smuggler, I'll probably end up tortured until I tell him where you are."

"Maybe I don't need it," Doran said with a hopeful glance at Cassia. "The bleeding could stop on its own."

"Stranger things have happened," she told him. "But the odds are slim. Do you feel lucky?"

Solara shook her head. "We're not gambling with your life, Doran."

"If I could reach my father—"

"But you can't," Solara interrupted. Twice over the last few weeks, they'd tried calling his father from the ship's transmission system, with no success. She looked down at her gloves and knew there was only one solution. "If nobody will sell us the drug, we'll steal it."

"Won't work," Renny said automatically, as if theft was the first thing he'd considered. "We'd have to put out feelers to see which smugglers have the Tissue-Bond. That alone will tip our hand because everyone knows about the fight."

"I never said we'd be stealing from smugglers," Solara told him.

One curious brow lifted above Renny's eyeglass lens.

"We're close to Obsidian," she said. "The beaches are in the tourist circle, which means food and shopping—and shiny medical centers with fully stocked supply rooms."

"Demarkus has men working in hospitals, too," Renny said. "That's where half his narcotics come from."

"Right," she agreed. "But people know me as Solara Brooks, a dirty, bruised-up felon from the streets." She jogged to her supply container and pried off the lid, then pulled out the ball gown she'd purchased, the one she never thought she'd wear. Holding it up, she batted her eyelashes and drawled, "Not Lacy Vanderbilt, a vacationing socialite with a busted ankle."

"Nice dress," Cassia observed.

"Thanks. Doran bought it for me."

"Must've slipped my mind," Doran said, narrowing his eyes at the gown. "How much did that little gift set me back?"

"Not important." She turned to Renny. "It's the narcotics they keep under lock and key, not the healing accelerants. With your quick fingers and me to distract the staff, they won't notice it's gone until we are."

The first mate dragged off his glasses as a slow smile uncurled across his lips. "Why, Miss Vanderbilt," he said, tipping an imaginary hat at her. "I like the way you think."

CHAPTER FIFTEEN

*O*nce they were alone, Doran watched his new friend unfasten the single mahogany braid at the base of her spine, then gently shake loose the plaits with her long fingers. The ball gown he'd "bought" for her hung on the wall, and she gazed lovingly at the luminescent waterfalls of fabric, occasionally pausing to glance over her shoulder as if to ensure he was alive.

"I'm still here," he said. "And I still think this is a terrible plan."

"I still don't care, so deal with it," she answered.

He hated the thought of her stealing. The risk was too great. But since she'd refused to change her mind, he held his tongue and pushed away invading tendrils of guilt, reminding himself that this was her idea, not his.

It helped that she obviously couldn't wait to get inside that dress. The way she admired its holographic sparkle, tipping her head to and fro with her lower lip caught between her teeth, made him wonder if she'd ever worn a proper dress before—not a hand-me-down frock for church Mass, but the kind of garment designed to turn a man's head and leave his chin dragging on the floor. She'd kept mostly to herself at the academy and hadn't attended any dances. With a pang of shame, he imagined how he might have reacted if she'd come to prom: the cutting looks and the thinly veiled insults he'd have used to make her feel unwelcome. He knew she would've touched the birthmark at the base of her throat when he called her *Rattail* because it jabbed at her fragile confidence, just as he'd intended.

He wanted to tell her he was sorry, and that he knew how it felt to wear a target on his back. After his mother left, some older boys had caught him crying in the bathroom, and he'd quickly learned that the first rule of academy life was *Tease or be teased*. And years later, when Solara had won the alumni award, he'd lost more than a trophy. He'd lost a bit of esteem in his father's eyes, the only family Doran had left. Now he saw that picking on Solara had been a cowardly move in so many ways, but he couldn't tell her that. Instead he said, "That's a Belladucci design from the newest eveningwear line. Every girl who sees you in it is going to turn twenty shades of green."

Her reaction wasn't what he'd expected. She cringed, peering at him with regret in her eyes. "It was five thousand credits," she whispered. But while her expression oozed repentance, her fingers reached toward the gown in a protective gesture that told him he'd only get it back if he pried it from her cold, dead hands.

Since laughter would hurt too much, he held his breath until the impulse passed, then exhaled slowly. "I want to see you in it. After all, I'm the one who'll have to explain the charges on my expense account."

Assuming he even had a job when this ordeal was over. He still needed to reach his ship on Obsidian and figure out the significance of the coordinates his father had given him. The more Doran thought about it, the more he suspected there was a connection between his mission and the Solar League's false charges. Someone had gone to great lengths to ruin his reputation, and for no logical reason. He knew that should infuriate him, but at the moment he only had room for so much suffering.

Solara gathered her hair to the side and frowned as if something had just occurred to her. "It'll take more than a gown to turn me into an heiress. I didn't think to buy matching shoes."

"Go barefoot," Doran suggested. "Girls always take off their shoes to dance. You can pretend you left them at the party."

"But what about my hair? And makeup. I've never—"

"Ask Cassia to fix you up. She's a society girl."

"What?" Solara spun to face him. "Who told you that?"

"Nobody," he said with a shrug that sent a ripple of pain down his side. He gritted his teeth until the throbbing passed. "I know my own kind. She walks around the ship like she owns it."

"That doesn't mean anything."

"Actually, it does," he insisted. Cassia carried herself with the authority of someone accustomed to power at an early age. Doran recognized it because he'd behaved the same way, until his father busted him for using company interns to schedule hot dates. After that, Doran joined the ranks of the interns to learn a lesson in humility. But he'd noticed physical evidence of Cassia's upbringing, too. She carried a clue right on her skin. "Have you ever smelled her?" he asked. "Really close-up?"

Solara recoiled like he'd demanded to know her bra size. "No. Have *you*?"

"Once." It had happened the morning of the Pesirus hellberry festival, after he'd spent an hour hauling and stacking crates. He'd accidentally collided with Cassia in the washroom, and although sweat had soaked the front of her shirt, nothing but the scent of orchids had emanated from her skin. Only one thing suppressed natural body odor like that, and the procedure was so painful and expensive that even he'd turned it down.

"She has perfume microbes implanted in her sweat glands," he said. "They're rare and invasive. I've only met one other person who had it done, and he's a Solar League diplomat. That means she's not just loaded; she's important."

He waited for Solara to say something, but she just stood there, glaring at him.

"What?" he asked.

She shook her head and slung the gown over one shoulder, then left without a word.

* * *

As Solara charged down the hall, she recalled something Doran had told her on board the *Zenith*: *Anyone who stinks like a toolshed is safe from my advances.* She'd forgotten about that, and now she wondered what she smelled like after a week with no shower.

Certainly not perfume.

It was none of her business and she didn't know why she cared, but under what circumstances had Doran smelled Cassia really close-up? The two hadn't spent much time together, at least not that she knew of, but then again, romantic trysts didn't take long. Cassia had openly announced that hookups were the best way to fight transport madness. Had the pair secretly decided to help each other *rev up those endorphins*?

Solara's stomach felt sick.

She shouldn't be doing this, speculating and jumping to conclusions as if she owned him. It wasn't like she wanted Doran to boost *her* endorphins.

So why was her face throbbing in time with her pulse?

"Let it go," she muttered. "It doesn't matter."

"What doesn't matter?" asked Cassia, leaning her fair head out the open door to her bedroom.

Solara stopped short, clutching the ball gown to her chest. She faked a smile and said "Nothing," but she couldn't help surveying the girl with new eyes. She looked past the dishwater blond dreadlocks, dull and coarse from months of neglect, and beyond the unmade copper-hued face to the mannerisms beneath.

Cassia had gone to great lengths to hide her privileged upbringing, but there it was—a slightly haughty lift of her chin that allowed the tiny ship hand to look down at Solara despite their height difference. Cassia's body language resembled Doran's in that way, self-assured and completely in control. He was right. They were two of a kind.

"You okay?" Cassia asked.

"I'm just nervous about the job," Solara lied. "Do you think you can make me pretty? I've never worn makeup before, so I need all the help I can get."

"No problem. Come on in."

When Solara followed inside, curiosity hijacked her body. She rushed Cassia in a hug, locking both arms around the girl under the pretense of gratitude while burying her nose for a deep whiff. An enchanted garden filled her senses, seeming to originate from beneath the skin instead of on the surface. It was heavenly. Cassia stiffened at the ambush, and Solara stepped back, battling a surge of envy. She wished she could smell of springtime breezes instead of engine grease.

"Thanks," Solara said. "You're the best."

Cassia's room bore a striking resemblance to hers, except with one bunk stacked atop the other instead of a full-size bed. She noticed Kane watching her from the top bunk, a protein bar suspended an inch from his lips. He wore the same puzzled expression as Cassia, their blond heads tipped at precisely the same angle as they tried to make sense of her abrupt display of affection.

Solara greeted him with a cool nod.

He recovered then, apologizing with his eyes. "Hey, I'm sorry about last night. I shouldn't have run my mouth like that. I didn't mean a word of it. That was the Crystalline talking."

Solara wasn't sure if she believed him. He'd seemed plenty sober to her.

"Doran's already banged up," Kane went on. "The last thing he needs is me making him feel worse." Dipping his head, he asked, "Did you tell him what I said?"

"No. Not yet."

"Then maybe we can keep it between us," Kane suggested. "I like Doran. He's a good guy, and I don't want the rest of the trip to feel awkward."

Solara rubbed the dress between her fingers, unsure of what to do. Kane seemed sincere, but her first loyalty was to Doran, and she still felt he had a right to know.

"I'll think about it," she said. To change the subject, she added, "We should hurry. Renny wants to leave soon."

"Sure." Kane's lips slid into an easy grin, as if nothing had happened. "But you don't need holographic goop to make you pretty."

"Of course she doesn't," Cassia agreed, and reached up for a bite of his snack. She tore off a chunk and handed it back, then pointed at her own face and clarified, "Well, except for the bruises."

"And the birthmark," Kane added. "It's cute, but it's an easy giveaway."

Despite having not fully forgiven him, Solara felt her mouth curve up. "You think my birthmark's cute?"

His impish grin widened, his voice dipping low and smooth. "I think every part of you is cute."

Cassia responded by climbing the bunk ladder and smacking her roommate upside the head. When he gaped in protest, she thrust a finger at him and hissed, "I like this one. Leave her alone."

Kane rubbed his head and scooted to the other end of his mattress, not that it afforded him any protection from the furious girl glaring at him hard enough to singe off his eyebrows. "I was just being friendly. What's wrong with that?"

"You and I both know what you were doing," Cassia snapped. "Now, get down here and help me."

The argument made Solara wonder, for the hundredth time, how the ship hands knew each other. Despite their sharp looks and harsh words, they moved through the *Banshee* like planets in orbit, sharing everything from meals to inside jokes with a comfortable familiarity unique to siblings. But if they really were brother and sister, why the differences in their body language? With his shameless stare and flirty smile, Kane acted like someone who'd regularly seduced for his supper, not a trust fund baby.

The two of them took a break from bickering long enough to decide that Kane would style her hair while Cassia handled the makeup. Then they ushered her onto a stool facing the bottom bunk and got down to business: Kane brushing her hair from behind while Cassia sat cross-legged on the mattress sorting through a box of cosmetics.

From her new vantage point, Solara noticed an assortment of photographs taped to the wall beside Cassia's bed. She spotted Kane in one of them, his arm slung playfully around Cassia's neck as they toasted each other with cups of red juice. Hellberry wine, maybe. The other photographs were of landscapes—lush, rolling hills of lavender giving way to an endless indigo lake, its ripples reflecting the glow of twin moons. Solara had never seen a place so breathtaking, and she caught herself frowning when Cassia blocked the view by leaning in to dust powder on her cheeks.

"Where were those pictures taken?" she asked. "They're beautiful."

Cassia lost her grasp on the powder puff, and it sailed to the floor. At once, her eyes found Kane's and softened in sadness. "Just someplace I used to live," she said. Kane finished a brushstroke and used his thumb to skim the outside of Cassia's wrist in a touch so brief that Solara would've missed it if she'd blinked. But she hadn't missed it, and in that sliver of a moment, she watched an exchange of pure intimacy pass between them.

Definitely not brother and sister, she thought.

Neither spoke after that, so she kept silent. But Solara couldn't stop prickles of worry from creeping over her. She and Doran had slipped into an easy trust with the *Banshee* crew, and yet she knew nothing about what had brought them all together.

Who were these people?

* * *

Doran battled a wave of dizziness, squinting hard to bring Solara into focus when she and the crew returned to his room. He had imagined how she might look in her dress, but nothing could've prepared him for the complete transformation that made her into a stranger—strikingly beautiful, to be sure, but so unfamiliar that the sight of her caused his brows to pinch together.

It was her eyes he noticed first, peering at him beneath long, iridescent lashes. Two butterfly wings fluttered out from her upper and lower lids, painted in autumn tones and treated with a holographic glaze so they appeared to blink along with her. When combined with the halo of silver ribbons woven through her braids, the effect was mesmerizing. But he couldn't reconcile those eyes with the pair he'd grown accustomed to watching across the dinner table each night during games of *Would You Rather.*

He let his gaze wander and took in the ball gown, which twinkled with the brilliance of a starry night sky. The strapless design hugged her curves like a second skin, highlighting her bare shoulders and arms, and through some miracle that defied gravity, her breasts were thrust upward in a display halfway to her chin.

Doran nearly swallowed his tongue, trying very hard not to stare and batting down the selfish urge to wrap her in a blanket so that nobody else could see her like this. He forced his eyes lower, all the way to the tips of her toes, which alternately flashed pink and purple with animated lacquer. Her fingernails were polished as well, and her tattoos concealed. In all her glitz and glamour, he could easily imagine her gracing the cover of a fashion magazine.

He didn't know how he felt about that.

Warring impulses tugged at him in a jumble of emotions he didn't understand. He wanted to keep looking at her, to tell her that she took his breath away, but at the same time, he wanted to ask her to wash off the makeup and put on her regular clothes, to remove the flashy polish and let the beauty of her naked toes shine through.

He wanted her to be the Solara he'd come to know—*his* Solara.

Cassia bumped Kane with her shoulder. "Look. He's speechless."

"We do good work," Kane agreed, admiring their creation.

When Solara glanced up at him again, Doran found his voice. "Wow," he told her. "I don't know what to say." But she deserved more than that, so he added, "Five thousand credits was a small price to pay. You're stunning."

Her answering smile warmed his heart.

"And you're forgiven," she announced. Before he could ask what he'd done wrong, she turned and padded away. He called after her to be careful, but he wasn't sure she heard.

Sometime later, as he lay awake in the darkness with nothing but his pain to keep him company, it occurred to Doran that once he reached Obsidian, he and Solara would part ways. She would continue on to her job in the fringe while he finished his father's errand and returned home to clear his name. Their paths might never cross again.

He didn't know how he felt about that, either.

Actually, yes, he did.

But before he had a chance to examine the reason for the new tightness in his chest, another dizzy spell came over him, along with a vicious chill that seemed to leach the marrow from his bones. Doran huddled beneath the covers while his insides pulsed like an abscessed tooth. He hoped Solara returned soon with his medicine. Otherwise they might part ways a lot earlier than he'd planned.

CHAPTER SIXTEEN

With its flashing billboards illuminating the craters of an anchoring moon, the retail satellite was impossible to miss by any pilot taking the direct route from the nearest outpost to Obsidian—the route the *Banshee* had carefully avoided. This place was a tourist mecca, a respite from the months-long voyage where travelers could cure their cabin fever with honeyed wine, laser quests, and chintzy souvenirs.

But none of that interested Solara.

She leaned forward in her seat and peered out the shuttle window, scanning past multicolored scrolling advertisements for QUICK SHUTTLE REPAIR! and LOOSEST SLOTS IN THE GALAXY! to the single security checkpoint located at the top of the static bubble shielding the complex. That narrow apex was the only way in or out.

Not the ideal blueprint for making a quick getaway.

"Please tell me there's a secret back door," she said to Renny, who cut the shuttle thrusters and steered toward the checkpoint, essentially casting them out of the frying pan and into the fire. Their craft drifted near enough for Solara to make out the silhouette of a cloaked laser canon, invisible but for the distorted space around it, which rippled like heat waves rising above asphalt.

"I could do that," he replied. "But I'd be lying."

Solara blew out a breath and strapped a gel pack around her ankle while Renny tugged at the cuffs of his dress coat, trying to lengthen its sleeves. If he wanted to look dapper, he should've swiped a jacket from a taller man.

"Remember," he said, holding up an ill-gotten credit fob. "I'm Uncle Jared, your mom's brother, and you're staying with me for the summer."

He piloted their shuttle to the automated checkpoint scanner, two panels on either side of a narrow passageway monitored by a guard keeping watch from inside the station. While invisible beams swept the shuttle for weapons, Renny pressed his stolen fob to the side window. Casual browsing wasn't permitted here, much like the auto-malls, and visitors had to supply proof of credit to gain entry. Through the station glass, the guard pointed a handheld scanner at the fob and asked Renny to state his name and identification code.

Renny tuned into the station's frequency and said, "Jared Rogers," followed by a series of letters and numbers. With no further delay, the guard disabled the security shield and allowed them to pass.

"That wasn't hard," Solara said, relaxing into her seat. She noticed that her palms had grown damp, and she glanced around for a place to wipe them, eventually settling on Renny's sleeve. When he drew back in offense, she shrugged and pointed to her dress. "It was five thousand credits."

He reached beneath his seat for a flask of Crystalline. "Take a sip of this, but don't swallow," he said. "Swish it around a little, then spit it in your hands and wipe it all over the front of you."

She did as he asked but carefully avoided the dress. Even drunk, no girl in her right mind would spill booze on this gown. Leaning in, she asked, "Do I smell like a raging party?"

"Close enough, but it'll evaporate soon."

All the more reason to snatch the Tissue-Bond and run. Playing dress-up was fun, but the reality of what they were about to do—and the consequences of failing or getting caught—had begun to set in, and Solara's heart pounded hard enough to rattle her rib cage.

Renny navigated past a strip of retail stores and dining establishments to the medical center at the far end of the complex. Instead of landing the shuttle near the emergency entrance, he alighted behind a ship twice their size.

"This'll be easy," he told her while cutting the engine. "But if anything goes wrong, come straight back here. The shuttle's the safest place to hide, and you know how to fly it back to the *Banshee* in case . . ." *They catch me and you have to run.*

He didn't have to say the last part. Solara understood from her time on the streets. As honorable as it sounded to leave no man behind, that was a naive policy that would result in more damage, not less. The Enforcers would arrest them both and try turning them against each other in the interest of a speedy conviction. If the guards nabbed her, she fully expected Renny to save himself and return the medicine to the *Banshee*. Doran's life was leaking out of him, and they didn't have time to be noble.

"Thank you," she told Renny. "I don't know why you're helping us, but I'm glad you're here. There's no way I could pull this off on my own."

He flashed the same genuine smile that had melted her heart the instant they'd met. She wished he really were her uncle; that blood would tie them together no matter how much distance stretched between them. It wasn't fair that people couldn't pick their own families.

"It's not an easy life out here," he told her. "I think you know that. So when fate places a kindred traveler in your path, you do your best to make the journey last."

"What's your story?" she asked. This might be their last chance to talk, and she felt suddenly desperate to know more about him. "How did you end up on the *Banshee*?"

He shook a chiding finger, as if scolding her for lack of faith. "I'll tell you this much. I had a home on Earth, with a good job and a woman who loved me more than I deserved. But my condition got in the way. I stole from the wrong people, the mafia, and it wasn't safe to stay there anymore." He patted her on the shoulder. "You'll have to wait till later to hear the rest."

He opened the shuttle doors, and Solara looped both arms around his neck when he came around to fetch her. As he carried her across the docking lot, she rested her head on his shoulder and grimaced in a show of pain, just in case the guards were watching the security feed. When the med-center's emergency doors parted, cool air washed over them, thick with the biting scent of antiseptic.

She released an audible groan while Renny rushed to the admissions counter and told the attendant, "It's my niece. She hurt her ankle at a party." He drew a breath and went on, each word tumbling out quicker than the last. "I never should've let her go, but she promised there wouldn't be drinking."

"*Heyyyy*," Solara slurred, jabbing a finger at his chest. "*It'sss* not my fault. They told me it was fruit punch."

Ignoring her, Renny made pleading eyes at the receptionist, a middle-aged woman wearing a pinched expression that said her shift was nearly over and, along with it, her patience.

"Tell me you have the meds to fix it," Renny said. "I can't send her back to my sister like this. I swore not to let—"

"How'd you hurt your ankle?" the woman interrupted, sliding her gaze to Solara's painted face.

"Turns out," Solara said, and hiccuped for effect, "I'm a really bad table dancer."

Renny hung his head. "Your mom's going to kill me."

With a barely contained eye roll, the receptionist pushed a data tablet across the desk and nodded toward the area behind them. "Fill this out and wait over there. Someone will call you shortly."

Renny situated them in the far corner of the waiting room, where Solara drew the gazes of at least two dozen bored patients, gawking at her like they'd never seen a debutante before. She couldn't blame them. Roles reversed, she probably would've stared the hardest. At first the attention made her nervous, but then she heard a familiar name on the news program playing above their heads, and the rest of the lobby ceased to exist.

"*Still no word on the whereabouts of Doran Spaulding,*" a female journalist said from the ceiling speakers, "*the Prodigious Academy alumnus wanted for the same crime that landed his father, president of Spaulding Enterprises, in jail without bond while he awaits trial.*"

In unison with Renny, she snapped her gaze to the telescreen, where Doran grinned at them in high definition, standing alongside an older, slightly taller version of himself in a three-piece suit. No wonder Doran couldn't reach his father—the guy was in lockup.

"*According to Solar League officials,*" the woman went on, "*both father and son orchestrated the theft of a substance known only as Infinium from a heavily guarded government transport. Prosecutors call the evidence damning, but the lead defending attorney continues to deny the charges on behalf of both men, despite the fact that DNA evidence at the scene has linked Doran Spaulding to the crime.*"

Infinium? What was that, and why was it so heavily guarded? Solara tried to picture Doran sneaking inside a military vessel and pulling off a heist. There was no way. Maybe he'd done something to accidentally implicate himself.

"*The young man is thought to be traveling with an indentured servant, eighteen-year-old Solara Brooks, a convicted felon wanted for questioning in a credit fraud investigation. She can be identified by her permanent tattoos and by the birthmark . . .*"

Solara didn't wait to see her mug shot appear on the screen. "Get me out of here," she whispered to Renny, clutching his arm hard enough to make him cringe. For the benefit of everyone watching, she pressed a hand to her lips and moaned, "Oh god. I think I'm gonna be sick."

He scooped her into his arms and returned to the sour-faced receptionist, who wasted no time ushering them into a private exam room once Solara started making gagging noises. In less than a minute, Solara was sitting on a padded table with a waste receptacle balanced on her lap. Renny whispered encouragements and rubbed her back until they were alone. Then he raked a hand through his hair and hissed a curse.

"Let's not panic," he said, contradicting himself by turning in a nervous circle. "With all the makeup you're wearing, your own mother wouldn't recognize you."

"I guarantee she wouldn't," Solara muttered. "Go look for the Tissue-Bond. If anyone asks why you're wandering the halls, tell them I sent you for Fizzy Ale to settle my stomach."

"Fizzy Ale," he repeated, nodding.

"Hurry. It won't take long for them to figure out my ankle isn't sprained. I'll stall the exam for as long as I can, but . . ."

He left before she finished the sentence.

Alone in the sterile room, Solara tried to calm the butterflies in her stomach by reminding herself that Renny was right. Every blemish that made her recognizable, from her birthmark to her tattoos, was hidden beneath a layer of holographic cosmetics. Her fake identity would hold up as long as she didn't give anyone a reason to question it.

Several minutes later, she heard the click of approaching footsteps and curled into a ball on the exam table, making herself as pitiful as her tight bodice would allow. The door slid open, and a man asked, "Miss Vanderbilt?"

Whimpering, Solara pushed into a sitting position and froze when her gaze landed on the boy in front of her—because with his smooth baby face and waiflike build, nobody would mistake him for a man. As young as he was, she thought he might be an orderly. But then she glanced at the badge affixed to his lab coat, which read DR. DEATH.

That had to be a joke.

"It's pronounced 'deeth,'" he said with a sigh, like he made that clarification a thousand times a day. "How are you feeling tonight?" Despite the polite inquiry, the flatness in his tone told her it was just a formality to move things along, clear one room and on to the next. His eyes shifted to a bone scanner mounted on the side wall, and Solara knew she'd have to be creative if she wanted to stall him.

"Much better . . . *now,*" she said, grinning and lowering the angle of her chin until she peered coyly at him beneath her lashes. She'd never flirted this way before, but it always worked in the movies.

His businesslike mask vanished, and his mouth opened as if he'd glimpsed an alien and wasn't sure whether to believe his eyes. Based on his reaction, Solara guessed that most girls found him invisible, and she felt a tug of sympathy for the young doctor. She boldly looked him up and down, from his cropped brown hair to the tips of his sensible shoes, then widened her smile to show that she liked what she'd seen.

"You're not what I expected," she told him.

He stammered for a moment and cleared his throat. "Neither are you."

"But in a good way, right?"

A bloom of color spread over his cheeks, and his gaze dropped to the floor. "Of course. You look real nice."

Real nice? If that was the best he could do, it was no wonder he couldn't get a date.

"You think?" she asked, feigning shyness while leaning down to display a deep line of cleavage. As intended, the movement didn't escape his notice. His eyes locked on her curves and glazed over while his face went dopey. But just when she thought she had him well and truly hooked, his brows lowered and his head tipped to the side.

"What's that?" he asked, pointing at her throat while he took a step closer. "Is it a birthmark? Or a scar, maybe?"

Solara touched the base of her neck and felt something sticky. When she pulled her hand away, her fingertips were covered in an oily peach goo. She frowned at the substance before realizing what had happened. The ninety-proof Crystalline she'd dribbled all over herself must've slowly eaten away at her makeup. She jerked her gaze to her knuckles, where black ink peeked out between gaps in the concealer.

That didn't escape the doctor's notice, either.

She hid both hands behind her back, but it was too late. She could see the questions forming in his mind as his gaze sharpened, refocusing on her throat. There was only one reason for a girl to cover her knuckles with cosmetics, and anyone smart enough to graduate from medical school would figure it out. And unless he lived in a cave, he'd recognize her birthmark, too.

The door slid open and Renny stood on the other side, assessing the mood with a quick glance. Instead of joining them, he patted his breast pocket and thumbed over one shoulder. "I'm stepping outside for a smoke. Hang in there, sweetie. I'll be back before you can blink."

Solara exhaled in relief. That was their signal—a message

that he'd stolen the Tissue-Bond and would wait for her in the shuttle. Now all she had to do was create a believable excuse to follow him.

"Okay," she said. "But I wish you'd quit. Those things will kill you."

"So will drunken table dancing," he replied with a wink, and strode away.

The young doctor didn't laugh. He watched Renny disappear into the lobby before turning back to Solara with his brow creased in deep concentration. She didn't need X-ray vision to see the puzzle pieces clicking inside his head. It was time to get out of here.

Rotating her ankle, she said, "The gel pack must have helped, because I feel a little better." She stood from the table and pretended to test her weight, limping when her bare left foot touched the floor. "Where's the bathroom?"

The young man's eyes widened by a fraction, and there it was—the unmistakable spark of realization that said he'd finally made the connection. He knew who she was.

"Let me find you a wheelchair," he told her, backing toward the exit. "Stay put."

Then he darted out and shut the door behind him.

Solara ran after him, but when she tapped the exit panel, the door refused to open. She grabbed the manual lever and tried hauling it aside, but no matter how hard she tugged, the door wouldn't budge. He'd locked her in.

The bottom fell out of her stomach.

Once he alerted security, the complex would go on lockdown. If she didn't make it to the docking lot soon, Renny would have no choice but to leave her behind. Which meant her life was as good as over.

Survival instincts kicked in, and she spun a rotation to check for windows or an air duct wide enough to crawl through. There was nothing, not even a heat register. Whirling back to face the door, she studied the exit panel—a thin, steely plate designed to respond to the touch. If she could pry the panel free, she might be able to override the lock.

She plucked a hairpin from her braids and wedged one narrow point beneath the panel's lip, working it back and forth until it slipped halfway underneath. Then, using a tongue depressor as leverage, she widened the gap between the panel and the wall until there was enough room to wriggle her fingers inside. With a gentle force, she pulled the plate free, making sure to leave plenty of slack for the wires connected to the other side.

Sweat slicked her hands, and she wiped them on her gown without a care for how much it cost. Right now nothing was worth more than her freedom. Squinting, she studied the tangle of electrical tubing and immediately picked out the grounders and hot wires, the ones to leave alone. Of the remaining cables, she began systematically pulling and reattaching them until she found the emergency override. The door slid open, and she didn't waste another second inside that room.

Hitching up her dress, she sprinted down the hall and into the lobby, rudely knocking aside anyone in her path. She never looked back, focusing only on the double doors leading to the docking lot. She was close enough to smell shuttle exhaust when she heard shouts of "Stop!" and "Seal the exit!" behind her. With only a few yards to go, she pumped her legs harder and faster, head down and barreling through the doors just as they began to close.

She made it into the lot, but the instant her feet met concrete, an invisible force jerked her backward, and she slammed into the sealed fiberglass doors. Whipping her head around, she discovered that half her skirts were trapped on the other side. She tugged the fabric in vain while her heart pounded a frantic staccato. A glance through the glass showed two security officers pointing at her and shouting orders at the receptionist. When her gown refused to tear, Solara reached a trembling hand behind her and jerked down the bodice zipper. She pushed the dress over her hips and stepped free, then ran like hell toward the shuttle, wearing nothing but a pair of government-issue underpants and the long strips of linen she'd used to support her breasts.

Renny must have seen her coming, because he'd already fired up the shuttle and opened the rear hatch by the time she reached him. She sailed inside headfirst, screaming for him to "Go, go, go!" and the craft lifted off the ground before the door had even shut. She sealed the hatch and scrambled on her hands and knees toward the cockpit, then strapped in beside him.

"You forgot your dress," Renny said, staring straight ahead while he white-knuckled the control wheel and jettisoned toward the security checkpoint.

"Never let anyone tell you," she panted, "that I don't know how to make an exit."

He laughed for an instant before his features hardened. When Solara followed the direction of his gaze, she understood why. Red alarms flashed all around the guard station while security officers scrambled like ants behind the wraparound glass. A billboard message flashed NO EXIT, and the line of shuttlecraft waiting to leave the complex jerked to a stop, nearly causing a pileup.

"Renny . . ." she said, then went mute.

Instead of slowing down, he pushed the accelerators to the limit, sending Solara jerking back in her seat. As they zoomed toward a single shuttle halfway through the exit point, she began to understand Renny's intentions. He was going to try to follow the craft out before the shield closed behind it. But if the shield caught their back end, the energy surge would destroy their circuitry, leaving them drifting right outside the satellite. They'd be easy pickings for the Enforcers, assuming the surge didn't electrocute them first.

"Hold on," he warned. "I'm gonna have to ram them to get out."

She gripped the armrests and held her breath, watching in horror as they approached the rear of the shuttle with dizzying speed. The guard station buzzed past her periphery, and she braced for impact. Instinctively, her eyes clenched shut. The scream of steel on steel tore through her ears as she slammed against her harness. Her head flew forward and back just as quickly, and the next thing Solara knew, they were outside the security shield with a chorus of alarms blaring inside the cockpit.

Renny's glasses had flown off, but he didn't miss a beat. He veered right, separating them from the other shuttlecraft and away from the cannon's line of fire. An energy blast nicked the port hull and forced them into a barrel roll, but he corrected quickly and hit the boosters. The shuttle rocketed toward the nearby moon, and an instant later, they were out of the cannon's range.

But that didn't mean they were safe.

Renny was too busy hugging the moon's gravity field for a slingshot of acceleration to tend to the dashboard, which lit up like a Christmas tree. The buttons and switches were unfamiliar to Solara, and without her diagnostic equipment, she couldn't tell which systems had failed.

"What can I do?" she shouted above the beeping alarms.

"Radio the *Banshee*," he said, and clutched the trembling wheel. "Tell the captain we need a track-and-intercept. He'll know what that means." Darting a glance at the dashboard, he added, "Make sure he knows our emergency system's fried. We've got, maybe, thirty minutes of oxygen left."

And nowhere safe to land, Solara thought. Then she realized that if they died, so would Doran, because the *Banshee* would never find them in time to deliver his medicine. The possibility made her shiver. She sent out a distress call, but there was no reply. "I don't know if our com is out, or just the receiver," she said.

"Keep trying."

She did, over and over again, until her skin puckered into goose bumps and her teeth chattered. Without heated oxygen coursing through the cockpit, the temperature had plummeted so low that her breath condensed into clouds—not the best conditions to fly half naked.

Renny shrugged out of his jacket. "Put this on," he said, then unbuttoned his shirt and handed her that, too. "And cover your legs."

The coat was warm with body heat, so she wrapped herself

tightly between the lapels before it cooled. When she thanked Renny, she noticed a scattering of pink lesions marring the bare skin on his shoulders. She frowned at the scars. Round and precise, they looked like laser wounds.

"What happened to your back?" she asked.

After engaging the autopilot, he reached blindly across the far end of the dash until he found his glasses, then grinned when he saw that they weren't broken. "Remember what I said about stealing from the wrong people?"

"They shot you?"

"Thoroughly," he said with a wry smile. "While I ran screaming for my life, a lot like how you did back there at the satellite."

Solara wondered if those men had known Renny couldn't control the impulse to steal, but she supposed it wouldn't matter to the kind of people who'd shoot an unarmed man in the back. "What about the lady?" she asked. "The one who loved you. Where is she now?"

Renny's mouth lifted in a sad smile. "I wish I knew . . . or maybe I don't." He shook his head. "Look at the mess we're in now. This is no life, running in the shadows, never settling in one place. I wanted something better for her—a real home and a family she could be proud of. That's why I left her behind." A faraway look crossed his face, and he sighed with so much longing that it plucked at Solara's heartstrings. "Some days, I hope she moved on," he said. "And some days I don't."

Solara didn't know what to say, so she took his hand, and they stared silently out the front window as the time and distance passed, along with their oxygen supply.

At some point, their grip loosened and it took a few tries to reconnect. They became clumsy in their movements, dizzy with confusion. Solara let her gaze wander around the cockpit but couldn't make sense of the blinking lights or remember where they were going. She gulped breath after breath, never able to satisfy her body. The sensation reminded her of the city trams on Earth, how stifling they'd become in the summer until the tram operator had to lower a window.

"Hey, we sh-should open the h-hatch," she stammered. "And let in some air."

Renny peered at her through his glasses and tried to scratch his chest, but his hand fell into his lap. "I don't think that's a good idea."

She was about to ask why when a sudden movement caught her eye, and she turned to find an old, ugly ship keeping pace beside them. She knew that ship—couldn't remember its name but desperately wanted to be on board.

Renny saw it, too, and released a whoop of joy. "We're coming in hot," he said, turning his gaze to the control panel. "Need to slow down."

But all he did was rub his forehead.

A set of thick, metallic cables snaked out from their shuttle and latched onto the ship, then towed them closer. As if by remote control, their engines fell silent and they nestled into the ship's port with a loud click. Solara tried standing from her seat, but straps held her in place until a boy with blond dreadlocks unfastened them.

He dragged her into the ship's cargo hold and then went back for Renny.

The air inside the ship was clean and pure, so refreshing that she filled her lungs in great breaths that strained the linen straps binding her ribs. Her mind seemed to sharpen with each rise and fall of her chest, and by the time Renny recovered, she was already hugging him and laughing hysterically.

*　*　*

A while later, after they'd given Doran his medication and made sure he was stable, the crew reconvened in the galley. There she'd learned that the captain had never received her transmissions. He had tracked the shuttle the entire time they were gone. Sitting at the table, she thought about what Renny had said, what he'd wanted to give his lady on Earth: *a real home and a family she could be proud of.*

Solara still didn't know this crew's secrets or how their paths had crossed, and yet these strangers had done more to protect her today than her own parents had done in eighteen years. In her opinion, that was definitely something to be proud of. Renny was wrong when he'd said this was no life.

In that moment, there was no place she'd rather be.

CHAPTER SEVENTEEN

*I*n the days that followed, Doran learned to dread nighttime.

He'd spent so long in bed that his body had forgotten its sleep schedule, and now the eight hours when the ship was still and quiet had become a mental prison sentence. He wished he'd lied and told Cassia that he needed pain pills. Then he would be in a medicated coma right now instead of lying awake, worrying about what Solara had told him.

Your father's in jail.

The echo of those words still had the power to make his stomach clench, because they revealed a terrifying truth—Doran was alone.

He couldn't remember a time when his father hadn't been there to help him. Even when he hadn't needed a hand, he'd moved through life with more confidence knowing that his dad would catch him if he stumbled. Now that the safety net was gone, Doran couldn't shake the sick sensation of falling.

And what about his father? Was he lonely and afraid, too, or had he transformed his cell into a makeshift office and let his lawyers do the worrying? Doran had no way of knowing, and he hated that. He missed the sound of his father's voice. He missed making his dad laugh. There was no way for them to talk now, and Doran had never learned what he was supposed to do once he reached the coordinates in the outer realm.

He would continue with his mission, but he no longer felt confident about clearing their names. Yesterday he'd borrowed a data tablet and learned a detail about the case that made him believe someone had framed them—someone within the government. The Enforcers claimed to have found Doran's DNA on a crate of stolen Infinium from their transport. But Doran had never set foot on board a government ship, and he'd never heard of Infinium. That could only mean the Enforcers had planted the evidence, and if that was true, he wouldn't get a fair trial.

Panic squeezed his rib cage, and it occurred to him that no matter how hard he fought, things might never be the same. His old life could be over, replaced by this new existence of running and hiding.

No. He shook those thoughts out of his head. His father was depending on him to stay strong and do his job. Whatever awaited him at those coordinates in the fringe was the key to their freedom.

He had to believe that.

✱   ✱   ✱

The next morning, he squinted against the starlight filtering through the porthole and glanced down at Solara's balled-up form, hidden beneath a heap of blankets so that only her nose peeked through.

"Why are you still sleeping on the floor?" he asked, then cleared the gravel from his throat. She couldn't possibly be comfortable down there. Just looking at her made his shoulders ache with the remembrance of those unforgiving steel panels.

To dispel the sensation, he reached both arms above his pillow and arched his bare back in a stretch, elongating muscles that had grown stiff with disuse. In response, a few wayward vertebrae popped into their rightful places along his spine. It felt so good that he repeated the movement, then pulled each knee to his chest to stretch his legs. Much like his shower privileges, he hadn't appreciated his full range of motion until he'd lost it, and he vowed never to take his body for granted again.

Solara yawned and rolled onto her back, her naked fists poking through the blankets in a stretch of her own. He was glad she'd quit wearing her gloves, but he kept his mouth shut about it. She was sensitive about her markings, and he could never manage to discuss them without pissing her off.

When she didn't answer his question, he indicated the empty space beside him. "It's a double bed, remember? There's more than enough room for two." He sniffed himself and added, "I don't smell. At least, I don't think so."

She sat up, grumbling and rubbing the side of her neck. She must've tossed and turned a lot in her sleep, because a riot of hair had escaped her braids and formed something resembling a bird's nest at her forehead. It made him smile.

"You know why," she said. "You need the—"

"Whatever." He waved off her excuse because that's exactly what it was. "There's nothing wrong with me." He pushed the blankets down to his waist and said, "Come and see for yourself."

Wearing nothing but a T-shirt that barely reached her thighs, she stood from the floor and took a seat on the edge of the mattress. She seemed to have lost some of her modesty, and Doran didn't mind that, either.

"You still have bruises," she criticized, pointing at the yellowy splotches beneath his flesh.

"But they don't hurt anymore."

With a dubious twist of her lips, she placed her warm palms on his sides, then ran them up and down the length of his rib cage while Doran's breath locked inside his chest.

Hot damn.

At her touch, every internal organ between his hipbones tightened—and a couple of external ones, too. His skin hummed alive beneath her fingers, like energy flowing through a completed circuit, and he was grateful as hell to have a thick layer of blankets concealing his lap.

"Am I hurting you?" she asked.

Doran shook his head. He felt an awful lot of sensations at the moment, but pain wasn't one of them. Maybe sleeping beside her wasn't such a good idea after all. He gathered her hands and held them at a safe distance from his body.

"See?" he said, and swallowed hard. "Soon I'll be good as new."

She studied the tips of her own fingers, not seeming to mind that they were trapped between his palms. "Then you'll be gone," she told him. "And I'll have the whole bed to myself. I might as well wait."

He didn't say so, but she had a point.

The *Banshee* had reached Obsidian yesterday, and they'd been hiding on a large orbiting meteor while Solara repaired the damages to the two-man craft. Once Doran felt well enough to travel, he would shuttle planet-side to the private ship waiting there. After that, he'd never see the *Banshee* or her crew again.

But he didn't want to think about that right now.

Instead, he turned Solara's knuckles to face him and skimmed a thumb over the codes tattooed on her skin. Strange how the markings didn't bother him anymore. If his assets weren't frozen, he'd hire a flesh forger to give her a new start. After everything she'd done for him, she deserved it.

"So you can stand to look at them now?" she asked.

"What?"

"That day in the washroom, right before the propellant cell broke. You told me that if you could stand to look at my tattoos, then so could I." She pulled her hands away and tucked them beneath her thighs.

"I didn't mean it like that," he said. "You never gave me a chance to explain."

"Okay, then." One eyebrow lifted in challenge. "Explain."

"It's a long story."

"I've got time."

Doran noticed that chills had broken out along her thighs—not that he was staring or anything. Just a casual observation. And since the problem in his shorts had abated, he lifted the covers and invited her to join him. She hesitated for a beat, then crawled in beside him, and soon they lay six inches apart in mirrored positions, facing the ceiling with their hands folded on top of their stomachs.

"All right," she said, cozying in. "Make it good."

"This story doesn't have a happy ending," he warned, and though he hadn't intended it, his voice sounded dark. She turned her neck to face him, but he stared straight ahead. It was easier that way. "A lot of this is public knowledge. I'm surprised you never heard about it."

"No gossip tabloids in the group home," she told him.

"It was a big deal when it happened, but that was a long time ago. Even if you saw it on the news, I guess you would've forgotten."

"Forgotten what?"

"I was abducted when I was nine," he said, the rote words rolling easily off his tongue. "Me and my brother, we were held for ransom. The nanny was in on it. She disabled the alarm and let the guys in the back door while everyone was asleep."

Solara pushed onto her elbows, forcing him to make eye contact with her. "You have a brother? I didn't know that."

"I don't," he said, and paused to let that sink in. "Not anymore."

A tattooed hand flew to her breast, and when Doran blinked, he saw the inky knuckles of the man who'd clapped a palm over his mouth and dragged him from his bed that night. There had been so many markings—rows and rows of them, right on top of each other—and he hadn't understood what they'd meant. Until the next day, when he was locked inside a closet with a concussion and a bloody lip. Then he'd learned.

Solara brought him back to the present with a gentle touch. "I'm so sorry," she whispered. "How old was he?"

"Same age as me. We were twins."

"Twins," she echoed. "That must have made losing him even harder. I've heard that twins have a special bond."

Doran couldn't say whether or not that was true, because he had no other siblings, and nothing to compare it to. He recalled that he and Gage were like two sides of a coin—made from the same mold but distinctive enough to anyone who paid attention. Doran took after their father, crushing the other kids' lemonade stands by undercutting prices, while Gage shadowed their mom in her laboratory, peering over the counter in awe of her experiments. But despite their differences, he and his brother were unstoppable partners in crime. They'd learned at an early age that the nanny couldn't tell them apart, and because she could never be sure which boy she'd seen jumping on the sofa or dropping marbles inside the piano, neither of them were ever punished.

Of course, she'd paid them back—in spades.

Doran realized he'd fallen silent, and he turned to Solara with an apology in his eyes. But Solara didn't seem to mind. She quietly lay back down and hooked an arm through his, then waited until he was ready to go on.

"Anyway," he finally said. "My father didn't trust the Enforcers to rescue us, so he hired a group of mercenaries to do the job." And to their credit, they had. No one could've foreseen what happened next. "They found us two days later in an ancient row house outside the city. The plan was to storm the place and take us by force, but when the team threw a stun grenade through the window, it sparked a gas leak, and the whole house went up in flames."

Even now, Doran could taste the bitter stun gas that had made his limbs heavy and his sight dim. The grenade had done its job, ensuring that no one in the house could move. From inside the closet, he'd lain on moldy carpet and listened to the screams of men too drugged to haul themselves out of the fire's path. Above the noise of chaos, he'd heard Gage wailing in agony. It was a horrible sound that no amount of therapy could make him forget, though not for lack of trying.

"One of the mercenaries found me in a closet," Doran said. "But by the time he carried me outside, the top floor had collapsed, and it wasn't safe to go back in."

A dozen men lost their lives that day: three inked felons, eight hired guns, and the other half of Doran's coin. The fire had burned so long and hot that investigators didn't expect to find any bodies. But Doran's mother had refused to give up until Gage was recovered, swearing that her son's last resting place wouldn't be in that house. She'd held firm, and the following week they found his remains, still bound at the wrists and ankles.

Doran wished he didn't know that detail.

"That's why you hate closets," Solara said.

"And felony tattoos," he added, lifting her hand to study her knuckles. "The men who took me had them."

In a blur, she jerked her hand away and detangled their arms. "Oh no," she said, bolting upright so quickly she shook the mattress. "It's a trigger for you. That's why you flipped out the first time you saw me without gloves. And why you kept quiet when I said this crew might ransom you."

Doran was about to say yes, but she didn't give him the chance.

She scrambled out of bed, apologizing over and over and ignoring him when he asked her to come back. Then, after rooting through her clothes, she pulled on those damned finger-less gloves again.

"No," he insisted as he propped himself on both elbows. "Take them off."

"It's fine," she said. "I don't mind wearing them."

"I mind, damn it!" He hadn't meant to shout, but if she started covering her knuckles again, it wouldn't be to protect his delicate sensibilities. "I want to see your ink. It's part of who you are."

"But—"

"But nothing. I don't care what we said before. The day you took off those gloves and told me your story was the day we became friends. If you hide from me now, it's like taking a step backward." He knew he shouldn't care. Soon he'd be gone and none of this would matter. But it *did* matter, to him. "Just take them off."

She hesitated.

"Please," he said. "For me."

She peeled the gloves from her hands but avoided his eyes afterward as she brushed and braided her hair. The conversation died, and when he offered to eat breakfast with her in the galley, she insisted that he stay in bed. He objected, making it only as far as the chamber door before a dizzy spell sent him back beneath the sheets.

Stupid traitor body.

More than the silent treatment, Doran hated lying around like an invalid while other people pulled his weight. Everyone on board the *Banshee* had a purpose: Renny navigated, Solara repaired, Cassia and Kane tackled the day-to-day chores, and the captain generally saved their asses. All Doran had accomplished was one lousy pirate divorce.

You'll never change, and you'll never make a difference. When you die, no one will miss you, because your life won't matter. You don't matter.

He knew Solara didn't believe those words now, but they still stung because, deep down, there was a kernel of truth to them. He was the reason the *Banshee* was hiding like an insect inside this asteroid. Half the quadrant was hunting him, and if the Daeva ever picked up his location, they'd use it to capture the crew. The kindest thing he could do for these people was leave. At least he'd make a difference in that small way.

✳ ✳ ✳

"Are you sure you're strong enough for this?" Solara asked, her gaze averted as she nudged his duffel bag with the toe of her boot. "There's no hurry."

No hurry. That was what the crew kept telling him, but another week had passed, and Doran couldn't stay here forever. The dizzy spells had subsided, and honestly, he'd felt fit for travel a while ago. But he couldn't admit to that, so he deflected with a question of his own. "Are you sure you won't come with me? It makes sense. We're both going to the fringe."

Yesterday he'd broken down and told her that his coordinates were located in the outer realm. His father wouldn't approve, but Doran didn't care. He trusted Solara, and he didn't want to make the journey alone.

"Thanks, but they need me here." She mumbled something about leaking coolant coils in the main engine. "Your ship probably runs like a gazelle."

"What about the Daeva?"

She shrugged. "No matter what I do, I'm not safe. If I stay here, it's the Daeva. If I go with you, it's Demarkus and the Enforcers. Six one way, half a dozen the other."

He couldn't really argue with that.

"But," she added, "I'll shuttle you to your ship."

"You don't have to do that," Doran told her. "Kane said he would."

"I want to." She finally peeked up at him, a hesitant grin sparkling in her eyes. "It's only fitting. I'm the one who started you on this wild ride."

"True. Did I ever thank you for that?"

She cocked her head in mock offense. "No, I don't believe you did."

"Not surprising," he said. "I'm an asshole like that." She rewarded him with a peal of laughter, and in that moment, he would've paid anything to bottle the sound. "Take this instead," he added, handing over the fuel chip necklace. "Money's more useful than words."

"Won't you need it?"

He shook his head. It was company policy to keep a sack of fuel chips inside all Spaulding-owned vessels. He would have more than enough to sustain him through this job and perhaps beyond. Solara fastened the leather cord behind her neck, then tucked the metal coins beneath her shirt. It made Doran think of something, and he smiled.

"I challenged Demarkus for you," he said. "And now you're wearing my token. You know what this means, right?"

She laughed again. "Look at me, jumping from one pirate husband to another."

"What would the nuns say?"

"I won't tell if you won't."

"It's a deal." He extended a hand to shake. "Our little secret."

But when Solara slid her palm against his, it wasn't enough.

Doran pulled her into an embrace and wrapped both arms around her shoulders, fully expecting her to pull back. She surprised him by locking both wrists at the base of his spine and resting a cheek on his chest, a reaction that pleased and shattered him in equal measure. Because now it would be twice as hard to walk away.

Long seconds ticked by, but her body felt so warm and soft that he resisted breaking the hug. He hadn't realized how much he'd missed human contact. So he buried his nose in the braids encircling her head and breathed in the lingering scent of oil vapors from the engine room, intoxicating when blended with her natural sweetness. He never imagined the combination could smell so good, and he wished he could bottle that, too.

In the end, she was the first to pull away.

"Ready?" she asked.

He hid his disappointment and slung his bag over one shoulder. Then he made his way through the *Banshee*, shaking hands and trading well wishes until there was no choice but to board the shuttle and head toward his destination.

They arrived at the ship's hiding place far too quickly for Doran's liking, a flat patch of onyx sand on the opposite side of Obsidian from the beaches, where an ancient salt ocean had long ago died and surrendered to the desert. No tourists ventured here. Nothing but jet-black dunes stretching for miles in every direction. He doubted that anything survived here at all.

He scanned the area and noticed a slight color variation in the sand, roughly the length of a small passenger craft. "There's the ship," he said, pointing. "It's under a tarp."

Solara nodded and landed nearby.

Once the thrusters died and they opened the shuttle doors, a scorching wall of heat slammed into them with the force of a tsunami. Wind danced over the arid landscape, offering no relief whatsoever. The air was so hot and devoid of moisture that it reminded Doran of aiming a blow-dryer at his face.

"So this is what hell looks like," Solara observed, glancing this way and that. "Does your father always hide his ships in the desert?"

"Just this one. He insisted on it." Doran found an edge of the tarp buried beneath the sand and began pulling it up. In seconds, the light task had him sweating like a linebacker. Solara helped, and before long, they had the ship uncovered. It was a sedan-class vessel, standard for the kind of traveling he'd done as an intern.

"Want me to stay awhile?" she asked. "I should at least make sure the engine starts."

"No, that's all right. I'll radio you if I need help."

"Then I guess this is good-bye."

"Yeah," he said, lifting a shoulder to blot the sweat from his face. "Guess so."

A gust of fiery air pelted them with smoldering bits of sand, ensuring this wouldn't be a drawn-out farewell. Solara jogged back to her shuttle to take shelter. Right before she closed the door, Doran shouted, "Wait."

Shielding her eyes, she turned to him.

"I never asked where you're going," he said. "In the outer realm."

"A brand-new terraform called Vega," she hollered.

"Vega," he repeated to help him remember. "If I'm ever out that way, I'll look you up."

"Make sure you do. And bring some birds."

She waved and disappeared behind the metal door, then gave him a minute to scale the ramp into his ship before she fired up the thrusters. Once he was safely inside the open cargo hold, her shuttle lifted off and spun to face southwest before speeding away. He watched the craft grow smaller in the distance until it faded from view. Afterward, he waited there for a full five minutes, expecting her to return.

She didn't.

While moving through the ship's narrow hallways, he told himself this wasn't really good-bye. Assuming he cleared the charges against him, his work for Spaulding Fuel would send him to the far reaches of the galaxy, occasionally to the fringe, where new elements were discovered every day. It was completely within the realm of possibility that he could find her on Vega.

But then he imagined what that visit might look like.

She would probably have a new circle of friends by then, a place within the budding community of outcasts and runaways.

What would he have in common with any of them? And what if she had a guy in her life? Doran felt a sharp tug in his chest when he pictured her with someone else.

Whatever, he thought. *I'll worry about that later.*

He reached the cockpit and searched the hidden compartment beneath the floor until he found a sack of fuel chips. After tossing a handful of chips in his pocket, he returned the rest to the cubbyhole and booted up the ship's navigational equipment. His father hadn't told him anything about his destination other than *You'll know what to do when you get there,* so Doran entered the coordinates and sat in the pilot's seat to read the results.

The map displayed a nameless moon-sized planet located at least a day's journey beyond the farthest fringe settlement. Classified only by its chart number, the tiny planet orbited too far from its sun to support human life, which meant it would never qualify for terraformation. Doran had seen worlds like these, nothing more than useless boulders in orbit. Why would his father send him to a place like that? For a new element, perhaps?

There was only one way to find out.

He'd just plotted a basic navigational course when, from outside, a ship's engine rumbled with enough force to vibrate his control panel. He shifted his focus out the front window, and what he saw made his stomach hit the floor.

The Enforcers had found him.

An armed Solar League vessel twice the size of his ship hovered above the dunes, its thrusters blowing clouds of ebony sand in every direction. For a fraction of a second, it occurred to Doran that someone had betrayed him, but then his mind shut to all coherent thought outside of escape. His hands flew into action, powering on the ship's engines and auxiliary systems. The thrusters on either side of his craft rumbled to life, ready for takeoff, and he grasped the wheel with trembling fingers.

As if anticipating his move, the Enforcers fired two perfectly aimed blasts that turned his thrusters to useless shards of metal.

The impact shook Doran out of his seat, and before he could gasp, he was on the floor with a chorus of fire alarms blaring from above. Tendrils of smoke crept and curled inside the cockpit, poisoning the air and forcing him to belly-crawl to the rear exit.

Fed by canned oxygen, the fire shot like lightning through the walls and shorted the electrical system. By the time Doran reached the rear hatch, not even the emergency lights were operational. Blindly, he felt for the hatch's manual lever and hauled the door open. Blazing sunlight spilled inside, along with a gust of hot air and a face full of sand.

He stumbled outside, shielding his eyes from the desert's assault while he spun in a circle to search for a safe haven. Logically, he knew there was no place to hide, but it took several moments for his eyes to get the message. He tried telling himself this was for the best, that eventually someone would've caught up with him—better the Enforcers than the Daeva or Demarkus Hahn. At least now he'd make it back to Earth in one piece, maybe even receive a fair trial.

By the time the Enforcers touched down, Doran almost believed his own lies.

But then he noticed another craft bearing toward him, so high in the sky that he had to squint to make it out. The colossus sailed nearer, blocking the sun while remaining just outside the planet's gravitational pull. Even from so far away, Doran recognized the battered ship, bigger than a lowland giant and twice as ugly—much like the pirate at its helm. Its belly opened and belched out half a dozen shuttles, which flew like arrows in his direction.

Doran sat back on the dune, not bothering to run. The kohl sand scorched his backside, and he dismissed that, too. Because no matter what he did, his ass was cooked.

CHAPTER EIGHTEEN

Sister Agnes used to say that trust was like a flower unfolding in the sun: The more you opened yourself to the warmth of this world, the more of God's blessings you would receive. But in Solara's experience, trust was like a switchblade: Give it away too quickly, and expect to find a knife in your back.

As much as she wanted to believe that Kane was a friend, she'd found it suspicious when he offered to pilot the shuttle to Obsidian. He'd never volunteered for extra duties before, so why would he start now? Even more suspicious was his reaction when he'd learned that she wanted the job. He'd gone pale and offered his services as if his life depended on it. Clearly he was hiding something. Behind the goodwill and the easy smile, she'd sensed a simmering anxiety that warned his feelings toward Doran hadn't changed.

That was why she'd insisted on flying here, and why she'd

spent the last several minutes surveying the desert for a safe place to watch the skies.

Just west of Doran's location stood a wide, curving cliff that surrounded a sooty valley resembling the Grand Canyon. Halfway up from the base of a long-dead river and concealed from above by a stone ledge, she'd discovered a crevasse just wide and deep enough to hide the shuttle. No sooner had she climbed out to stretch her legs than an Enforcer craft appeared on the distant horizon. It seemed Kane had cashed in on the reward.

A cold weight settled in her heart. She'd predicted this, but she didn't want it to be true.

She strapped into the pilot's seat and made two incog radio transmissions, first to the captain, asking him to let her shuttle go off the grid for twenty-four hours. If her plan went sideways, she didn't want him wandering into this mess. As for the second transmission . . . that might've been a mistake. But the deed was done, and now she had to let the chips fall.

Traveling due east, she pushed the shuttle to the limit and arrived just as complete and utter hell broke loose.

A swarm of mismatched pirate shuttles circled like vultures above the smoking ruin of Doran's ship, seeking a safe place to land and dodging cannon fire from the Enforcers on the ground. She peered through the dark fog and spotted Doran sitting twenty yards behind his craft, its shell consumed by flames that stretched toward the clouds. With any luck, the smoke would provide enough cover to scoop him up and make an easy getaway.

Keeping the flaming ship between herself and the Enforcers, she touched down dangerously close to Doran, hoping he'd have enough sense to get out of the way and open the passenger hatch. Sand flew in every direction, but she couldn't afford to cut the engine and wait for it to restart.

For the longest five seconds of her life, she bounced a heel against the floor and waited for him to join her. When he didn't appear, she opened the pilot's hatch and lifted a hand to protect her eyes.

"Doran!" she yelled, earning herself a mouthful of sand.

She spat downwind and scanned the dunes, her stomach dipping when she spotted a red uniform heading toward her. If one Enforcer had made it to this point, others wouldn't be far behind.

From somewhere above her head, the scream of metal rent the air, followed by the sickening crunch of a shuttle as it crashed to the ground. She needed to get Doran out of here before the cannons disabled her craft, too. She called his name again and found him striding into view with his T-shirt pulled over his nose and mouth. He seemed to realize who she was, and then he finally snapped out of it.

A foot soldier moved into Doran's path, but that didn't faze him. Doran bent and charged the Enforcer, planting a shoulder in the man's midsection. The soldier flipped forward in a blur of red, and the next thing Solara knew, the passenger hatch opened and Doran leaped inside.

She lifted off without a moment's hesitation while Doran wrestled the door shut. Another pirate shuttle went down in flames, nearly clipping their starboard wing as it spiraled toward the ground. Solara rolled away while trying to hug the sand. The closer she stayed to the dunes, the better her chance of avoiding the cannon blasts raining from above. As soon as she cleared the battle scene, she sped toward her hiding spot in the canyon.

"What are you doing here?" Doran asked.

She cut her eyes at him. "I think what you meant to say is, 'Thanks for saving my pretty hide, Solara.'"

"But you—"

"Never left."

He watched her while picking grains of sand off his tongue. "Why not?"

"I had a feeling someone would sell you out." While Doran reached over to fasten her harness, she explained everything. "I should've told you sooner, but I didn't want to believe it."

"Kane," Doran said, sounding wounded. "He even called Demarkus."

"Um, actually . . ." She trailed off, focused on finding her bearings, then veered farther west. "I'm the one who radioed Demarkus."

A moment of silence followed. "Come again?"

"I had a feeling he'd be lurking near Obsidian. So I called in an anonymous tip." She shrugged and added, "I just didn't mention that the Enforcers were here."

Though she couldn't see Doran's smile, she heard it in his voice. "You were banking on them fighting each other instead of me."

She couldn't help smiling in return. "Looks like it worked."

"You're diabolical. No wonder he married you."

A rogue shuttle rammed them from behind, sending Solara lurching forward in her harness straps. Her heart lodged in her throat, and she wished she'd given Doran the wheel. He had plenty of experience with flying. She could barely land, let alone pull off evasive maneuvers.

"How do I shake him?" she asked. A glance at the nav screen showed the shuttle still trailing her. "I'm going as fast as I can."

Doran placed a steadying hand on her shoulder. "You can do this; I promise. I'll talk you through it."

She drew a deep breath and blew it out slowly.

"On my mark," he said, "pull up as hard as you can and come full circle. Don't look out the window or you'll get disoriented. Watch the screen, okay?"

Solara nodded.

A few moments later, he shouted, "Now!"

With both hands, she gripped the wheel and tugged it all the way back, never taking her eyes off the nav screen until she'd completed a full rotation and the shuttle was upright again. As soon as she leveled off, she discovered the pirate craft in front of her.

"Now be ready," Doran said. "Because he's either going to do the same thing or circle around horizontally. When he does, I want you to use the nose of the shuttle to clip his outside wing—not hard, just a love tap."

"A love tap?"

He nodded. "Any harder than that, and we'll go down with him."

Gritting her teeth, Solara stared at the craft in front of her for the slightest change in his trajectory—anything to betray his next move. When he veered right, she was ready. Her hands took charge as if operating independently of her brain. She steered sharply to the right and dipped the shuttle just enough to bump his wing, then pulled a hard left as his craft barreled out of control.

When she circled back around, the pirate shuttle was upside down in the sand.

Doran gave a loud whoop and ruffled her braids. "You're a natural!"

She laughed while her fingers trembled from the adrenaline surge. Tears flooded her vision, but they were the happy kind. Her body simply needed a release. Doran seemed to understand. Instead of telling her to calm down, he rubbed her neck. Then he finally said, "Thanks for saving my pretty hide, Solara," and her tears turned to laughter.

After making sure no one else had followed them, she descended into the great smoky valley and found her secret hiding place.

"Let me guess," he said. "Now we wait for the coast to clear?"

Solara cut the thrusters and rubbed her palms together. She was still shaking. "We should disconnect the battery while we're here. Even with the engine turned off, we'll emit a low-enough electrical pulse—"

"To trip a scanner," he finished, nodding with an appreciative grin. "I'm loving your criminal mind right now."

She rolled her eyes while levering open the hatch. "Careful, you're speaking Jackass again."

"It was a compliment." Doran unlatched the hood and held it open while she unplugged the battery and fuel cables. "I wish I had your instincts. They're a lot more useful out here than the business classes my dad made me take."

"I wish I had your calm under pressure," she told him, wiping grease on her pants. "A solution's no good if it comes five minutes too late." As soon as she spoke the words, she remembered how she'd once called Doran helpless, and she realized with a stitch of guilt how wrong she'd been about him. He had plenty of skills, just different from hers. That was what made them such an effective team. "But speaking of instincts," she said, returning to the problem at hand, "what're we going to do about Kane? I don't have any proof that he turned you in, just a gut feeling. That won't convince the crew."

"It'll be our word against his," Doran agreed. "We have to dig up some dirt on him. Until then, we can't let him know anything's wrong, or he might destroy the evidence."

"I'll check the ship's outgoing transmissions as soon as we get back. If he deleted a record, I'll be able to tell by resetting the log."

Doran blew out a breath, shaking his head in a way that said he didn't want to talk about Kane anymore. "I guess you're stuck with me for a while longer."

"All the way to the fringe," she said, not bothering to hide her smile. "Just my luck."

She was grateful for the extra time with him. The journey to the fringe was four rings out from their current position inside the tourist circle, so that meant Solara would have several more weeks in Doran's company. Thinking about it sent a gradual warmth through her limbs until the shaking stopped.

The sensation lasted until the sun went down.

It was amazing how quickly the oppressive desert heat vanished, leached from the cave's dark stone walls as the first shadows crept in. The temperature plummeted, and she began shivering again. At least she had a jacket. Doran had left his on the ruined ship, along with a sack of fuel chips and everything he owned.

She told him to search the shuttle for an emergency pack while she checked for activity outside. Taking a seat at the mouth of the cave, she peered at the night sky, expecting to see the orange glow of thrusters. Nothing glowed in the heavens except for two moons and a ribbon of stars twisted into a nebula. But though the activity seemed to have died, the *criminal instincts* Doran loved so much warned her to stay put for a while longer.

"I found something." Doran's voice echoed from the rear of the crevasse, where the absence of starlight made it impossible to see his discovery.

She detected a rustle of fabric. "A blanket?" she asked, afraid to hope.

"More or less." He joined her and held up a strip of foil-like cloth the approximate size of a bath towel. "Hope you don't mind sharing."

"Will that thing cover both of us?"

"Only one way to find out," he said, and started glancing around at the floor. "Where do you want to sleep?"

A new shiver rolled over her, one that had nothing to do with the temperature. When she'd resolved to spend the night here, it hadn't occurred to her that she and Doran would need to huddle for warmth.

When she didn't answer, he asked, "We're staying till morning, right?"

Clearing her throat, she nodded and pointed at the spot

beside her. "We'll camp here, so we can keep an eye out for trouble."

If he felt the same nervous tingling at the prospect of sleeping beside her, he didn't let it show. He unbuckled his belt—just for comfort, she hoped—then lay on his side with his back pressed to the cave wall and one arm curled beneath his head like a pillow. By way of invitation, he extended his other arm to her.

Solara reminded herself that this was no big deal. People shared body heat all the time in emergency situations. But despite all her encouraging self-talk, she curled onto her side and barely touched him. Doran fixed that problem by wrapping an arm around her waist and tugging her backward until they nested together like two spoons in a drawer.

Solara's breath hitched while her skin buzzed with awareness. Every inch of him was molded to her, so hot that she doubted they'd need the blanket at all. His heart beat against her shoulder in a strong, steady thump. If he could feel hers, he would know it was trying to pound its way out of her chest.

He spread the meager blanket over their joined bodies and then slid his arm beneath, where he settled it squarely under her breasts and hugged her even closer. With his chin resting atop her head, he asked, "Better?"

She gulped.

This was so much better . . . or worse, depending on whether she wanted to get any actual rest tonight. With all the atoms in her body pinging against one another in a manic dance, sleep wasn't going to happen. She wished she were as unaffected by his touch as she pretended to be. As she lay beneath the glamour of a thousand twinkling stars, she wondered if Doran felt the same magnetism.

"If you're still cold," he murmured, his warm breath stirring her hair, "we could take off our shirts and try this skin-to-skin."

Her whole body flashed hot before she realized he was joking. She delivered a light elbow to the belly and told him, "Keep dreaming."

"Just trying to be helpful."

"You're such a gentleman."

His thumb brushed the base of her rib cage, forcing her to release a shamefully loud sigh. "See?" he said. "At least I'm good for something." Then he felt the need to add, "I've been told my body's a furnace."

And just like that, the spell broke.

Because with those words came a painful reminder that she wasn't the first girl Doran Spaulding had held like this, and she wouldn't be the last. Even if he felt the same stirrings of attraction that she did, where could it possibly lead? He would forget her as soon as he returned to his life on Earth and all the pink-haired princesses waiting for him. She and Doran were cut from different cloth. They were friends now, but only by circumstance.

She needed to remember that.

"Go to sleep," she said, and pushed against his arm until he loosened his grip. She required body heat, not comfort. "I'll take first watch."

"Okay." He didn't seem to notice the shift in her mood. After slinging his arm loosely over her hip, he settled in and exhaled, long and slow. A few minutes passed in silence, and just when she thought he'd drifted off, he said, "One more thing."

"What?"

"Since we're stuck together for a while longer, I think we should reevaluate our ground rules."

She hadn't been expecting that. Intrigued, she cocked an ear toward him. "Does this mean I get my stunner back?"

"As long as you promise not to use it on me."

"Agreed."

"And second," he said, "nobody sleeps on the bedroom floor. That's nonnegotiable. I won't camp down there again, and I'm tired of feeling guilty because I'm comfortable and you're not. There's plenty of room on the mattress, and I won't try anything, if that's what you're worried about."

Solara scoffed. But on the inside, she fought to push down the annoyingly persistent tingles that reappeared behind her belly button. "I know where to put my knee if you get too close."

From behind her, his hips withdrew an inch. "So we don't have a problem?"

"If anyone will have a problem sharing the bed, it won't be me," she told him. "You'll stay on your side, and I'll stay on mine." It sounded so simple, yet even as she spoke the words, she caught herself nestling against his body.

Solara forced her eyes shut, hoping she hadn't made herself a liar.

CHAPTER NINETEEN

*T*hey returned to the *Banshee* early the next evening and told the crew everything that had happened. Solara brushed off their encounter with the Enforcers as a freak coincidence, all the while seething in rage every time her gaze landed on Kane. Recounting the story made her realize even more clearly the danger he'd put them in, and she couldn't wait to expose him for the traitor he was.

At the dinner table, she sat facing him, smiling sweetly while she tightened one fist on her lap. "The chili's amazing," she said. "Did you do something different?"

"Actually, yes." He perked up and launched into some spiel about replacing one spice with another, but Solara wasn't listening. Instead, she studied him for signs of guilt: inconsistent eye contact, fidgeting, widened pupils, flaring nostrils. He betrayed nothing, which made him either a natural-born actor or a sociopath. Probably the latter. "Thanks for noticing," he added.

"My pleasure."

A sudden rustling noise shifted their attention to the cabinet, and Kane pulled it open to discover Acorn's head buried in a bag of lentils she'd torn wide open. Some of the tiny dried beans spilled out, clinking to the floor. Acorn seemed to know she was busted. Her furry body disappeared completely into the bag.

"Damn it," Kane swore, gently scooping her out. "There goes tomorrow's supper."

The captain reached across the table and took Acorn in his palm. "It's your own fault," he told Kane while stroking Acorn's head with his thumb. "Food belongs in bins, not bags. It's in her nature to forage."

Unaware of the trouble she'd caused, Acorn closed both eyes and purred contentedly. In Solara's next life, she wanted to come back as a sugar glider. *Must be nice to have no worries.*

"It's your turn," the captain said to her. "Ask us a question."

"Make it good," Renny added.

Solara pursed her lips, tapping them with an index finger to feign deep thought when, truthfully, she'd chosen her question hours ago. "Okay, how about this? Would you rather confess your darkest secret to the whole galaxy, or tell your best friend's darkest secret to their worst enemy?" The question was designed to test Kane, so she looked at him first. "What's your answer?"

"That's easy," he said. "The first one."

She raised a challenging brow. "Your secrets must not be that dark."

"You'd be surprised," he told her, and stared at the scattering of lentils on the floor. "But I'd do anything to protect my best friend." He flicked a glance at her and stressed, "Anything."

Solara frowned at his response. It wasn't what she'd expected.

One by one, the rest of the crew gave the same answer until the meal ended, and then empty bowls were piled into the sink, and tin mugs were gathered in preparation for customary after-dinner drinks around the fireplace.

Doran caught her eye and gave a slight nod—a signal that he would keep the crew occupied in the lounge while she rifled through Kane's bunk.

"I'm heading back to my room for a minute," she told the group. "Go ahead and start without me."

She strode upstairs and passed through the lounge, then continued to her open doorway and waited there for Doran's next signal. The ship's quarters were connected to the lounge by one short hallway, making her easy to spot by anyone who moved to the far end of the room. So she stayed put until she heard Doran challenge the crew to a poker game and then for the noise of bodies settling into chairs before she tiptoed into Cassia and Kane's chamber.

The room carried traces of Cassia's floral scent, so subtle that Solara wouldn't have noticed it had she not known about the implants. She felt a twinge of guilt for pilfering through Cassia's things, but not enough to stop her from searching every drawer built into the storage wall.

Beneath a stack of Kane's shirts, she discovered a small pouch containing twenty fuel chips, which was about two months' wages for a ship hand. Nothing out of the ordinary. In his sock drawer, she found an assortment of basic possessions: an older-model data tablet with a cracked screen; a few photographs, all of Cassia; assorted souvenirs; a Solar League ID fob bearing the name KANE ARRIC.

There was no evidence of a reward, nor of an electronic credit account. He didn't even own a laser blade, which explained why he kept using Cassia's. A peek beneath the bottom cot didn't reveal anything but dust balls, and if there were any hidden panels in the room, Solara couldn't find them. It wasn't until she swept a hand under the bottom mattress that she discovered something interesting.

For the second time in her life, she touched gold. But this necklace made Demarkus's choker look like costume jewelry. At the end of a thick, sturdy chain dangled a palm-sized amulet with a faceted blue stone at its center. Even in near darkness, the stone captured the glow from the exit lighting and sprayed prisms over her sleeve. Peering closer, she admired the intricate design work that adorned the piece in an interwoven circle of flowering vines. That kind of artistry proved it hadn't come off an assembly line. She turned it over and noticed the other side was damaged by light scratches, but not badly enough to conceal the name carved there in bold script.

Princess Cassia Adelaide Rose

Solara dropped the necklace and had to perform a feat of acrobatics to keep it from hitting the floor. Blinking hard, she read the text two more times in case her eyes had deceived her.

They hadn't. Cassia was royalty.

But from which planet? Dozens of colonies were classified as monarchies, either by active reign or as symbolic figureheads of a democracy. As long as Solar Territory laws were obeyed and taxes rendered, the League didn't care how the colonies governed themselves. Narrowing down Cassia's home world would take time and research.

The bigger question was why any girl would trade a life of royalty for a career as a ship hand—in the company of fugitives, no less—or why Cassia hadn't returned to that life once she'd discovered the Daeva were tracking the ship. Something terrible must've happened at home if she felt compelled to stay here. And how did Kane fit into the puzzle? He seemed to belong to the same race, but judging by his possessions, he was a man of simple tastes, not royalty. Solara had found no trace of reward money in his room, and she was beginning to think that wealth didn't matter to him anyway.

She tucked the necklace back into its place beneath the mattress while chewing the inside of her cheek. Had she misjudged Kane? Or did he have a different motive for wanting Doran off the ship?

*   *   *

Not surprisingly, Doran's first reaction to the news was to gloat.

"Told you she was important," he said, kicking off his boots at the foot of the bed. He pulled off his shirt and tossed it over one shoulder, then dropped his pants. "Looks like I was right."

Solara whirled to face the other direction, but it was too late. The image of Doran in his shorts had burned itself into her retinas. For some reason, she'd pictured them continuing to sleep fully clothed when she'd agreed to share the bed. "Whatever. You didn't know she was a princess."

"Not exactly, but it doesn't surprise me."

"Well, this will surprise you," she said, staring at the door and seeing the hard planes of Doran's abs instead. "I checked the outgoing transmissions, and there's nothing there. I even rebooted the system. Nobody's made a call since last week."

"Huh. Maybe we were wrong about Kane."

"I was thinking," she said. "There's one possibility we overlooked. The Enforcers might've found your ship through the tracking system. That would explain why they showed up right after you powered on the navigator."

"But to do that, they had to know exactly which ship they were looking for. My dad didn't even tell *me* that information."

"They probably seized his records during the investigation."

"I guess that makes sense," Doran said, and then sheets rustled in the background, along with the creaking of mattress springs. "It's safe to turn around now, by the way."

"Face the wall," she told him.

"Why?"

"So I can admire the back of your head," she said sarcastically. "Why do you think?"

"Oh, come on. I've seen you undressed."

"That was when you were sleeping on the floor. Want to revisit that arrangement?"

He grumbled a few colorful words and flopped onto his side.

As soon as his back was turned, Solara wiped her clammy palms on the blanket and released a shaky breath. She'd dreaded this moment ever since they left the cave, where she'd awoken so wrapped up in Doran that she was literally on top of him.

He'd gloated about that, too.

She double-checked the bolt before turning off the light and shedding her pants. The sheets were warmer than usual when she slid between them, already gathering heat from the human "furnace" lying inches away from her. She felt his body radiating energy, not near enough to touch but too close for comfort.

"Scoot over," she whispered.

The mattress shook with his movement.

"A little more," she said.

"If I get any closer to the wall," he hissed, "I'll have to buy it dinner."

She grabbed her pillow and wedged it between them. "There, that's better."

"Are you sure you're okay with this?"

"Of course I'm sure."

"All right, then," he whispered, and she could sense him smiling. "This time, try not to mount me in my sleep."

She kicked him in the shin while her face went hot. "Keep joking, and I'll make sure you don't wake up in the morning."

"Good night, Solara," he crooned.

"Sleep tight," she told him. "*Way* over there."

CHAPTER TWENTY

Doran didn't sleep with girls, not if he could help it.

Years of trial and error had taught him that dating was like chemistry: Some elements weren't safe to mix—overnighters and fooling around, for example. Put those two together and expect "fun" to turn into "feelings," right before it all blew up in your face.

But even he could get used to this.

Every morning for the past two weeks, he'd awoken to Solara's bare arm draped over his chest and her breath caressing his skin. It didn't matter how far he backed toward the wall. She would inevitably kick off the covers and gravitate toward him in nothing but a T-shirt and a pair of white cotton panties that looked surprisingly hot on her. When morning came, she'd blink awake and scowl at him, as if he'd chased her into a cuddle instead of the other way around. Then he'd smile and point at the vacant stretch of mattress behind her and tease, *What's wrong? Did you wake up on the wrong side of the bed again?* Which never failed to make her whole face turn red.

All in all, it was an excellent way to start the day.

He particularly enjoyed using the end of her braid to tickle her awake. This always earned him a smack on the chest, but it was worth it. And because today was a special occasion, she might not punish him.

Moving as little as possible, he reached behind the pillow to retrieve the end of her braid, then swept it down the middle of her face, holding in his laughter when her nose twitched like a rabbit's. She groaned and scrubbed a fist over the spot before snapping awake and moving to strike.

He caught her hand in midair and said, "Remember what today is?"

She gasped, teeth flashing in an instant smile. "Shore leave!"

"That's right," he said, figuring it was safe to release her. "Not even *you* can be mad."

Firing her usual glare, she scooted back to her own side of the bed and rubbed the sleep from her eyes. "Unless we have to leave early, like on Pesirus. Then the whole crew is dead to me."

"Hey, I did my part. Nobody's looking for me here."

Last week, Doran had placed a few strategic transmissions to his friends back home, telling them—after they'd sworn to secrecy, of course—that he was on his way back to Earth to hide out in his father's lake house. He'd figured at least one of them would blow the whistle, and they had come through like champs. Now the Enforcers were scouring the wrong end of the galaxy for him, and hopefully Demarkus was, too. Captain Rossi had pulled a clever bait and switch of his own, using a fake ship name to schedule a cargo pickup at a planet called Cargill. And because the Daeva had no way of tracking them to the settlement, he'd awarded the crew a day of freedom. More than anything, Doran needed a temporary distraction from his worries. He'd been looking forward to this.

"So why are we still in bed?" Solara asked.

"Speak for yourself."

Doran playfully shoved her face in the pillow while leaping off the mattress. A race ensued, in which he beat her to the washroom and back to their quarters to dress. It was neck and neck for a moment, but he pulled into the lead and reached the galley just ahead of her.

The clomp of their footsteps drew Kane's attention. He turned from the steaming vat of porridge on the stove and grinned at them. "That excited for my breakfast, huh? I knew I had skills."

Doran returned the smile without having to fake it. He hadn't uncovered any information to implicate Kane, so it looked like the Enforcers really had used the tracking system to find him. It felt good to let go of all that resentment, or at least shift it to the right people.

Cassia shared a knowing look with Renny, who sat beside her, nursing a cup of coffee and feeding Acorn a bean. "You've got skills, all right," she quipped. "Mostly for being an—" She cut off when the captain hobbled into the room, then finished with a stiff smile. "Amazing cook. How do you make the porridge taste so sweet?"

"With an extra scoop of love, of course," Kane forced through his teeth.

Captain Rossi barked a laugh and lowered onto the opposite bench. He eyed the ship hands while massaging his bad knee. "You can cut the act. I won't revoke your leave privileges for fighting."

Both blonds sighed with relief, apparently exhausted from ten seconds of being nice to each other. But their smiles turned genuine when they shared a glance. The promise of fresh air and wide-open spaces seemed to hang in the air like a second sun, lifting everyone's mood. Even the captain had an extra pep in his step this morning . . . or rather in his limp.

"We've been in a pressure cooker lately," he continued. "So I want you to blow off some steam." Lifting a knobby hand, he clarified, "*Quiet* steam—the kind that floats up from a boiling pot, not the kind that comes screeching out of a teakettle. Keep your heads covered, and don't draw too much attention. That means no getting locked up, and no passing out naked in the middle of the town churchyard. Understood?"

Renny chuckled behind his coffee cup while both ship hands turned the color of ripe raspberries. They nodded, gazing into their laps.

"It's none of my business how you spend your wages," Rossi continued, "but remember that we're lying low, and that means fewer jobs."

"No worries, Cap," Kane said. "I'm only taking two chips with me."

"Smart move," the captain told him. "We're not in the tourist ring anymore, so watch your coin purse, and don't bring anything with you that you don't want stolen. We'll meet back here at sunrise."

Cassia gasped with excitement. "We get all night?"

"You've earned it." He pointed his crutch at the stove. "Now, finish your breakfast and go have fun. I hear there's a harvest festival in town. Might be a good place to start."

After that, bowls and spoons went flying in a blur of activity, and in less than ten minutes, Doran and Solara led the way toward town with Cassia and Kane walking closely behind, bickering about whose turn it was to do laundry in the morning.

The crunch of dried grass created a lively percussion as Doran lifted his hands and face in worship to the sun's rays. It was fall here, and the crisp breeze carried hints of wood smoke and kettle corn—autumn's signature scent no matter what planet he visited. If he closed his eyes, he could pretend he was home, tailgating at a college football game with his friends. But those memories made him ache with longing and stirred up fears that he might never return to that life. So he zipped his borrowed jacket tightly over his chest, tugged down his knitted cap, and gazed toward the festival in the town square.

Right away, he noticed the no-frills architecture and the absence of flashing billboards that set this place apart from the planets within the tourist ring. Most technology was manufactured on Earth, so by default, the farther removed the settlement, the more primitive it became. Cargill was located in the third ring, mostly producing grain. Next would come the ore mines, then the prison settlements, and finally his father's coordinates in the outer realm.

Doran had never been to the fringe, but he'd heard the settlers there farmed crops by hand. He couldn't fathom living that way. Then again, he'd never experienced the overcrowded slums of Houston, so he really had no right to judge. These people hadn't done anything to deserve their fate. They worked as hard as he did, probably harder, because they had to scrape for the basic things he took for granted. He glanced at Solara and wondered if she would be happy on Vega.

The townspeople here seemed content with their simple lives, chatting animatedly as they browsed the vendor tables lining their crudely paved streets. A group of children chased one another in a clumsy game of tag, tripping over their own feet in overly large shoes probably handed down from older siblings. It reminded Doran that he needed to buy clothes to replace the coveralls he'd lost in the fire.

"I'll meet up with you," he told the group, and then strode toward a table piled high with secondhand garments.

Just half a fuel chip bought him three pairs of pants, several pullover shirts, a parcel of socks and shorts, and a knapsack to carry it all in. A bargain, he learned, because Spaulding Fuel cost twice as much on this planet than on Obsidian. Despite the sudden increase in his currency's value, Doran frowned as he walked away. He couldn't see any reason for the steep markup. Fuel cost more to transport to remote planets, but not *that* much more.

He found his friends playing carnival games in a field behind the town hall. Kane held a rifle stock in the bend of his shoulder and fired lasers at moving holographic targets in the air. Judging by Cassia's laughter, he hadn't landed a shot yet.

"It's busted or something," Kane muttered, scrutinizing the rifle's eyepiece.

"If by 'it,' you mean your head," Cassia said, "then I agree."

The carny running the booth, a stout man with a barbell piercing in his lower lip and the words BORN TO KILL tattooed across his neck, slapped a palm on the counter and growled, "Ain't nothing wrong with my equipment. Let the lady try."

Kane made a show of glancing around the field. "Lady? I don't see a lady here."

"You scatweed," Cassia said, snatching the rifle. She jabbed him in the belly with it, then raised the weapon smoothly toward the targets and fired. In response, a bubble exploded into a twinkling shower of fireworks. "See?" she announced, and shoved the gun back at him. "The only thing that's busted is your aim."

"You two are such easy marks," Solara said, burying her hand in a bag of roasted nuts. "The rifle's laser isn't calibrated to match the targets." She pointed a nut at the carny before tossing it into her mouth. "He's triggering the hits with a foot pedal. It's the oldest trick in the book."

The carny gave her a glare that would melt steel. "Are you accusing me of thievery?"

Solara shrugged. "Everyone knows these games are rigged."

"Rigged?" asked a new voice from behind.

When Doran spun around, his gaze landed on the hardest-looking woman he'd ever seen—not so much unattractive as lethal. He caught himself drawing back. At six feet tall and about thirty years old, she had a striking face with regal cheekbones and an ice-cold smile that would send any lucid man running for his life in the opposite direction.

"I provide the finest traveling amusements in this system," the woman said. "Anyone who says otherwise is attacking my livelihood, and that of my employees." Her upper lip curled, revealing an incisor so sharp that she must have filed it. "Do you know what the punishment is for slander, little girl? I could have your tongue slit for this."

Solara stepped forward with fire in her gaze, but Doran put her behind him and said, "She didn't mean anything by it."

The woman's frigid blue eyes narrowed to slits. "That girl accused my worker of tampering with the game. Now you're saying she didn't mean it?"

"No, she didn't," Doran told her.

"Then she disparages reputations for fun? I don't see how that's any better."

"We don't want any trouble. Let's just—"

"What you want," she interrupted, "is irrelevant. You've got trouble. All that remains to be seen is how you'll pay for it."

Doran was considering whether he should grab Solara's hand and run when Kane slung the laser rifle casually over one shoulder and sauntered up to the woman.

"You'll have to forgive my cousin," he said in a voice that dripped honey. He tapped his forehead and let loose that punch-worthy crooked grin of his. "She's a bit touched by God, as my mum used to say. Never been the same since the black fever of . . ." He paused, tipping his head in wonder at the woman.

"What are you staring at?" she asked.

"I'm sorry," Kane said. "It's just . . . there's a place on Louron, my home world, where the river meets the sea in a shallow bank of pristine white sand. When the sun hits it just right, the water turns the most incredible shade of blue. It's almost too beautiful to bear." He reached toward her face, then pulled back. "I never thought I'd see that color again, until a moment ago, when I looked into your eyes."

While Doran suppressed the urge to vomit, the woman lifted a hand to her heart and blushed—actually *blushed*—as a soft gasp parted her lips.

She was really falling for this tripe?

"You're breathtaking," Kane whispered. "I hope you don't mind me saying so."

The woman flapped a dismissive hand.

"You might slap me for this," Kane murmured, "but I have to tell you . . ." Then he pressed his mouth to her ear and said something that made her giggle harder than a freshman at a slumber party.

Doran took that as his cue to make an exit.

He retreated a pace, and then another, while towing Solara along with him. Once they reached a safe distance, he flagged Cassia over, and the three of them made their way quickly to the other end of the festival grounds.

"So much for lying low," Solara said into her bag of nuts.

"Don't worry about it," Cassia told her. "Kane could seduce the wings off a bird. It's his one useful talent."

"Does he do that often?" Solara asked.

Cassia laughed while helping herself to a handful of nuts. "He's been charming his way out of trouble since we were kids."

That caught Doran's attention. "You grew up together?"

"Yes, but not on Louron. He was lying about that."

"Where, then?"

The shift in her expression warned that she would dodge the

question, which she did with a flick of her wrist. "Just a small colony in another sector. You've probably never heard of it."

Worried she might shut down completely, Doran decided not to press for the planet's name. Instead, he asked, "How'd you end up on the *Banshee*?"

He noticed that Cassia started rubbing her throat, but she dropped her hand when she saw him watching. Then she fixed her gaze on the ground. "Things are complicated at home. We'll go back someday, when it all dies down."

Her typically sharp tone was full of so much sadness that Doran couldn't bring himself to ask any more questions. Something terrible had obviously prompted her to leave home, and prying information out of her felt like kicking a puppy.

They wandered in silence back to the town square to browse the vendor tables. Cassia's mood brightened when Kane caught up with them.

"So, did you make a new friend?" she asked with a teasing grin.

Kane wrinkled his nose and stopped to spit on the street. "Yeah. A friend who chews hash leaves. She kissed me, and now I'll never get the taste out of my mouth."

"Here," Solara said, holding out the bag of nuts. "Maybe this will help."

Cassia intercepted the bag and arched a haughty brow at Kane. "Considering the kind of girls you date, this should be an improvement."

"You seem to care an awful lot about my love life," Kane told her, snatching the nuts. "If I didn't know better, I'd think you were jealous."

Cassia drew a breath loud enough to tell anyone within listening distance that Kane had plucked a nerve. "Not in your most twisted fantasies!"

Kane leaned down until their eyes met. "My fantasies aren't all twisted. I'll tell you about them if you ask nicely."

The girl's lips parted, and then Kane smiled—not the oily grin he used like a weapon, but a barely noticeable curve of his mouth with warmth dancing behind his eyes. Doran had never seen that smile before, so he presumed it was the real thing.

And he'd given it to Cassia.

It was then that Doran understood. Kane was in love with a girl who outranked him by a thousand rungs on the social ladder. It wasn't clear whether Cassia felt as strongly, but even if she did, she probably wouldn't let herself get serious with him. Not if she intended to return home. Doran almost felt sorry for the guy. The tension inside their quarters had to be combustive enough to launch a missile. No wonder they fought all the time.

The look Solara gave him said she'd noticed it, too.

Cassia spun around and turned her attention to a jewelry display. Kane barely had time to dodge the girl's flying dreadlocks when she reached out blindly and clutched his arm.

"Kane," she breathed, eyes locked on the table.

"What's wrong?" he asked.

They all gathered around the table and watched as Cassia lifted a necklace from its stand. It was a simple design, just a black cord with a blue marbled pendant set in tarnished silver. Doran didn't see what all the fuss was about.

The vendor, a wrinkled man with tufts of gray chest hair

protruding from his collar, swept a hand toward the necklace. "It's an Eturian prayer stone, used for—"

"I know what it is," Cassia snapped. "How much?"

He motioned for her to come closer, then whispered in her ear.

"*What?*" she cried, recoiling. "Are you mad? That's a month's wages."

The vendor's answering shrug said he didn't care. "It's a simple issue of supply and demand. No one's been able to export from Eturia since the war began."

Cassia's hand went slack, dropping to her side. "What war?" she asked in barely a whisper. "When did it start? Which kingdoms are fighting?"

Another shrug. "Even if I knew, it wouldn't change my price."

Cassia seemed to have stopped breathing. Kane took the necklace from her and hooked it back onto the display, then wrapped an arm around her shoulders and led her across the street.

Solara touched Doran's elbow and stood on tiptoe to reach his ear. "I think it's obvious where they're from," she whispered. "What do you know about Eturia?"

"Nothing," Doran said. There were more than a hundred colonies within the Solar Territories, and at least a dozen more in the fringe. He'd only studied those that mattered to the company. "Cassia was right. I've never heard of it."

He peered above the crowd and saw Cassia's face buried in Kane's chest. An influx of shoppers thickened the street, and when Doran finally lost sight of the pair, he turned to the vendor and asked for more information about Eturia.

"It's a small colony," the man said. "On the most beautiful planet you'll never see."

"*Never* see?" asked Solara.

"Visitors and immigrants aren't allowed past the atmosphere shield." He indicated the wares spread across his table. "That's what makes these so valuable."

"What about the war?" Doran asked. "Do you know why they're fighting?"

The man frowned, likely sensing this wouldn't result in a sale. "Like I already told your friend, I don't know anything. And even if I did—"

"It wouldn't change your price," Doran finished. He thanked the man and backed into the street with Solara. "So what now?" he asked her. "We could talk to the other vendors. Someone else might know more."

"We could do that. Or we could enjoy our shore leave." Pointing at the sky, she added, "That's a real sun up there, not a lamp to keep us from getting transport madness, but an actual star shining above solid ground."

"And we only have until morning to soak it in," Doran agreed. "Point taken."

"Come on." She linked their arms and steered him in the other direction, where a giant harvest maze had been erected in a schoolyard. "Let's lose ourselves in some corn."

CHAPTER TWENTY-ONE

D oran kept his elbow linked with Solara's and didn't let go the entire time they wandered through the maze. Neither of them was in a hurry. They strolled aimlessly among the rows of brown cornstalks while children raced past them toward the finish line. There was no conversation between them, but it was a contented silence. The fresh breeze, the warm rays, and the music of laughter blended into an intoxicating cocktail, and they drank it up until they accidentally found the maze's exit.

By that time, their stomachs rumbled, so they found a concession stand and loaded up on fire-roasted corn, mulled cider, meat on a stick, and enough fried funnel cake to send them into a sugar coma. They carried their feast to a flat patch of grass and gorged themselves until they lay sprawled in the sun like bloated walruses.

"I might die," Solara groaned, rubbing her belly. "But I'll go with a smile."

Doran loosened his belt a notch, then reclined with an arm folded under his head. "Do me a favor and die tomorrow. That way I'll have a partner for the barn dance tonight."

She snorted a dry laugh. "I guess with that face, you never had to learn how to sweet-talk girls."

"You have to remember I'm speaking Jackass."

"Well, try it again in English."

Doran rolled onto his side and took her hand, then pressed it to his chest. "Solara," he crooned. "Will you do me the honor of accompanying me to a Podunk barn dance tonight? I can't promise not to step on your feet, but I swear I won't let you pass out naked in a churchyard." He winked. "Unless you're up for that. In which case, you can count on me to make it happen."

She tried scowling at him, but her lips twitched into a grin. "It's a good thing I like you, or you'd be dancing alone tonight."

Her words did funny things to his stomach. "You like me?" he asked, threading their fingers together. "How much?"

"Not enough for naked churchyard shenanigans."

"That's a shame."

She watched their linked hands and fell silent for a moment. "Hey, do you think you'll ever come visit me?" she asked. "When I'm living on Vega?"

"Visit? If I can't clear these charges, I'll be your permanent sofa crasher."

"I mean it. Be serious."

Doran didn't say so, but he was only half joking. He had a new theory about why his father had sent him to the outer realm, and if he was right, neither of them would ever be free again—at least not within the Solar Territories. He'd have to start over in the fringe. Assuming anyone would hire an eighteen-year-old business intern with no useful trade skills.

"Wait." Solara brushed a thumb over his knuckles. "You don't really believe that, do you?"

"I don't know," he told her. "I think I figured out what Infinium is."

"What's that got to do with sleeping on my sofa?"

"Remember what I told you about my job collecting new elements?"

"Yes," she said. "For product development."

"Sometimes we find one that's too unstable for fuel but perfect for blowing things up. When that happens, my father destroys the sample and deletes all the data from our archives. He says he doesn't want to be responsible for creating the next weapon of mass destruction."

"And that's what you think Infinium is?"

"It makes sense," Doran said. "I think my father discovered something dangerous, and the Solar League got their hands on it. That's why he sent his men to steal it from the transport and why he sent me to the fringe. Maybe he wants me to destroy what's left of Infinium before the League finds it."

"A government conspiracy?" she asked. "That's a little far-fetched, isn't it?"

"Have you got a better idea?"

"Actually, I do." She rolled onto her side to face him. "Let's quit talking about Infinium and enjoy our shore leave."

When her amber-green eyes locked on his and she unleashed

that dimpled smile, all of Doran's worries dissolved the way springtime melted the last dregs of winter. As he lay so close to her in the soft grass, their hands linked between them, it was easy to forget everything but the dusting of freckles on her cheeks and the scent of powdered sugar on her breath. His heart ticked to a new rhythm, one that warned he was in trouble. Because this girl had left a mark on him, deep down where time wouldn't erase it.

He used his free hand to cup her chin. "I'll visit you."

"Promise?"

"Just try to keep me away."

Relief flickered on her face, and it warmed him inside to know that he'd left a mark on her, too. "Now back to our shore leave," he said. "What should we do next?"

She unlinked their fingers and pushed to standing, then peered across the schoolyard toward the town square. "I heard there's a hayride around here somewhere. Want to check it out? I'm too full for anything else."

"All right. But on the way, let's walk down the vendor street again." He wanted a souvenir of this perfect day, a physical memento to hold when Solara's hand was on Vega.

"What are you looking for?" she asked.

He lifted a shoulder. "I'll know it when I see it."

But after making a full pass along the vendor tables, he hadn't spent a single chip. There was no shortage of goods for sale—wood-carved figurines, ceremonial knives, handmade candies, body art, and every type of jewelry imaginable.

None of it reminded him of Solara.

They crossed paths with Kane, who was haggling over the

price of the Eturian prayer necklace that'd caught Cassia's eye that morning. Kane had obviously returned to the ship for more money, because he opened a pouch of fuel chips for the vendor to see. The poor bastard really had it bad. Doran decided not to interrupt them. Instead, he veered away and led Solara to the town churchyard.

Once there, they climbed aboard a wooden skid padded with fresh straw and hitched to a hovercraft that had seen better days. The craft lifted them into the air just high enough for their dangling feet to skim the tops of the tall weeds, then it set off at an easy pace. They sat with their shoulders touching, swaying together as the hovercraft towed them through the field and into the woods beyond. Doran never thought he would enjoy something so simple as a slow glide through the trees, but when the ride was done, he paid for them to go again.

Once the sun dipped below the horizon and two moons arose to take its place, they walked to the community center, which was decorated like a barn with hay bales, wood planks, and a scattering of straw on the floor. The dance was already in full swing, filling the night air with a chorus of fiddles and stomping feet, along with the musky odor of too many bodies in one place.

A young man slouched near the entrance, both arms folded across his chest and clearly unhappy with the job of collecting admission while his friends were inside. But he perked up when he spotted Solara, grinning and wagging his eyebrows. "Hey," he said. "Want to have some fun?"

Doran frowned at the guy and settled a hand at the base of Solara's spine. "That's why we're here."

Unfazed, the local extended a hand, palm up. "Good. That'll be three bits." After receiving payment, he dug into his pocket and produced a leather pouch, then handed them each a piece of dried apple. "Enjoy," he said, and waved them inside.

That seemed odd, but Doran didn't question it. He and Solara popped the bites into their mouths and walked inside to join the party. It only took an instant to realize he wasn't chewing on apple. Bitter and musky, it tasted like bad fungus. He glanced around for a place to spit it out while Solara clapped a palm over her lips and did the same. Soon they found a waste receptacle in the corner and cleaned out their mouths.

"What was that?" she asked. "Some kind of mushroom?"

"A rancid one," he said, and spat again into the trash bin. "But it's nothing a cup of cider won't fix."

That did the trick. With their palates freshly cleansed, they took to the dance floor.

Doran had no idea how to move to this kind of music, so he captured Solara's waist between his hands and led her in a basic quickstep. As soon as she gripped his shoulders, he knew she couldn't dance to the music, either, but they eventually synched their steps well enough to follow the crowd's circular path around the room. Embracing their clumsiness, they laughed and twirled until the band changed the pace with a slow ballad.

This was what Doran had secretly hoped for. He pulled Solara closer than he probably should have, and when she didn't object, he eliminated another pocket of space between them. She locked both her wrists behind his neck and rested her chin on his chest, grinning up at him as they moved in a lazy sway. Her cheeks were flushed pink, and her eyes practically glowed from exertion. In that moment, he wondered how he'd ever believed she was anything less than spectacular.

She glanced at their fused bodies and told him, "The nuns would say we're not leaving enough room for the Holy Spirit."

It took a second for Doran to find his breath because she'd stolen it. "That's all right. The Holy Spirit doesn't belong here. He would just get in the way."

The longer they clung to each other on the dance floor, the lighter Doran's limbs felt. It started in his toes as a fizzy sort of warmth and bubbled through his veins until a sensation of euphoria overtook him, stronger than any champagne buzz he'd ever known. And strangely, the music sounded better. The vibrations created so much pleasure inside his ears that he rested his forehead against Solara's and groaned.

"Hey," she said. In the seconds since he'd last looked into her eyes, her pupils had grown wide and chased away all the amber. "Do you feel kind of . . . drunk, but not? Like all your skin is trying to float away?"

For some reason, Doran found that hilarious. He began chortling and couldn't stop. "I think I know what that mushroom really was," he said between chuckles.

"The magical kind?"

"Uh-huh." And if he felt this blasted now, he was lucky he hadn't eaten the whole thing. He worried about how sick he'd feel in the morning, but then a ticklish warmth settled over him like a blanket, and a delicious shiver rolled down his spine.

Solara peered up at him with a wide grin. "You're sparkly."

He noticed that she was, too. Her skin shimmered as if she'd dipped her face in diamond dust. He cupped her dimpled cheek and simply took her in, so moved by the girl staring back at him that it hurt to breathe. "And you're beautiful," he told her. His gaze landed on her birthmark, followed by the sudden urge to trace it with his tongue.

"I'm not beaut—"

Before she could finish, he tipped back her face and licked the base of her throat. Her skin was salty with a hint of sweetness layered beneath, so perfect that he did it again and again, until she let her head loll back. He wanted more, so he moved to the side of her neck and sucked a trail from ear to shoulder, right there in the middle of the crowded dance hall, without a care for who might see.

When she pushed away, her eyelids were heavy. "Is it hot in here?"

"God, yes," he said. "So hot."

"We should get some air."

"Air is good. Let's do that."

They ran outside, and a dozen heartbeats later, he had Solara flat on her back in the cool grass behind the barn, her legs wrapped tightly around his hips while he lay atop her and sucked his way down the other side of her neck.

His heart was about to explode and he couldn't catch his breath, but nothing mattered except tasting more of her skin. When he reached the base of her shoulder, he tugged aside her collar to expose a fresh patch, and then raked his teeth across her flesh. The drug had somehow rerouted half his nerve endings to his tongue and the other half to his ears, because everything below the waist had gone numb while all her little noises and sighs vibrated his eardrums in a surge of pleasure that made him see stars.

"Doran," she whispered.

He lifted his head to glance at her lips, and it struck him that he hadn't kissed her yet—something he'd fantasized about for weeks. But when he lowered his mouth to hers, he felt nothing. There was no brush of skin, no meeting of tongues, no thrill of contact. The deadened sensation reminded him of a trip to the dentist.

She must have sensed the invisible barrier, too, because she turned her face aside and panted, "It's not working. I can't feel you."

"Me neither." He shifted his weight to one elbow and paused to catch his breath. "My lips are numb. My skin's numb. Everything's numb."

She pushed his chest, and he rolled off her and into the grass. After their breathing slowed, they lay there for a while, side by side, occasionally giggling or commanding the moons to stop spinning. Doran was about to say that the mushroom they'd eaten would make a better anesthetic than a drug when a thought struck him and he sat upright.

"I know what I want for a souvenir," he said.

"Yeah?"

He took her wrist and brushed a thumb over the delicate skin there. "Let's get matching tattoos, so we never, *ever*, forget this day."

Her lips parted in a gasp of delight. "That's a great idea!"

"Really? So you'll come with me?"

"Of course I will," she said. "Let's hurry before we change our minds."

*   *   *

"Rise and shine, you crazy kids."

Someone kicked Doran's boot, jerking him into consciousness. He didn't have to open his eyes to know the sun was up. It pierced his brain right through both lids, causing his whole head to throb. Groaning, he rolled onto his side and clutched his temples. Something dry and scratchy tickled his hands, and he cracked open one eye to find brown grass beneath him.

Grass?

"You look kind of rough," came the voice again. It sounded like Kane. "But hey, at least you're not naked on the lawn of First Pesirus Presbyterian. There's no living that down."

"Nope," Cassia added. "I can testify to that."

"The captain said to get your drunk asses on board—his words, not mine," Kane said. "We should've lifted off an hour ago."

Doran pushed into a sitting position, though half his muscles ached in protest. "We're not drunk," he whispered in a dry throat. Damn, he was thirsty. He glanced beside him and found Solara lying next to the barn wall, massaging her forehead with one hand, and a strip of white gauze covering the wrist below it.

At the sight of that bandage, all his memories from last night came rushing back in a sucker punch to the face. He didn't have to look at his wrist to know it was covered, too. And the skin there wasn't numb anymore. In fact, it burned like hellfire.

"Oh no," he said. "What did we do?"

It was a hypothetical question. He recalled every word, every giggle, every clumsy grope, and, most of all, the ink-stained needle that ensured he would never, *ever*, forget any of it. Doran had wanted a souvenir, and he'd gotten one—in the shape of four antique pirate swords curving into a figure eight.

The symbol for the Brethren of Outcasts.

Have fun explaining that to the shareholders, he thought.

Solara slung an arm over her eyes. "Please tell me that was a dream. Please tell me we weren't inked by a retired accountant who took up body art last month." Then she peeked beneath her bandage and whimpered. "Nope. Not a dream."

"I'd ask what you've been up to," Cassia said, "but I can already tell." Smiling, she leaned down to inspect Solara's neck. "You two are animals!"

Kane laughed and elbowed her. "It's always the quiet ones."

Doran's eyes locked with Solara's before he glanced at her throat and felt all the blood drain from his face. Her skin was covered in hickeys. She was going to kill him once she looked in the mirror.

"I'm sorry," he said, but then he remembered how the mushroom had rewired his brain and given him some kind of eargasm, and the whole thing was so crazy that he couldn't stop a laugh from bubbling up. "I haven't," he choked out between chortles, "given anyone a hickey since seventh grade."

Her face turned so red it almost matched her neck. "You owe me a visit to the flesh forger," she said, standing up. "And this"—she pointed back and forth between them—"will never happen again."

She stormed away, and Cassia followed, clearly struggling to keep a straight face.

Doran was still laughing, though he knew that wouldn't last long. The tension in his stomach warned that he'd soon be kneeling in front of the merciless toilet gods.

Kane gave a sympathetic wince and offered his hand. "I've heard that before. Last year after the hellberry festival."

"She'll get over it," Doran said, accepting the help. "Eventually."

Kane hauled him up with a laugh. "That's what I thought, too." He clapped Doran on the shoulder and said, "Good luck. You're going to need it."

CHAPTER TWENTY-TWO

*T*he hickeys faded after a week, but the crew's nightly wise-cracks in the galley were much like the scent of burnt porridge—never-ending.

"No scarf tonight?" the captain asked, pointing at Solara's neck. "I guess you finally beat that cold virus."

"I don't believe she had a cold," Renny said thoughtfully. "I'll bet it was the Hoover flu. You know, named after the old vacuum cleaners on Earth?"

"Oh, I've heard of that disease," Cassia chimed in. "Doesn't it cause a rash that looks like suction marks? Highly contagious when mixed with cute guys and Crystalline?"

Renny nodded. "That's the one. Nasty business, the Hoover flu. It can lead to a serious fever."

Solara hid her annoyance behind a heaping bite of beans, but if the ribbing didn't let up soon, she might consider staging a mutiny with her newly recovered stunner. A girl could only take so much.

The captain chuckled to himself and nodded at Doran. "Are you up to reporting to the bridge after supper? Or do you feel a fever coming on?"

If the jokes bothered Doran, he didn't let it show. Solara glanced up and caught him watching her from above the rim of his cup, his lips curved in the same unsettling smile he'd worn since their night together on Cargill. There was something different in the way he looked at her now, as if he'd seen beneath her skin and knew all her secrets. It never failed to knock her sideways. She couldn't count the number of times she'd opened her mouth to speak and had drawn a blank, or forgotten why she'd walked into the room. In fact, she couldn't quite recall why she'd felt so annoyed a moment ago. . . .

"I have been running hot lately," Doran said, never taking his eyes off her. "But who says I want the cure?"

The whole table erupted in laughter and wolf whistles.

Oh, yes. That was why she'd felt annoyed.

Solara drew a breath and geared up for a snarky comeback, but once again, he'd sent her world tumbling off its axis. Damn him.

"Report to the bridge anyway," the captain said. "We need to narrow down your destination so I'm not flying all over hell's half acre once we reach that nameless planet of yours."

For the first time that night, Doran's grin faltered. It seemed that the closer they traveled to the fringe, the less he wanted to talk about his father's errand. Solara couldn't blame him. His whole future depended on finding a substance he'd never seen on a planet he'd never visited . . . and maybe thwarting a government conspiracy to boot. She was secondhand nervous just thinking about it.

"I still don't know what I'm looking for," he admitted. "But since there's no real settlement there, a quick scan for electronics should pinpoint—"

The galley lights flickered and died, followed by an abrupt silence that told Solara the auxiliary engines had shut down. Before she could blink, her plate clattered and she bounced one time in her seat. It felt as if the *Banshee* had hit a speed bump. The disturbance lasted only a second, but no lights returned other than the emergency strips glowing along the floor.

The captain scooped Acorn out of his pocket and handed her to Cassia. "Cage her," he said. "But first wrap her in one of my shirts so she has my scent."

Cassia recoiled, stretching out both arms like she was holding a live grenade. "Gross, she licked me. Now I'm covered in her germs."

"Don't talk about her like that," the captain scolded.

"She doesn't speak English."

"But she can sense your feelings," he hissed. "Whether you like it or not, that creature is bonded to us. We're the only—"

"Family she's got," Cassia finished on a sigh. "I know, I know."

After she strode away, the captain gathered his crutch and asked Solara to inspect the engine room while he returned to the bridge to check the equipment readings. Doran volunteered to go with her, and together they followed the dim arrows down the stairs. His fingers kept curling around her waist, and she shot him a questioning look in the darkness.

"In case we hit more turbulence," he explained.

"You think you'll catch me?"

"Maybe. Or at least break your fall."

She removed his hand, holding on a few beats longer than necessary because her mind and body weren't on speaking terms. The truth was she craved his touch—so much that she sought it in her sleep. And that scared her. Because one day soon, she would be alone on Vega while he warmed someone else's bed.

"I don't want you to break my fall," she said, and continued ahead of him.

Just as she reached the auxiliary engine room door, the captain's voice crackled over the com system in a broken command. "Don't . . . inspection . . . geomagnetic storm . . . electrical systems . . . have to . . . planet-side until it passes."

The message was clear enough. They returned upstairs to strap in for a bumpy landing, then reconvened in the galley after touchdown.

"Where are we?" Kane asked, wiping spilled beans off the table.

Cassia took the rag from him and resumed cleaning the mess, her prayer necklace bobbing with each movement. "Is it breathable outside? Or will we need the suits?"

"No suits," Captain Rossi said. "We're on New Haven."

Solara felt her brows jump. "But that means we're—"

"In the outer realm," he finished. "And no, the Enforcers

can't touch us here. But don't get too excited. There's a reason they don't patrol these colonies."

Solara didn't argue, but that reason depended on who you asked. Politicians claimed the fringe was a drain on public resources, that the outer settlements didn't generate enough revenue to merit the protection of the police force. Others implied that the colonists had devolved into animals, and it wasn't safe to patrol there. But according to stories she'd heard, the real reason the Enforcers stayed away was because the fringe settlers refused to be controlled.

She liked that last reason the best, so that was what she chose to believe.

"I picked up a distress call from the northern settlement," Captain Rossi said. "Figured I'd check it out." He nodded at Solara. "Why don't you tag along and get a feel for this *new life* of yours."

Something in his tone put her on edge, but she nodded. She wanted to see how a fringe town operated.

"I'm coming, too," Doran said. He settled a hand on her shoulder, which she promptly shrugged off.

"Suit yourself," the captain told him. "But the shuttle's a two-seater, so you'll have to volunteer your lap." The captain hobbled toward his chamber and called over one shoulder, "If you've got any weapons on board, bring 'em—the bigger, the better."

Doran cut his eyes at her. "That doesn't bode well."

She agreed but didn't say so. Instead, she retrieved her hand-held stunner and told herself the captain was overreacting.

*   *   *

271

An hour later, she found out he wasn't.

"My god," Doran breathed, peering out the shuttle window at the decimated landscape below. His arms tightened around her waist, either as a protective gesture or from the shock; she couldn't tell which. "What happened here?"

Solara shifted on his lap and leaned closer to inspect the town, or what was left of it. She'd never seen destruction like this. Wood buildings were flattened, their timbers pounded to the dirt in splintered fragments. None of the ruins were charred by fire, and she didn't see any evidence of a flood. It looked as if a giant boot had simply descended from the heavens and stomped the settlement into the ground. Stranger still, the surrounding fields of leafy-green crops were untouched, including a reaping machine half covered in vines.

"A weapon, maybe?" she said.

The captain shook his head and steered the shuttle east. "A lightning spout."

"A what?"

"It's a side effect of sloppy terraforming. When the atmosphere's not stable, it causes weird storms. Like twisters that build up pressure and strike in a single bolt. See how the damage is contained?"

She nodded.

"That's how you can tell." He grumbled to himself and said, "The settlement brokers colonize these terraforms too soon. They lure folks out to the fringe with the promise of free acreage, then leave 'em stranded here for life . . . however long that lasts."

"Why don't the settlers go back?" Doran asked.

"With what money?" the captain said. "They sell everything they own for the broker's fee and a one-way ticket to the promised land. Once they get here, they spend whatever's left on seed, equipment, and the fuel to operate it. That doesn't leave much for transport fare."

"What about fuel?" Doran asked. "If you wanted to fill your tank here, how much would it cost?"

The captain shook his head. "Only a fool would do that."

"Humor me. How much per unit?"

"Not sure," Rossi said, lifting a shoulder. "At least a hundred credits, maybe more."

Doran's jaw dropped. "But it was only two credits on Obsidian."

"You're not on Obsidian anymore."

"That's price gouging," Doran said. "How do the settlers run their equipment?"

Solara recalled the mechanical reaper she'd seen abandoned in the field. "I guess they don't," she said, and her mind wandered to Vega. How long would they need a mechanic if they couldn't afford to use their machinery?

"Anyway," the captain went on. "Assuming the colonists hitched a ride back to Earth, they'd have nowhere to live, except crammed into a one-bedroom flat with a half dozen other families. That's why they left in the first place."

"And they can't make a life anywhere else," Solara said. "Not without money or a prearranged job." A chill gripped her stomach. Even if she found work in the tourist ring, that would put her within reach of the Enforcers and another felony charge. When faced with the choice between Vega and a prison settlement, she'd have to take her chances in the fringe. She told herself it would be okay, that she'd prepared for this.

It felt like a lie.

"So they stay," the captain said.

"And make the best of it," she finished. "Like I will."

Doran held her close with one hand while using the other to tug on his earlobe, something he only did after an argument or when he had to apologize to her. She wondered if he was worried about sharing her fate, assuming he couldn't clear the charges against him.

"It's all right," she whispered. "Your dad's probably got loads of money stashed away. I'm sure you won't end up crashing on my sofa."

He scrubbed a hand over his face as if he hadn't listened to a word she'd said, and then he refocused on the landscape. "If someone sent a distress call, there were survivors. Where's the nearest town? Maybe they went there."

"About a four-day walk south of where we landed the *Banshee*," the captain said. "But their wounded wouldn't be able to make the journey. They probably built a temporary camp." He pointed to a thin finger of smoke curling up from a vacant stretch of landscape with no structures or people in sight. "Like that one."

The captain landed the shuttle on a hilltop about twenty yards away, but instead of opening the side hatches, he raised an antique pistol for show, the kind that fired metal slugs instead of energy pulses.

"Ever shoot one of these?" he asked. When they shook their

heads, he handed them each a sheathed dagger. "Then tuck this in your belt. And don't be afraid to use it."

"I thought we were here to help," Doran said.

The captain strapped a pistol across his chest. "You've never tried to save a drowning man, have you?"

"No," Doran said, wrinkling his forehead. "What's that got to do with—"

"He panics," the captain interrupted. "Grabs on to you and pushes you under. He can't help it. He'll do anything for one more breath." Rossi pointed a second pistol at them before adding it to his holster. "Desperate people kill to survive. I'll do what I can for these settlers, but not at the expense of losing one of my own. Are we clear?"

They nodded.

"Good," he said, unlocking the hatch. "Now, watch each other's backs."

The noise of the shuttle had drawn a dozen survivors from their hiding places. The settlers blinked at them with bloodshot eyes that seemed to bulge from their skulls. So much filth covered their faces and matted their hair that Solara couldn't tell the men from the women, or even their ages. Their clothes hung in tatters from sharp, thin shoulders, and bony ankles jutted from torn trouser hems.

Whatever they'd been eating, there wasn't enough of it.

"Picked up your distress beacon," the captain said, making sure to open his jacket and display both pistols. "Might be able to transport your injured. How many are there?"

One person stepped forward and answered in a man's deep

timbre. "None. At least, not anymore. The last one bled out a few days ago."

"Survivors?"

"What you see here." The man hitched a thumb over his shoulder. "Plus fifty more in the dugouts."

Now that Solara paid attention, she noticed a few shelters excavated from the hillside behind the group, basically caves made of dirt. A small fire crackled in the center of camp, smoking a few strips of meat into jerky. Sudden movement caught her eye, and she spotted a mud-streaked child poking his head out of his cave to study her. The whites of his eyes grew when they met hers, but someone quickly snatched him out of view.

"If you want transport to the next settlement," Captain Rossi said, "we can probably arrange it."

"Thank you, friend," the man replied with a coolness that negated his words. "But we'll stay and rebuild. There's only a month till harvest, and the crop looks good this year. It'll get us through the winter."

"What will you eat in the meantime?" Rossi asked. "I don't see any livestock."

The man indicated the long red strips dangling over the fire. "We just butchered our last steer. The meat's well preserved."

"Will it be enough?"

One bony shoulder lifted in a shrug. "If not, the slave traders will come around soon. They always do. Our weakest will fetch a bushel of grain per head."

"You would sell your own people?" the captain asked, not sounding surprised.

"Better a life of servitude than death by starvation." A spark of inspiration lit the man's eyes, and he added, "We have widows. And orphan girls. They'd make excellent traveling companions for your crew. If you're willing to trade—"

"I don't deal in flesh."

The man looked taken aback, as if insulted by the quick dismissal. He tipped his dirty head and studied each of them in a way that raised the hairs at the back of Solara's neck. Then his gaze returned to the captain's pistols, and he asked, "How many are in your crew?"

Solara's pulse throbbed with fear because she knew what the man was thinking. Slave traders would pay a lot more than one bushel of grain for her, and an even higher price for a strong boy like Doran. She sensed the man sizing them up, calculating how many shots the captain could fire before he succumbed to an attack. She rested a hand on her knife hilt, but even armed, they were no match for a group of sixty.

On a whim, Solara rolled up her shirtsleeve to display her tattoo. "More than enough," she blurted. "Considering who we are."

Eyes went wide, and the group leader retreated a pace. As an outcast himself, he obviously recognized the symbol for the Brethren of Outcasts and knew its implications. Anyone bearing that mark belonged to a network of ruthless fighters. To provoke one was to provoke them all.

Doran caught on quickly and displayed his own wrist. He looked down his nose at the group and said in a menacing voice, "You've heard stories of Demarkus Hahn, the pirate chief with fists like sledgehammers. I'm the man who laid him flat and took his bride."

To validate his story, Solara gave a tight nod.

"He may rule the quadrant's inner circle," Doran went on, "but the fringe belongs to me. All Brethren in this realm will answer to Daro the Red." He cracked his knuckles and cocked his head to the side in a flawless imitation of the pirate lord. "Or else challenge me now, before these witnesses."

Nobody volunteered.

"We have no quarrel," the group leader said, taking another backward step as he lifted both hands in supplication. "Let's part as friends . . . and allies."

After pretending to think it over, Doran nodded as if he'd done the man a favor. Then they climbed inside the shuttle and didn't look back.

✳ ✳ ✳

Late that evening, when the *Banshee* was locked up tight and the rest of the crew slept in their bunks, Solara stood in front of the bedroom mirror and unfastened her braids with cold, clammy fingers. She couldn't stop picturing the bones that had protruded from the settlers' clothes, or the way their hollow eyes had made them look more like scarecrows than human beings.

Would a year on Vega do the same thing to her?

Yes, she realized. *If someone doesn't sell me first.*

The captain had warned her about this months ago, but she'd stubbornly clung to her dreams of independence and belonging—of being revered for the calluses on her palms and the grease under her fingernails. There was no freedom here— not really. She'd just traded one form of oppression for another.

Whether on Earth or on Vega, her life would never be anything more than a bare-knuckled fight to survive.

Tears welled in her eyes, but she blinked them away and focused on Doran's reflection in the mirror. She could tell his mind was somewhere else, too. He sat hunched on the edge of the bed, resting both elbows on his knees and staring at his hands. They were nice hands, strong and rough from months of labor, but she doubted he was really seeing them.

"You okay?" she asked. "You've been quiet tonight."

He flashed an empty grin, all lips and no eyes. "Just thinking."

"I *thought* I smelled smoke," she teased. When the joke didn't rouse him, she turned around and tipped his chin with an index finger. "What's wrong?"

He watched her for a moment, then shrugged. "I think I found my purpose in life."

The flippancy in his tone shocked a dry laugh out of her. "Is that all? Try not to act so excited. You might pull a muscle."

"There's nothing to be excited about. At least not yet. Discovering your purpose and making it happen are two different things."

His message hit home, and she dropped her gaze to the floor. Until today, she'd thought she had a purpose. Now she wasn't sure.

"I can make a difference here," Doran told her. "Just by putting an end to the price gouging. Think of the impact that cheaper fuel would have on the fringe—more crops, better technology, the freedom to travel off world. It would be a total game changer."

She glanced up at him and noticed a passion in his eyes she'd never seen before. Clearly he'd given this a great deal of thought. But his smile was sad when he added, "I could help people."

"What's the problem?"

"I can't do anything unless the Enforcers drop the charges," he said. "And even if the Spaulding board reinstates me, it could take months before we see changes in the fringe." He leaned forward and delivered a pointed look. "This place isn't safe. A lot of terrible things will happen before then. A lot could happen to *you*."

She'd managed to forget about Vega for a moment, and the reminder sent needles of anxiety prickling along her spine. "Don't worry about me. I'll be fine."

"No, you won't," he said. "And neither will I—not if you ask me to leave you here."

She shook her head. "You don't owe me anything."

"Actually, I do. But my motivations aren't that pure."

"What does that mean?"

"It means," he said, standing from the bed, "that if I clear my charges, I want you to come back to Earth and stay with me. For good."

"Stay with you?" For a brief second, her heart soared. But then she remembered the reason she'd left Earth in the first place. "And do what?"

"Anything you want."

"Have you forgotten about the fraud charges?"

"It was my credit account you used. I'll tell the investigators you had permission to buy whatever you wanted."

"But I'm only trained to do one thing," she said. "There

weren't enough mechanic jobs when I left, and nothing's changed since then."

"I'll make sure Spaulding hires you. We always need mechanics. Or if you want, I'll teach you another career, maybe product development. Then we can travel together like we do now."

"And how would that look?" She glanced at her tattooed knuckles and imagined what the gossip magazines would say: SPAULDING HEIR SLUMMING IT WITH LATEST FLING. "A convicted felon working side by side with the future company president?" She shook her head. "Are you even listening to yourself?"

"I'll hire a flesh forger to erase your record."

"But I still won't fit in. I'm not cultured or beautiful like your—"

"Stop saying that," he interrupted. "You *are* beautiful."

"*You* stop saying that," she fired back. "Because I know you don't mean it!"

His blue eyes flashed and he took a step closer, erasing the distance between them.

"Don't tell me what I mean," he said, his voice rough. "When I walk into a room, you're the only person I see. My brain doesn't get a choice anymore, because there's something inside you so rare it radiates out and blocks everyone else. You have the kind of beauty that can't be manufactured—the kind that comes from in here." He tapped a finger against her chest. "I didn't know what real beauty was before I met you, but I get it now. So trust me when I say you're the most breathtaking girl in my world."

Solara's eyes burned with tears. She tried blinking Doran

into focus, but something hot and painful welled inside her until his face became a wet blur.

"I like waking up in sheets that smell like you," he said, gentler this time. "And I like the little wrinkle that shows up between your eyes every time you look at me. When I think about giving that up, I can't breathe." He took her face between his warm, callused hands. "Today, when I imagined what it would feel like to leave you behind, I realized that I can't do it. And don't think I'm being noble."

"Doran," she whispered with a weak smile, "I would never accuse you of being noble."

"Then you know me." Smiling in return, he stroked her cheek with his thumb. "My reason is totally selfish—I need you. Wherever you are is where I want to be."

Solara shook her head as tears leaked down her cheeks. She wanted to believe him, but deep down she worried that he'd only grown attached to her out of isolation. Once he had other options, he might feel differently.

"You think that way now," she said, pulling away. "But that doesn't mean it's real. We've been through a lot together. It's normal to have feelings for someone when you're alone like this."

"So you think I fell in love with you by default?"

She nodded.

"You know," he said with a twinkle of amusement in his gaze, "I've never told a girl I loved her before. This is kind of a big deal for me, and you're ruining the moment."

That forced an undignified snort of laughter out of her. She used a sleeve to wipe both eyes and repeated what Doran had said weeks ago. "Not surprising. I'm an asshole like that."

He moved in close, capturing her face again. "Then we're a perfect match, aren't we?"

Before she could even draw a breath to answer him, Doran brushed her lips in a kiss that wiped her mind clean of everything but the electric thrill of his mouth on hers. At the barest contact, her insides did backflips, and when she rose onto tiptoe for more pressure, her blood simmered to a boil. Right then, she decided that their kiss behind the barn on Cargill didn't count. Because it hadn't made her feel anything like this—as if her skin were alive with energy and about to burst into fireworks.

This was their first kiss.

And if she thought that was mind-blowing, it was nothing compared to the moment their tongues met. Her nerve endings ignited, and what little control she had snapped in half. She wrapped both arms around his neck as his hand slipped under her shirt, and the next thing she knew, they were stumbling toward the bed and landing on their sides in a tangled heap.

While Doran caught his breath, he watched her beneath heavy lids, his gaze flickering like a blue flame. She saw the raw emotion on his face and felt it in the desperate press of his fingers. It was then that she finally believed him. Doran had given his heart to her. At the realization, something in her own heart shifted and grew, spreading outward until there wasn't room for anything else inside her chest.

"My answer is yes," she whispered.

Doran rolled her beneath him and interlaced one of their hands high above her head, gazing down at her with so much gratitude that it tightened her throat. "You'll come home with me, when all this is over?"

She nodded against the pillow, breathing in the scents of soap and oil vapors that their joined bodies had made. It was unique to them, and sweeter than any perfume implant in creation. "I'll go anywhere with you."

As she locked her legs around his waist, a shiver spread out from her navel all the way down to her toes. Soon their hips grew restless, and their breathing turned choppy. He whispered one more time that he loved her and lowered his mouth for a kiss.

After that, there was no more talking.

CHAPTER TWENTY-THREE

"Hand me the two-thirds hydraulic wrench, will you?" Solara asked, facedown in the shower's filtration system while her backside wiggled in the air, turning Doran's thoughts far from repair work. She must've known he wasn't paying attention, because she clarified, "The one with the blue handle."

"Uh-huh," he said, still staring.

"Doran!"

He tore his gaze away and handed her the blue wrench, then leaned forward and glanced over her shoulder to see if she was almost finished. The tangle of tubes beneath the floor looked like disemboweled innards, so the answer was probably no.

His shoulders slumped.

In the days since they'd waited for the geomagnetic storm to pass, Solara had taken it upon herself to give the *Banshee* a full tune-up—a nice gesture, but Doran was tired of sharing her with the ship. He kept daydreaming about whisking her away to someplace tropical, just the two of them. In his fantasies, life had returned to normal and he had full access to the Spaulding toys.

"Have you ever seen the ocean?" he asked.

"Once," she called over her shoulder. "The nuns took us on a day trip to Galveston. It rained the whole time, but we had fun. Sister Agnes let me bury her to the neck and sculpt her into a mermaid."

"I want to take you to the Caribbean," he said. "We'll borrow one of my dad's smaller yachts so we can drop anchor in the island shallows." That way they'd have total privacy—no hotels, no touristy beaches, not even a crew to disturb them. "We can snorkel and swim right off the boat."

"A personal yacht? What's next, a private shuttle?"

"Well, yeah," he said. "How else would we get to the marina to fetch the boat?"

Solara righted herself and leaned on one elbow, smiling at him. "If you're trying to spoil me, it won't work. I can earn my own keep."

He returned her smile while his whole heart melted. His feelings for her were nearly tangible, swelling like billows inside his rib cage, and he found himself constantly consumed by the need to express it. Each night he did his best to show how much he loved her—until they were breathless and weak—but it wasn't enough. He wanted to give Solara closets full of glistening ball gowns, to take her to exotic places and fill her belly with the finest foods. There was no better reward than seeing her happy, so from now on he was going to pamper her like it was his job.

"I'm highly motivated," he said. "So I suggest you don't fight it."

She leaned in for a quick kiss before returning to her work. "You're getting ahead of yourself. We might not be able to go back."

Doran frowned. He knew that better than anyone. "A guy can dream."

The captain's voice came over the *Banshee*'s intercom system and put an end to the reverie. "Looks like the worst of the storm has passed, so prepare for takeoff. We should arrive at Planet X by morning."

Planet X—the site of Doran's errand. That meant his ordeal was almost over, though whether it would end in his favor remained to be seen.

"Want to talk about that?" Solara asked.

"No," he said.

He didn't want to think about it, either. In the last few weeks, he'd nearly thought himself to death trying to puzzle out how to save himself and free his father. Now that he realized how many lives in the fringe depended on his return to Spaulding Fuel, he felt a weight on his shoulders so heavy that sometimes he caught himself stooping over. What if he failed? Or if someone else found out about the coordinates and beat him there?

No, he definitely didn't want to talk about it.

"Well, scratch that," Captain Rossi grumbled over the intercom. "The storm must've shorted the main transmitter. I don't want to lift off until it's fixed. Lara, can you come take a look?"

Solara hauled herself out of the coils of tubing beneath the floor. "Sure, just give me a minute."

"I think the parts are fried," the captain said. "Maybe you can salvage what we need from the other system."

"What other system?" she asked, scrunching her forehead.

"The emergency com. It's a decent backup, but between the two, I'd rather have the main transmitter running."

"I didn't know we have a backup."

"You're not supposed to. It's hidden under the console."

Solara shared a long, silent glance with Doran—one that told him they were both realizing they'd left a stone unturned during their search of the ship. As much as he didn't want to backtrack, he couldn't ignore the possibility that Kane had used the emergency com to alert the Enforcers.

"All right," Solara told the captain. "We're on our way."

Ten minutes later, Doran was lying underneath the pilot-house control panel, squinting at a tiny com screen while Solara rebooted the hardware from beside him.

The ancient screen blinked to life, asking him to input a recipient frequency. He wasn't accustomed to this operating system, so it took a few tries to navigate to the main menu, but once there, he tapped the SENT file and waited for the data to populate. Soon, pages of lines filled the screen, each one detailing a date, time, frequency, and length of transmission for every call that had left the *Banshee*. He scrolled through the previous month, looking for the signature Solar League code that ended in a series of zeroes.

As he searched the data, a sick feeling of foreboding uncurled in the pit of his stomach. It reminded him of the time he'd snooped on his first girlfriend and discovered her with another guy. Looking back, he hadn't needed the proof. His gut had told him something was wrong, and since then he'd learned to trust his instincts. Right now, those instincts told Doran he would find a government frequency in the ship's system.

And he did.

A brief, one-way transmission had been sent to the Enforcers weeks ago, on the morning he'd left to shuttle to Obsidian. He read the information twice and triple-checked the date until finally there was no denying it.

Kane had betrayed him.

Doran wasn't prepared for the blow that came next. An ache opened up behind his chest—the kind of pain that only a friend could inflict. But the suffering didn't last long. On the heels of that pain came a rage so hot it tunneled his vision and turned it red. He had barely enough forethought to duck out from beneath the console, and then all logic flew out the window. He didn't care about strategy or timing. All that mattered was finding an outlet for his fists, and he knew exactly where it would be.

Ignoring Solara's questions, he slammed aside the pilothouse door and flew down the stairs, not bothering to silence the clamor of his boots. A furious pulse pounded in his head, and he couldn't have held back if he wanted to. The scent of onions led him to the galley, where he paused in the doorway just long enough to scan past Cassia and Renny to the dreadlocked boy standing at the stove.

After that, Doran charged.

When Kane glanced over one shoulder, his eyes flew wide and he dropped his ladle to brace for impact. A microsecond later, their bodies collided with a rewarding smack that sent Kane stumbling backward into the storage wall. Cabinets shook, sending loose tin cups clattering to the floor while voices bellowed from behind Doran. Kane flailed both arms in a struggle to right himself, but Doran didn't give him the chance. Bracing one hand against the wall, he sank his opposite fist into Kane's stomach, then drew back to deliver a right hook to the jaw.

Doran's knuckles screamed at the impact of bone on bone, but he ignored the burn. He'd just wound up for another blow when a powerful set of arms locked around his chest and dragged him back toward the table.

"Enough," Renny said in his ear. Doran thrashed and kicked like an animal. He landed his boot so hard in the oven door that it left a dent, but he couldn't escape the hold. Renny was stronger than he looked. "That's enough," he repeated. "Don't make me stun you."

Doran's eyes locked on Kane, who had the nerve to glare back at him. Kane dabbed at his bloody lip and demanded, "What the hell's wrong with you?"

"What's wrong with *me*?" Doran shouted, and fought to free himself again. He struggled in vain until all the hurt and anger welling up inside him crested like a wave. "I know what you did, you asshole!" he yelled. "I know it was you!"

He noticed a flicker of awareness on Kane's face, followed by the unmistakable look of a guilty man realizing he'd been caught. Kane shook his head but didn't try to deny what he'd done. He only opened and closed his mouth without sound, proving that for once, he couldn't charm his way out of a problem.

The captain appeared in the doorway with Solara by his side.

He surveyed the dishes scattered across the galley and pointed his crutch at the dented stove. "Sounds like Armageddon in here. Someone better start talking."

"Go ahead," Doran said to Kane. "Tell them." His voice went hollow as all the fight inside him died. Since he'd quit struggling, Renny released him. "Tell them how you sold me out for the reward."

Something in Kane's expression hardened, almost as if he was proud of what he'd done. Folding both arms, he admitted, "Yeah, it was me. I did it for the money. And I'm not sorry, either."

While jaws dropped and silence blanketed the galley, Cassia stepped in front of Kane, shaking her head at him. "Stop it," she ordered, and then faced Doran. "He didn't turn you in. I was the one who made the call."

"Don't listen to her," Kane said, nudging her aside. "I did it."

Cassia whirled on him, curling her tiny hands into fists. "Shut up, Kane! I don't need you to protect me!"

"You don't think so? Because my busted lip says otherwise!"

The captain put a stop to the nonsense by slamming his crutch on the floor and bellowing, "What in damnation is going on?"

"That's what I want to know," Doran said. "It wasn't an accident when the Enforcers found me on Obsidian. Someone told them I'd be there."

"That someone was me," Cassia said. "Kane had nothing to do with it. I didn't tell him at first, but as soon as he found out, he tried to help you by—"

"Piloting the shuttle," Solara finished. "That's why he

volunteered. I practically had to arm-wrestle the job away from him."

Cassia nodded, keeping her eyes fixed on Doran. "He was going to take you somewhere safe and pretend the shuttle was broken until the Enforcers left."

"But why?" Doran asked. "What did I ever do to you?" He knew it shouldn't matter—either way he had a knife in his back—but he needed to know. "Do you hate me that much?"

"I don't hate you at all."

"You have a funny way of showing it."

"Believe it or not, I had good intentions," Cassia said. "I thought you were soft, that you were just a pampered rich boy who didn't understand how dangerous life is out here." She glanced down at her feet. "Because that's exactly how I was when I left home. I thought it would be best if the Enforcers took you back to Earth. So you'd be out of harm's way."

Doran scoffed. He didn't believe for one second that her reasons were so pure. "You were doing me a favor? I can't wait to repay you."

Kane placed a hand on Cassia's shoulder. "Give her a break. There was more to it than that."

"Of course there was," Doran said. "I'm not an idiot."

"You don't know what's at stake," Cassia told him. "If the Daeva catch you—"

"They'll torture me to death," Doran interrupted. "I already know that."

"No, they won't." She peeked up, her eyes full of fear. "They'll torture you until you tell them where I am."

Doran cocked his head to make sure he'd heard her right.

"It's my name on the contract," Cassia went on. "Mine and Kane's. But he didn't do anything wrong, except stand by me. If the Daeva catch us, they'll kill him, and then they'll take me home for something even worse."

"Why?" asked Solara. "What did you do?"

For a few beats, Cassia seemed to struggle for her next words. It wasn't until Kane took her hand that she told them, "I ran away from Eturia and started a war."

"It wasn't her fault," Kane said. "Two of the ruling families have been at each other's throats for ages. The war is way overdue."

"But my marriage was supposed to stop it," Cassia muttered, her gaze fixed on the floor. "My parents called a meeting with the enemy house. They agreed to join our families by promising me to a prince named Marius." Her upper lip hitched. "I wanted nothing to do with him. I threw a dozen fits, but my parents wouldn't budge. They said I was being selfish—that it was my duty to bring an end to all the fighting. We argued about it for months. At one point, we quit talking. Then the week before the wedding, my parents hosted a banquet for Marius, and I overheard him telling one of his men that he didn't want anything to do with me, either. And his family's goal wasn't peace. He was supposed to marry me, then kill my father so he'd rule both kingdoms."

"Not to mention," Kane added, "scoop out Cassy's melon and turn her into a puppet."

Cassia nodded. "His family invented the same technology the Daeva use to block their prefrontal cortex. They had it all figured out—the perfect takeover. But when I told my father, he didn't believe me. I guess after all the tantrums, he thought I was pulling another stunt to delay the wedding." Her eyes met Kane's, and she gave him a weary smile. "So I went to my best friend and asked for help. He dropped everything and followed me out the door, even though his clerk's apprenticeship was almost finished."

Kane squeezed her hand. "Palace life was overrated anyway."

"A few weeks later, we met the captain," she said. "We were begging for work at every port, and he was the only one to take us—"

"Wait a minute," Doran said, rubbing his temples. "This is all very touching, but what does any of it have to do with selling me out to the Enforcers?"

"I panicked and I made a mistake," Cassia told him. "I thought you'd be easy to break, or you'd lead the Daeva to us." She splayed both hands in an unspoken apology, but it didn't escape Doran's notice that she hadn't bothered to say she was sorry. "I was wrong. You're tougher than I gave you credit for."

"Here's a news flash, Your Highness," Doran snapped, his anger building again. "You're more of a threat to this crew than I ever was. If you wanted someone thrown off the ship, you should've started with yourself."

"Hey, back off," Kane warned. "She said she was wrong. There's no harm done."

"No harm done?" Doran repeated with a glare at Kane. "Do you really believe the words coming out of your mouth, or are you just desperate to score with your princess?"

Kane puffed up like a bear and took two threatening steps forward. "Don't talk about her like that."

"You hypocrite," Doran spat. "And I'll say whatever the hell I want!"

Renny wedged himself between them and shoved in opposite directions. "Knock it off, both of you," he said. "This has gone far enough. Either shake hands so we can discuss this like adults, or I'm putting you on lockdown."

Doran narrowed his eyes. He wanted to give Kane a good shake, but by way of his throat, not his hand.

"Fine, then," Renny said. "Back to your quarters. You first, Kane." When all that moved was Kane's flaring nostrils, Renny barked, "That's an order!" Once Kane had charged away and slammed his door, Renny nodded at Doran and told him to do the same. "And don't come out," Renny called, "until you're both ready to make nice."

* * *

It wasn't until six hours later that hunger forced them out of their rooms for a stiff handshake and a round of meaningless apologies. As far as Doran was concerned, he would coexist with Cassia and Kane, but their friendship was over.

Dinner that night was more awkward than a hug from death.

Nobody made eye contact, and the only sounds were the scrapes of utensils against plates. Even Acorn seemed to sense the tension. She hid inside the captain's pocket throughout supper, occasionally reaching out a paw for a new raisin.

Halfway through the meal, the captain cleared his throat. "Listen," he said to no one in particular. "Everyone panics and makes stupid choices, even me. I'm still wanted on Earth for desertion in the last war." He glanced at Doran and asked, "Did I ever tell you that?"

Reluctantly, Doran shook his head. He could tell a lecture was coming, and he was in no mood to hear it.

"I was about your age," the captain said. "It was the night before my first battle, and I was piss-scared. Got up from my bunk and told the sergeant I had to use the latrine, then ran away without bothering to put on my pants." He grunted to himself. "Let me tell you, there's not much worse than turning tail in your underwear."

Doran poked at his dinner and tried to imagine the stone-cold captain running away from a fight. He couldn't picture it.

"I couldn't go home and face my father," Rossi continued. "So I joined a crew and ended up out here. Never saw my folks after that, but I swore I'd never shame them again. And I'm proud to say I kept my word." He fed Acorn another raisin and said, "We're all allowed a moment or two of weakness. Everyone makes mistakes."

"True," Doran agreed, and shut down the sermon with his next words. "But some mistakes are bigger than others."

After that, Renny wisely changed the subject. "Whose turn is it tonight?"

The captain jerked his spoon toward Kane.

"Do you have a question ready?" Renny asked.

"Yeah, I've got one," Kane said out of the corner of his mouth. He took a swig of water and set down his cup, pausing until Doran looked at him. There was still plenty of resentment in Kane's eyes. "Would you rather ruin the lives of two innocent strangers," he asked, "or watch someone you love die a violent death?"

The subtext behind that question was about as subtle as a pipe bomb. Doran brought his mug to his lips and tipped it back, refusing to be the first person to answer. When the rest of the crew chimed in, everyone gave the same response. If given the hypothetical choice, they wouldn't hesitate to sacrifice innocent lives to protect the one they loved. The captain went a step further, reminding them of the settlers on New Haven and how he'd placed the safety of his crew above that of an entire village.

All eyes landed on Doran for his answer. He felt Solara squeeze his hand under the table, and when she peered up at him with that dimpled grin, he was forced to admit to himself that he would have done the same thing in Cassia's and Kane's position. That didn't mean he trusted them, and it didn't mean he was ready to forgive. But he gave a begrudging nod along with his answer.

"That's what I thought," Kane said, and returned his attention to his bowl. "You're no different from us."

CHAPTER TWENTY-FOUR

Much as Doran had expected, Planet X was a frozen wasteland.

Its distant sun, visible as a pinprick of warmth on the horizon, cast a slanted glow over the landscape that seemed to create more shadow than light. The contrast allowed him to see that its hills were made from belts of ice stacked into tiny steps. Everywhere else, the terrain was relatively flat, dented with shallow pockmarks that reminded him of a scarred face. If any useful or dangerous ore existed down there, he'd need an industrial drill to find it.

What did his father expect him to do at these coordinates?

As Doran stood in the pilothouse and scanned the desolate panorama, it became clear there were no signs of life down there—plant or animal. And yet the *Banshee*'s sensors detected enough electrical current to power a town. Something was lying to him, either the equipment or his eyes.

"When was the last time you had your sensors checked?" he asked the captain.

"There's nothing wrong with my equipment," Rossi said, stroking his beard and staring out the windshield with a frown. "If we're picking up a charge, there's machinery running."

"Maybe it's cloaked," Doran said. "Or buried underground."

They ran a scan for metals and detected a disk embedded in the ice near the heart of the power source. From the computer's preliminary sketch, it appeared to be an air-lock hatch, which supported his theory that something was operating beneath the planet's surface.

"Whatever's down there must be huge," the captain mused. "It's using a ton of juice."

"Try to land by the hatch," Doran said. "I'm going to suit up and see if I can get inside."

"Take Renny and Kane with you," the captain told him. "Armed, just in case."

Doran hesitated. He didn't want Kane anywhere near him. "I can manage without—"

"Renny *and* Kane," the captain repeated. "That's not up for debate."

Doran knew better than to argue.

He made his way to the cargo level, and by the time the *Banshee* alighted on the planet's surface, the three of them were securing oxygen helmets to their pressurized suits.

To test out the suit's com-link, Doran glanced at Renny and warned, "I don't know what's down there, but I think Infinium might be a weapon. And if I'm right, whoever's building it won't appreciate a visit."

"Not a problem," Renny said. "We've got your back."

Kane froze for a second while pulling on his gloves. His lips tightened beneath the fiberglass helmet, but he nodded in agreement. Renny handed them each a pistol, and after strapping the weapons to their hips, they exited the ship.

The insulated suits didn't do much to keep out the chill, and even with weights at their ankles, their boots slipped and skidded over the icy ground as they fought their way toward the hatch. A fierce wind howled across the stark landscape, fighting their every move and creating a creepy whistle when mixed with the steady release of oxygen inside Doran's helmet. By the time they reached the hatch, his skin was covered in goose bumps, more from the eerie surroundings than the temperature.

They couldn't find an automatic switch, so Doran grabbed the manual lever and tugged it aside while Kane hauled open the thick metal door. One by one, they descended the ladder leading to the air-lock chamber. Doran was about to close the hatch when a new helmet appeared out of nowhere, and he flinched, nearly losing his grip on the steel rung.

It was Solara.

"There's no way I'm missing this," she said through the com-link.

Doran exhaled in relief. She'd promised to stay behind until they knew it was safe, but secretly he was glad to have her here. "Fine, but hurry. That wind is killing me."

After she descended the ladder and closed the hatch, they flipped on the oxygen switch and listened to the low hum of heated air filling the chamber. A green light flashed to indicate optimal pressure and oxygen saturation, and a door in the chamber wall clicked ajar. Doran removed his helmet and hooked it to the utility belt on his hip, then pulled open the door and peeked through to the other side.

"It looks like a bunker," he said, taking in the concrete walls and floors of the dimly lit hallway. It led to a corner about ten yards ahead, then continued to the right. He noticed the slightly stale scent of recycled air, but nothing out of the ordinary. No reek of decay or musty odor of neglect. But despite that, his instincts told him this place was no oasis.

"I don't see anyone." He cocked one ear and added, "Or hear anything."

A computerized voice called out from the chamber ceiling, making everyone jump in shock. "Interior air-lock port closing in ten seconds," it said, and began counting backward.

Doran shared a nervous glance with the others. Because it seemed they had no choice but to continue or turn back, they made their way inside the corridor and removed their helmets as the air-lock door sealed behind them. In tentative steps, Doran led the way into the bunker. As soon as he rounded the corner, motion sensors activated a strip of overhead lights, causing him to shield his eyes from the brightness.

Solara squinted while hooking her helmet to her belt. "These sensors might report to a centralized system," she warned. "We should be prepared for company."

"Draw your weapons," Renny told them. "But set the safety catch."

Having never used a pistol before, Doran had to watch Kane

to learn what to do. He removed his gloves and used a thumb to flick a switch near the trigger, then fisted the weapon and continued down the empty hallway.

After turning two more corners, they reached a set of double doors bolted from the outside. Without a glass pane or any labeling, there was nothing to indicate where they led. Doran glanced down the hallway at another corner, torn between continuing on and staying to investigate.

"You and Solara stay here and check it out," Renny suggested, nodding at the doors. "Kane and I will see what's down that way."

"Sounds good," Doran said, even though he didn't like the idea of separating. He agreed to check in using the suits' comlink, and then watched half the group walk away.

Solara took his hand and gave it a fortifying squeeze. Together they unlocked the bolt and inched open the doors while Doran pointed his pistol inside. The motion triggered another set of overhead lights, and a wide room came into view. His eyes automatically scanned for life, and when he found the room empty, he allowed himself to look closer.

The space was pristine, with white walls and glossy tiled floors. Several tables stood along the perimeter, covered in computers, microscopes, and an assortment of machinery. It didn't take long to figure out the room's purpose.

"It's a lab," he said.

Solara peeked around his shoulder. "What kind? Medical?"

"I don't know." Since it seemed safe, he holstered his gun and entered the room. "Let's find out."

They explored opposite halves of the room, starting at the

entrance and working their way toward the back. As Doran moved from one table to the next, he detected a familiar scent, something that plucked at his memories of his internship with new product development. The smell was slightly sharp and metallic, like melting ore. Then he noticed a glass-paned furnace in the wall with a chunk of metal burning inside, and everything clicked into place.

"I've seen this before," he said. "It's fuel development."

"Not just any fuel." The sudden flatness in Solara's tone prompted him to face her. She trailed her index finger along a data tablet affixed to the wall and added, "The one you're accused of stealing."

He rushed to her side and glanced at the screen, instantly spotting the word *Infinium* in several places on the page. The rest of the text was a nonsensical jumble of numbers and formulas, so he tapped the panel and returned to the main data directory.

He found a file called G.S. INFINIUM LABORATORY JOURNAL and selected it, then scrolled through the entries while Solara read along with him.

G.S. ENTRY #1: Solar Day 3, Cycle 9. Discovered Highly Unstable Ore With Unusually Long-Burning Properties.

"Look." Doran pointed at a small clear bag of rocks resting on the table, labeled INFINIUM RAW ORE SAMPLES. "It's like I said. I'll bet my father found out how dangerous this was and wanted it destroyed."

The next several entries confirmed his theory as the scientist detailed the challenges involved with stabilization. On its own, the metal was highly combustible to the point of weaponry use. But then the journal took a different turn. After several months of trial and error, G.S. found a combination of additives that allowed the ore to ignite and generate energy without exploding. Once the process was complete, he named the new matter Infinium, because it seemed to burn eternally.

G.S. ENTRY #243: Infinium is now stable, but its temperature output is too high for use in current engine systems.

They'd just scrolled through another week's report when the com-link in their suits activated, and Renny's voice crackled from inside their collars.

"Report back," he said. "You two okay?"

"We're fine," Doran answered. "We found the Infinium lab, and we're getting caught up on the data files. How about you?"

"There's a private residence down here," Renny said. "Stocked with—"

"More like a mansion," Kane cut in. "This place is swank. Theater screens in every bedroom, a full gym, showers so big you could drown. There's even a heated pool with sun lamps and a beach simulator."

"It's true," Renny said. "I've never seen anything like it."

"Is the house abandoned?" Solara asked.

"It don't think so," Renny said. "There are dishes in the sink and food in the cooler, but we haven't seen a soul."

"Neither have we," Doran added, feeling the urge to check behind him. No one was there, but that didn't put his anxiety to rest.

"The hangar is empty, so whoever lives here may have flown off world," Renny said. "Keep your eyes peeled, and we'll check in again soon."

Doran exchanged a heavy glance with Solara. The posh living quarters, the hidden lab. Clearly his father had rewarded someone lavishly to stay here and experiment with Infinium, far from the reach of the Solar League. But nothing about the data led Doran to believe there was a weapon of mass destruction here.

He leaned in and skimmed the screen until he found the next entry describing the scientist's progress. It took several months, but G.S. finally created a sample of Infinium that was interchangeable with Spaulding fuel.

G.S. ENTRY #360: To test compatibility, I rewired our compound's power source to the ignition tank in the lab, fueled by a twelve-ounce sample of Infinium. The outcome was successful with no interruptions in energy supply. I will document the time lapse until the sample is depleted.

Doran scrolled through the next two months' entries but couldn't find any indication that the original sample had run out. He turned and stared across the room at the hunk of rock burning inside the laboratory tank, then had to force himself to blink.

"You mean to tell me," he said, "that a tiny rock has been powering this whole complex? For *months*?"

Solara touched his arm. "If it's true, think about what this means."

He didn't need prompting. His mind was already reeling with the implications of Infinium on the open market. A lump of this super-fuel would burn a lifetime in the farming machines that now lay dormant on fields across the outer realm. Homes would stay heated for generations. Travel expenses would plummet, opening new trade routes and freeing settlers to come and go as they pleased. Commerce would flourish, and lives would be saved.

Infinium had the power to change everything.

But what none of this told him was why his father had sent him here or how his DNA had ended up on the supply crate. All Doran knew was that he'd never touched these samples. He glanced around the lab until he noticed a strand of long jet-black hair on the floor, and an idea came to mind. Using a pair of tweezers, he picked up the hair and carried it to the lab's genetic scanner.

"Let's find out who G.S. is," Doran said.

After he inserted the sample, the machine buzzed for several minutes, and the words MATCH FOUND scrolled across the screen. He tapped the DISPLAY option and leaned closer, pulse ticking in anticipation. But when the result flashed on the panel, his own face stared back at him, along with the text DORAN MICHAEL SPAULDING, HOUSTON, TEXAS: EARTH.

"That can't be right," he said. "You saw that hair—it's not mine."

"Has your hair ever been that long?" Solara asked. "Maybe someone planted it here."

"No, never."

"Then we have to assume it's your genetic code."

"But it's not."

"Are you sure?" Solara dipped her head and peered at him intently. "Doran," she said with a gentle touch of her hand. "Think about it. A long time ago, there was someone who shared your DNA. I think he's the one who invented Infinium, or at least that he handled the crate your father supposedly stole from the Solar League transport."

Doran's twin? The implication was so absurd that he nearly laughed. "My brother's gone. We found his body."

"Did you see the remains?"

"Of course not. I was nine years old."

"What was his name?" she asked. "You never told me."

"Gage," he said. As soon as the word left his lips, the hair along his forearms stood on end. "Gage Spaulding."

"The initials fit. It *all* fits."

"No," Doran whispered. "That's crazy."

He shook his head again and again, never stopping, because denial was the only way to bat down the prickle of hope quickly swelling inside him. He couldn't afford to hope. It would only hurt that much more when reality set in again. His brother couldn't be alive, otherwise Doran would have sensed it somehow. And what about his parents? If their other son had survived, they'd know it, and they would never keep a secret like that from him.

Solara was wrong. She had to be.

But then the lab doors swung open and revealed something that shifted his very center of gravity. Renny and Kane strode inside with their hands folded behind their heads, both of them forced forward at gunpoint by a furious, distorted mirror image of himself.

At once, a memory washed over Doran—an emotional snapshot from his childhood that he'd nearly forgotten. On the night he was snatched from his bed, he recalled lying blindfolded on the cold floor of a shuttle and holding his brother's hand. Fear had choked him in tandem with a musty rag shoved inside his mouth, but the grip of Gage's fingers had kept Doran grounded, connected to something safe and familiar.

Now those fingers were curled around a pulse pistol.

Doran had to remind himself to breathe. Impossible as it seemed, Gage Spaulding was alive and well. But how much of the boy Doran remembered was still in there?

CHAPTER TWENTY-FIVE

"G age," Doran whispered, his body as stiff and motionless as a tomb.

The twin's eyes moved toward the sound of his name, then flew wide in a way that told Solara this encounter was just as shocking for him as it was for the rest of them. He studied his brother, no doubt taking in the subtle differences that set them apart. Gage's skin had the slightly golden hue of someone who bathed in artificial light instead of natural sun, with a silver web of scar tissue tugging down the corner of his left eye. He wore his hair in a low ponytail that disappeared behind a pair of broad shoulders that could pass for Doran's. And both of them had the same arrogant tilt to their chins, the one she'd taken months to recognize as a defense mechanism. Each boy peered at the other through an identical mask of reserved wonder, as if afraid to believe what their eyes were telling them. The similarities were uncanny.

Except this twin knew how to wield a gun.

When Doran took a step toward his brother, Gage aimed at him and warned in a shaky voice, "Drop your pistol and stay back. I'm pretty sure I know why you're here."

Doran tossed his weapon to the floor and held both palms forward. His mouth seemed to have stopped working, because it took a few tries before he spoke. "How are you alive?"

Gage faltered, as if the question had caught him off guard. "The same way you're alive. I got out of the house before it burned down."

"But we buried you. There was a body."

Gage didn't look too surprised to hear that. He glanced away from his brother, staring thoughtfully at the discarded pistol before picking it up and tucking it inside his waistband. "The body wasn't mine. I ran for two blocks and hid behind a garbage bin. That's where Mom found me. She wanted to keep me safe from Dad, so she let him think I was dead. But she said you knew our secret. She never mentioned it to you?"

"Never mentioned it?" Doran echoed. "She sat next to me at your funeral." For a long time afterward, Doran went very still and quiet. His eyes were shimmering with unshed tears when he finally broke the silence. "And then she left me with Dad and brought you here to live with her for all these years. Because you were the science prodigy, not me. I was just average. I wasn't . . ."

Useful to her.

Solara didn't need to hear the final words—they were written on Doran's face. Her heart broke as she watched him try to blink away the moisture welling in his eyes. Abandonment was one thing, but his mom had left him in favor of another child. Solara had never told anyone, but that was the real reason she refused to seek out her birth parents. She couldn't bear the possibility that they'd started a new family without her.

"Is Mom here now?" Doran asked, and wiped a sleeve across his eyes.

Gage shook his head.

"Good," Doran muttered. He swallowed hard, his gaze turning sharply to ice. "As far as I'm concerned, she died that day instead of you."

That seemed to ruffle Gage's feathers. His chin jerked up, along with the barrel of his pistol. "Watch your mouth."

"You're defending her?" Doran asked, flinching back like he'd been slapped. "She faked your death and kept us apart for almost a decade. And for what? To take revenge on Dad? To invent the perfect fuel and drive him out of business? It's sick!"

Solara agreed. The Spauldings made her glad to be an orphan.

"And Dad's a total saint, right?" sneered Gage.

"Maybe not, but he's a victim in all this, too."

"A victim?" Gage snapped, rage burning behind his eyes. "He knows me! Mom let me call him months ago, to tell him about what I created—how Infinium was going to change everything, and how the Solar League paid a fortune for my first batch. But do you think he asked me to come home?" Gage made a noise of disgust. "No. He begged me to bury the project, just like Mom said he would. He told me Infinium would make Spaulding Fuel redundant and ruin the family legacy. When I refused to play along, he stole the batch from the transport.

Then he traced our location and threatened to send someone here, either to destroy my research or to steal it; he didn't say which." Gage's voice sounded broken when he added, "I just didn't know it would be my own brother."

Doran's shoulders sank. He had to be reeling with the fact that not only were both his parents liars, but also that the future he'd envisioned no longer existed. Once Spaulding Fuel collapsed, there would be no company to inherit.

"And here you are," Gage said flatly. "In my lab, looking through my computer. Mom told me you were just like Dad. I guess she was right about that, too."

"No," Doran told him. "Dad sent me here, but I had no idea why. I would never destroy your work. The fringe needs it too much."

"Right." Clearly unconvinced, Gage flicked his aim at Solara, then at Renny and Kane. "Who are your friends?"

Before any of them could answer, the com-link speakers activated, and Captain Rossi called through their suits, "Time to wrap it up. Cassia found a tracker on the *Banshee*'s front landing gear. I'm guessing someone on New Haven planted it there to claim the reward for Daro the Red. So far the skies look clear, but who knows how long that'll last."

Solara went cold. "We have to go," she told Gage. "Now."

"She's right," Doran said. "There's a pirate named Demarkus on the way, and you don't want to meet him while you're wearing my face."

Gage lifted his pistol. "Nobody's going anywhere. Not until I figure out what to do with you."

Her pulse hammering, Solara glanced around the lab for

a weapon to use against Gage or a way to distract him long enough to make it back to the ship. Her gaze landed on the bag of Infinium ore samples, and she made a snap decision. With one hand, she snatched the bag off the table and dashed out the open doors and into the hall, hoping Gage was smart enough not to shoot her and risk blowing them all into next week.

She heard the stomp of boots and the metallic clang of a bolt sliding into place. Glancing over her shoulder, she saw that Gage had locked everyone inside the lab. He'd set down his pistol and was pulling on an insulated suit with the kind of speed that prompted her feet to move faster.

While she ran, she stuffed the ore samples in her suit pocket and fastened her oxygen helmet. If she could reach the ship before Gage, she and the captain might be able to disarm him and free the others. She beat him into the air-lock chamber and shut the interior door, then wasted no time in climbing the ladder to the surface. With a mighty heave, she pushed open the top hatch and stepped outside.

Instantly, she froze in place. The pirates were already there.

At least a dozen mismatched shuttles had landed in a circle surrounding the *Banshee*, whose lowered cargo ramp showed that she'd been boarded. Solara's heart jumped, and she darted glances in every direction looking for Cassia and the captain. The fact that he hadn't warned her through the com-link suggested the pirates had captured him.

Or worse.

But there was no sign of the crew . . . or of anyone.

Gage caught up with her, but she ignored the pistol pressed against her ribs and pointed at the night sky, where a distant moon illuminated the pirates' tank of a ship hovering just outside the planet's gravitational pull. She was about to explain when an iron hand settled on her shoulder, and she whirled around so quickly that she landed on her backside. That same hand smacked the pistol from Gage's grip and sent it flying.

With pain radiating from her tailbone, Solara craned her neck to take in seven solid feet of muscle encased in a thermal space suit. She couldn't hear Demarkus's voice, but she watched his lips curve in a familiar smile, equal parts charming and chilling. Those lips moved in a phrase she recognized easily.

"Hello, little bird."

CHAPTER TWENTY-SIX

*I*t took Doran and the crew twenty minutes to remove the lab doors from the hinges with a screwdriver they'd found in a drawer, twice as long as it should've taken because the shock of everything Doran had just learned was making his hands clumsy.

He couldn't think straight. Nothing made sense anymore. The mother he'd missed for half his life cared more about vengeance than her own children. The father he'd idolized since he was old enough to toddle in the man's footsteps had placed the family business ahead of his actual family. And Gage. The dead had risen. It was all too much to take in.

"Doran!" Kane snapped his fingers an inch from his face. "Wake up!"

Doran blinked, suddenly alert as he followed Renny and Kane into the hallway. He couldn't afford to let his thoughts distract him, not if he wanted to reach Solara. She was counting on him to keep a clear head, and he wouldn't let her down.

"The com-link's dead," Kane announced, tapping the button on his chest.

"Then someone shut down the system," Renny said darkly. "And the only way to do that is from the pilothouse."

That was all Doran needed to hear. He donned his oxygen helmet, and the three of them jogged toward the air-lock chamber. By the time he crawled onto the planet's surface, he was tensed and ready for a fight.

Fists raised, he spun in a circle . . . and found nobody.

He lowered his arms, confused as he glanced to and fro. The icy landscape looked exactly the same as when he'd left it. Nothing seemed out of the ordinary—until he turned his gaze skyward and noticed the pirate ship looming overhead, its hangar door closing behind a convoy of shuttlecraft. Then realization hit, and the fear of losing Solara and Gage caused him to push so quickly to his feet that he expected to rocket to the moon.

With a firm shake, Renny redirected his attention to the *Banshee* and her shuttle, still docked on the opposite side of the air-lock hatch. Doran's legs moved to run, but Renny jerked him to a stop and used two fingers to communicate *We'll check it out first.*

Once Doran forced himself to calm down, he nodded in agreement. Pirates weren't likely to leave behind anything useful, like a ship and all her cargo. Some of them were probably still here.

Renny led the way to the boarding ramp. Once they reached the bottom, Doran peered inside and caught a glimpse of movement. He quickly drew back, but not before the two pirates rummaging inside the cargo hold had spotted him. One shouted to the other, and they clomped down the metal ramp to investigate.

Doran's heart lodged in his throat, and he backed into Kane, who was futilely glancing around for a place to hide. There was nothing to conceal them, not even a boulder.

While they continued backing away, Renny ducked beneath the ramp until the men passed him by. Then he climbed up behind the pair and crept silently toward them. In the time it took Doran to blink, Renny swiped a pistol from one man's holster. The pirates spun around, and he instantly shot them both in the chest. Before the smoke had even cleared, he used hand signals to announce that he was going inside and disappeared up the ramp.

Doran tried not to notice the steam rising from the bodies. He took the other man's gun while Kane pilfered himself a pair of knives, and they joined Renny in scouring the *Banshee*. After searching every crevice of the ship and finding no other scavengers, they met in the bridge to discuss what to do next.

Boots paced the floor, none of them able to stand still.

"We can't spend any more time here," Doran said, tapping a nervous finger against the helmet latched to his hip. "We have to go right now. Demarkus could be—"

"Agreed," Kane cut in. "Let's get airborne and figure it out as we go."

Renny tried reasoning with them, lifting a hand. "We're up against a fully armed battleship, and the only weapon we have is the element of surprise. That's why I haven't activated the com-link yet. If we go off half-cocked, we don't stand a chance. We can't help anyone if we're dead."

Doran understood, but he couldn't stand around while Demarkus killed everyone he loved. There was a simple solution, and it would only work if they hurried. "It's me Demarkus wants. So take me to him."

"Out of the question," Renny objected, pulling off his glasses to rub his eyes. "Demarkus is smarter than you think. He won't let anyone go; it would make him look weak."

"I'll make sure they get out," Doran said.

Kane arched a curious brow. "How?"

"They have to be suited up, right? Otherwise they couldn't have boarded the pirates' shuttle," Doran pointed out. "If they still have their oxygen helmets, I can—"

"Flush them out an air-lock, or an open hangar," Kane finished, shifting his gaze to Renny. "It could work if you're there to pick them up in the *Banshee*."

"I'm hearing a lot of *ifs* in this plan," Renny said.

Ignoring him, Kane turned to Doran. "I'm coming with you."

Doran shook his head. "We need you in the shuttle to collect anyone Renny misses."

Kane gnawed on the inside of his cheek, silently turning the idea over until he locked eyes with Doran and made a single demand. "Promise you'll watch after Cassy. I know what she did to you was wrong, but—"

"I'll bring her back," Doran said. "Or die trying."

"All right. Then I'm in."

Kane extended his hand, and for the second time since their fight, Doran shook it. But this gesture was more than an empty peace offering. When they clasped palms, a look of understanding passed between them, an unbreakable trust that they would do whatever it took to bring their people home.

CHAPTER TWENTY-SEVEN

Solara peered out the multipassenger shuttle window and watched the pirates' hangar door close. It didn't seem so long ago that she'd entered this ship willingly. Now she would eject herself into empty space if given the chance. She didn't want to be here when Demarkus realized he'd nabbed the wrong twin.

Glancing at her lap, she strained both wrists against her bindings, but they held firm and delivered a light electric shock as punishment. She jumped in her seat, bumping Gage's shoulder and drawing the gazes of Cassia and Captain Rossi, who occupied the seats directly across from hers.

The captain brought both bound wrists to his helmet to unfasten it. "No use wasting your oxygen supply," he said. "Might as well breathe the shuttle air for free."

Cassia followed suit.

Stretching her spine, Solara peered toward the front of the

shuttle and noticed that the pilots had left. She pulled off her helmet. "I escaped from this ship once, and I can do it again. But first I need to unlock these cuffs."

As soon as Gage removed his headpiece, Cassia and the captain did a simultaneous double take. "Who's this?" Cassia asked.

"Oh, him?" Solara said, scanning the floor for something to use as a lock pick. "That's Doran's evil twin."

Gage rolled his eyes. "Excuse me for wanting to protect everyone stuck out here in the armpit of the galaxy. Which is exactly the point of my research, by the way."

"If I were you," Solara advised, "I'd shut up about that research. If you think your father's bad, wait until the pirates find out what you can do." Thumbing at him, she told Cassia and the captain, "Meet Gage Spaulding, the inventor of Infinium. His mom faked his death nine years ago, and they've been living out a twisted revenge fantasy ever since."

"Wow," Cassia said, wrinkling her nose. "And I thought I had baggage."

"Enough about me," Gage dismissed. Leaning forward, he peered out the window at the cluster of men chatting at the far end of the hangar. "What does this Demarkus person want with Doran?"

"To kill him as an example to his men," Solara said.

"I imagine he'll do the same to me," the captain added. "For shooting him in the chest last year." He lifted one broad shoulder. "Can't say that I blame him."

Cassia squirmed in her seat, clearly worried about her own fate. "I think he'll do a lot worse than kill us."

Gage snapped his eyes to hers. "What could be worse?"

"A trip to the slave auction," Cassia said. "That's probably where we're headed. Pirates are scum, but they're not stupid when it comes to business. They know we're not worth anything dead."

"Except for me," the captain said with a half grin, rubbing the spot above his Beatmaster 3000. "They can sell my carcass for spare parts."

Cassia nudged him with her elbow. "Don't joke like that."

"Who's joking?"

A lump of fear rose in Solara's throat, but she held her breath and counted backward from ten. The only way she would solve this problem was by staying calm, and by God, she did *not* come to the outer realm to be sold as a slave. When the countdown finished, she closed her eyes and imagined all the tools within her reach. An idea came to mind, and she touched her pocket to make sure the ore samples were still there.

"You know those rocks I stole from your lab?" she asked Gage.

"Like I'd forget."

"How combustible are they?"

He slanted her a glance. "*Very*. Why?"

"Because I think I know a way out of here." She twisted her hip and brought both hands to the bag in her pocket. The act cost her a dozen electric shocks, but she was able to fish out a few bits of ore and hand them to the others. "Hold on to these. When I give the signal, we'll make them go boom."

Gage laughed. "And then what?" He raised an index finger and added, "Assuming we can ignite the ore and we don't end up with a chest full of shrapnel."

"Then we return here and steal a shuttle," she said. "Look, I know it's not an airtight plan, but unless you've got a better . . ." She trailed off when she noticed Demarkus break away from the men in his group and move in her direction.

The giant chief had never looked so content, grinning broadly as he approached the shuttle in the bouncing strides of a rich kid on Christmas morning. But his grin died when he hauled open the shuttle door and caught a glimpse of Gage.

Forehead wrinkled, Demarkus reached across the seat and grabbed Gage by the suit collar. "Who are you?" he demanded. "Where's Daro the Red?"

From her position sandwiched between the two, Solara felt Gage's muscles lock with terror. His breath hitched, and he said in a trembling voice, "Daro is dead. I'm his brother."

While Demarkus pondered this news, Solara crept her fingers along his utility belt, feeling for anything she might use as a lock pick. She struck gold, her grip landing on a small key ring. She slipped it free and tucked it under her sleeve just in time to avoid Demarkus's hand as he unsheathed his knife.

"Not anymore," he said, and sliced off Gage's ponytail. "You'll have to do." He tossed the hair aside and ordered the four of them to exit the shuttle. "I've assembled my men for a rematch." Slapping Daro's substitute on the back, he added, "Don't worry, boy. I'll make it quick."

As they marched toward the air-lock, Gage elbowed Solara and whispered, "Feel free to work your magic. Preferably before I die."

She covertly tried each key on the ring until one connected with a click. Keeping her hands inside the loosened cuffs, she calculated the risk of returning to the shuttle and locking themselves inside. She could probably hot-wire the ignition, but without anyone to open the hatch from the guard station, they'd be trapped inside the hangar like a bug in a jar. Seeing no other option, she was about to slip her cuffs when one of Demarkus's men shouted, "A transmission just came in, Chief."

Demarkus made a *so what?* gesture.

"From Daro the Red," the man said. "He's requesting permission to come aboard."

Solara went numb as she watched Demarkus's face transform with rapture. "Well, it seems our friend has been resurrected," he said, sliding an amused glance at Gage. "Who am I to deny this miracle? Bring Daro to the great hall so I can return him to his maker."

They made their way to the entrance of the great hall, where Solara received more than her share of dirty looks from the pirates she'd once held hostage there. The bald guard with eyes tattooed on his head seemed especially pleased to see her in cuffs. While he stood outside the boxing ring and puffed on his cigar, she took stock of her surroundings, particularly the number of men within lunging distance.

A dozen, she thought. *All with pulse rifles at their hips.*

She leaned into Gage and whispered, "I see one way to ignite the ore. Pulse pistols."

He jerked his head toward a pig roasting over an open flame at the other side of the hall. "Make that two ways. If you've got a good arm, and even better aim."

Footsteps sounded from behind her, and she spun around, instantly locking eyes with Doran while searching his expression for clues. The steadiness in his gaze told her he had a plan, but not much more. Seeing his face brought a flood of relief—but also fear, because she knew he had no weapons. The guards by his side would've made sure of that.

When he reached her, he took her face between both hands and kissed her like a man heading for his own execution. He was so convincing that for a moment she doubted it was an act, and dread gripped her heart. But then he whispered in her ear, "Do you have your oxygen helmet?"

She nodded, feeling its weight hooked to her suit.

"Does the crew?"

Another nod.

"Good," he whispered. "Be ready to put them on and run back to the hangar. Renny's waiting outside to catch you. Kane, too."

"You're coming with us," she insisted, and pressed a chunk of ore into his palm. "When the time is right, throw this—"

A guard pried him away before she could say anything more.

While he strode into the room to meet Demarkus, Solara summoned false tears and rushed to Cassia and the others for "comfort." Huddled around them, she quietly passed along the message and the handcuff key. She only hoped that Doran had understood what she'd put into his palm.

The crowd silenced their murmurings when Doran reached the center of the great hall. He stood tall in front of Demarkus and announced in a firm voice, "I'm here for my friends. If you let us leave, nobody has to die."

Laughter broke out, Demarkus's throaty chuckle rising above the rest. "I do like your spirit," he said with a regretful shake of his head. "In another life, we might've been crewmates. But in this life, I'm going to break you in half." He grinned in a way that contradicted his next words. "I hope you know this gives me no pleasure."

"Last chance." Doran rested a hand on the helmet hooked to his belt. When his warning was met with another round of laughter, he pressed his com-link and said, "Renny. Kane. Get ready for us."

Demarkus sobered up enough to deliver a quizzical look. His lips formed a question that he never had a chance to ask, because Doran hurtled his rock into the fire with flawless precision, and an instant later, an explosion rocked the ship.

The floor shook beneath Solara's feet, sending her stumbling for balance. Just when she'd righted herself, a second detonation thundered in her ears, twice as hard as the first. It seemed Gage had ignited one of his samples as well. Sirens blared and smoke filled the air as men scrambled toward the exits.

Solara slipped her cuffs and grabbed a pulse pistol from the nearest holster. When its owner spun on her, she fired off several rounds, none of which managed to hit him. He bolted in the other direction, and she paused to fasten her helmet. In the few seconds since the blast, the air had grown frigid and thin. It told her the hull was breached, and the ship had yet to seal off the damaged areas. The ore must be more powerful than she'd thought.

Cassia and Gage appeared on either side of the captain, helmets already secured.

"You know what to do," the captain ordered through the com-link. "Everyone book it to the hangar."

Solara motioned for them to go ahead while she stood on tiptoe and searched through the smoky haze for Doran. She spotted him sprinting her way, a group of men close on his heels. He caught up with her and snagged her hand, and they were off, tearing down the hallway so fast they passed the crew. They'd nearly reached the hangar when Solara glanced over her shoulder and realized they were a man short.

"The captain," she said, squinting to bring his lumbering form into focus. He kept stumbling against the wall, pounding one fist against his chest. "Something's wrong."

They circled back and noticed Demarkus flanked by several guards, all running toward them from the other end of the hall. Solara raised her pistol and fired. The men ducked for a moment, and then, seeing she hadn't hit any of them, continued in pursuit.

"I'm not saying you have bad aim," the captain said with a pained smile. "But you couldn't hit water if you fell out of a boat." He took the pistol and squeezed off several shots, but Solara wasn't paying attention to his targets. Her eyes moved over his face, which had grown waxen and sweaty beneath the glass. "I'm fine," he said when he caught her staring. "The Beatmaster needs a recharge. Happens all the time. Let's go."

Doran and Gage each took one of the captain's arms to help him move along, but they weren't fast enough. Demarkus was closing the distance, plodding onward with his pistol raised, despite the lack of oxygen that clumsied his steps. A whirring noise from the overhead duct system said the ship was filling with heated air, which meant Demarkus and his men would soon get a second wind—literally.

A few moments later, the corridor twisted to the left, and Solara ran through the open air-lock doors into the hangar. Escape seemed so near, but she stopped short as soon as she crossed the threshold. There was a problem. Someone had to open the hangar hatch from the guard station, and the interior air-lock door had to be shut in order for that to happen. It was a safety mechanism, just as she'd told the pirate guard all those weeks ago. That meant one of them had to go back inside and face Demarkus.

The others must have realized it, too, because nobody said a word.

Tapping his com-link, Doran started to say, "I'll do it," but the slamming of the air-lock door cut him off, and they spun around to find the captain watching them from the other side of the thick windowpane. Doran grabbed the door handle and shook it with both hands, but the captain had already locked himself inside.

"Go," Captain Rossi said. He held up his pistol along with a chunk of ore. "I'll open the hatch and send a few pirates to hell while I'm at it."

Solara's breath caught when she understood his meaning.

"No!" Cassia yelled, banging both fists against the window. "We'll wait for you!"

From behind the glass, Rossi delivered a stern look and thrust a finger toward the hangar door. "You'll move your ass, Cassy Rose. That's an order. I want you at that exit and ready for pickup when I hit the switch."

"But . . ." she began, and choked on a sob.

"No *buts*." The captain disappeared into the guard station.

They couldn't see him, but they heard his final words through the link. "Don't you dare cry for me. I've lived twice as long as most men do, and I've finally found something worth dying for. That's a blessing." His voice turned soft. "Now, go, and take care of each other. It's been an honor to have you as my crew."

The next sound they heard was the synchronized click of a dozen shuttles releasing from their docking ports, followed by the hum of the hangar door opening. The pressure changed, sweeping Solara off her feet as her body drifted toward the exit. She thrashed her limbs, unprepared for zero gravity, until she caught hold of a rudder and used it to steady herself.

Shuttles floated into space, and beyond them hovered the *Banshee*, cargo ramp open and ready to welcome her inside. As Solara launched herself toward the exit, she listened for the captain's voice, hoping more than anything that he would join them. But when a sharp *boom* rang out from the guard station, tears flooded her vision, and she had to hold her breath to keep her heart from cracking in half.

She forced herself to focus on the scene outside. It was an obstacle course of floating debris—everything from shuttle-craft and hull fragments to a few frozen bodies. Once a path cleared, she used both legs to push off into the icy chill of space and braced herself to collide with the *Banshee*'s cargo hold. She met the end ramp with a thud and grabbed on tight, hauling to the top as Gage and Cassia followed. When she turned around, the tail end of the pirate ship was practically torn off from the captain's detonation, blowing even more debris outside. She scanned the carnage for Doran but couldn't find him.

"Doran," she called through the link. "Where are you?"

He didn't answer.

She gripped the edge of the ramp while frantically searching for him. Part of her view was obstructed by a floating sheet of metal. Once she pushed it aside, she spotted him, and her stomach lurched so hard she nearly heaved inside her helmet. Because there, far below the ruined pirate ship, Doran was caught in the planet's gravitational pull, tumbling out of control and free-falling to his death.

CHAPTER TWENTY-EIGHT

*D*oran couldn't scream. His fear was beyond that.

He flailed both arms to right himself, but stars and soil alternated in his field of vision until he couldn't tell up from down. The spiraling images triggered his gag reflex, forcing hot bile up the back of his throat. He shut his eyes, swallowing hard as he curled into a ball and focused on filling his lungs. Each of his gasps seemed amplified, like breathing underwater through a snorkel. So he counted breaths—*one Mississippi, two Mississippi*—and tried to ignore the question burning at the edges of his mind.

When will I hit?

He reached twelve when voices invaded his helmet.

"Kane!" Solara shouted. "Do you see him out there? He's falling!"

"I see him," came the reply. "Doran, I'm on my way. The

shuttle hatch is open. All you have to do is grab on and climb inside."

Doran opened his eyes and tightened his core, extending all four limbs in an effort to provide enough wind resistance to keep from tumbling. It didn't work right away, but after a few tries, he finally faced the planet below, then yelped when he noticed the surface rising up to meet him.

He tapped his com-link and shouted, "Kane!"

"Right behind you," Kane said. "I'm almost there."

Doran tore his gaze away from the planet and glanced over his shoulder. The nose of the shuttle kept pace at his heels, not quite fast enough to catch him. Kane must have known it, because he shut the hatch to eliminate air drag and increase his speed.

It worked. The shuttle accelerated, but now Doran had no way to get inside.

He made the mistake of looking down and nearly wet himself. If something didn't happen in the next ten seconds, the crew would be cleaning his splattered remains from the shuttle windshield. He turned his head to the side and made eye contact with Kane, who flew next to him on the right.

"New plan," Kane shouted, zooming ahead of him. "I'm dispatching the tow cables. Grab one and don't let go."

Doran's first thought was that it wouldn't work, that the weight imbalance would send the shuttle into a tailspin, or his grip wouldn't hold. But then he looked down and saw the landscape so near he could make out a pirate's toilet seat that'd hit the ground ahead of him. That was all it took to send his arms into action. He reached ahead and gripped one of the metallic coils snaking out from the rear of the shuttle, ignoring the slap of a second cable against his shoulder. He struggled to wrap the cable around his wrist for more security, but the line was too tight.

"Hold on," Kane said, and pulled the shuttle up hard enough to send Doran swinging forward like a monkey on a vine. The frigid wind sliced through his gloves as a jolt of raw pain ricocheted from his wrists to his fingertips.

When the backward swing came, he held firm while his muscles trembled. A quick glance below showed the landscape whizzing past in a blur of ice about four feet from his boots, probably near enough for him to survive the fall. But as predicted, the burden of his weight caused the craft to wobble. Kane overcompensated for the imbalance, which resulted in Doran's arms jerking halfway out of their sockets. His hands ached, and he knew he couldn't hold on much longer.

"I have to let go," Doran yelled.

"Give me a second," Kane told him. "I'll slow down as much as I can."

As the shuttle teetered closer to the surface, Doran mentally calculated the best way to meet the frozen ground without fracturing every bone in his body.

Kane had just announced, "This is the best I can do," when Doran lost his grip on the cable. With inertia propelling him forward, he crossed both arms over his chest and tucked into a roll. The impact took his breath away. His helmet absorbed a blow hard enough to make his ears ring. Rocks jabbed at his shoulders and forearms. He tumbled fast and hard until an upward hill decreased his momentum. Then, as abruptly as the fall had begun, Doran found himself lying on his back, staring at the stars.

And blessedly alive.

His lips spread in a manic grin, and he filled his helmet with so much laughter that his stomach cramped. He moved his limbs one by one to test them. He'd broken his left wrist for sure, maybe a few ribs as well, but despite that, the smile never left his face. Pain could be treated and bones healed, but all the medicine in the galaxy couldn't fix dead. And he wasn't dead. He couldn't wait to tell the crew.

"I'm okay," he reported. "A little banged up, but nothing major. Kane, when this is over, I'm going to have your baby!"

Still grinning, he waited to hear Solara chime in with a laugh or for Kane to quip that he'd settle for a month of galley detail instead. No one answered.

He tapped his link again, wondering if the impact had shattered it. "Can anyone hear me?" He pushed onto one elbow and scanned the moonlit horizon for the shuttle. "Kane? You all right?"

The link crackled to life, and he detected Renny's voice. "Copy that, and glad to hear it," he said. "From the suit trackers, it looks like Kane went down about half a mile north of you. Sit tight while we check it out."

"Is he okay?" Doran asked.

When he didn't receive a response, he sat up to peer at the sky for the North Star, then remembered that he wasn't on Earth. His only hope of finding Kane was to reach a vantage point high enough to spot him at a distance. The act of standing up told Doran he'd twisted an ankle. He limped his way uphill and scanned the terrain in every direction.

No luck. He would have to wait.

Figuring he'd be easier to spot here, he took a seat on the ground and let the adrenaline work its way out of his system. With nothing but the whistling wind to fill his ears, the thoughts he'd banished an hour ago began creeping back in—questions about his parents, his newfound brother, and, most of all, his future. But Doran wasn't ready to face any of that yet, so he turned his attention to the sky and studied what was left of the orbiting pirate ship.

A great crack divided the rear of the hull from the rest of the ship, but if the emergency systems were operational, there should be survivors within the sealed-off areas. He was thinking about the best way to reach them when a shuttle engine roared nearby. He glanced over his shoulder to flag it down. Solara must have stolen one of the pirate crafts.

The shuttle landed, and he limped down the hill to meet it. As the side hatch opened, an unfamiliar pair of boots swung into view, definitely not Solara's. They were attached to a man of average height and built like a bull. His chest was so broad that it stretched the silvery fabric of his thermal suit to its limits. Doran stopped in his tracks. The man seemed to be alone, though judging by the array of gadgets hanging from his belt—two curved blades, three pairs of cuffs, and a coil of electrified rope—he didn't need backup.

Multiple restraints, Doran thought, taking a backward step and feeling along his hip for the pistol that wasn't there. *A bounty hunter, or maybe a slave trader.*

But then the man turned his head, and the light from his shuttle glinted off something inside his helmet. Metal studs dotting the skin at his temple—prefrontal cortex blockers.

Doran scrambled up the hill so fast he fell to the ground, where he frantically kicked and clawed his way over the ice to put some distance between them. His hand flew to his throat, but much like the pistol, his cyanide pendant was locked away on the *Banshee*.

A dozen gruesome scenarios played out inside Doran's head, all of them ending in his death. Which wouldn't be an easy one. His fingers trembled so hard it took three tries to press his com-link. "Renny," he said, voice cracking. "If you can hear me, get Cassia out of here—and do it now. One of the Daeva found us."

* * *

Solara and Gage were on their hands and knees, searching for extra weapons in a hidden storage bin beneath the floor when Renny's voice came through the cargo hold speaker.

"We're almost there."

Solara glanced out the nearest porthole into the blackness, wishing Doran was safe on board. He'd said he was fine, but his com had gone silent since then. "If the shuttle's not too banged up," she said, "I can find Doran while you guys tend to Kane. Or maybe the captain can—" She realized her mistake and cut off while a lump rose in her throat. She kept forgetting the captain was gone, and each reminder was an icicle to the heart.

After that, she fell silent and went back to her work of searching the compartment. Gage didn't try to strike up a conversation. He seemed to know that now wasn't the time to talk, not with two crew members unaccounted for. And he was right. The words and grief could come later, after they'd safely reunited the family.

Family.

She hadn't realized it until that moment, but that's what the people on this ship were to her. At some point during this haphazard journey, she'd fallen in love with a bespectacled kleptomaniac, a star-crossed seducer and his displaced princess, and, most of all, an infuriating blue blood who used to call her Rattail. She'd learned that home was a fluid thing, and whether on a planet, on a satellite, or on a rusted bucket of a ship, this crew was her home.

She refused to lose another one of them.

When the *Banshee* landed, Cassia was the first person down the ramp, already suited up with the medic bag tucked beneath one arm. Solara fastened her helmet and jogged after her. In the time it took Solara to reach the crash site, Cassia had already climbed onto the shuttle and was peering through the windshield.

One look at the craft told Solara it wasn't flight-worthy. Its nose had crumpled like an accordion and the passenger-side wing was bent at a ninety-degree angle, indicating that Kane had gone down headfirst when he'd lost control.

There seemed to be no movement inside.

Solara glanced at the moonlit stretch of landscape in the distance. Doran was out there somewhere. A sense of urgency churned in her stomach, but when she looked at the shuttle, she couldn't make her feet move. If nothing else, she knew Doran was alive. She couldn't say the same for Kane.

"How is he?" she asked through the link.

"He's unconscious," Cassia answered. Without missing a beat, she crawled across the wing to manually open the pilot's hatch. She tugged on the lever, but it didn't budge. "It's jammed. Renny, bring the crowbar."

"I'll get the hydraulic pliers, too," Solara said. "Just in case."

She ran back to the ship and returned to the shuttle to find that Renny and Gage had already forced open the hatch. Tossing aside the heavy pliers, Solara moved closer and peered on tiptoe at Kane. The pilot's harness kept his body upright, but his helmet hung low between unmoving shoulders.

Fortunately for all of them, Cassia didn't waver. She plucked a vial of ammonia gas from her kit and filtered it into Kane's helmet. The smelling salts made their way into his oxygen supply, and he jerked awake so quickly that his face shield struck Cassia's, sending her tumbling into Gage, who in turn fell off the wing and landed on his backside.

Cassia scrambled to Kane's side and blurted in a rush, "Are you okay? Does it hurt to breathe? Is anything broken?"

Groaning, he tipped back his head. "How's Doran?"

Cassia replied by smacking his helmet. "Answer me!"

"Okay," Kane called, shielding his head. "Yes, no, and maybe."

Cassia released a long breath through the com. Her shoulders rounded, and then she abruptly began crying. In between sobs, she probed Kane's shoulder and asked him if it hurt. When he told her no, she slugged him hard and shouted, "I thought you were dead!"

"Ow!" He rubbed the spot and started to make a wisecrack, but Cassia shut him up by raising both their face shields and kissing him hard on the mouth. He didn't seem to mind the oxygen loss. The way he gripped the back of her neck and held her close said he'd rather suffocate than break the kiss.

That was when Solara knew they could manage without her.

"I'm going on foot to find Doran," she announced. She set her com-link to track his signal, then followed the beeps until she faced the right direction. "He's not very far. I'll report back when I get there."

Gage handed her a pulse pistol and mouthed, *Take this.*

She tucked it beneath her utility belt, nodding in thanks.

✳ ✳ ✳

Doran couldn't run forever—or at all, really—so he decided to hold his ground. If he was going to die anyway, he might as well go down fighting. He didn't have a utility belt stocked with gadgets, but fate had gifted him a quarterback arm and all the rocks within reach.

They would have to do.

He palmed a stone and stood tall as the bullish man approached. After testing the rock's weight in his hand, he drew back and hurled it at the Daeva's face, where it dinged off the side of his helmet and disappeared into the night.

Unaffected, the man marched slowly forward until Doran could see his eyes, cold and hemorrhaged into a webbing of red where the whites belonged. With a slight tilt of his head, the

Daeva fixed his crimson gaze on Doran and held it there for a few moments as if scanning him through a database, which was a very real possibility.

The man tapped his com's external speaker. "Doran Spaulding," he said in a flat, robotic distortion that chilled the blood. "Where is your shipmate? The girl called Cassia Rose."

Doran snatched another frozen stone from the ground and swung it at the man's knee, but the Daeva was twice as fast, grabbing Doran's wrist and squeezing until the rock fell from his fingers.

"Where is she?" the Daeva repeated.

"Gone," Doran yelled, wincing in pain as the vise on his wrist tightened. "She changed ships at the last outpost."

"You're lying."

"I swear! She took a medic job on a luxury liner. I think it was called the *Zeni*—"

Quick as a cobra strike, the man clutched the base of Doran's throat and lifted him up until both boots dangled in the air. Doran's windpipe constricted under the pressure. Hungry for breath, he clawed at the fingers gripping his neck. His face tingled and swelled, eyes throbbing as they met the bloody gaze in front of him.

"Let's try again," the Daeva said. He turned and dragged Doran toward the shuttle. Once there, he set Doran on his feet and allowed him to breathe right before slamming his helmet into the steel hull. "Where is the princess?" the Daeva said.

He pounded Doran's head against the shuttle until his face shield cracked wide open. Steam poured from the gap, and Doran fell to the ground, disoriented. To compensate for the breach, his helmet released a burst of heated air in a steady hiss that ate through his tank's reserves. With his helmet spewing oxygen, he had a few minutes left—at best.

"Suffocation is a horrible death," the man said, and swept a gloved hand toward his shuttle. "I can fill my craft with warm air for you—if you take me to the girl."

Against Doran's will, his eyes turned to the cushioned pilot's seat, visible through the open hatch. He was tempted to say yes, and then sabotage the man during flight or lead him in the wrong direction. But if Kane's shuttle had crashed half a mile away, it was only a matter of time before the Daeva spotted the *Banshee* on his own.

Doran had to keep the man on the ground. "You can take that warm air," he growled, "and blow it up your ass."

The Daeva bent down, tracing a finger along the edge of his blade. "Once your lungs are flat and screaming, you'll change your mind. Or maybe I should carve the information out of you. That would be faster."

"So arrogant," Doran muttered. "Guys like you never learn." He kicked the man squarely between the legs, but his boot met the resistance of a plastic cup.

For the first time, the Daeva smiled—a mechanical curve of lips revealing two rows of dull, metal teeth. "You've never met anyone like me," he said, and unsheathed his blade. With one hand pressing Doran's helmet into the ice, he used the other to slash through the open face shield.

Doran cried out in pain, his cheekbone burning as warmth oozed over his skin. The Daeva drew back to make another cut, but he halted when pulse fire sounded from behind them. His

341

head whipped around, and in a flash, he sprang to his feet and ran to the open door, leaving Doran bleeding on the ground.

Doran pushed to his elbows and found Solara aiming a pistol at the shuttle. She fired two warning shots, which struck the hull on either side of the Daeva.

"Shoot him," Doran told her. "Don't hold back!"

"I'm trying," she yelled.

When another round of fire failed to strike him, the Daeva leaped onto the pilot's seat and closed the side hatch. Soon the engine rumbled to life. The craft lifted off the ground, its thrusters sending gusts of heat that scattered pebbles in every direction.

Solara ran over to protect Doran from the debris, but he shook his head and pointed at the shuttle. "It's the Daeva. He's going after the crew; we have to stop him."

"What about the explosive rocks?" she asked, pulling a bag from her pocket. "I still have some left."

Doran took the bag and shook its contents into his palm— two chunks of ore. "Two chances," he murmured. "That's all we get."

"You throw and I'll shoot," she told him. Doran didn't point out her questionable aim, but she must've known he was think-ing it, because she added, "I won't miss."

Nodding, Doran rose to his feet and gauged the distance between himself and the departing shuttle. Then he drew back his good arm and launched the first rock into the air. The ore sailed into range behind the craft, and Solara fired three blasts in quick succession.

She missed.

"Again!" she shouted.

With the shuttle gaining speed, Doran took his last bit of ore and gimped forward in a jog. When he knew he couldn't create any more momentum, he used every muscle in his core to hurl the rock at the shuttle, grunting as he released it.

Don't miss, he prayed while he watched the ore fly into the distance.

This was their last chance.

Please don't miss.

Gripping the pistol in both hands, Solara fast-tapped the trigger and filled the dim evening sky with pulses of brilliance. Doran lost count of how many shots missed the mark and bounced off the hull. But then a ball of light appeared, growing brighter until he had to shield his eyes. A thunderclap rent the air, and he peeked between his fingers as the tail end of the shuttle blew apart. The blast must have breached the fuel tank because another explosion took hold, and the next thing Doran knew, engine parts were raining from the sky.

Twisted ankle be damned, he grabbed Solara's hand and ran toward safer ground. Metal fragments pounded the landscape, each one spurring his adrenaline until he couldn't feel anything except the drag of half-empty air into his lungs. They'd just dodged a sheet from the hull when Doran's body collapsed beneath his weight.

He couldn't go any farther, not without air.

Solara dropped to her knees beside him and yanked free his oxygen tube, replacing it with hers. He started to object, but she shushed him.

"We'll share it," she said. "Cover your face to slow the leak."

From within his hissing helmet, Doran heard the com-link fizzle to life, followed by Solara's message to the crew. "Renny, I need an immediate track-and-intercept," she said. "We've got five minutes of oxygen to split between us. Do you copy?"

At first, there was only silence. Then Renny's voice came through the link with four of the finest words in the English language: "We're on our way."

CHAPTER TWENTY-NINE

"Y our chief is dead," Doran shouted to the fifty or so pirates kneeling before him in the great hall later that night. This was the largest room on board with an oxygen supply, so the survivors who'd surrendered their weapons had gathered here. Rows of men bent their heads toward the floor, fingers laced behind their necks as they awaited judgment. He had no plans to kill them, but they didn't need to know that.

"You're alive by the mercy of Daro the Red," Solara continued, resting a hand on the pulse rifle slung over her shoulder. "If you choose to bear his mark, you'll leave here on shuttles that I've repaired for you. But on two conditions. First, that you never return to this wreckage site, or to the planet below it. And second, that you'll repay Daro's kindness if he ever calls on you for a favor."

"If anyone objects to those terms," Doran said, "I'm happy to escort you to the nearest air-lock."

Not surprisingly, there were no objections.

The pirates remained on their knees until Doran summoned them, one by one, to the stage at the front of the room. There they swore allegiance to him and rolled up their sleeves to expose both wrists. Each previous chief had made a coin-size mark in the flesh, visible now as thin scars or faded tattoos. The younger Brethren wore only a single image, having served no one else but Demarkus Hahn, while seasoned veterans had brands halfway up the lengths of their forearms. Doran added his mark above the rest, an interlocking DR monogram stamped in thermal ink that would cool if he activated it.

"When this grows cold," he explained, "you'll know I'm calling for you." Then he provided a radio frequency where he would leave instructions if that day ever came.

Once the pirates accepted Doran's mark, Solara ushered them to the last functioning transport air-lock, where Renny and Gage filled the shuttles to capacity and sent them on their way. The crew kept the process moving, and in the span of a few hours, they'd fully evacuated the ship.

With that task completed, they returned to the *Banshee* to tend to broken bones, lacerations, and laser burns. Doran meant to ask his brother if they could spend the night in the comfort of the underground bunker, but his brain shut out coherent thought as soon as Solara fastened a splint around his wrist. He kissed her on the cheek and collapsed onto the bed, fully clothed and neglecting to eat dinner.

Cheating death was exhausting.

*   *   *

At first light the next morning, Doran changed into fresh clothes and scrubbed his face, then gathered with the crew in the galley. Even Gage joined them, electing to take the seat at the farthest end of the table. The thick scent of porridge hung in the air, but bowls remained untouched as each of them stared at the metal crutch resting on the table.

It was all they had left of their captain.

Acorn padded into the room, her nose twitching as she sniffed for her lost "mother." She climbed the wall and glided onto the table, where she scurried up and down its length in desperation. When she couldn't find the captain, she let out a heartbreaking whine that sent Cassia rushing out of the galley. She returned wearing a faded blue jacket that hung to her knees, her hands lost somewhere inside the depths of its enormous sleeves. It must have been one of the captain's, because the instant she sat down, Acorn chirped and took a nosedive into the breast pocket.

Cassia stroked Acorn's head with a thumb. "Now we can start."

Renny gave her a nod and stood from the head of the table. "I met Phineas Rossi when I was at the lowest point in my life," he said. "About six months after I left home. We were in this seedy outpost bar in the middle of nowhere, and he caught me picking his pocket." Renny smiled as if replaying the memory. "He bloodied my lip. Then, when he realized I'd taken a grease pencil instead of his money, he laughed and bought me a drink."

Kane chuckled softly, and Cassia rested her head on his shoulder.

"He'd just bought a small cargo ship from a repo man," Renny continued. "He told me the *Banshee* wasn't much to look at, but if I wanted to join him, it'd probably beat stealing pocket lint from strangers. I had nothing to lose, so I came on board as a general hand. A week later he learned I could navigate, and he promoted me to first mate—just like that. Without knowing anything about me, except that I made his pills disappear." Renny paused to remove his glasses and scrub away a tear. "He gave me a new life, and in the years after that, he gave me his friendship. I don't know which I value more, because I needed both."

"Remember when his Beatmaster charging paddle went missing?" Cassia asked with a sniffle. "Everyone blamed you, except the captain. And he was right. It turned out I was the one who'd stuck it in the wrong drawer."

"It takes a big man to trust a thief," Renny agreed.

Doran felt Solara sit up straighter beside him. She studied her tattooed knuckles and seemed to hesitate for a few beats. "That's what I loved most about him," she said. "I used to hate looking at my markings. But the captain taught me they don't mean anything. Because I'm more than the sum of my mistakes."

Doran took one of her hands and interlaced their fingers. "Captain Rossi showed more faith in me than my own father did." He tried not to think about when he'd see his father again, if ever. The wound was too fresh. "I always put my dad on a pedestal, but he must've had a low opinion of me if he thought I'd turn against my own brother."

Gage didn't respond, but color fanned out on his cheeks.

348

Probably because not too long ago he'd shared that same low opinion.

"Biology doesn't make anyone a parent," Cassia added as she tucked her Eturian prayer stone beneath her shirt. She kissed her fingertip and pressed it on Acorn's head. "The captain would've died before letting me go to auction. I can't say the same for my parents. They only ever saw me as a commodity."

That silenced the room until Gage cleared his throat. He poked at his porridge with a spoon, never looking up when he said, "I didn't know Rossi for very long, but he seemed like a good man. I'm sorry he's gone."

"Thank you," Renny said in that gentle way of his. "We're going to miss him." He spoke without a hint of resentment, as if Gage hadn't held the crew at gunpoint and locked them inside his lab twenty-four hours earlier.

That was when it occurred to Doran that Captain Rossi wasn't the only person who'd changed everyone on board the ship. They owed their lives to the first mate, too. Placing one hand on the crutch in front of him, Doran said, "Nobody can replace the man we lost. But the *Banshee* needs a captain, and I nominate Renny for the job."

"Seconded," Solara said with a firm nod.

While Renny blinked behind his glasses, Kane asked, "All in favor?"

"Aye," called five synchronized voices, including Gage's.

Doran turned to Renny. "It's unanimous. The job isn't easy and the pay probably sucks, but I can't imagine anyone else but you at the helm. Do you accept?"

After much blushing and stammering, Renny told them yes, and they sealed the deal with a toast of watered-down Crystalline from his private reserve.

"So where to next?" Renny asked, setting down his drained glass. "The cargo hold will be empty soon, and our paying passengers have turned into crew. I can probably pick up a few jobs under the radar, but nothing's changed."

Nobody had to ask what that meant. Each of them was a fugitive from something or other—the law, the mafia, a distant kingdom at war. It seemed their only option was to make a life in the fringe, a prospect Doran had once considered worse than prison. Now he found himself grinning.

He settled a hand low on Solara's back, confident that with her by his side, he could be happy anywhere. He thumbed at his brother. "I have an Infinium connection. Just think what we could do if we never had to buy fuel again."

"We could work as traders," Solara suggested. "That's half-way respectable."

"As long as the other half is shady," Kane teased. "Otherwise, where's the fun in that?"

"Half-shady traders," Doran said, testing it out. "That sounds like us." He glanced down the table at his brother, already knowing his response but needing to ask anyway. "Want to come along? That fancy compound has to feel small sometimes."

Gage answered with a smile that was barely a smile at all. It probably didn't look like much to anyone else, but to Doran it spoke volumes. The twinkle in his brother's eyes was the same he remembered from their childhood, and for a brief moment they weren't on the *Banshee* anymore. They were laughing beneath the roof of a blanket fort, using flashlights to illuminate their gap-toothed faces. He knew change wouldn't happen overnight, but the warm feeling behind his breastbone promised that one day they'd laugh like that again.

"I'll take a rain check," Gage said. "Right now I have my own work to do." He started to say something more, but then he reached into his pocket, and his smile died.

"What's wrong?" Doran asked.

"My data drive," Gage said, standing from the bench and frantically patting himself down. "I had it with me yesterday. All my research is on there. If anyone finds it, they can access my files and sell them to the highest bidder."

While the crew scanned the floor and peppered Gage with questions—"Where did you see it last?" "Is it in another pair of pants?"—Renny quietly emptied the contents of his pockets onto the table: three fuel chips, a marble, some bits of plastic, a small pink device, and, most important, one golden file drive. The group released a collective breath as Renny slid the data drive across the table.

"Sorry about that."

Cassia snatched up the pink tool and shook it at him. "What is it with you and my laser blade? It's like a conspiracy to keep me hairy."

"Told you I didn't take it," Kane said, slanting her a glance.

"*This* time," she retorted with a flip of her dreads.

"Don't start, you two," Solara warned them. "There's still some juice left in my stunner, and I'm not afraid to use it."

Renny reached deeper into his pocket and produced her handheld stunner. "Then you'll want this back."

Doran couldn't help laughing. He glanced at his brother, expecting to find a horrified expression on his face. But Gage watched the exchange with fascination, and another emotion Doran recognized from his own time on the *Banshee*: a desire to belong. He'd wanted that as well. Maybe they weren't so different.

"Come on," Doran said, and clapped his brother on the shoulder. In three days, their mother would return, and he intended to be long gone by then. "I hear there's a perfectly good beach simulator in that complex of yours."

Gage nodded, a challenge behind his gaze. "*And* a flag football set."

"No way."

"Way."

"You know what this means, right?"

"Yeah, I know," Gage said, and delivered the kind of menacing grin that only a brother could get away with. "It means you're going down."

CHAPTER THIRTY

Warmth was a rare delicacy in space.

Solara had almost forgotten how exquisite sunlight felt on her skin, and she couldn't stop humming with the simple pleasure of it. These simulator lamps were almost as good as the real thing. Reaching both arms over her head, she stretched out on the beach towel until her fingers and toes met the silky caress of sand. The fine grains had absorbed the heat from above, and she buried both hands to soak it up. They only had a few hours before it was time to leave. She didn't intend to take one second for granted.

"Mmm," she said again, smiling. "This is heaven."

Though her eyes were closed, she knew Doran was watching her. She could tell by the way he circled her navel with an index finger. He didn't seem to share the opinion that she looked ridiculous in her makeshift bikini of shorts paired with a cutoff T-shirt. It wasn't long before his touch began to wander, straying to the ticklish curve of her waist.

With a giggle, she rolled onto her stomach and rested one cheek on the towel. "When you promise a vacation, you really deliver," she said. "If I get any more relaxed, you'll have to scoop my melted body off the sand."

"It's no private yacht in the Caribbean, but it'll do."

"No private yacht," she repeated, mocking him. "This room is a wonder."

Squinting against the light, she opened her eyes to take in the turquoise water gently lapping at the sand. The wave pool was designed to mimic the ocean, an effect achieved by its sloping floor, and it resembled the real thing if she didn't look too closely.

"I changed my mind," Doran said, walking two fingers along her lower back. "Forget yachts and snorkeling in the open sea. This vacation is perfect because it gives us the one thing we can't find on Earth."

"Hmm?" she asked. "What's that?"

He leaned down until the warmth of his bare chest met her shoulders. Then his mouth was at her ear, whispering, "Total privacy."

Before she could agree with him, he brushed his lips along the sensitive bend of her neck and rendered her speechless. With his body so close, a new kind of heat settled between her hipbones, quickening her breaths in time with her pulse. She rolled over for a kiss, but instead of lowering his mouth to hers, he lay on his side and propped on one elbow, gazing at her with the expression of someone seeing the stars for the first time.

The shift in him caught her off guard. "What's the matter?"

At first he didn't say anything. He brushed back a stray tendril of hair that had escaped her braid and caressed her cheek while his eyes moved over her face. Then he wrinkled his brow as if trying to solve a quadratic equation. "Sometimes I look at you, and it feels like my chest is caving in. How do you do that to me?"

Solara's lips parted. How did she do it? She could very well ask him the same question, but she didn't. Because like so many other times when she was alone with Doran, the words wouldn't come. She didn't know why, only that there seemed to be a disconnect between her heart and her voice. Maybe she loved him more than words.

Instead of talking, she threaded her fingers in the dark hair behind his neck and pulled him down for a kiss with all her heart behind it. She hoped that someday she would be able to turn feelings into conversation. Until then, she'd have to show him. And she did. They were so tangled up in each other that they didn't hear the door open.

"Aw, come on," Kane drawled. "Take your burning love somewhere else."

"Seriously," Cassia agreed. "Some of us are trying to keep our lunches down."

While Solara threw them a withering look, Doran groaned, keeping both eyes shut as he swiveled his face in their direction. "Didn't you read the sign?"

"What sign?" Kane asked, glancing around for the best spot to plant his folding chair.

"The one I hung on the door this morning," Doran told him.

"Oh," Cassia said. "The board that says 'Stay Out'?"

"That's the one."

"I thought that only applied to pirates," she told him, and spread a blue-striped towel on the sand. "Or the Daeva."

"Public beach, guys," Kane added with that flirty grin—the one he knew didn't work on them but insisted on using anyway.

Solara exhaled long and slow. She asked in Doran's ear, "What's that you were saying about yachts and privacy?"

He laughed without humor. "The open sea isn't looking too bad now, is it?"

"Neither is that grassy spot behind the barn on Cargill."

"Before I forget," Cassia said while digging inside her beach bag. "I have something for you. Renny gave me these before he went topside with Gage to refuel the ship. He said to return them with the usual spiel about how he's sorry and he can't help it." She twirled a hand. "Blah, blah, blah."

Since private time was over, Solara sat up to find out what was in the bag. She didn't expect to see a pair of silvery bracelets, and it took a moment to recognize them as the indenture bands that had once linked her to Doran as his servant.

"Look," she told him while taking the bracelets in her hand. They were heavier than she remembered, but she had no problem recalling the high-pitched beep that used to call her in the middle of the night. "I wonder how long Renny's had these. I forgot all about them."

Doran frowned at the bands, reaching out to touch the MASTER emblem and then pulling back. He didn't seem to enjoy looking at them. When his gaze shifted to the birthmark at the base of Solara's throat, she wondered if he was thinking about that day in the ticketing station.

Let's get something straight, Rattail. If I agree to finance your passage, the only words that will leave your mouth for the next five months are "Yes, Mr. Spaulding."

She gazed into the electric-blue eyes of the boy sitting beside her on the sand. Instead of a tuxedo and a haughty smirk, he wore baggy secondhand cutoffs and a frown of contrition. This version of Doran had abandoned a life of privilege to travel on a decrepit ship with a crew of fugitives. She couldn't reconcile him with the other Doran, the one who'd hired her to wash his floor and fetch his champagne.

Taking his injured wrist, she carefully faced it up to expose the tattoo that matched hers, then traced the inky swords with her fingertip. "Seems like a lifetime ago when we wore those bracelets, doesn't it?"

He wouldn't meet her gaze. "Two lifetimes."

"Neither of us had any idea what we were getting into."

"One of us did." He peeked at her through dark lashes. "I had no intention of making it easy on you. If we'd stayed on the *Zenith*, I would've run you into the ground, just because I could. You don't know how awful I was."

"Trust me," she said with a grin. "I knew." Holding up the indenture bands, she asked, "So what should we do with these?"

"Burn them."

Solara found herself gripping the steel bands in case he tried to take them away. It was ridiculous to want them so badly when until a few minutes ago, she'd forgotten they existed. But she and Doran had a history, and these bracelets had set every wild moment of it in motion. The bands were as much a part of her as the tattoos that branded her a felon, and she had no plans to erase those, either.

"I'm not sorry it happened," she told him.

Doran turned to meet her eyes, shaking his head as he took her face in his palm. "Me neither," he said. "I'm sorry *how* it happened."

"Semantics," she dismissed with a wave. While kissing him on the nose, she tucked the bracelets out of sight beneath her beach towel. She wasn't giving them up. "But enough of that. You promised me a vacation."

"So I did."

"Then let's get back to it. Playtime's over in a few—" She cut off with a gasp, her face drenched from the mighty splash of Cassia pushing Kane into the water. A second spray came shortly afterward when Kane hauled his princess over one shoulder and took his revenge. Cheeks dripping, Solara finished, "A few hours."

Doran laughed and used his discarded shirt to blot her face. It smelled like him, and that made her smile. "I predict they'll be bickering again in three . . . two . . . one."

He was right, of course. But Solara wouldn't have it any other way, because these were her people and this was their journey together—messy and wild and wonderful. She had no idea what the future would hold for any of them, beyond possibilities as infinite as the stars.

And really, that was enough.

ACKNOWLEDGMENTS

Writing a book never gets easier for me, even after nine completed manuscripts. Clever one-liners, witty dialogue, and plot twists can't be reused, so with each new story, I'm forced to dig deeper to reach the source of my creative well. I couldn't do it without the help of some very special people who work hard behind the scenes, digging right alongside me.

Many thanks to my editor, Laura Schreiber, for taking my books to the next level with thoughtful, in-depth suggestions that never fail to amaze me. I draft with more confidence knowing your edit letters will arrive in my in-box. We make a great team, and I'm so glad that fate brought us together.

Speaking of which, much gratitude to my literary agent, Nicole Resciniti, for finding the right home for my novels, and for being my fiercest advocate. You rock!

Big hugs to my dear friend and critique partner, Lorie Langdon, and to Stacey Kade and Lea Nolan for taking the time to read *Starflight* and share your thoughts with me. Not only are you ladies excellent beta readers, you're phenomenal authors, too.

Much love to my family and friends for their continued support, and a huge shout-out to my readers, who warm my heart with every e-mail, tweet, video, and Instagram post. You are the very best part of my job!

TURN THE PAGE FOR
A SNEAK PEEK

CHAPTER ONE

*L*ight seemed sharper in space. The eyes tended to latch on to anything luminous, starved for a sense of direction in the thick black void. After the first year of living off world, Cassia noticed her sight had adapted to the sensory deprivation. All it had taken then was the glow of a distant star through her bedroom porthole to bring her boots into focus. Now, after her second year in residence on the SS *Banshee*, she moved through the ship like a cat at midnight, her retinas magnifying the barest hint of a spark, so she rarely needed to turn on the overhead bulbs.

She couldn't decide if that was a good thing.

When she'd left her home world of Eturia—or fled, really—it had been with a heavy heart and the intention of returning before the next gathering moon. But that was twenty-six moons ago. She'd counted. Each passing cycle was starting to feel like a defeat, and some days she wondered if she'd ever see home again.

She rotated on her narrow bunk to face one of the pictures taped to the wall, a panorama of her royal ancestral lands unfolding in great, rolling fields that gave way to an even greater lake of vivid indigo. This photograph was one of three items she'd managed to grab during her hasty escape. Since then, she'd spent so much time gazing at it she could trace a fingertip along the lavender-covered hills with her eyes closed. Sometimes in the twilight moments between dreams and awareness, she swore she heard the rustling of leaves on the breeze and smelled the scent of freshly clipped grass. But then she'd blink and find the spell broken, her senses jarred by the throaty snores of her roommate, Kane, and the musky smell of his antiperspirant.

He was snoring now.

She kicked the bunk above her, and he grumbled a curse before shifting on the mattress and dangling one brown arm over the edge. The sight of his blond-dusted knuckles made her smile. Kane was the second "item" she'd brought from home— her childhood best friend since the day he'd rescued her from a goose attack by sacrificing his cookie to the bird, buying her time to get away. Kane talked too much, he chewed with his mouth open, and he had a tendency to use her laser blade without permission. But without him, these years in exile would've been darker than the south side of hell.

So for that, she put up with him.

"Stop it," he grumbled, his voice rough from sleep.

"Stop what?"

"Pining. You're staring at the picture again."

"No, I'm not."

He didn't bother calling her a liar. "You're thinking about the good times because we've been away for so long. There's a reason we left, Cassy."

As if she could forget.

She touched the gold disk tucked beneath her shirt. That was the third item to make the journey from home, a royal medallion identifying her as PRINCESS CASSIA ADELAIDE ROSE. But even when she removed the necklace and hid it beneath her mattress, she felt its ghost weight tugging at her shoulders—a constant reminder that she'd abandoned her people during a time of war. All of Eturia hated her. The bounty on her head made that clear.

"It's not your fault," Kane said.

She drew a breath and ran a finger around the edge of her medallion. Logically, she knew he was right. Her marriage to the prince of a rival house would have prevented the war, but she'd discovered the man's true intent was to murder her family and rule both kingdoms. Her parents hadn't believed her when she'd told them. That much was her fault. If she hadn't fought so hard against the match and thrown so many tantrums, maybe her word would have counted for something.

"They wouldn't have listened," Kane added.

"Get out of my head."

"But it's so breezy and vacant in there. Plenty of room to stretch out."

Biting back a laugh, she punched his cot.

"Come on." He swung his bare feet into view. "We're going planet-side today. All you need's a little sun to set you right."

At the reminder, she perked up. Real sunlight was such a rare treat that cargo drops seemed more like a vacation than work. And if there was any wiggle room in the schedule, the captain might award them a day of shore leave. "What are we delivering?"

"The grain we picked up on Cargill."

She wrinkled her nose. Stacking crates of grain always left her covered in dust, not to mention whatever eight-legged critters hitched a ride from the last colony. But the prospect of fresh air, firm soil, and warm rays set her legs in motion.

A few minutes later, she was in the washroom for her daily sponge bath, as showers were limited to once a week. She'd just finished pulling on her canvas pants and T-shirt when a flash of auburn fur caught her eye, and she turned to find Acorn, the ship mascot, perched above the doorframe, preparing to launch.

There was a time when Cassia would have ducked and ran, but now she cupped both hands and extended them toward the sugar glider. Acorn spread her wing-like arms and coasted into Cassia's palms, then scurried up to one shoulder and began seeking her favorite pocket. She found it, the one above Cassia's heart, and burrowed in headfirst.

"At least you love me, girl," Cassia said with a smile. "Though you don't really have a choice, do you?"

Acorn's breed was highly social, to the point where she could die without enough affection. She'd bonded with the previous captain, and after his death, adopted Cassia as a foster mother. Acorn's tiny claws still sent the wrong kind of shivers down Cassia's spine, especially when they were tangled in her hair, but secretly she liked feeling needed.

After handing Acorn a dried lentil, Cassia faced the washroom mirror and unfastened her ponytail. The instant it came loose, she narrowed her eyes at the blond waves brushing her shoulders. She still didn't recognize herself without her waist-long dreadlocks. If she was lucky, the bounty hunters wouldn't recognize her, either.

Kane strolled inside, rubbing a hand over his own newly shorn head. The act lifted the hem of his shirt high enough to reveal a trail of golden curls encircling his navel and disappearing below the waistband of his pants. Against her will, Cassia's pulse hitched. She and Kane looked so much alike with their tawny skin and light hair that people often mistook them for siblings, but her body had no such misgivings.

Neither did Kane's. He kept making that clear.

He moved behind her and laced his long fingers through her hair, holding her gaze in the mirror while his lips curved in an appreciative smile. "I like it," he said, low and smooth. "I couldn't do this before."

Chills broke out along her backbone—the *right* kind of shivers. But she shut down the sensation and pulled her waves into a sloppy ponytail before things went too far again. She couldn't afford any more slipups. It wasn't fair to either of them.

Kane's grin fell in a way that said she'd hurt his feelings.

"Breakfast will be late," she reminded him, glancing at her

boots because the expression on his face made her insides ache. "I'll get started while you wash up."

Then she backed into the hallway and did what she did best. She left.

CHAPTER TWO

Kane scrubbed himself from head to toe and pulled on his shirt one slow sleeve at a time. He combed his hair until his scalp prickled. Twice, he shaved his face with Cassia's laser blade before checking in the mirror for any spots he'd missed. When he couldn't stall any longer, he set off for the galley and hoped she had finished her breakfast and gone somewhere else. *Anywhere* else, as long as he wouldn't have to spend another awkward meal sitting across from her at the table while the rest of the crew cast sideways glances at them and asked what was the matter.

She'd locked him in the friend zone again. That was the matter.

The instant he crossed the threshold, he scanned the galley and took in three faces, none of which belonged to Cassia. There was no sign of her at all, not even of the jacket she usually left balled up on the counter when working over the burners made her hot. The only proof she'd been there was a vat of porridge left simmering on the stove. He released a breath as the muscles in his shoulders unclenched. He was safe, at least until the next time their paths crossed on this sardine can of a ship.

"Morning," Renny greeted from above the rim of his coffee cup. Steam fogged his glasses, and he scrubbed the lenses with a cloth napkin before scrutinizing Kane more closely. "You feeling okay?" he added, probably worried about transport madness. "Spending enough time under the lamps?"

"I'm fine, Cap'n," Kane said. It felt strange calling the former first mate captain, and he wondered if he'd ever get used to it. Renny was a good man and they all loved him, but nobody could replace Phineas Rossi, the crotchety old half-mechanical battle-ax who'd taken them in and made them a family.

"Catch a few watts after breakfast. And soak up all the rays you can when we stop on Vega." Renny nodded at him. "You've lost some pep in your step. I don't like it."

Kane didn't like it, either. He kept his thoughts to himself, but he wondered if a change in sleeping arrangements might help. It wasn't easy bunking three feet above Cassia every night, listening to the little moany noises she made in her dreams and ignoring the floral scent wafting up from her perfume microbes. That was enough to shake any guy's screws loose.

With only three cabins on the *Banshee*, that left him the option of bunking with Renny, or asking Solara to switch rooms. Kane shifted a glance at Solara, who sat on Doran's lap with both arms locked around his neck while he used the end of her long chestnut braid to tickle her nose. Those two were permanently joined at the hips. No way they'd give up their private quarters.

"Hey, Cap'n," Kane said. "Mind if I bunk with you?"

Renny didn't ask why, one of the many reasons Kane liked him. "Suit yourself. But I snore."

"Me too." At least that was what Cassia claimed.

"It's a deal, then." Renny held up an index finger and dug inside his coat pocket, then produced Kane's watch. It was an antique, passed down from Kane's great-great-grandfather, and the only thing his dad had ever given him besides a tarnished last name. Renny handed it over with an apology in his eyes. "You might want to lock this up. I can't seem to stay away from it."

Kane fastened the metal band around his wrist. "As long as you don't lift the key to my lockbox." Renny had done that before. The man had compulsively sticky fingers, a condition that'd forced him to flee Earth after he'd stolen from the mafia.

Renny grinned. "I make no promises."

Doran tore his gaze away from Solara long enough to ask, "What's our ETA?" But he kept one hand on her thigh and used the other to rub her back with all the dedication of a guy trying to summon a genie from its bottle.

Kane made a face, but the pair didn't notice.

"About noon, Vega time," Renny said. "We'll dock there

overnight, so feel free to use the shuttle if you want to meet up with your brother."

That got Kane's attention. Doran's twin brother had invented a super-fuel called Infinium, which was quickly becoming the most valuable substance in the galaxy. The guy was loaded, and he lived below the surface of a nearby planet in a swanky compound that included a beach simulator. "I want in on that."

"But the shuttle only holds two people," Solara pointed out.

"Then I'll curl up in the rear hatch."

"For a two-hour ride?"

"For as long as it takes."

"You must really want out of here."

She had no idea how much.

Renny excused himself to check the autopilot, and Solara leaned forward, resting both elbows on the table. "What's up with you and Cassia?"

Shrugging, Kane told a deceptively simple truth. "Nothing."

"I noticed you two don't fight anymore."

"And that's bad because...?"

"Because bickering is what you guys do," Doran cut in. "Some people write sonnets. Other people draw hearts. You two yell at each other. It's your twisted love language."

The use of the L-word didn't escape Kane's notice. It hit home like a fist to the chest, forcing him to face the stove to hide whatever emotions were pulling down the corners of his mouth. It was no secret he'd loved Cassia since he was too young to tie his boots—enough to drop everything and follow her out the door two years ago. And she wanted him, too. The way her skin flushed every time he touched her made that obvious. But wanting and loving were two different things. The real desire of Cassia's heart was to go home and rule their colony, which she couldn't do with the bastard son of a merchant by her side.

Kane stirred a pinch of cinnamon into the porridge. "We're friends. That's all."

His tone warned them to drop it, and they did. But when breakfast was over and the crew left him to clean up the mess, their words replayed inside his head. They were right. The dynamic on the ship had shifted, and a knot was building inside his chest, pulling a little tighter each day. Something had to change before that knot snapped him in half.

He decided to forgo the sunlamps and returned to his room, where he stuffed everything he owned inside a spare storage box. He'd just grabbed his pillow when Cassia walked in and stopped short at the doorway.

Her honey-brown eyes flew wide, darting from the box in his hands to his now empty bunk. "What's going on?"

Kane knew he hadn't done anything wrong, but that didn't stop his stomach from sinking. The sensation reminded him of the time his mother had caught him hiding a broken figurine under the sofa. He fixed his gaze over Cassia's head and into the hallway. "The room's all yours. Now you don't have to listen to me snore."

"But where are you—"

"With Renny. I think it's best."

For a long time she said nothing. Then her mouth pressed into a hard line while her eyes flashed with anger. "Perfect," she spat, reaching behind her neck to unfasten the Eturian prayer necklace he'd bought for her—the one that had cost him two months' wages. She stood on tiptoe and shoved the necklace into the box, right beside his pillow. "Don't forget this."

Before he could tell her to keep it, she spun on her heel and took off toward the common room. The clang of her boots on the stairs soon followed.

Ignoring the heaviness in his gut, Kane left his old room and kicked the door shut. His brain understood this distance was long overdue. Now he needed the rest of him to get the message.